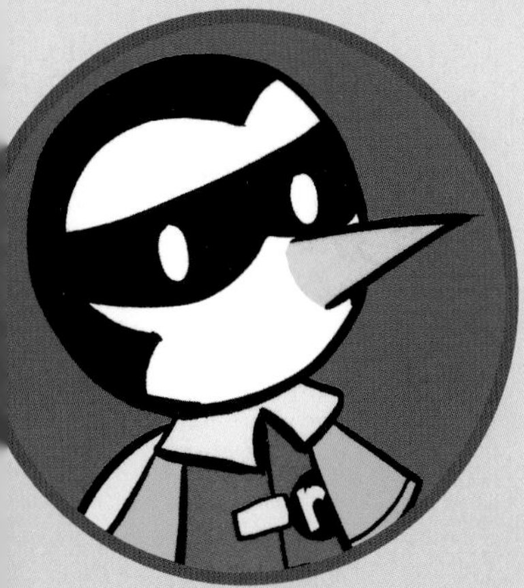
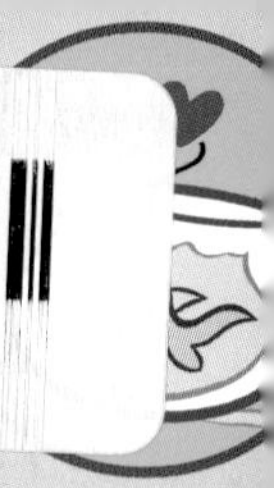
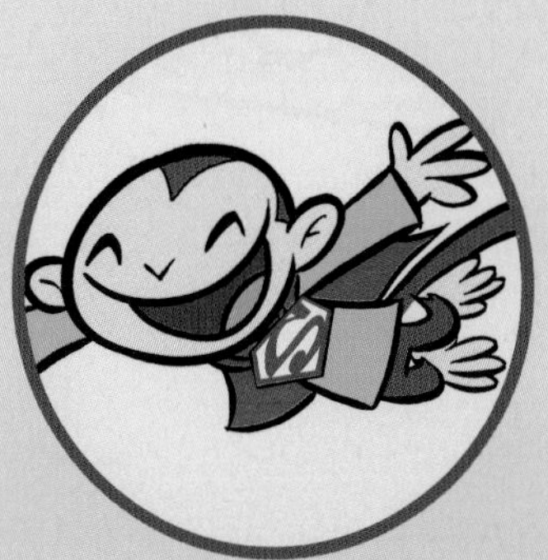
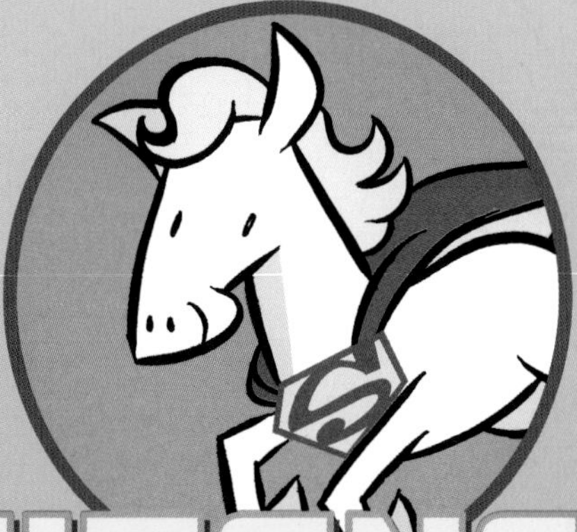
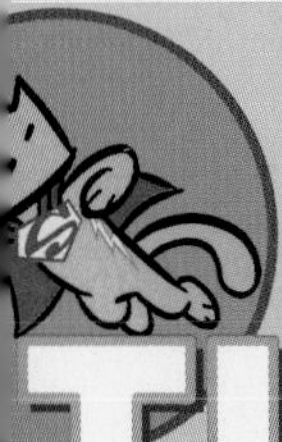

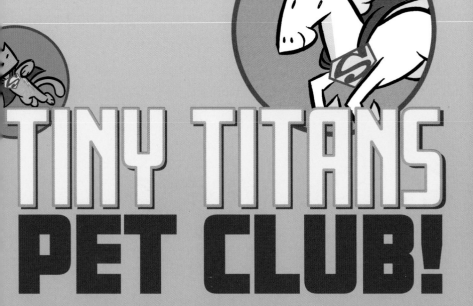

TINY TITANS
PET CLUB!

by
ART BALTAZAR
writer & artist

and
FRANCO
writer

TINY TITANS
PET CLUB!

JANN JONES
ELISABETH V. GEHRLEIN
Editors - Original Series

STEPHANIE BUSCEMA
ADAM SCHLAGMAN
SIMONA MARTORE
Assistant Editors - Original Series

ROBIN WILDMAN
Editor - Collected Edition

STEVE COOK
Design Director - Books

AMIE BROCKWAY-METCALF
Publication Design

KATE DURRÉ
Publication Production

MARIE JAVINS   Editor-in-Chief, DC Comics

DANIEL CHERRY III
Senior VP - General Manager

JIM LEE
Publisher & Chief Creative Officer

DON FALLETTI
VP - Manufacturing Operations & Workflow Management

LAWRENCE GANEM
VP - Talent Services

ALISON GILL
Senior VP - Manufacturing & Operations

NICK J. NAPOLITANO
VP - Manufacturing Administration & Design

NANCY SPEARS
VP - Revenue

MICHELE R. WELLS
VP & Executive Editor, Young Reader

TINY TITANS: PET CLUB!

Published by DC Comics. Compilation and all new material Copyright © 2021 DC Comics. All Rights Reserved. Originally published in single magazine form in *Tiny Titans* 3-6, 8, 9, 11, 13-15, 17, 19-21, 23, 28. Copyright © 2008, 2009, 2010 DC Comics. All Rights Reserved. All characters, their distinctive likenesses, and related elements featured in this publication are trademarks of DC Comics. The stories, characters, and incidents featured in this publication are entirely fictional. DC Comics does not read or accept unsolicited submissions of ideas, stories, or artwork. DC - a WarnerMedia Company.

DC Comics, 2900 West Alameda Ave., Burbank, CA 91505
Printed by Worzalla, Stevens Point, WI, USA. 3/26/21. First Printing.
ISBN: 978-1-77950-930-7

Library of Congress Cataloging-in-Publication Data is available.

FSC
MIX
Paper from
responsible sources
FSC® C002589
www.fsc.org

CONTENTS

Batcave Action Playset 6
May We Take a Bat-Message? 13
Pet Club 20
Pet Club: Atlantis 24
Pet Club: Penguins 28
Pet Club: Paradise Island 37
Stay for Dinner 45
Pet Club: Bunnies 47
Bee Bee 57
Battle for the Cow 60
New Recruits 64
To the Batcave! 66
Alien Pets 75
Pet-Tronics 81
Club Hoppin' 83
Ice to Meet Ya! 94
Driving Me Batty 98
All in the Batman Family 100
Got Cow? 114
Sound Check 116
Banana Splittin' 118
Streaky 124
Super-Pet Club 125
Super Fetch 129
Giant-Sized! 131
Find Fluffy 133
Tiny Titans Word Search 134

Preview: *ArkhaManiacs* 135

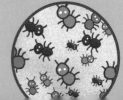

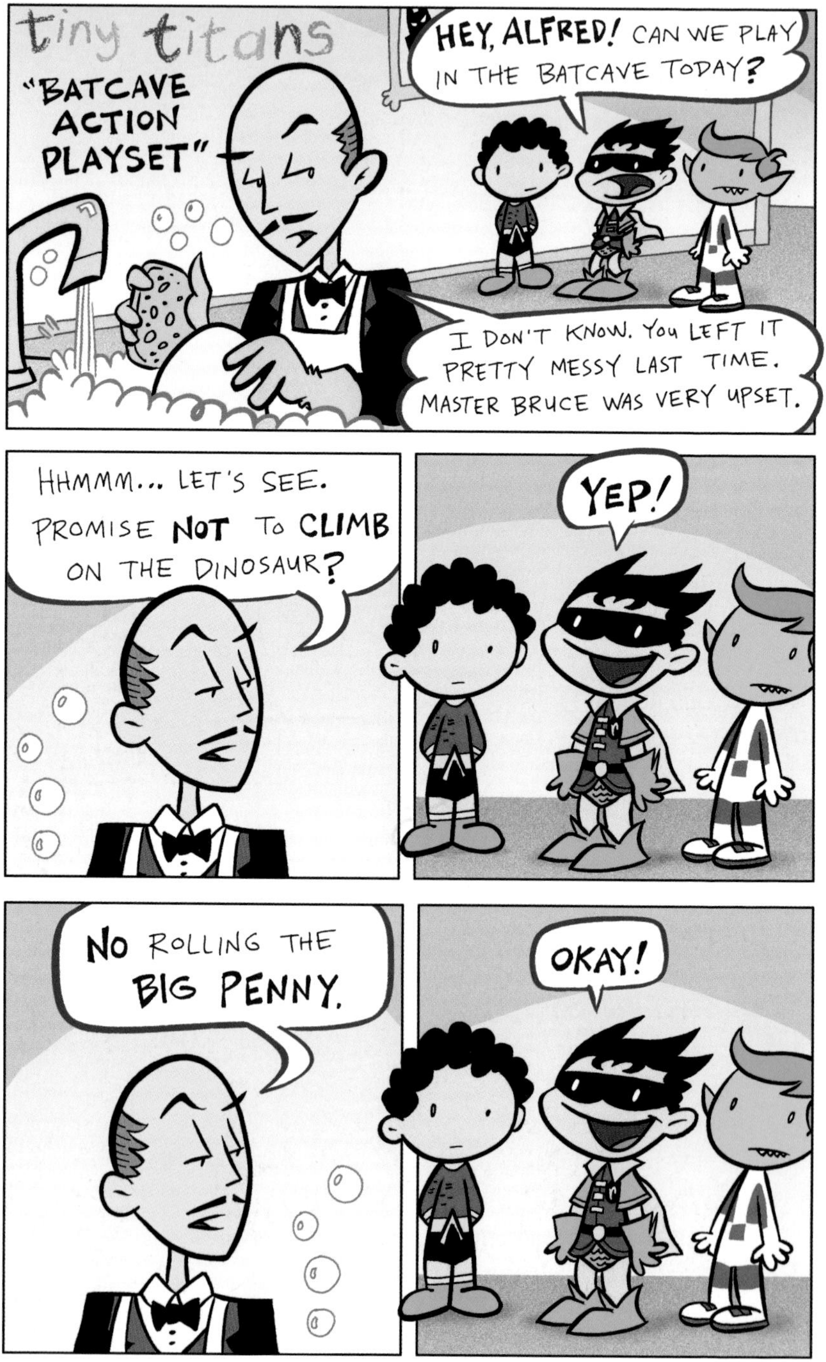
tiny titans
"BATCAVE ACTION PLAYSET"
HEY, ALFRED! CAN WE PLAY IN THE BATCAVE TODAY?
I DON'T KNOW. YOU LEFT IT PRETTY MESSY LAST TIME. MASTER BRUCE WAS VERY UPSET.
HHMMM... LET'S SEE. PROMISE NOT TO CLIMB ON THE DINOSAUR?
YEP!
NO ROLLING THE BIG PENNY.
OKAY!

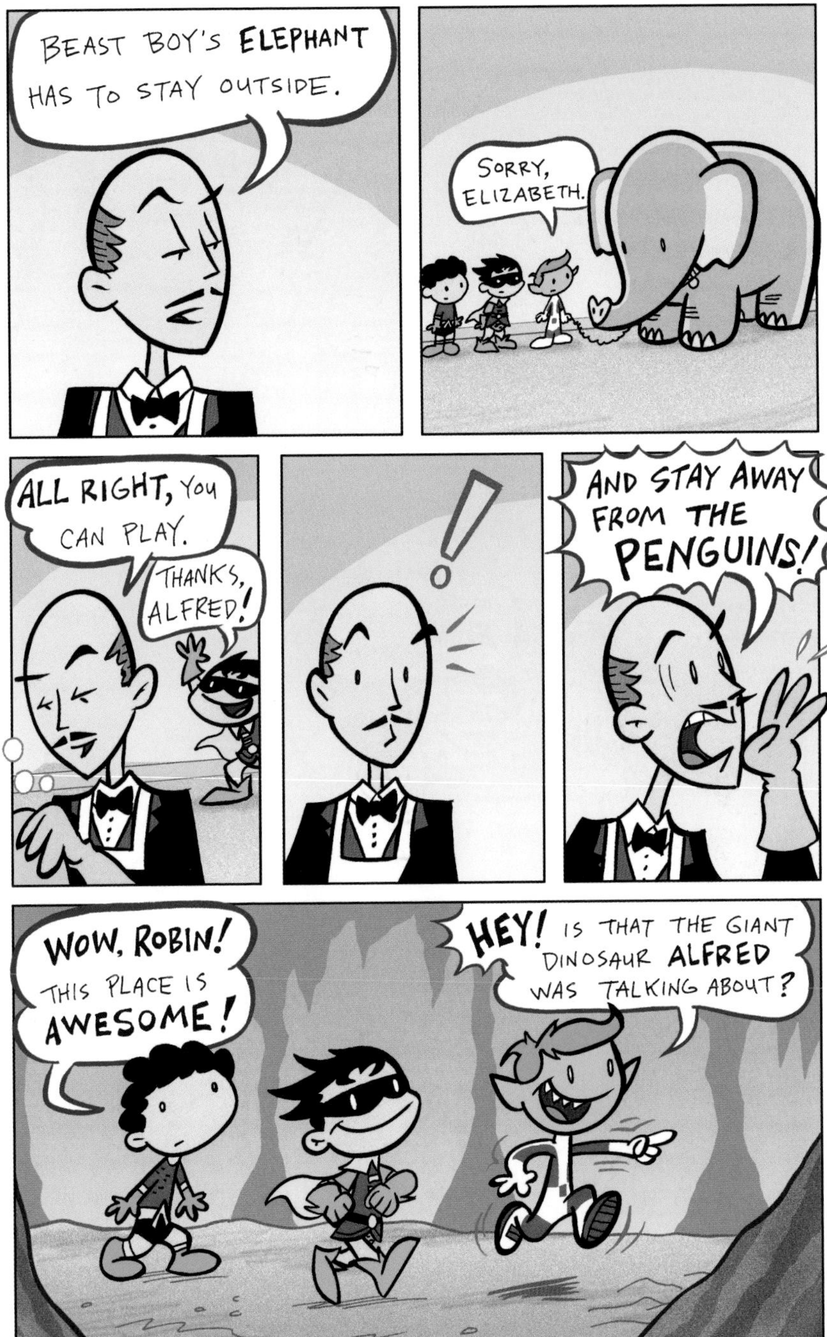
BEAST BOY'S ELEPHANT HAS TO STAY OUTSIDE.
SORRY, ELIZABETH.
ALL RIGHT, YOU CAN PLAY.
THANKS, ALFRED!
!
AND STAY AWAY FROM THE PENGUINS!
WOW, ROBIN! THIS PLACE IS AWESOME!
HEY! IS THAT THE GIANT DINOSAUR ALFRED WAS TALKING ABOUT?

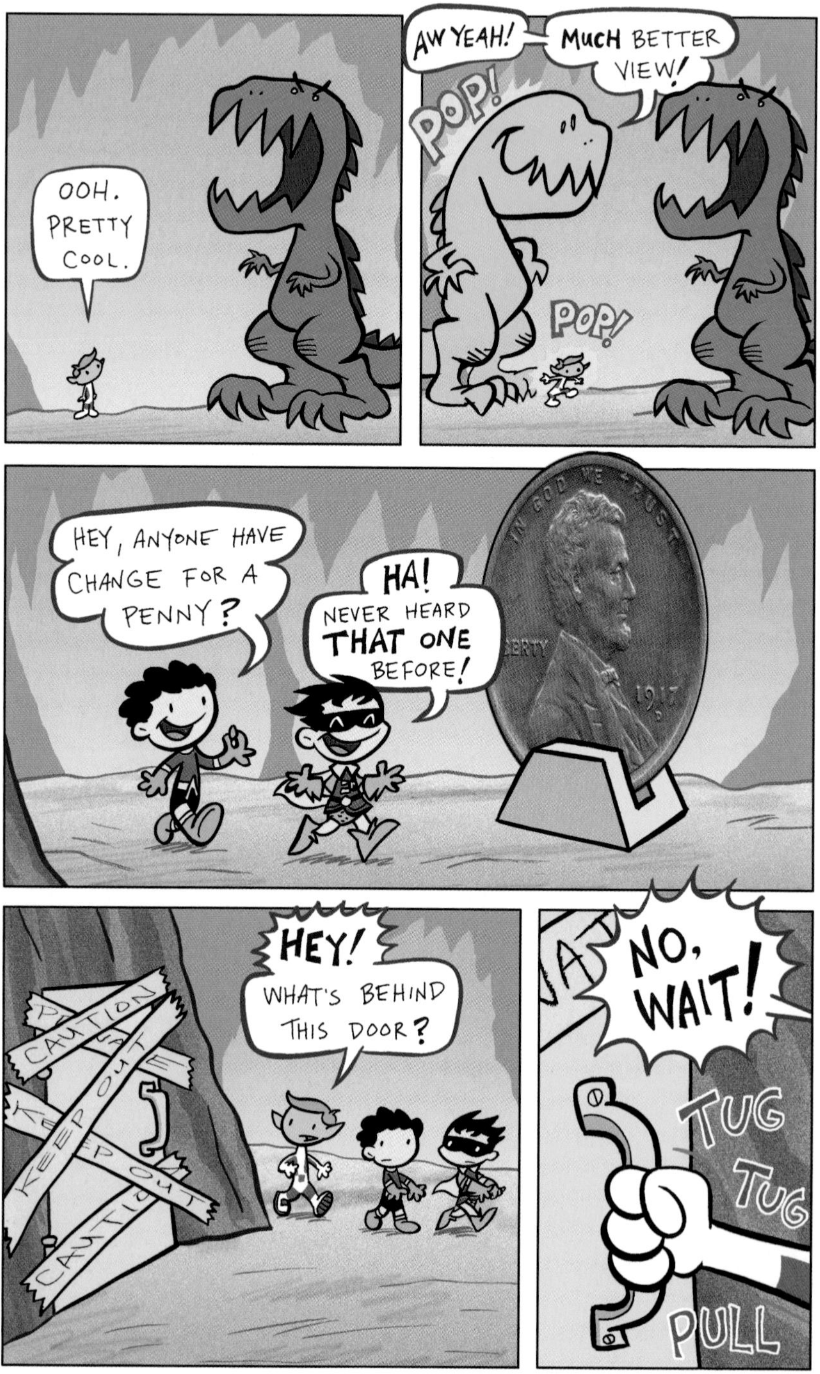
OOH. PRETTY COOL.
AW YEAH!
MUCH BETTER VIEW!
POP!
POP!
HEY, ANYONE HAVE CHANGE FOR A PENNY?
HA! NEVER HEARD THAT ONE BEFORE!
IN GOD WE TRUST
1917
HEY! WHAT'S BEHIND THIS DOOR?
CAUTION
KEEP OUT
KEEP OUT
CAUTION
NO, WAIT!
TUG
TUG
PULL

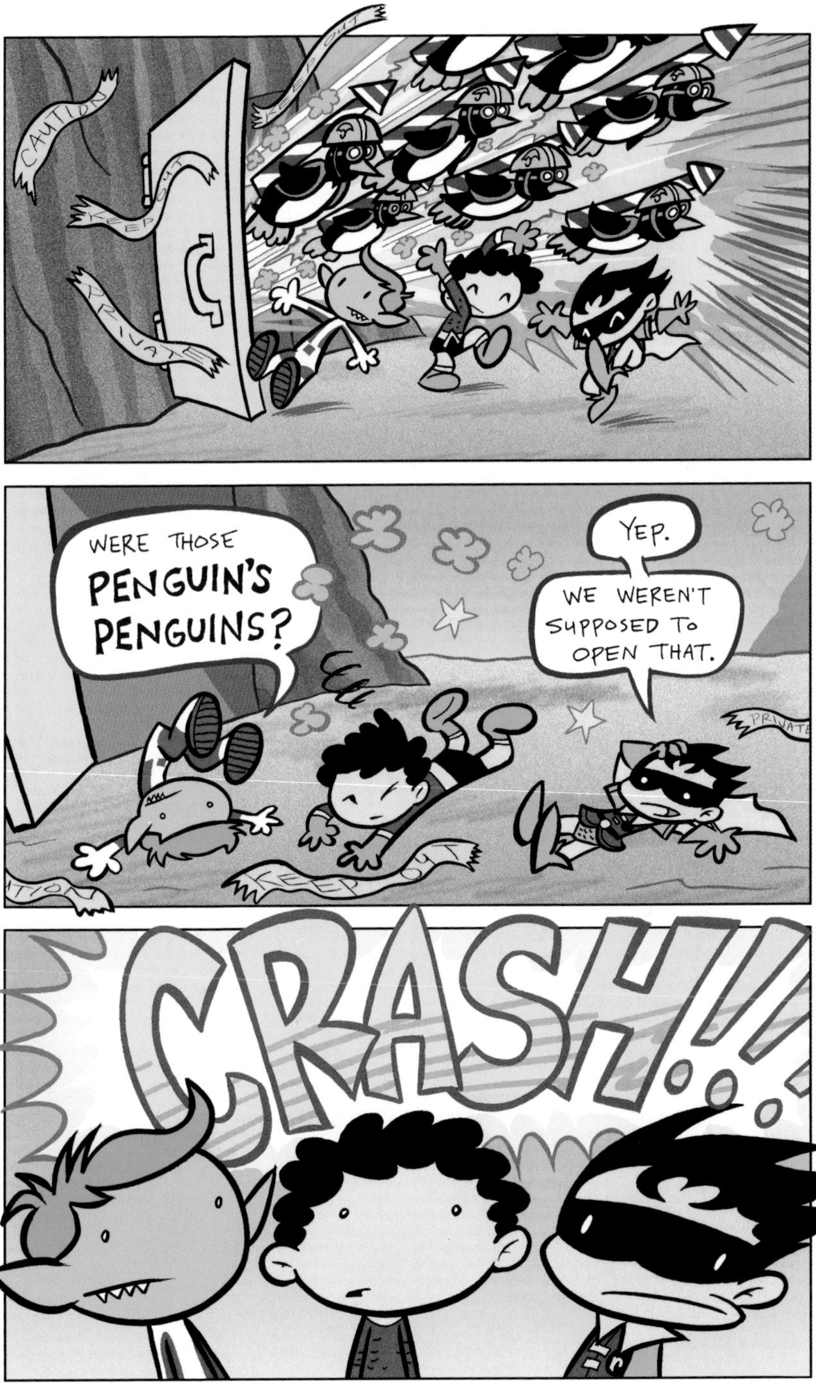
CAUTION
KEEP OUT
PRIVATE
KEEP OUT
WERE THOSE PENGUIN'S PENGUINS?
YEP.
WE WEREN'T SUPPOSED TO OPEN THAT.
PRIVATE
KEEP OUT
CRASH!!

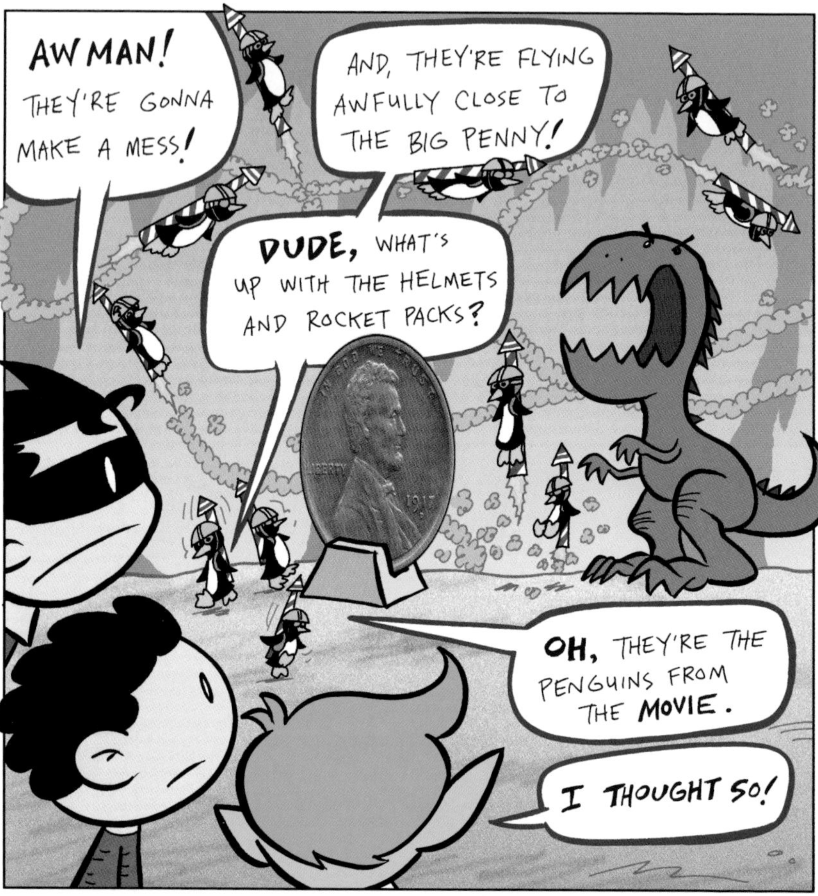
AW MAN! THEY'RE GONNA MAKE A MESS!
AND, THEY'RE FLYING AWFULLY CLOSE TO THE BIG PENNY!
DUDE, WHAT'S UP WITH THE HELMETS AND ROCKET PACKS?
OH, THEY'RE THE PENGUINS FROM THE MOVIE.
I THOUGHT SO!

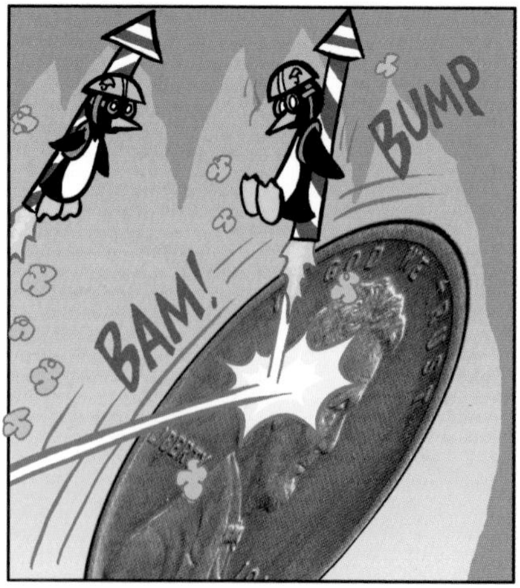
BUMP
BAM!

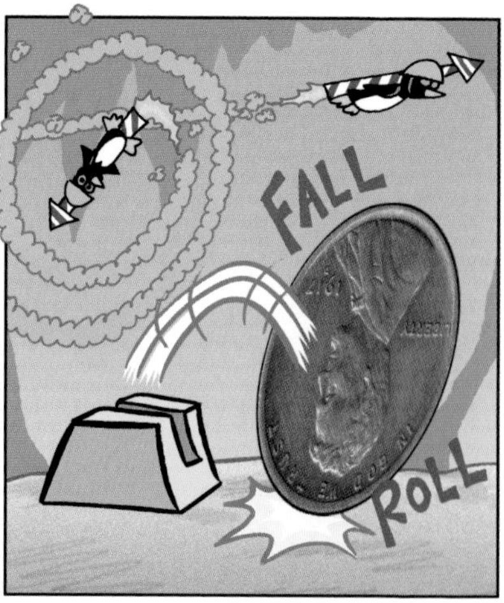
FALL
ROLL

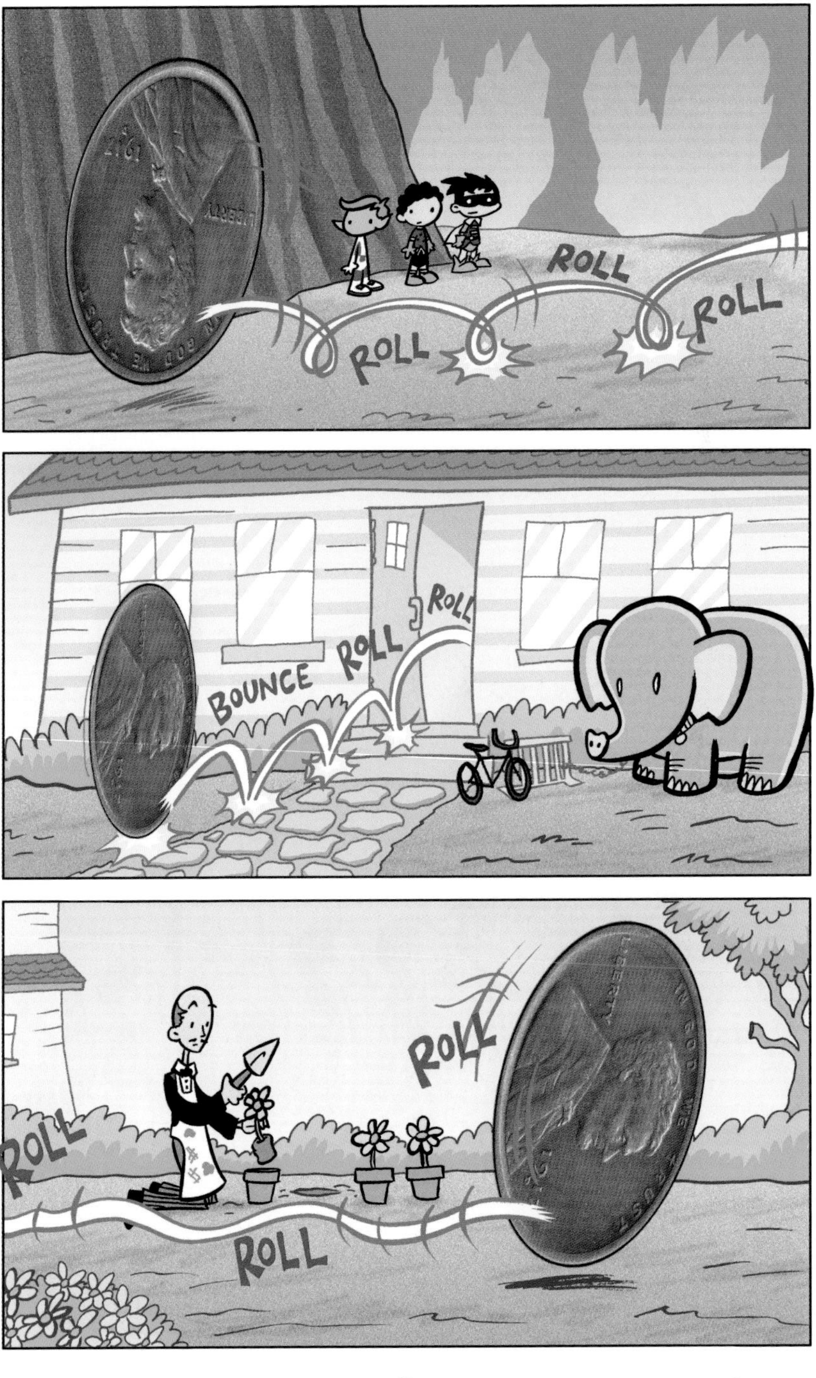
ROLL
ROLL
ROLL
BOUNCE
ROLL
ROLL
ROLL
ROLL
ROLL

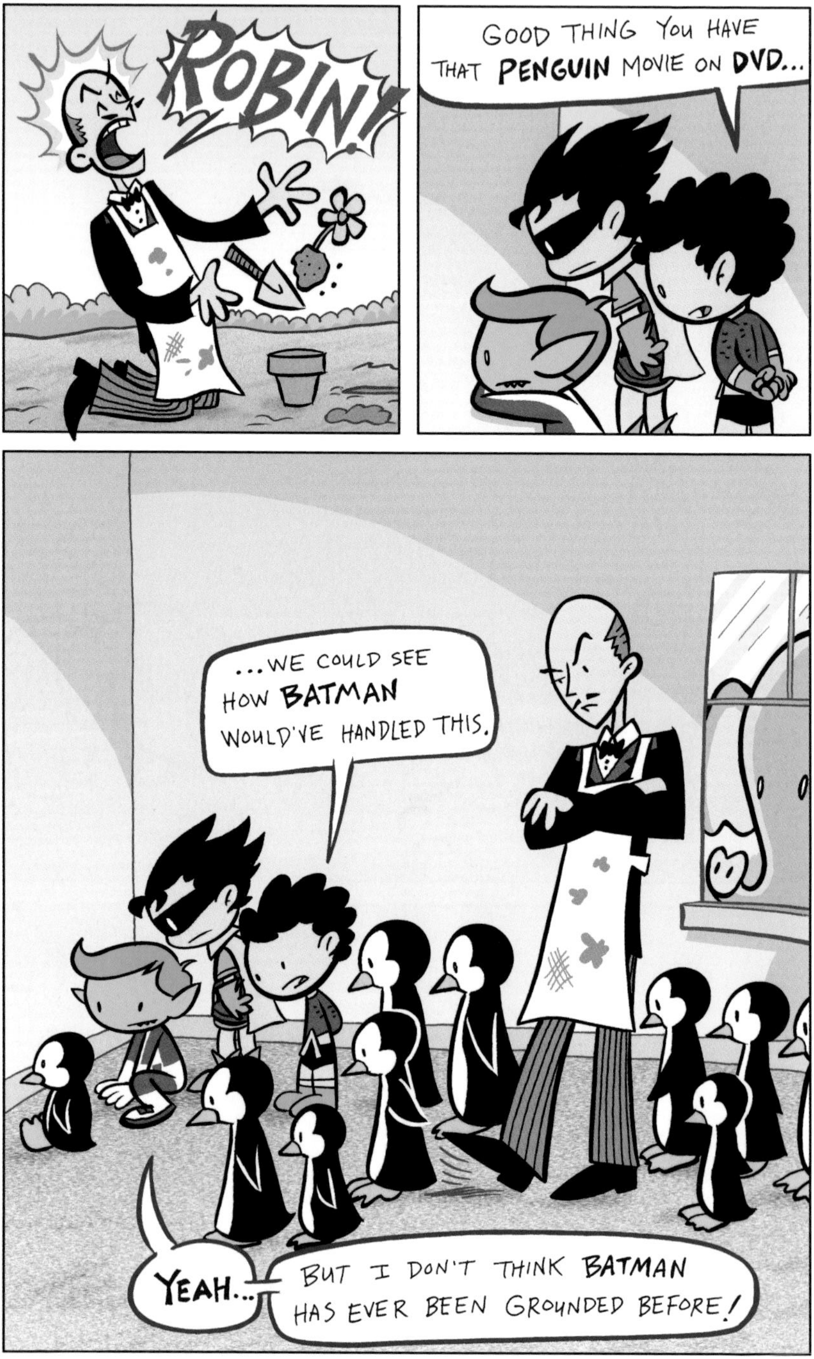
ROBIN!
GOOD THING YOU HAVE THAT PENGUIN MOVIE ON DVD...
...WE COULD SEE HOW BATMAN WOULD'VE HANDLED THIS.
YEAH...
BUT I DON'T THINK BATMAN HAS EVER BEEN GROUNDED BEFORE!

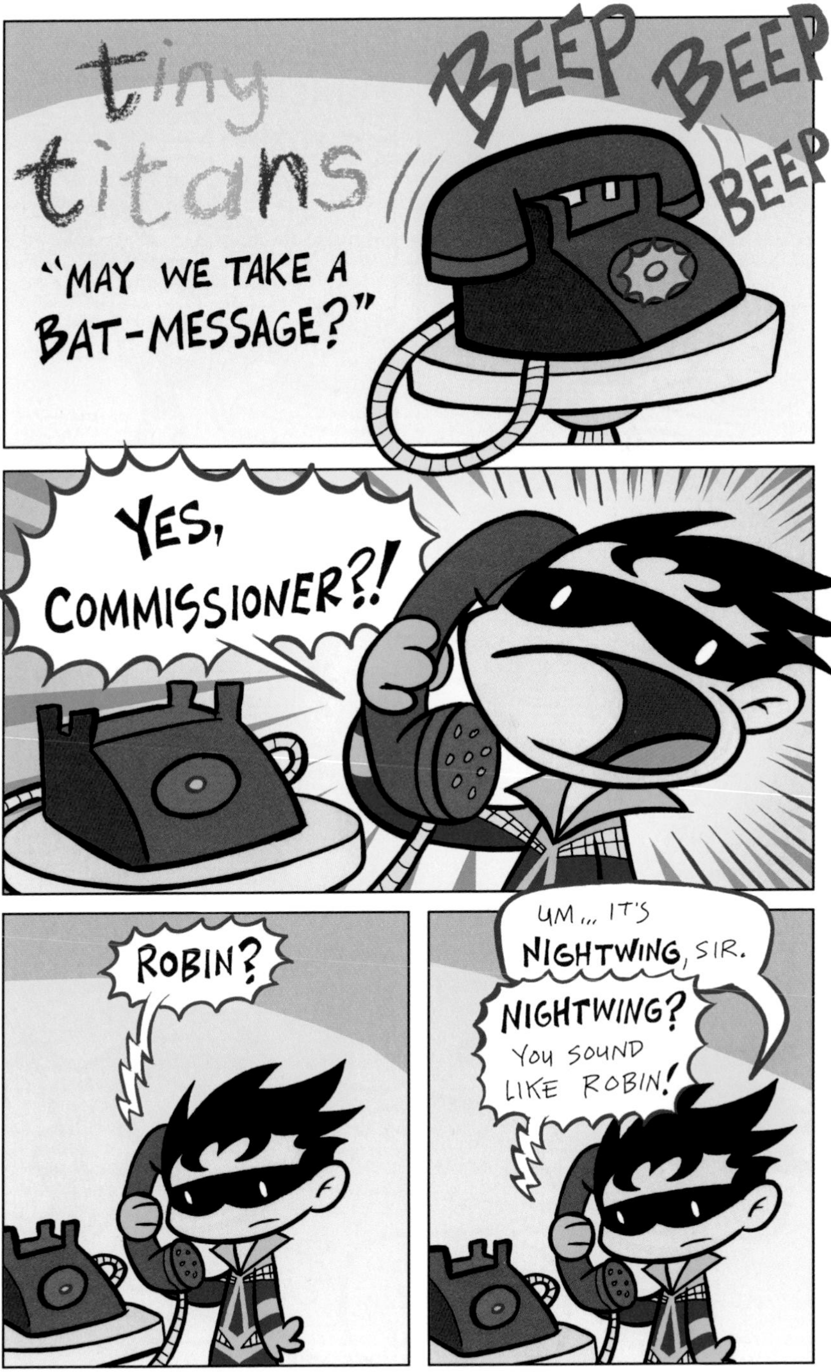
tiny titans
BEEP BEEP BEEP
BEEP
"MAY WE TAKE A BAT-MESSAGE?"
YES, COMMISSIONER?!
ROBIN?
UM... IT'S NIGHTWING, SIR.
NIGHTWING? YOU SOUND LIKE ROBIN!

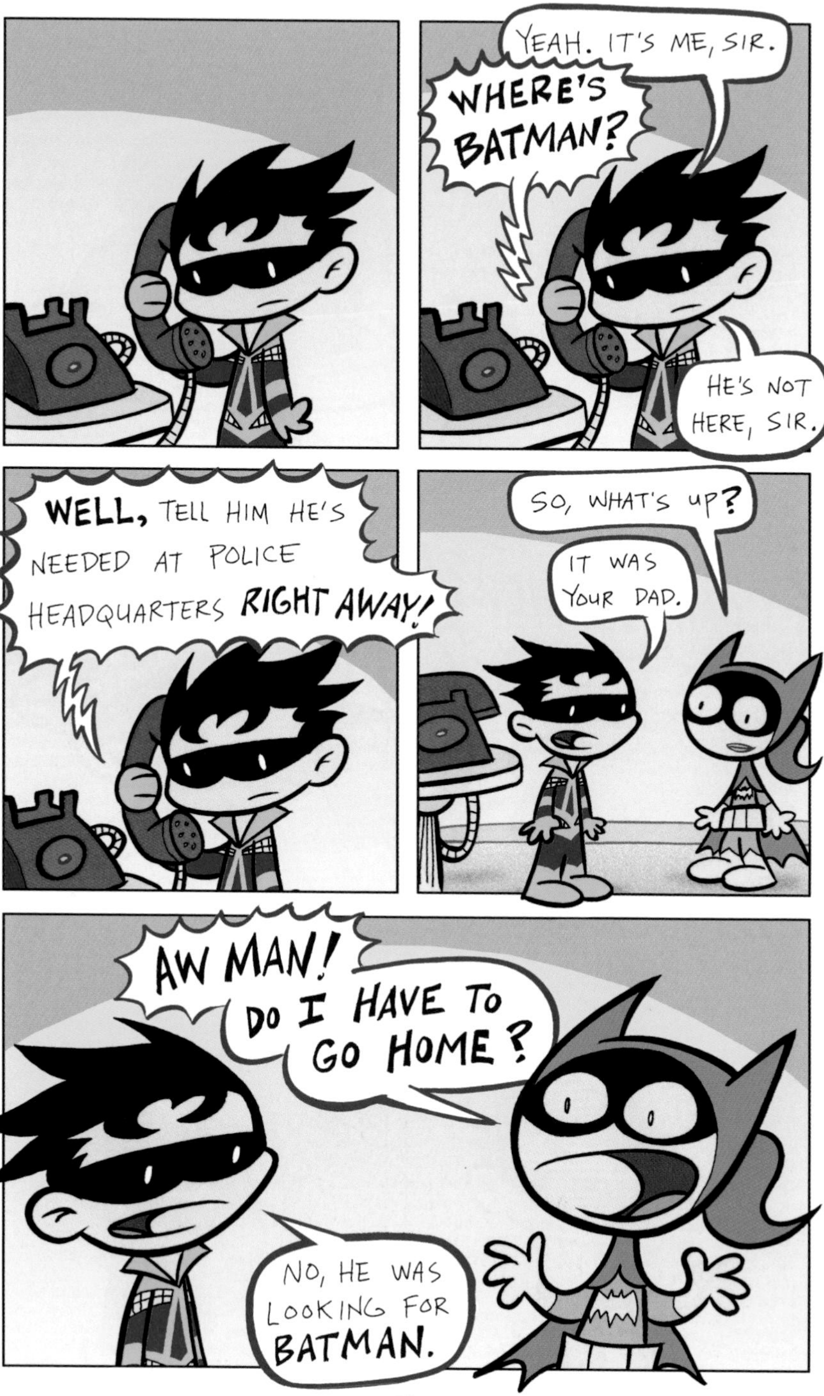
YEAH. IT'S ME, SIR.
WHERE'S BATMAN?
HE'S NOT HERE, SIR.
WELL, TELL HIM HE'S NEEDED AT POLICE HEADQUARTERS RIGHT AWAY!
SO, WHAT'S UP?
IT WAS YOUR DAD.
AW MAN!
DO I HAVE TO GO HOME?
NO, HE WAS LOOKING FOR BATMAN.

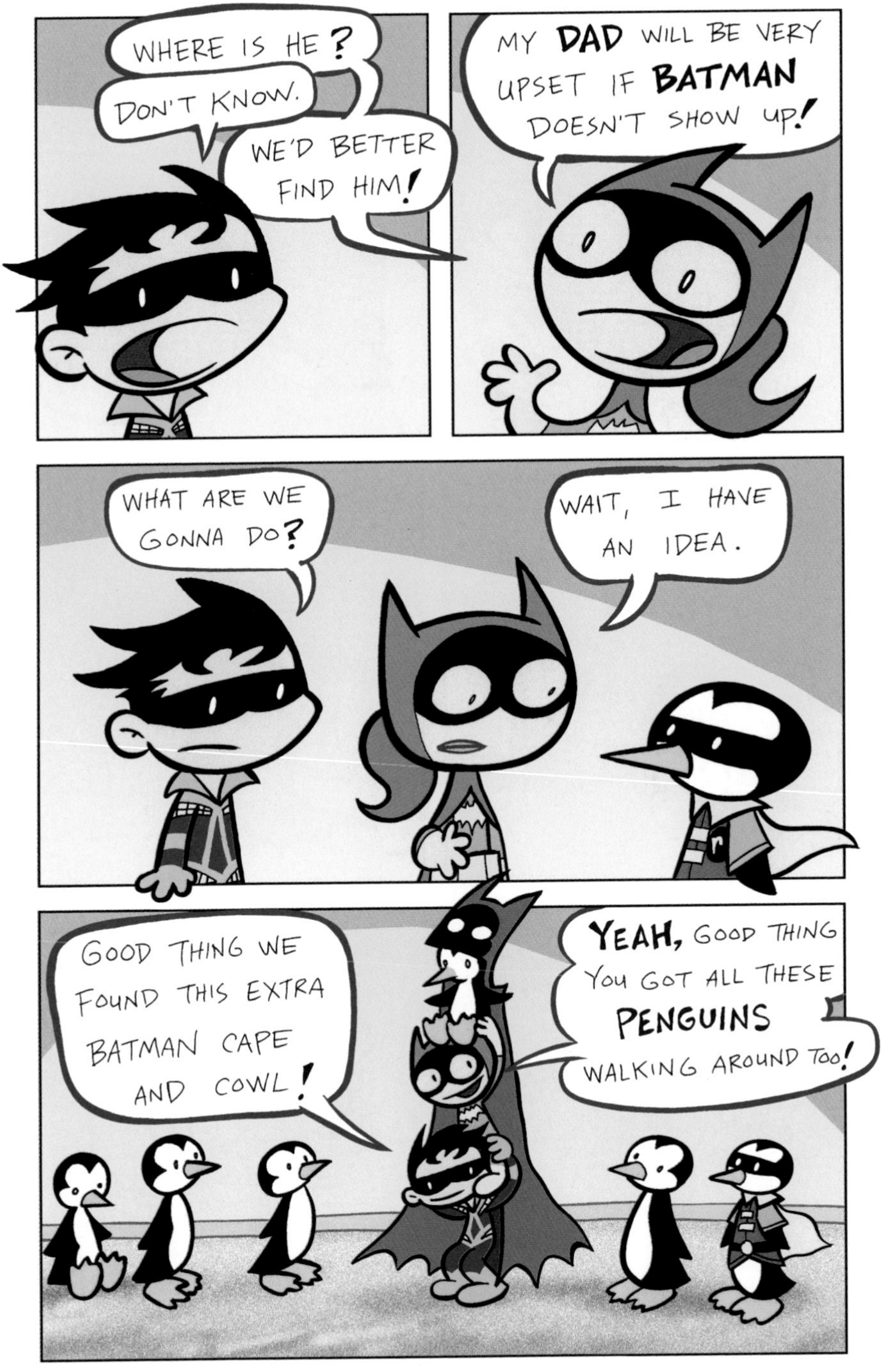
WHERE IS HE?
DON'T KNOW.
WE'D BETTER FIND HIM!
MY DAD WILL BE VERY UPSET IF BATMAN DOESN'T SHOW UP!
WHAT ARE WE GONNA DO?
WAIT, I HAVE AN IDEA.
GOOD THING WE FOUND THIS EXTRA BATMAN CAPE AND COWL!
YEAH, GOOD THING YOU GOT ALL THESE PENGUINS WALKING AROUND TOO!

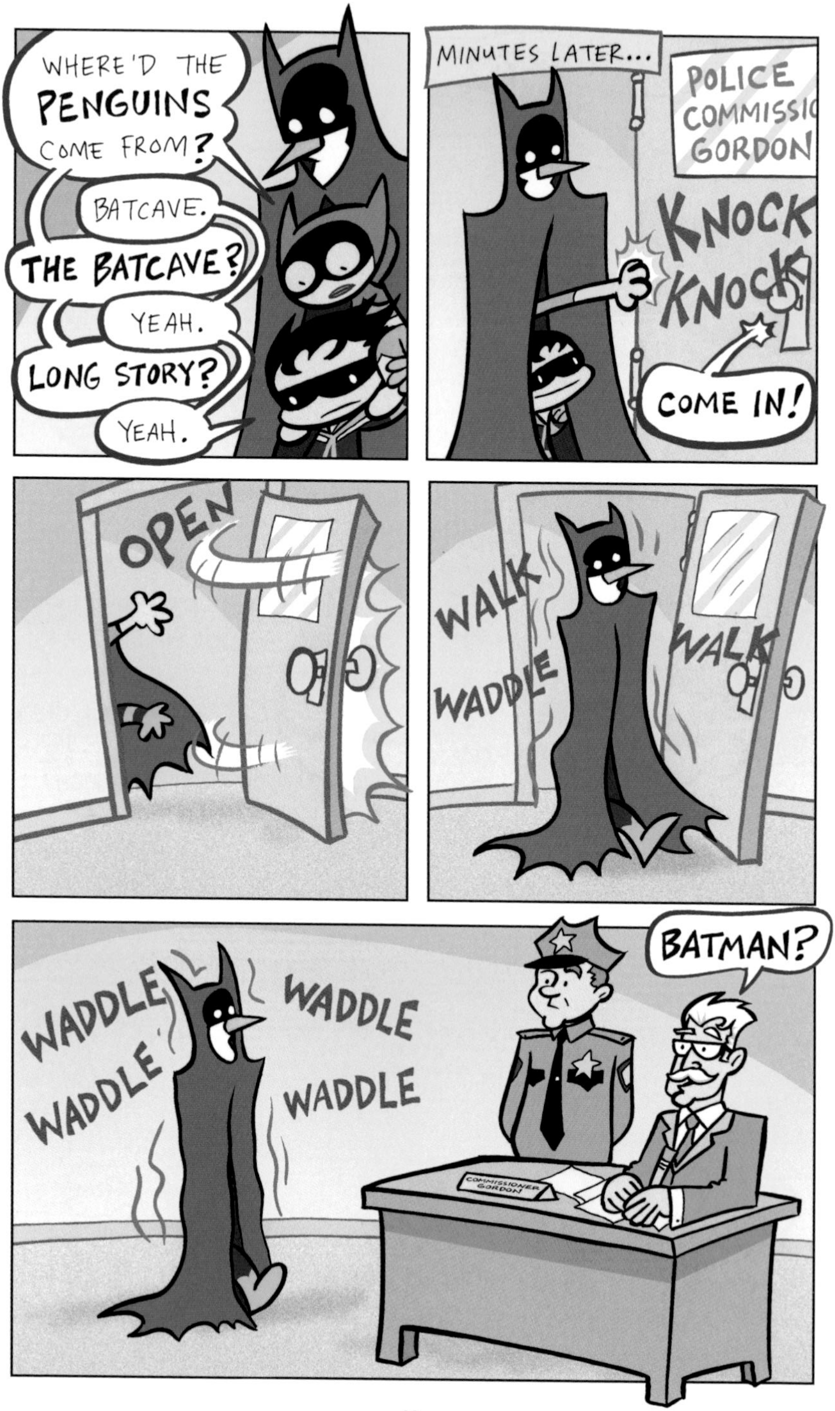
WHERE'D THE PENGUINS COME FROM?
BATCAVE.
THE BATCAVE?
YEAH.
LONG STORY?
YEAH.
MINUTES LATER...
POLICE COMMISSIO GORDON
KNOCK
KNOCK
COME IN!
OPEN
WALK
WADDLE
WALK
WADDLE
WADDLE
WADDLE
WADDLE
BATMAN?
COMMISSIONER GORDON

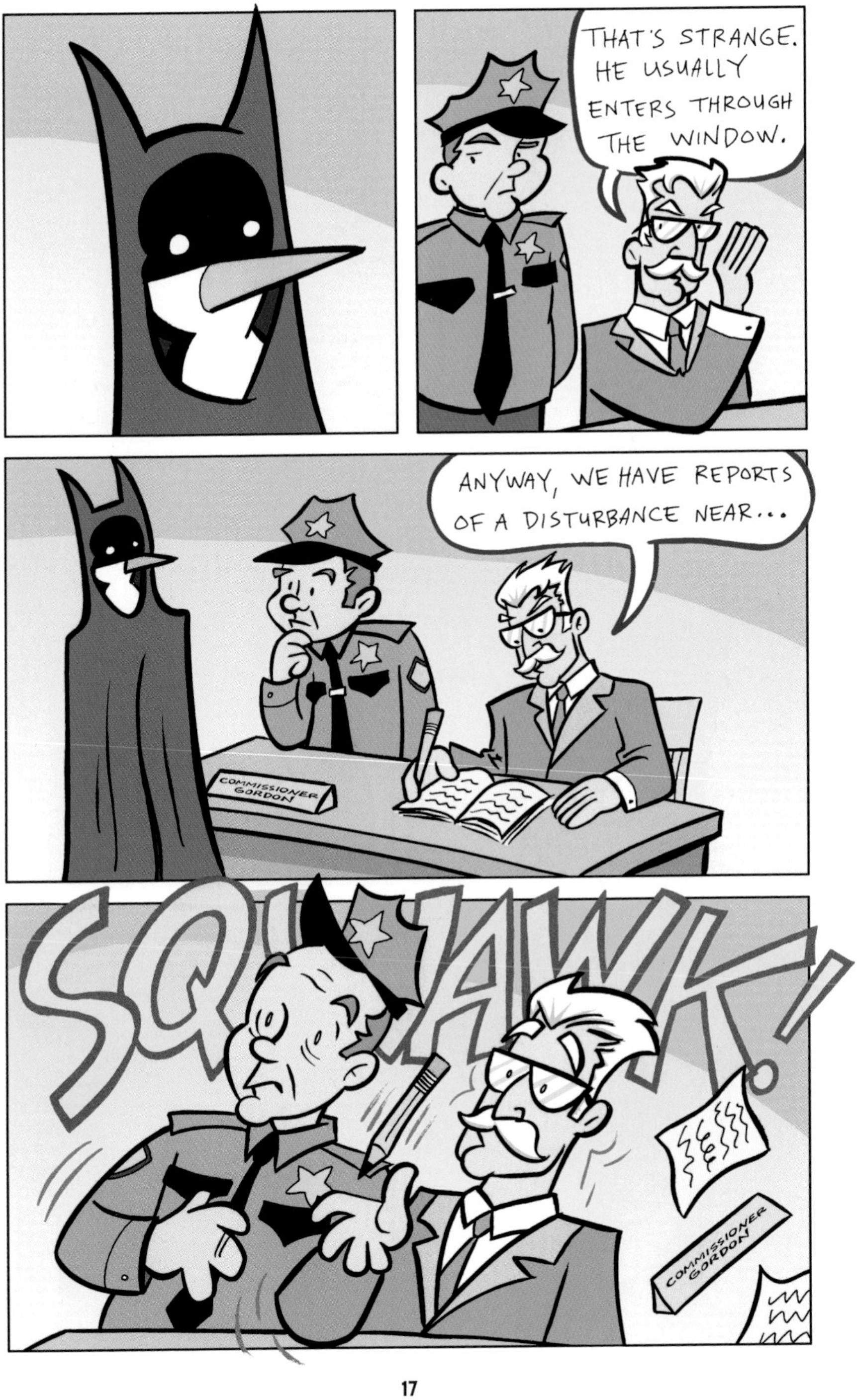
THAT'S STRANGE. HE USUALLY ENTERS THROUGH THE WINDOW.
ANYWAY, WE HAVE REPORTS OF A DISTURBANCE NEAR...
COMMISSIONER GORDON
SQUAWK!
COMMISSIONER GORDON

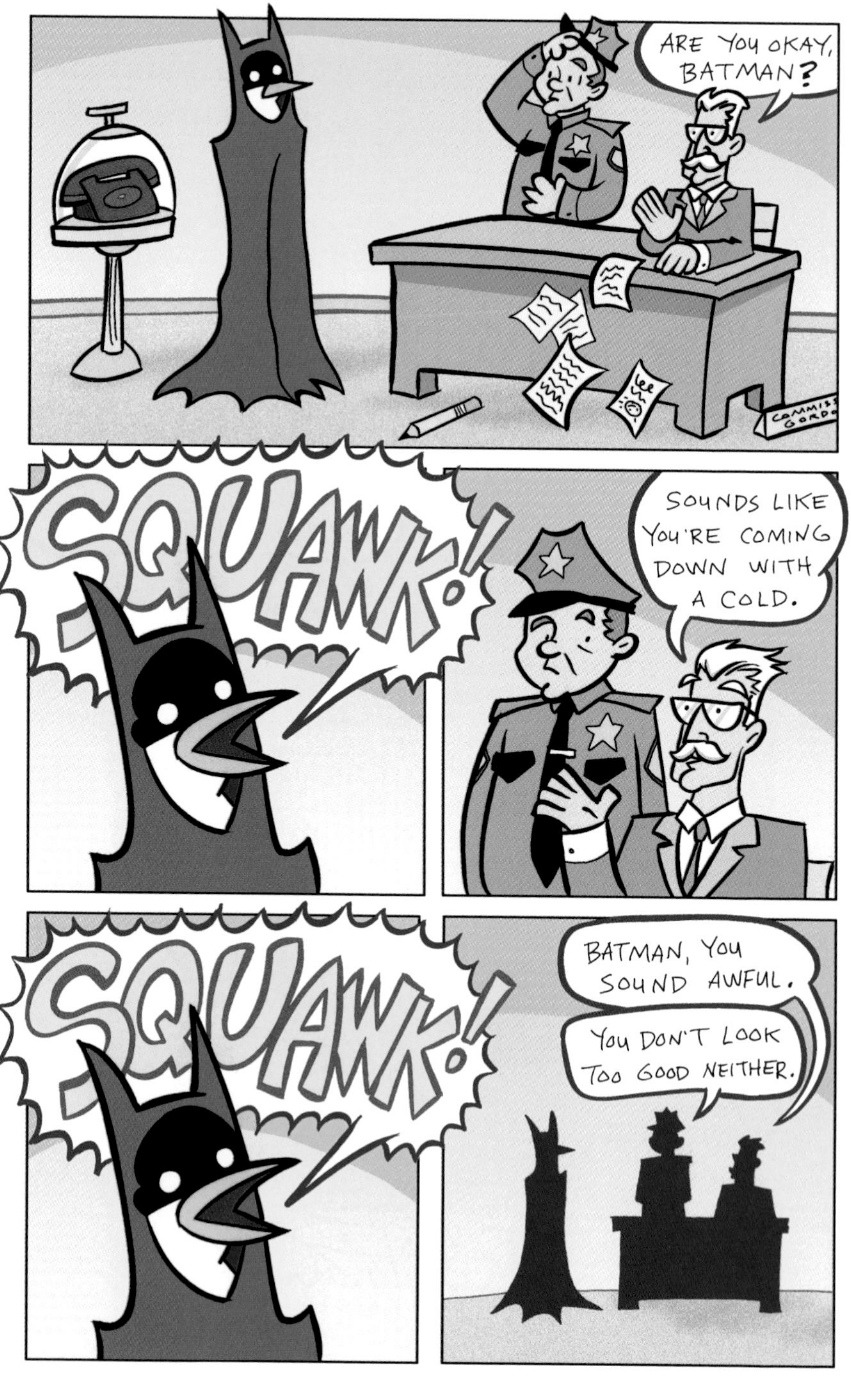
ARE YOU OKAY, BATMAN?
COMMISS GORDO
SQUAWK!
SOUNDS LIKE YOU'RE COMING DOWN WITH A COLD.
SQUAWK!
BATMAN, YOU SOUND AWFUL.
YOU DON'T LOOK TOO GOOD NEITHER.

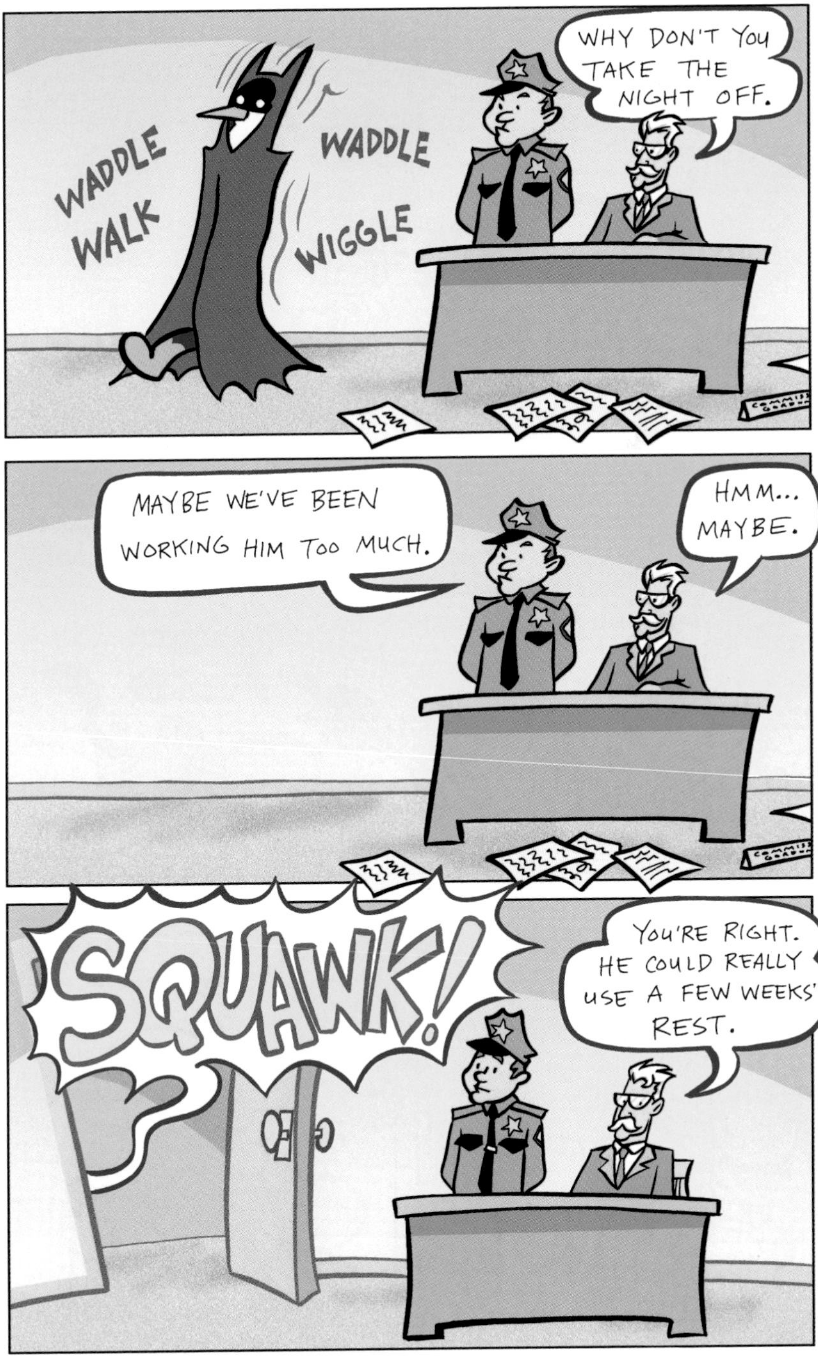
WADDLE
WALK
WADDLE
WIGGLE
WHY DON'T YOU TAKE THE NIGHT OFF.
MAYBE WE'VE BEEN WORKING HIM TOO MUCH.
HMM... MAYBE.
SQUAWK!
YOU'RE RIGHT. HE COULD REALLY USE A FEW WEEKS' REST.

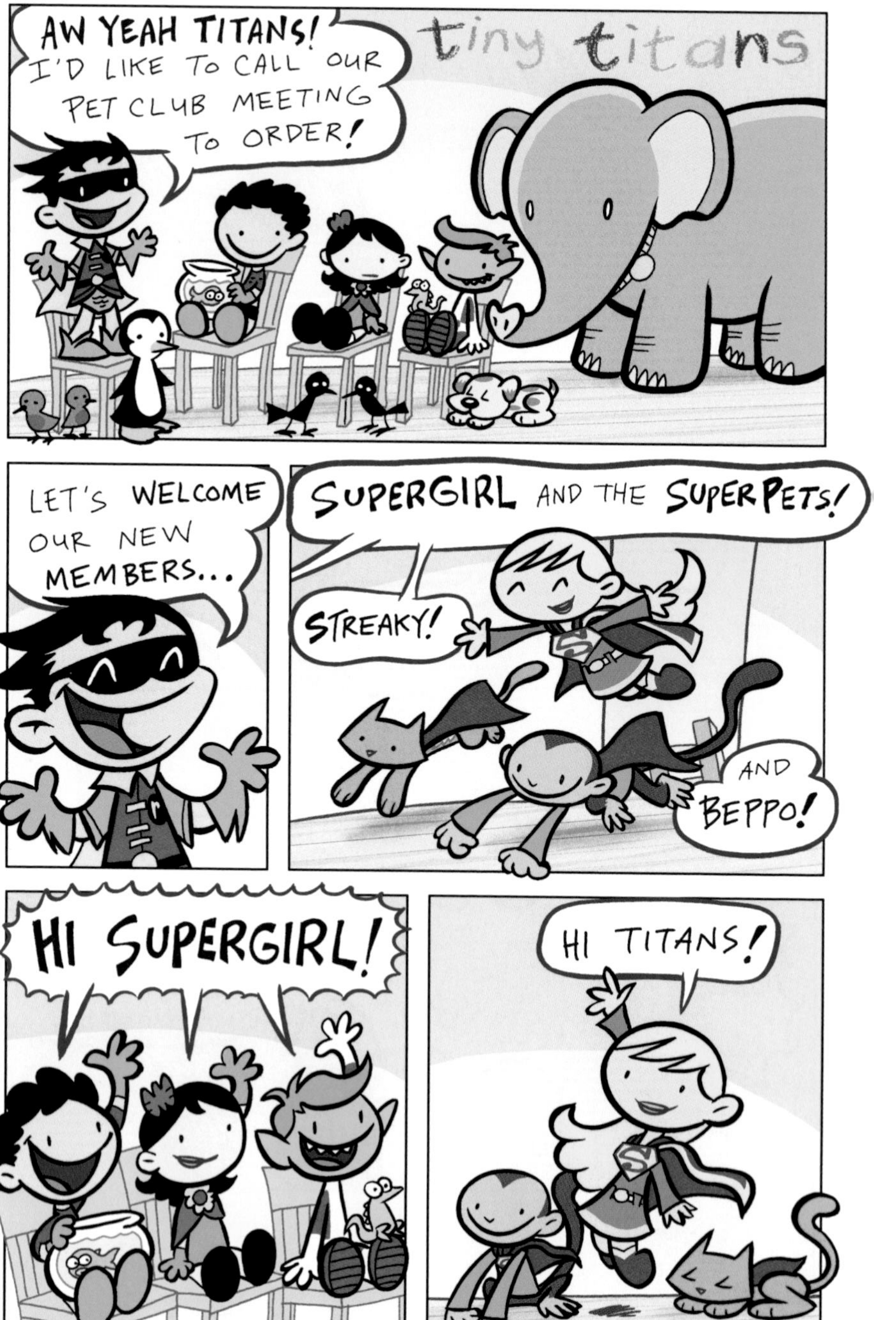
tiny titans
AW YEAH TITANS! I'D LIKE TO CALL OUR PET CLUB MEETING TO ORDER!
LET'S WELCOME OUR NEW MEMBERS...
SUPERGIRL AND THE SUPERPETS!
STREAKY!
AND BEPPO!
HI SUPERGIRL!
HI TITANS!

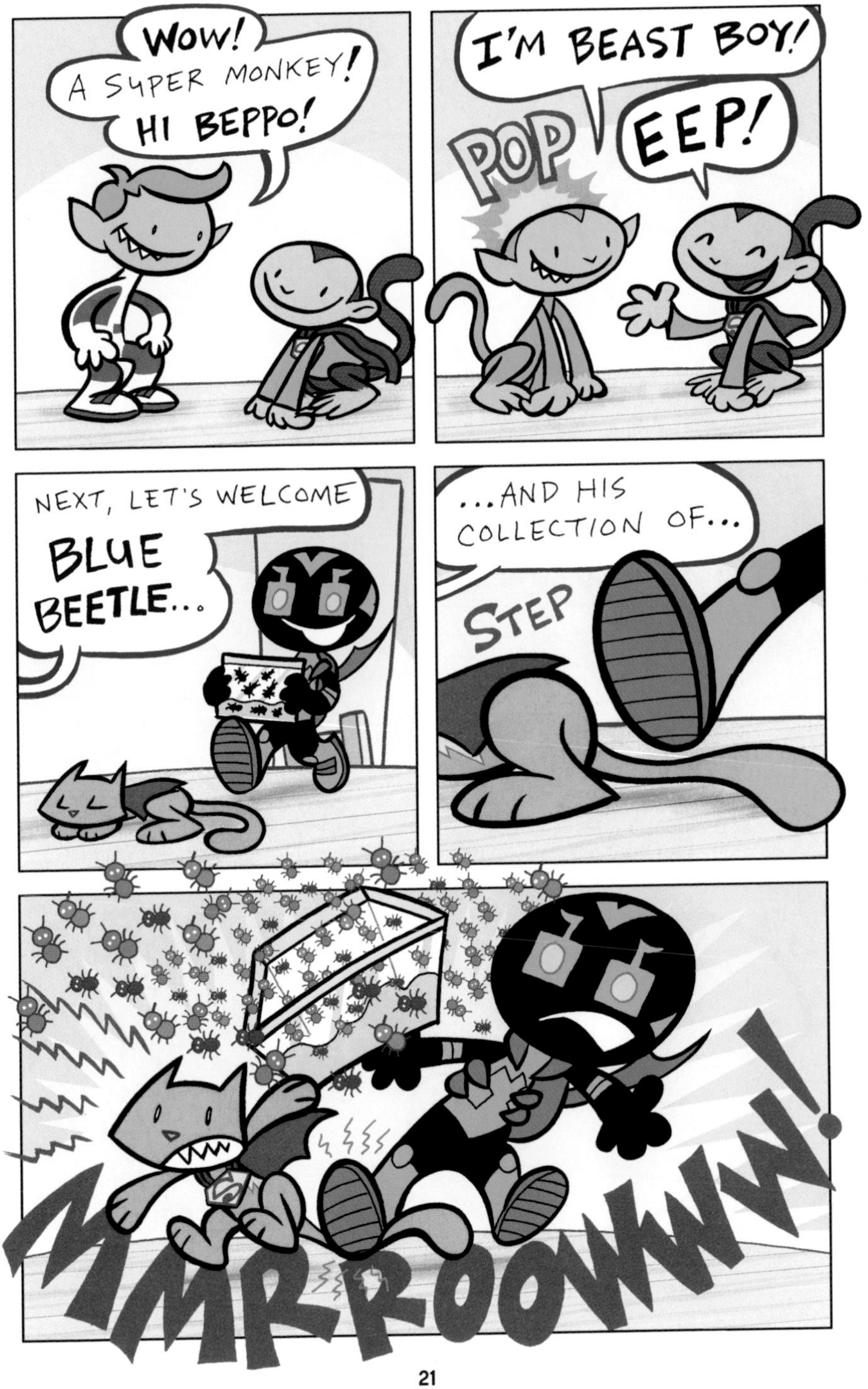
WOW!
A SUPER MONKEY!
HI BEPPO!
I'M BEAST BOY!
POP
EEP!
NEXT, LET'S WELCOME
BLUE BEETLE...
...AND HIS COLLECTION OF...
STEP
MMRROOWWW!

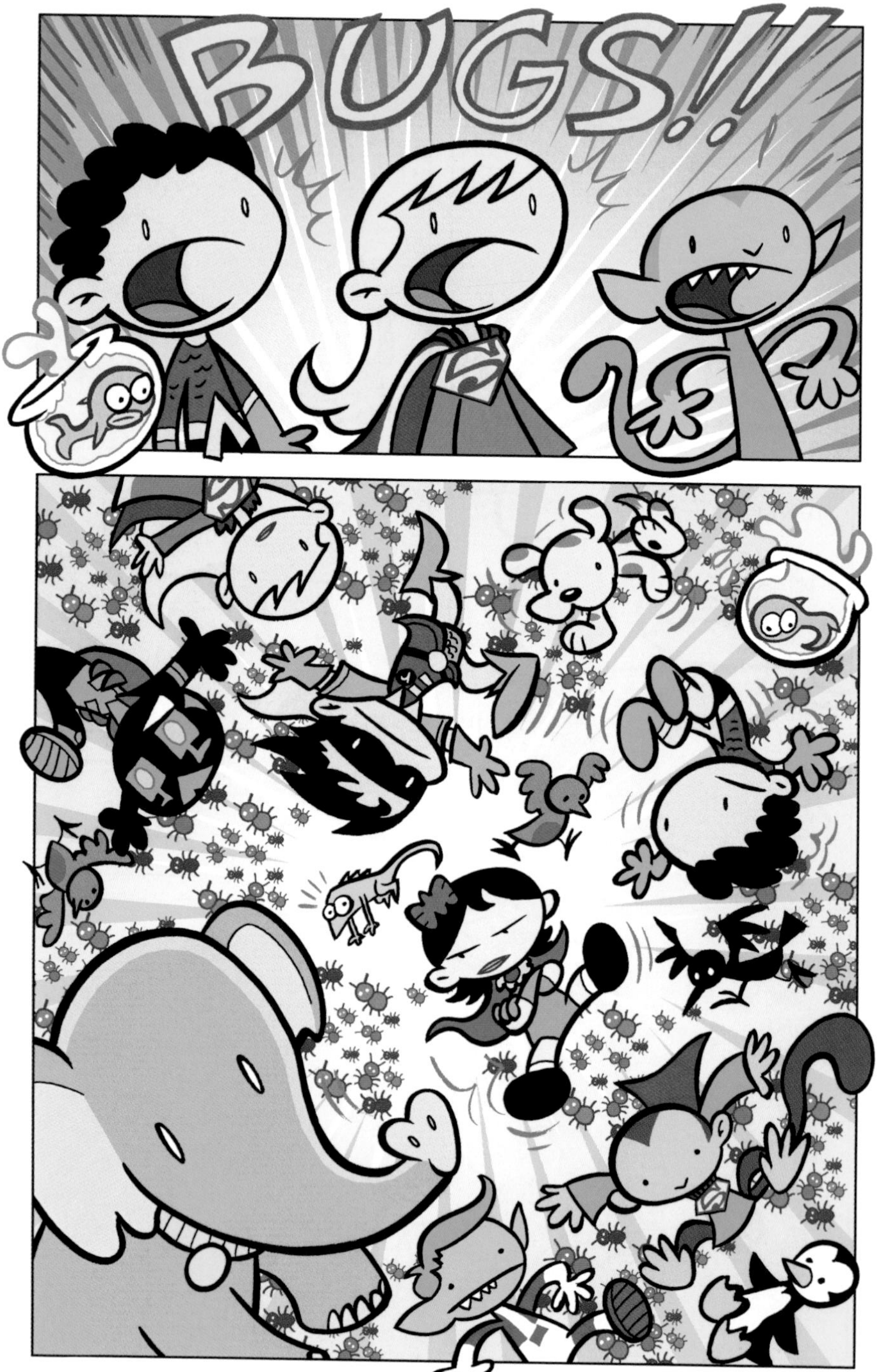
BUGS!!

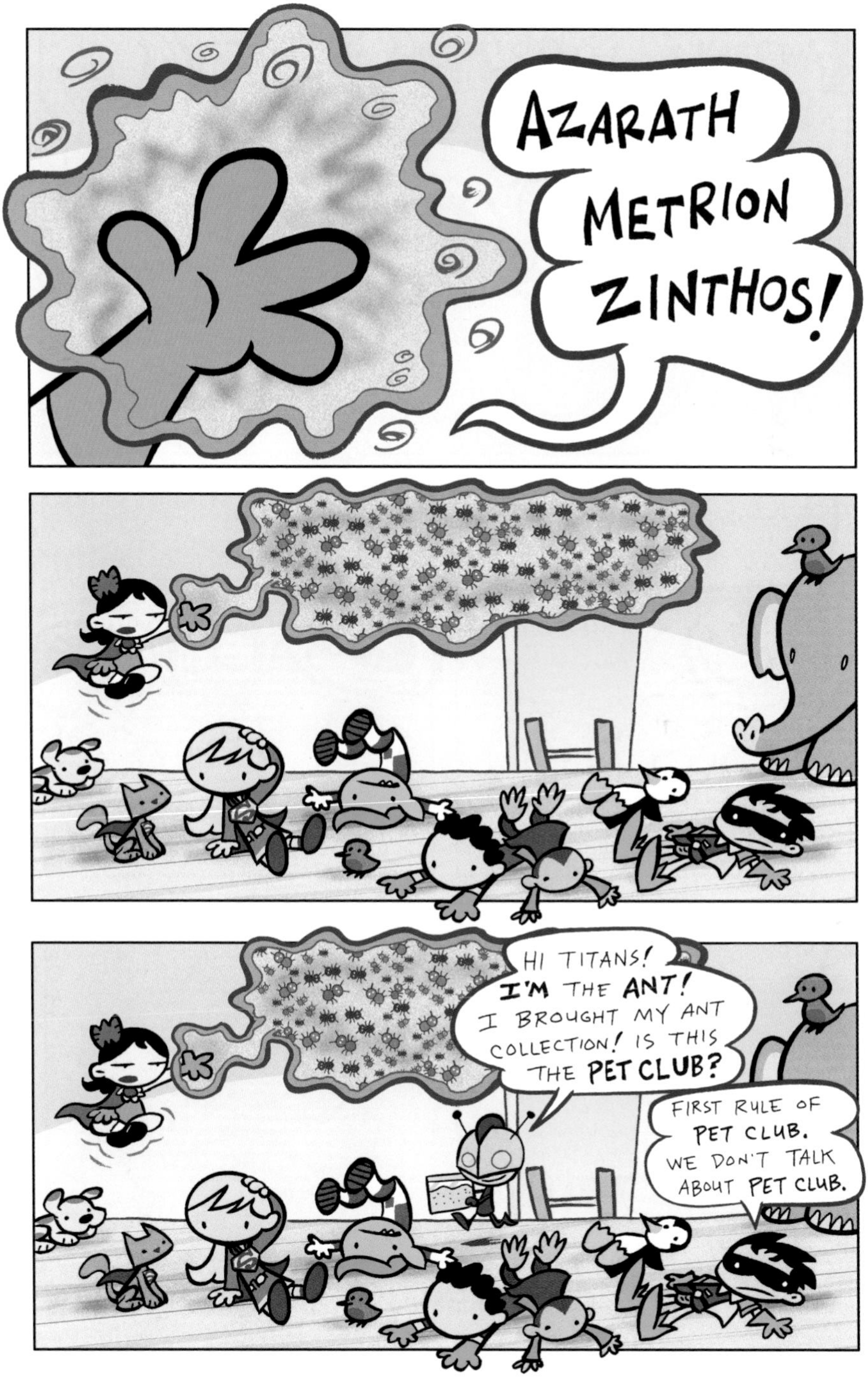
AZARATH METRION ZINTHOS!
HI TITANS! I'M THE ANT! I BROUGHT MY ANT COLLECTION! IS THIS THE PET CLUB?
FIRST RULE OF PET CLUB. WE DON'T TALK ABOUT PET CLUB.

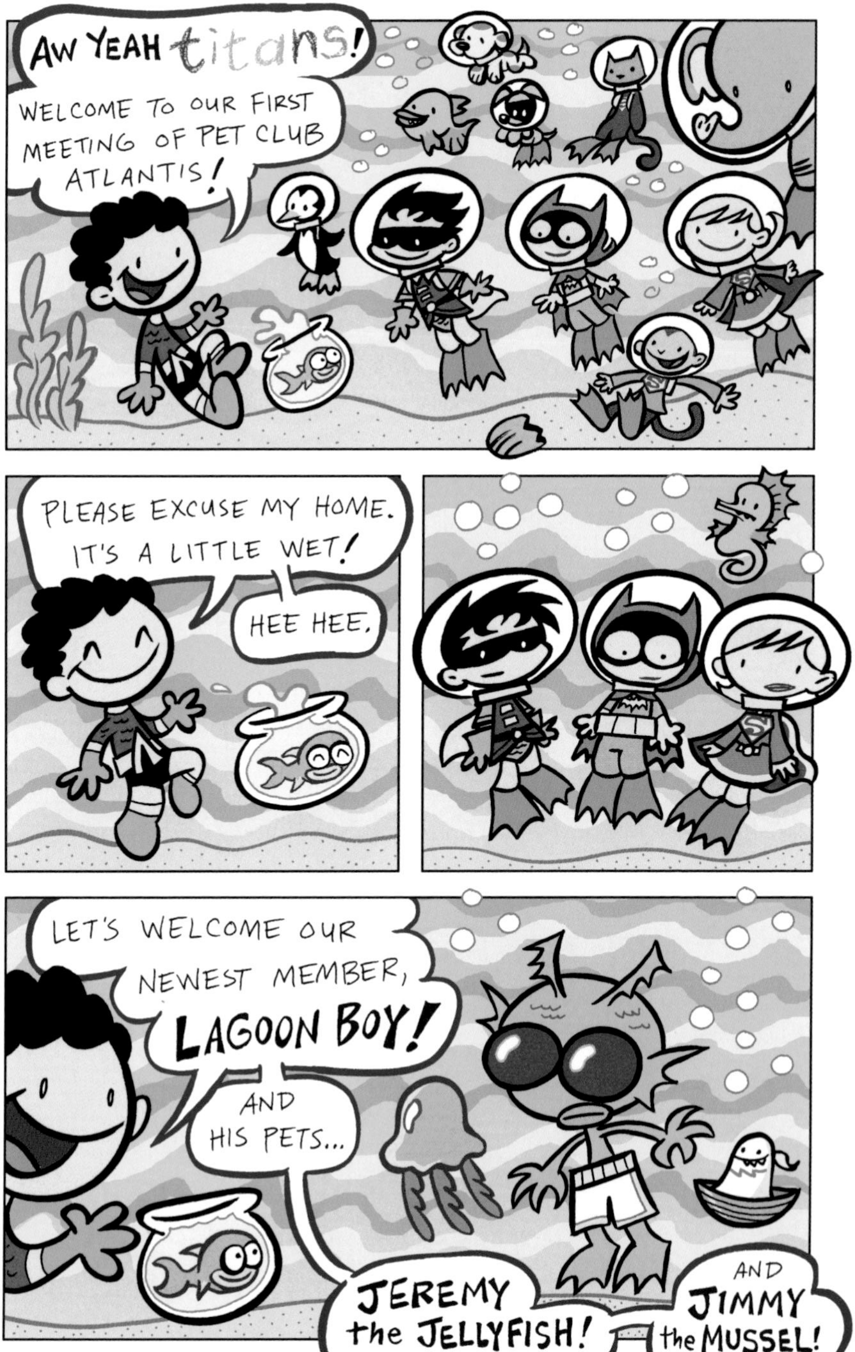
AW YEAH titans!
WELCOME TO OUR FIRST MEETING OF PET CLUB ATLANTIS!
PLEASE EXCUSE MY HOME. IT'S A LITTLE WET!
HEE HEE.
LET'S WELCOME OUR NEWEST MEMBER, LAGOON BOY!
AND HIS PETS...
JEREMY the JELLYFISH!
AND JIMMY the MUSSEL!

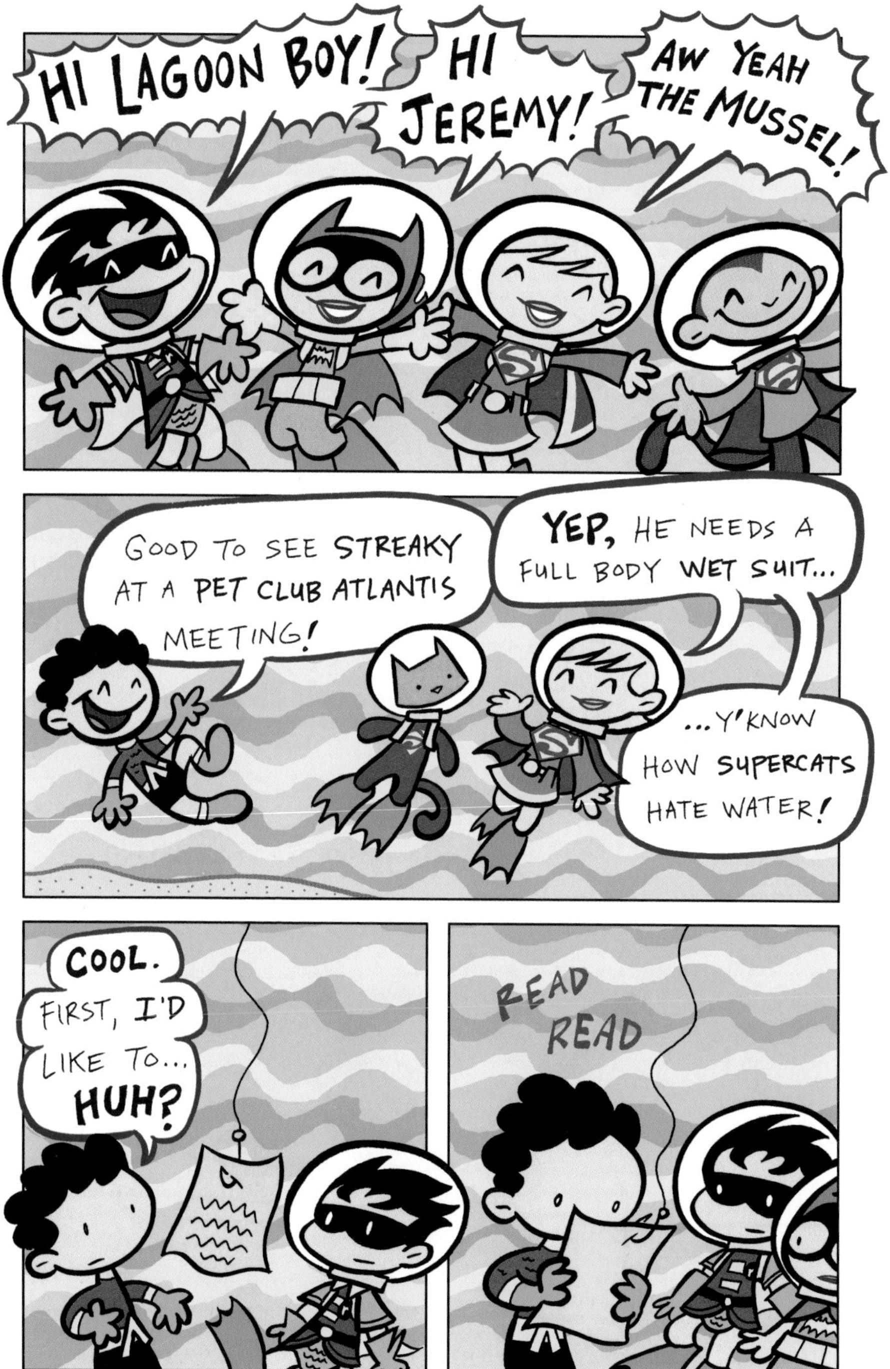
HI LAGOON BOY!
HI JEREMY!
AW YEAH THE MUSSEL!
GOOD TO SEE STREAKY AT A PET CLUB ATLANTIS MEETING!
YEP, HE NEEDS A FULL BODY WET SUIT...
...Y'KNOW HOW SUPERCATS HATE WATER!
COOL. FIRST, I'D LIKE TO... HUH?
READ READ

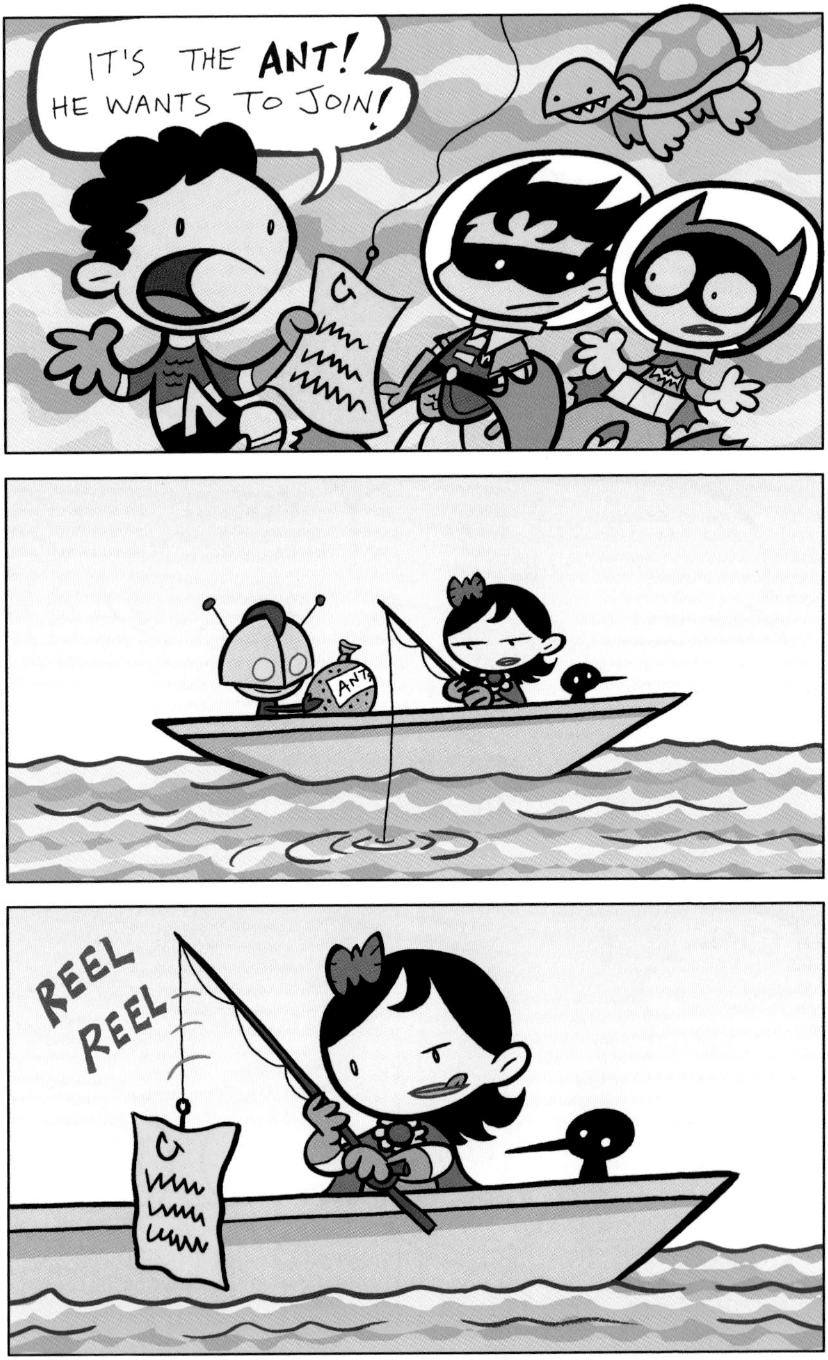
IT'S THE ANT! HE WANTS TO JOIN!
ANTS
REEL
REEL

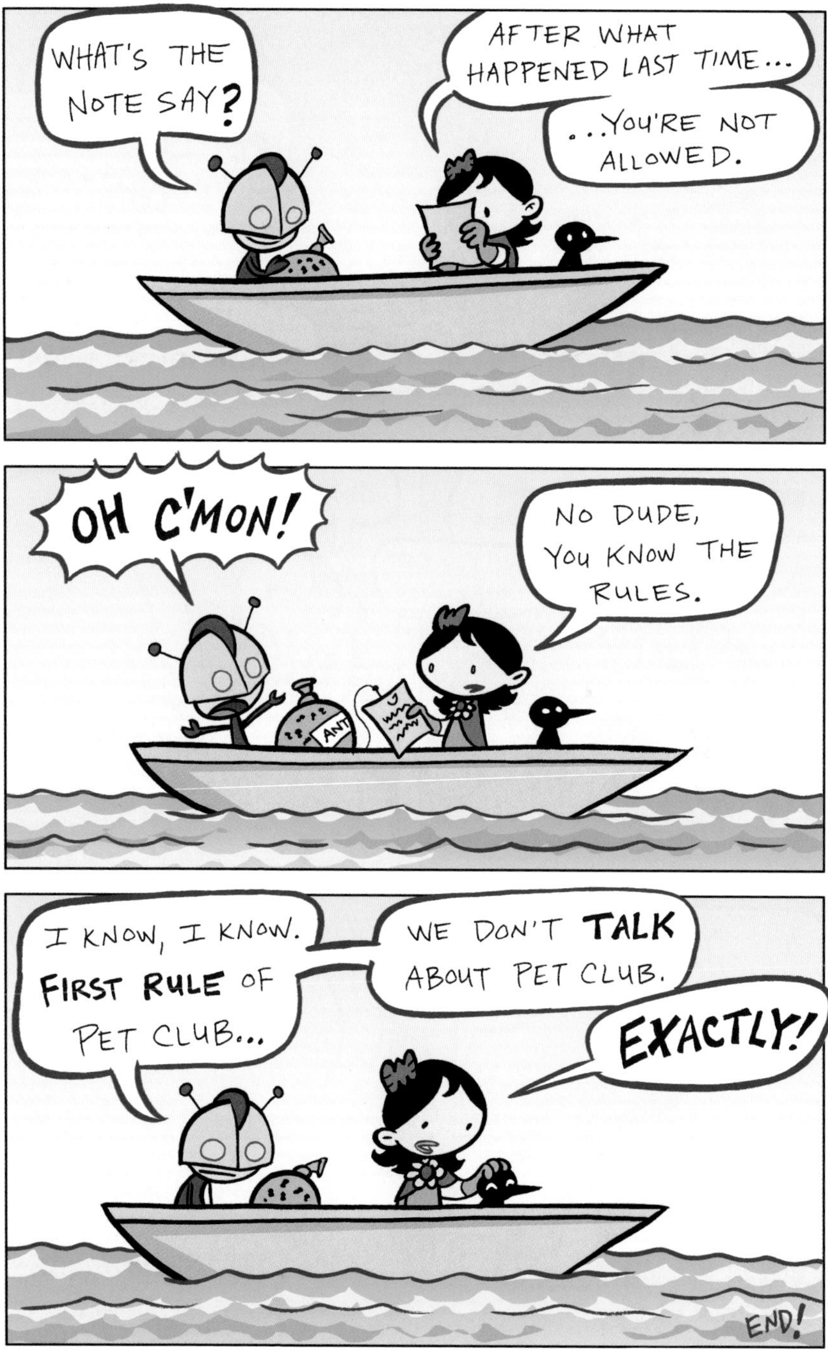
WHAT'S THE NOTE SAY?
AFTER WHAT HAPPENED LAST TIME...
...YOU'RE NOT ALLOWED.
OH C'MON!
NO DUDE, YOU KNOW THE RULES.
ANT
I KNOW, I KNOW. FIRST RULE OF PET CLUB...
WE DON'T TALK ABOUT PET CLUB.
EXACTLY!
END!

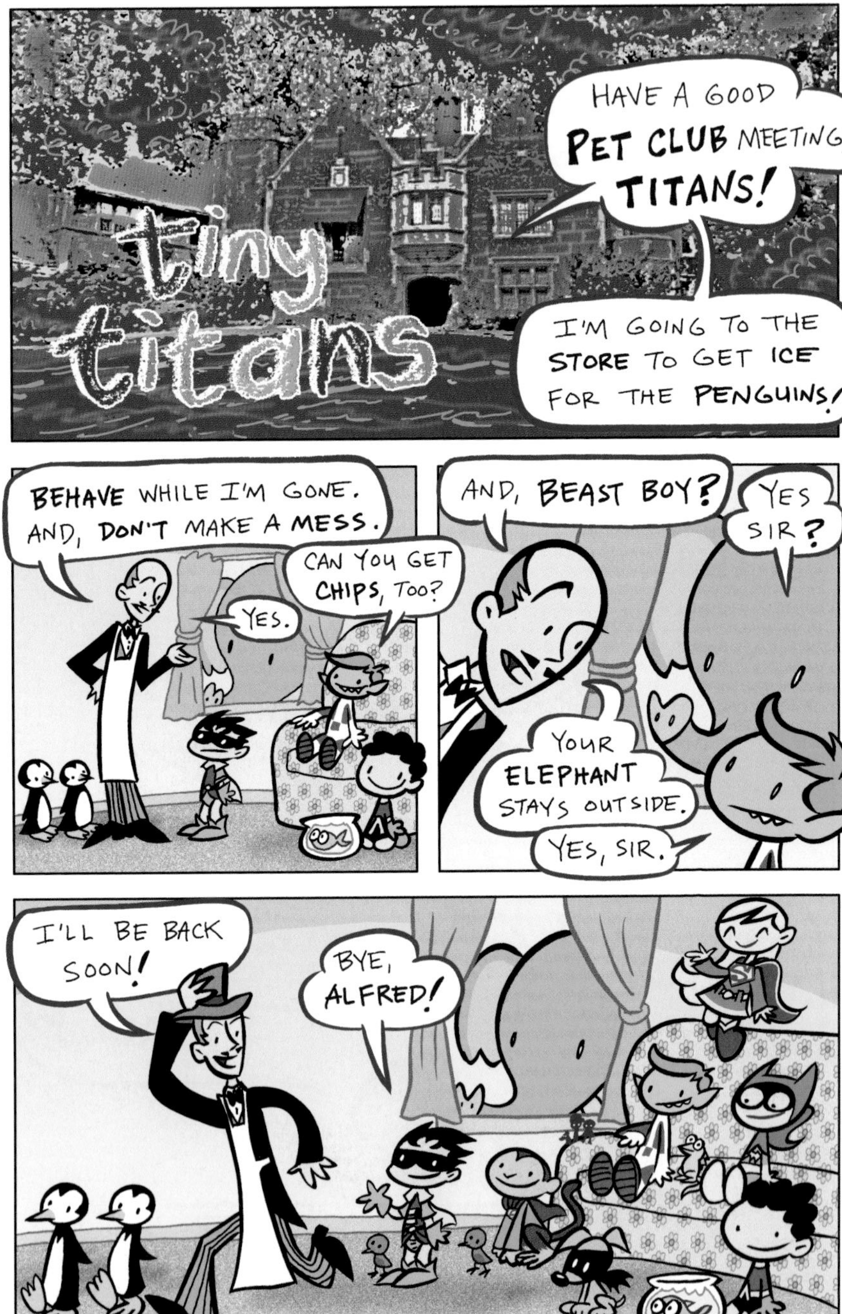
tiny titans
HAVE A GOOD PET CLUB MEETING, TITANS!
I'M GOING TO THE STORE TO GET ICE FOR THE PENGUINS!
BEHAVE WHILE I'M GONE. AND, DON'T MAKE A MESS.
CAN YOU GET CHIPS, TOO?
YES.
AND, BEAST BOY?
YES SIR?
YOUR ELEPHANT STAYS OUTSIDE.
YES, SIR.
I'LL BE BACK SOON!
BYE, ALFRED!

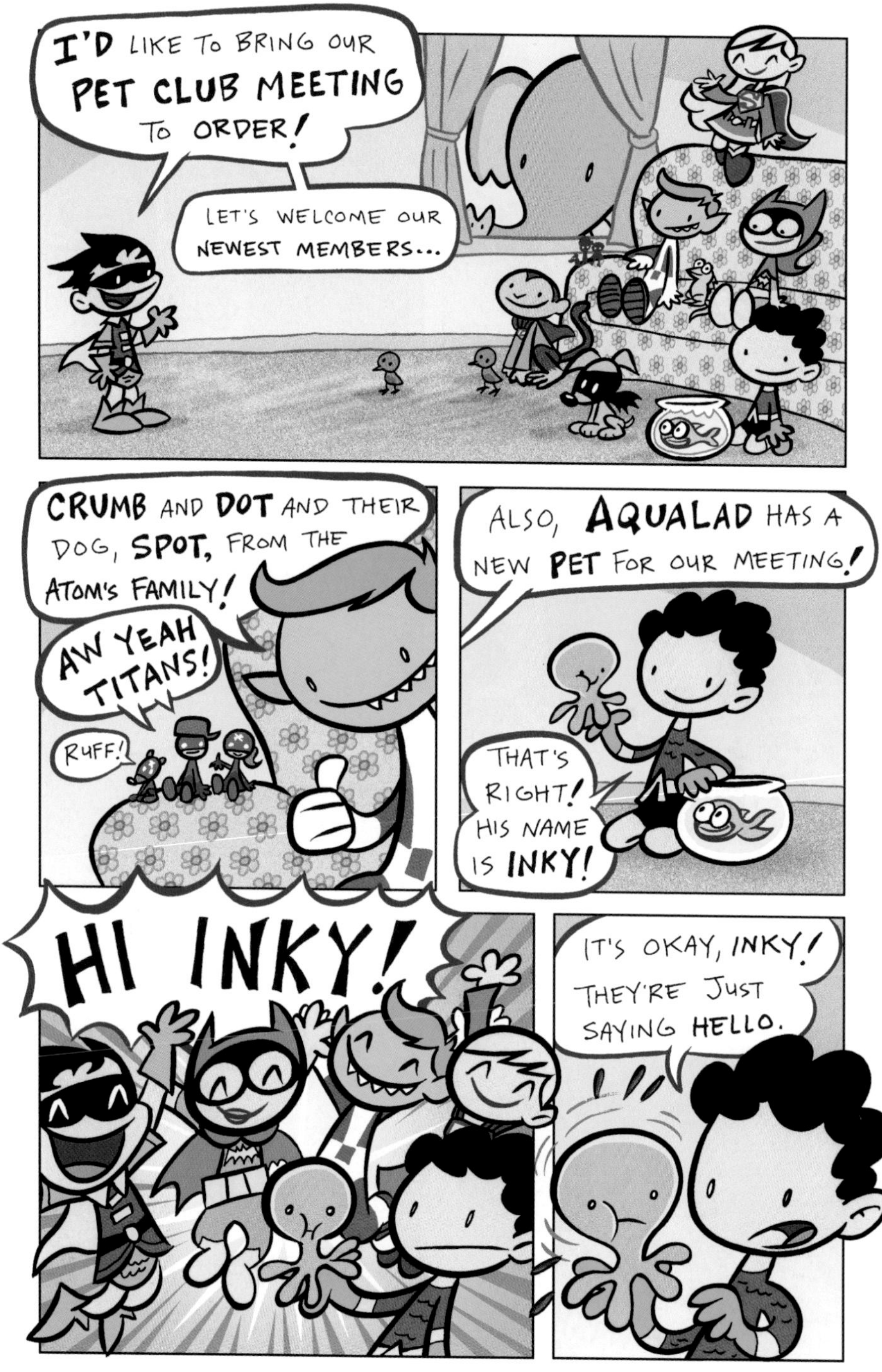
I'D LIKE TO BRING OUR PET CLUB MEETING TO ORDER!
LET'S WELCOME OUR NEWEST MEMBERS...
CRUMB AND DOT AND THEIR DOG, SPOT, FROM THE ATOM'S FAMILY!
AW YEAH TITANS!
RUFF!
ALSO, AQUALAD HAS A NEW PET FOR OUR MEETING!
THAT'S RIGHT! HIS NAME IS INKY!
HI INKY!
IT'S OKAY, INKY! THEY'RE JUST SAYING HELLO.

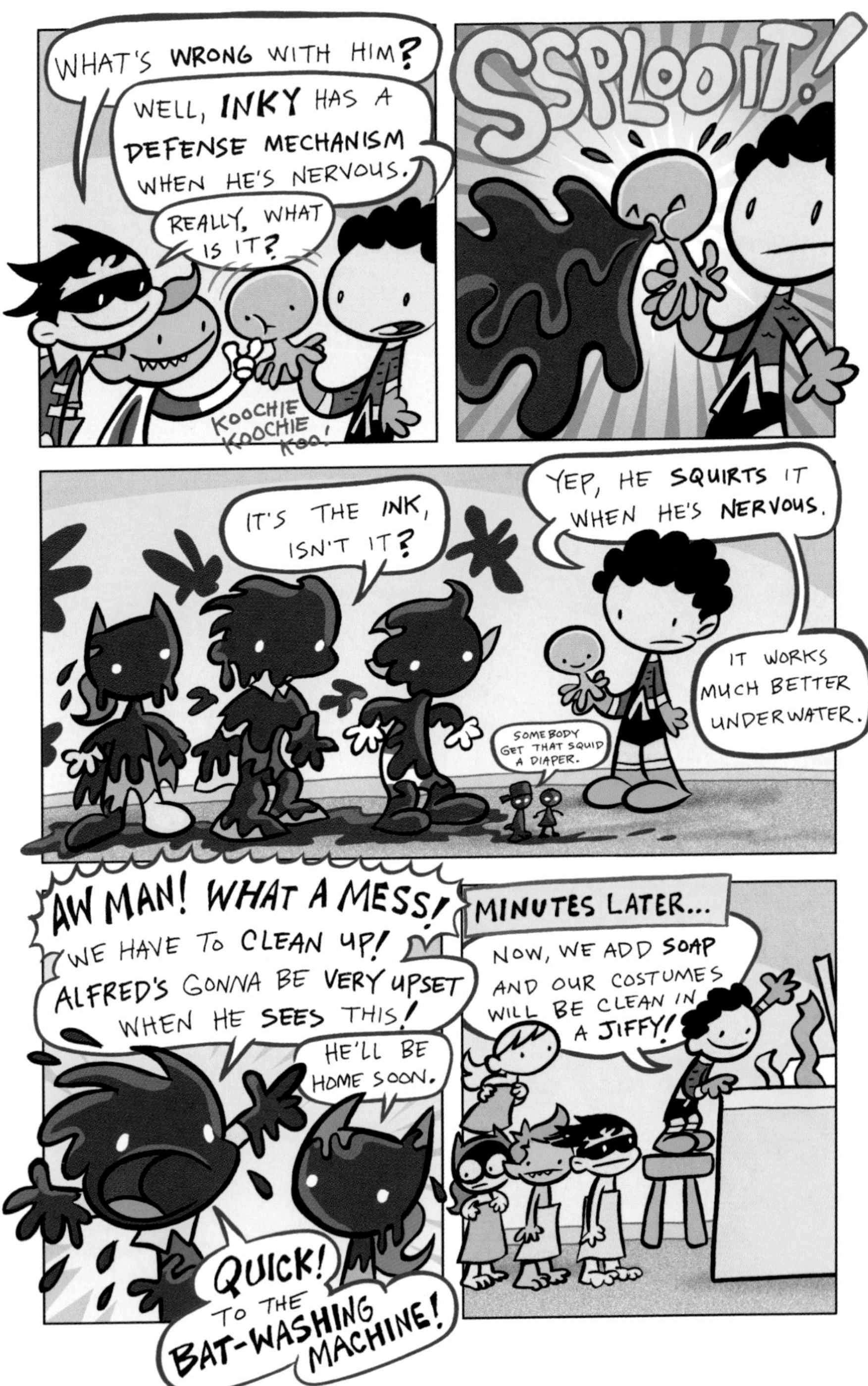
WHAT'S WRONG WITH HIM?
WELL, INKY HAS A DEFENSE MECHANISM WHEN HE'S NERVOUS.
REALLY, WHAT IS IT?
KOOCHIE KOOCHIE KOO!
SSPLOOIT!
IT'S THE INK, ISN'T IT?
YEP, HE SQUIRTS IT WHEN HE'S NERVOUS.
IT WORKS MUCH BETTER UNDERWATER.
SOMEBODY GET THAT SQUID A DIAPER.
AW MAN! WHAT A MESS!
WE HAVE TO CLEAN UP! ALFRED'S GONNA BE VERY UPSET WHEN HE SEES THIS!
HE'LL BE HOME SOON.
QUICK! TO THE BAT-WASHING MACHINE!
MINUTES LATER...
NOW, WE ADD SOAP AND OUR COSTUMES WILL BE CLEAN IN A JIFFY!

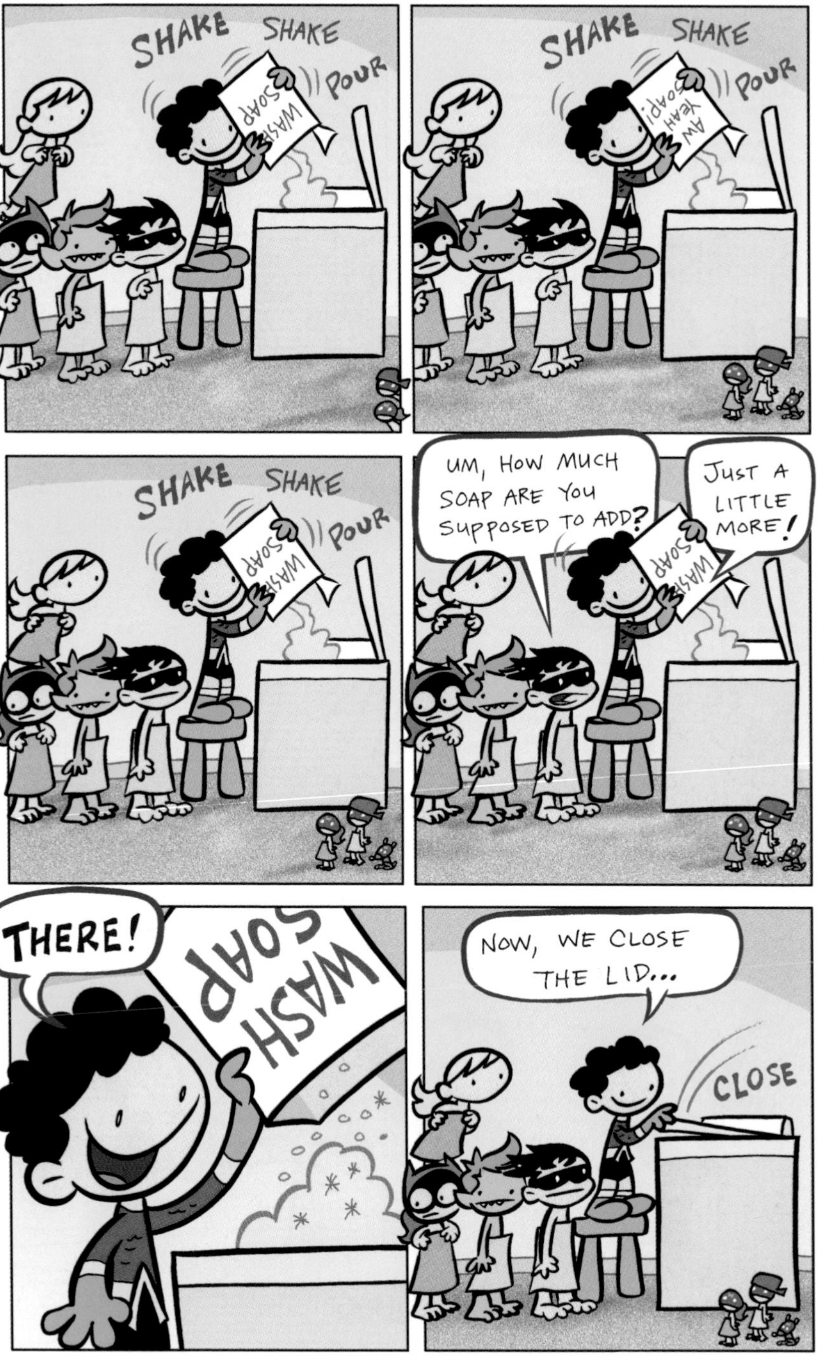
SHAKE SHAKE
POUR
WASH SOAP
SHAKE SHAKE
POUR
AW YEAH SOAP!
SHAKE SHAKE
POUR
WASH SOAP
UM, HOW MUCH SOAP ARE YOU SUPPOSED TO ADD?
JUST A LITTLE MORE!
WASH SOAP
THERE!
WASH SOAP
NOW, WE CLOSE THE LID...
CLOSE

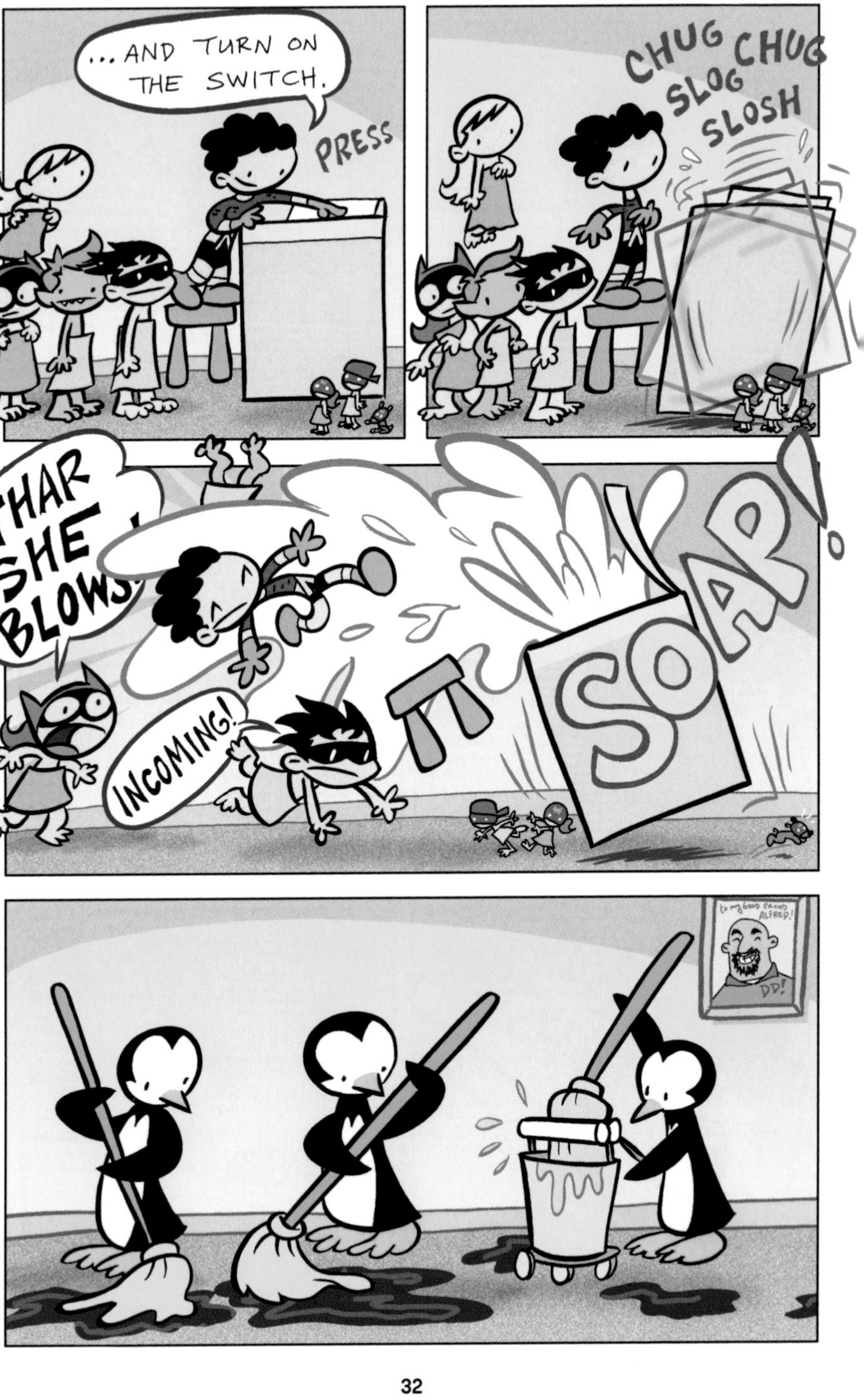
...AND TURN ON THE SWITCH.
PRESS
CHUG CHUG
SLOG
SLOSH
THAR SHE BLOWS!
INCOMING!
SOAP!
to my GOOD FRIEND ALFRED!
DD!

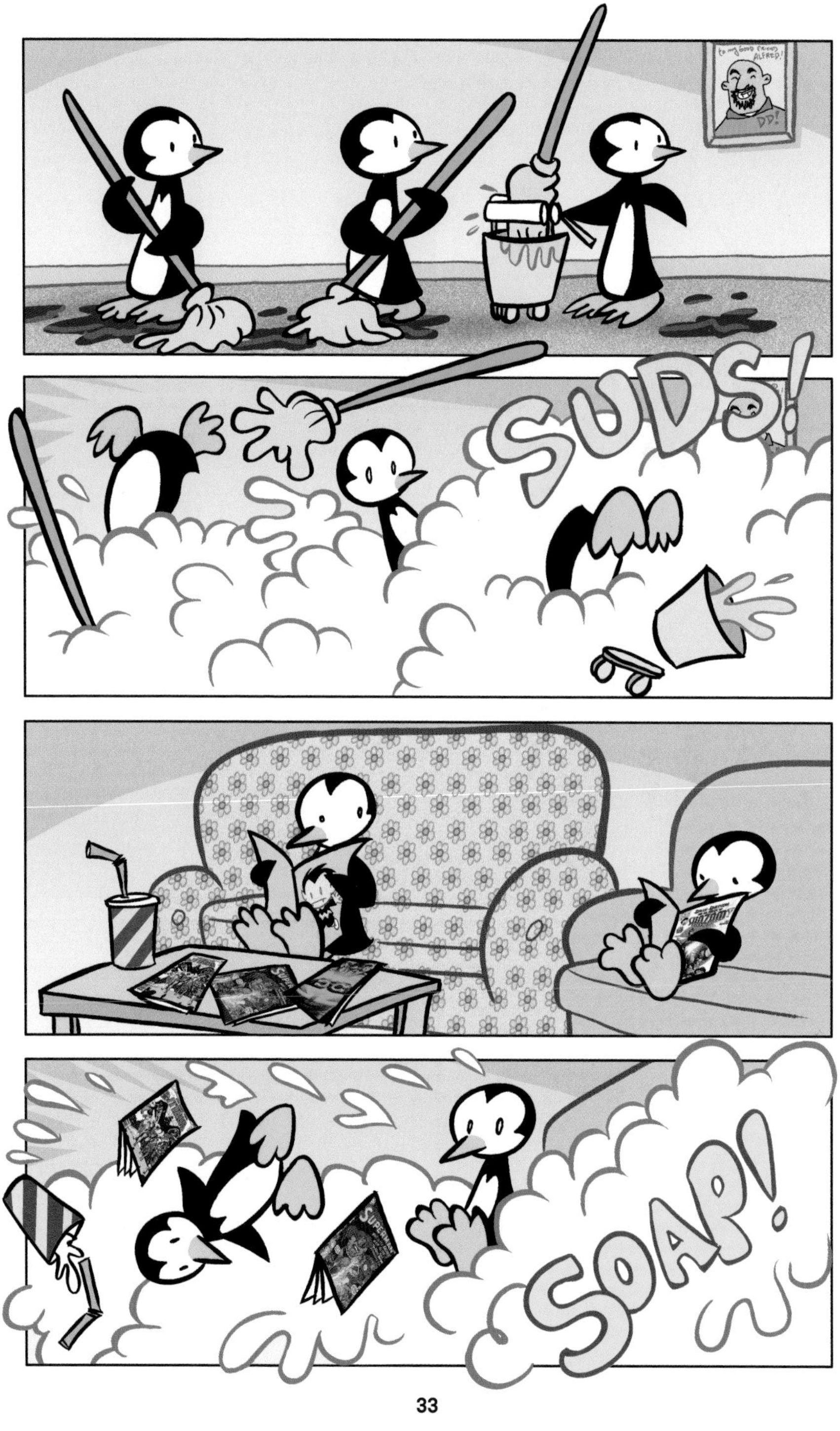
to my GOOD FRIEND ALFRED!
DD!
SUDS!
SOAP!

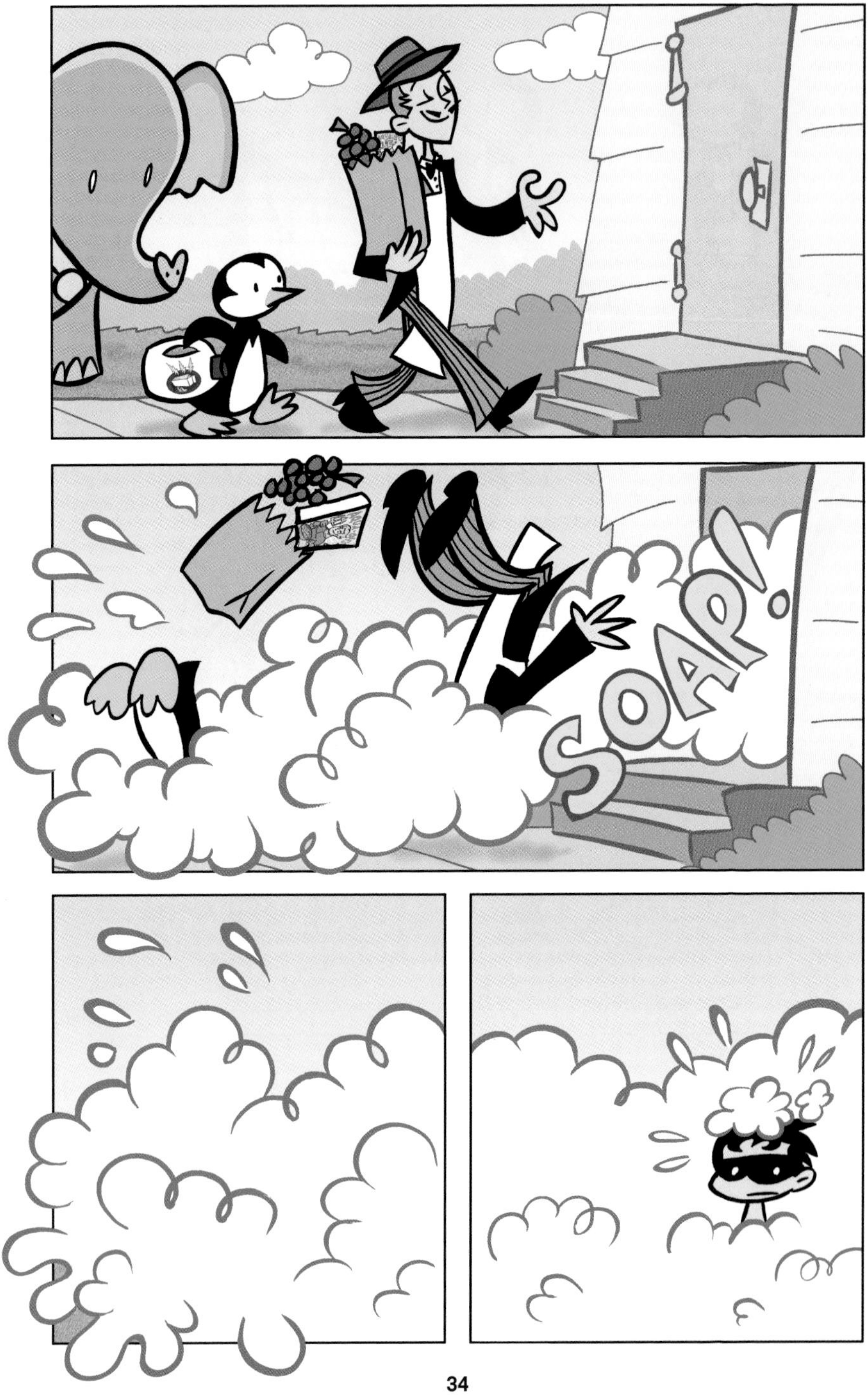
SOAP!

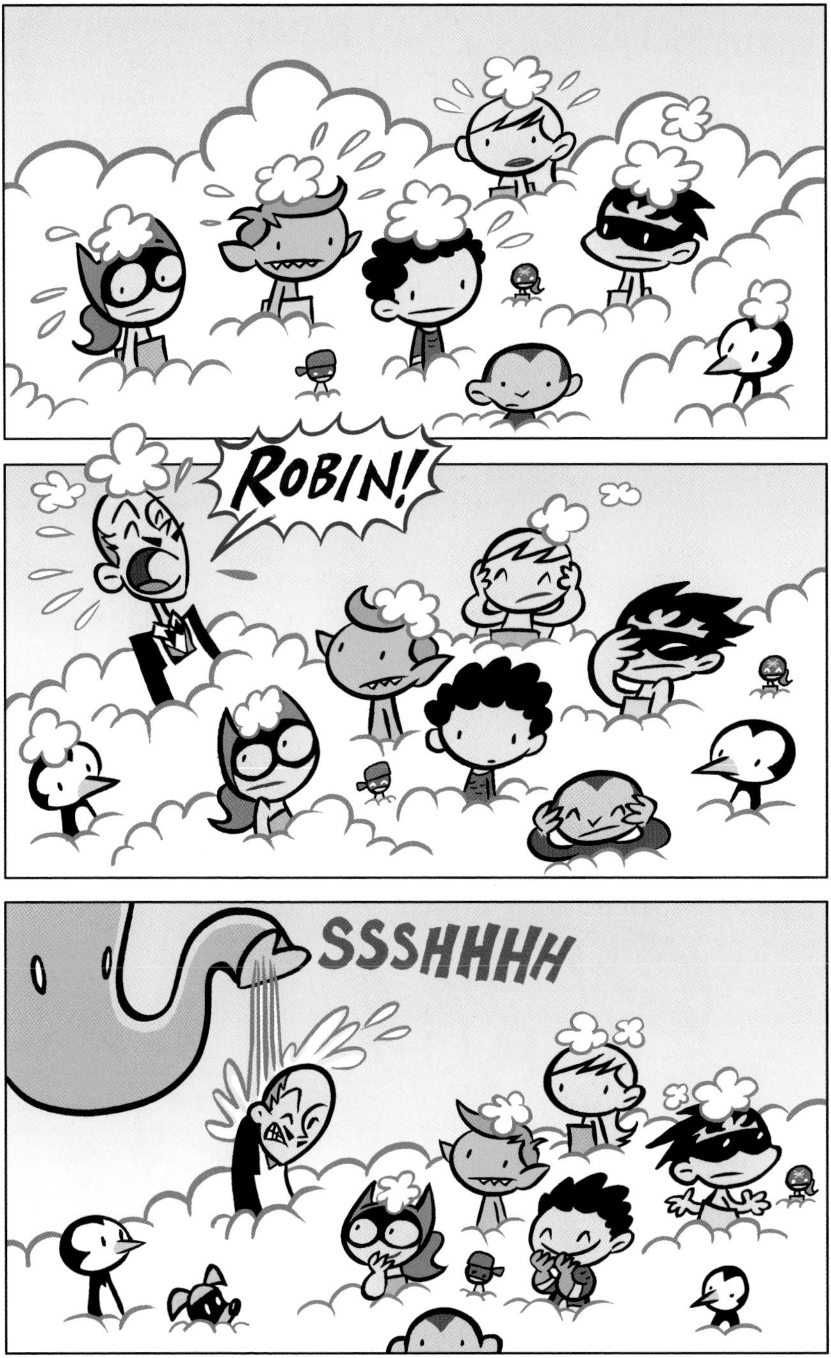
ROBIN!
SSSHHHH

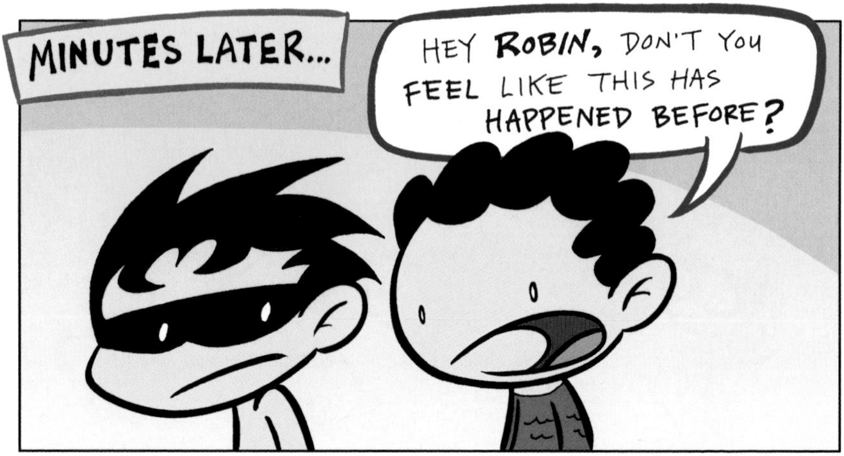
MINUTES LATER...
HEY ROBIN, DON'T YOU FEEL LIKE THIS HAS HAPPENED BEFORE?

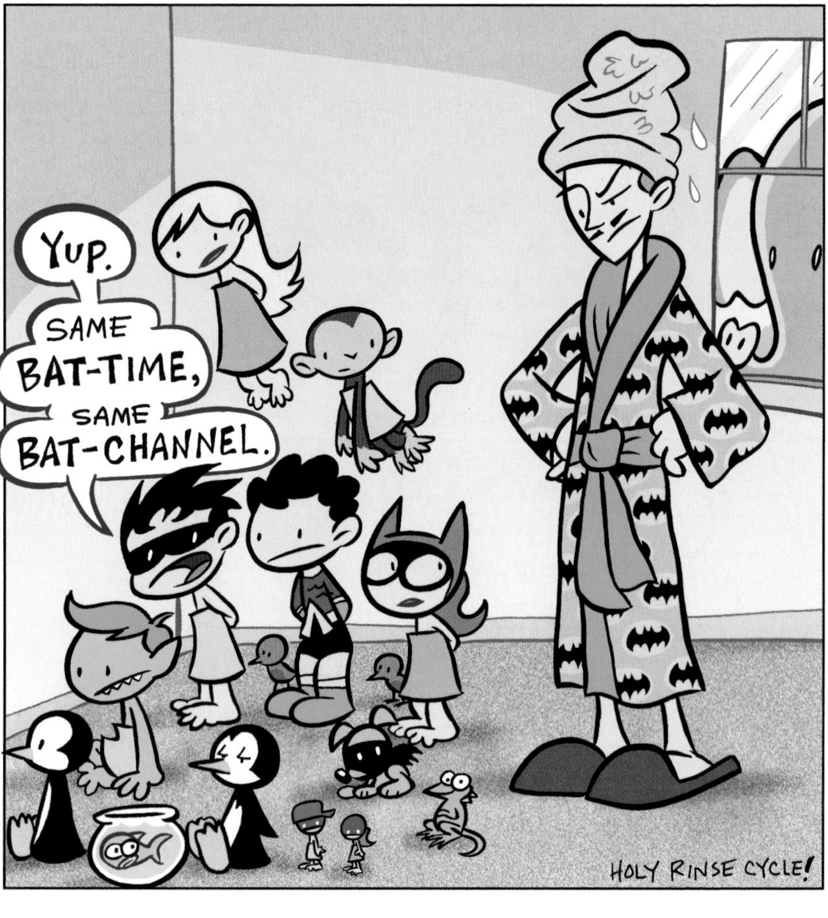
YUP.
SAME BAT-TIME,
SAME BAT-CHANNEL.
HOLY RINSE CYCLE!

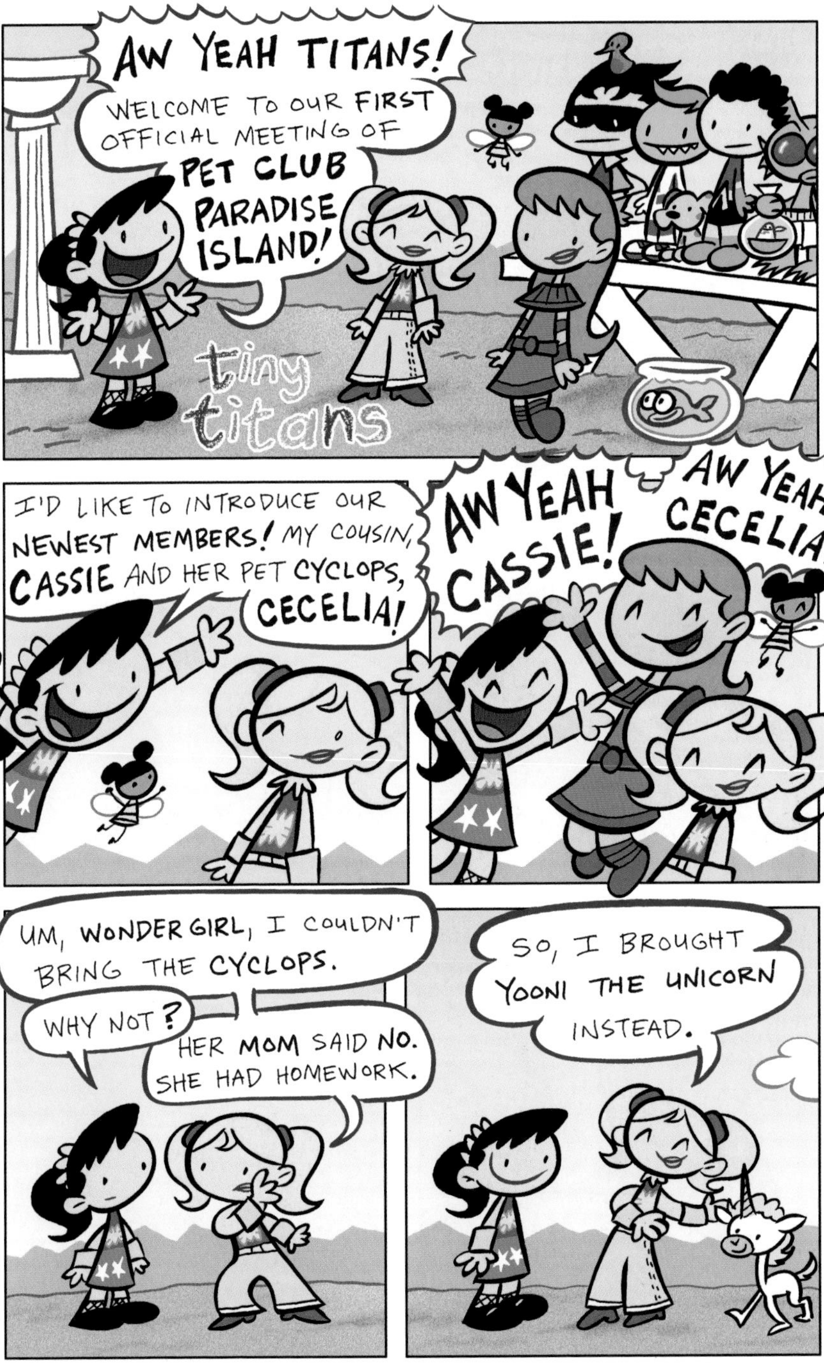
AW YEAH TITANS!
WELCOME TO OUR FIRST OFFICIAL MEETING OF PET CLUB PARADISE ISLAND!
tiny titans
I'D LIKE TO INTRODUCE OUR NEWEST MEMBERS! MY COUSIN, CASSIE AND HER PET CYCLOPS, CECELIA!
AW YEAH CASSIE!
AW YEAH CECELIA!
UM, WONDER GIRL, I COULDN'T BRING THE CYCLOPS.
WHY NOT?
HER MOM SAID NO. SHE HAD HOMEWORK.
SO, I BROUGHT YOONI THE UNICORN INSTEAD.

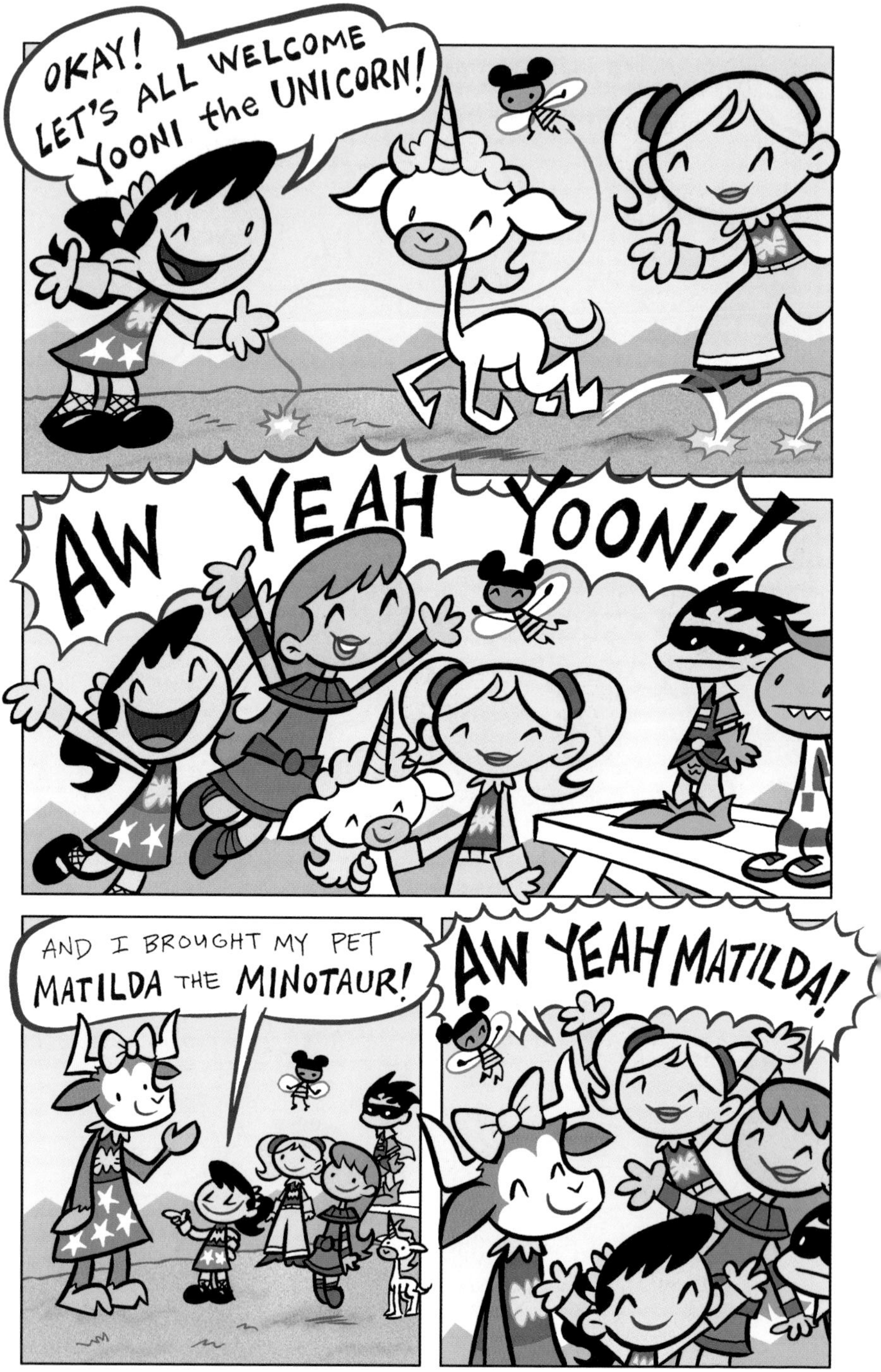
OKAY! LET'S ALL WELCOME YOONI the UNICORN!
AW YEAH YOONI!!
AND I BROUGHT MY PET MATILDA THE MINOTAUR!
AW YEAH MATILDA!

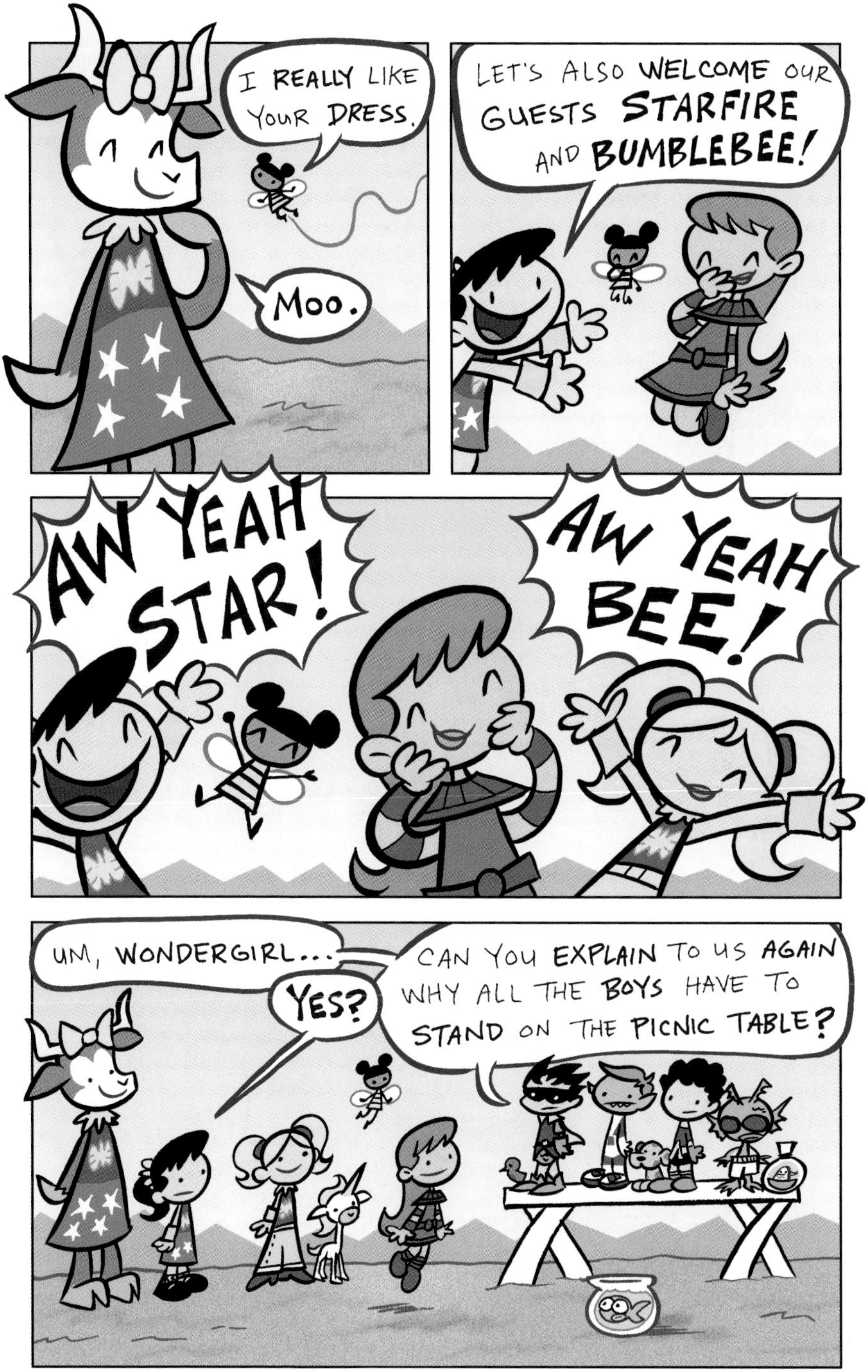
I REALLY LIKE YOUR DRESS.
MOO.
LET'S ALSO WELCOME OUR GUESTS STARFIRE AND BUMBLEBEE!
AW YEAH STAR!
AW YEAH BEE!
UM, WONDERGIRL...
YES?
CAN YOU EXPLAIN TO US AGAIN WHY ALL THE BOYS HAVE TO STAND ON THE PICNIC TABLE?

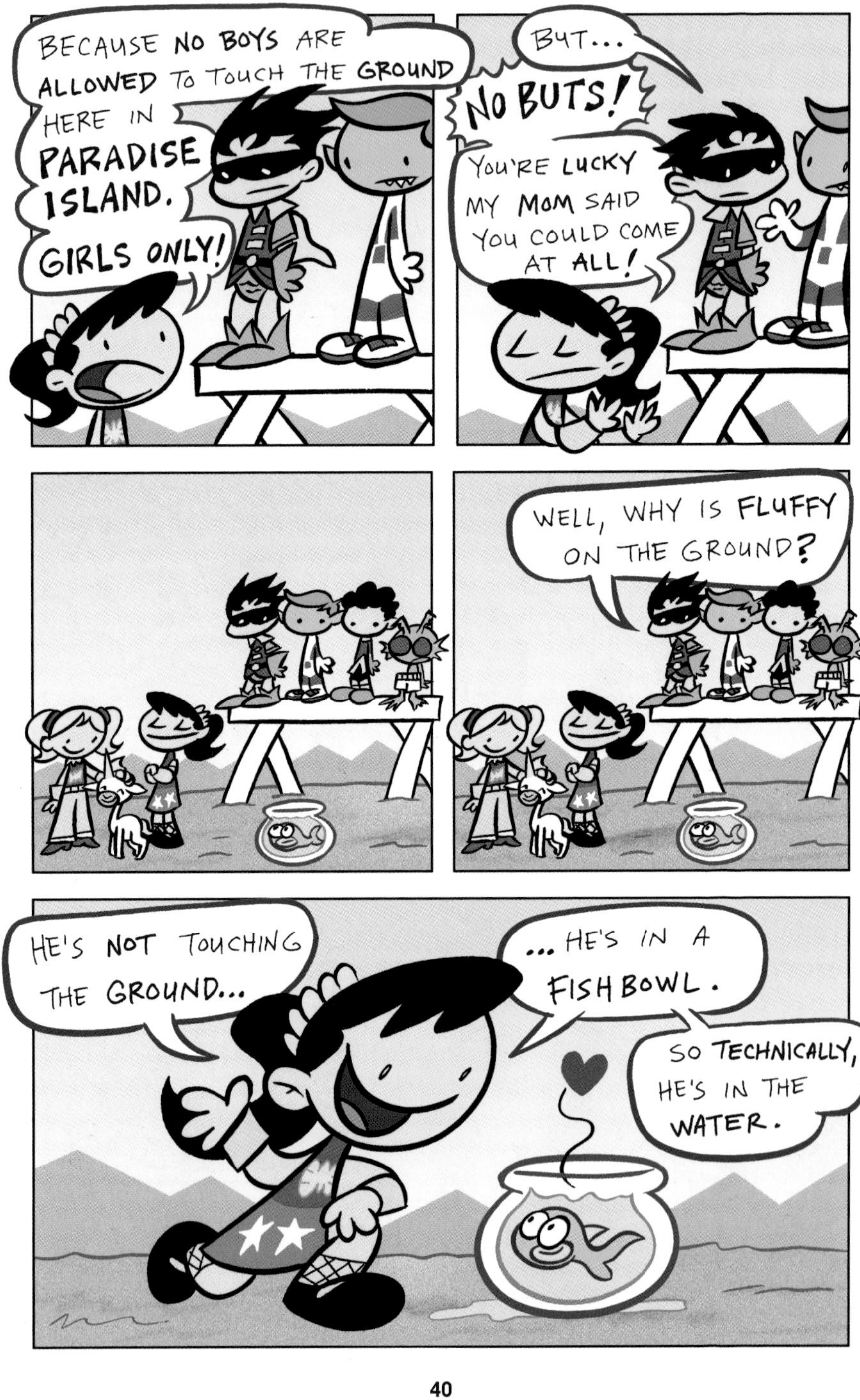
BECAUSE NO BOYS ARE ALLOWED TO TOUCH THE GROUND HERE IN PARADISE ISLAND.
GIRLS ONLY!
BUT...
NO BUTS!
YOU'RE LUCKY MY MOM SAID YOU COULD COME AT ALL!
WELL, WHY IS FLUFFY ON THE GROUND?
HE'S NOT TOUCHING THE GROUND...
...HE'S IN A FISHBOWL.
SO TECHNICALLY, HE'S IN THE WATER.

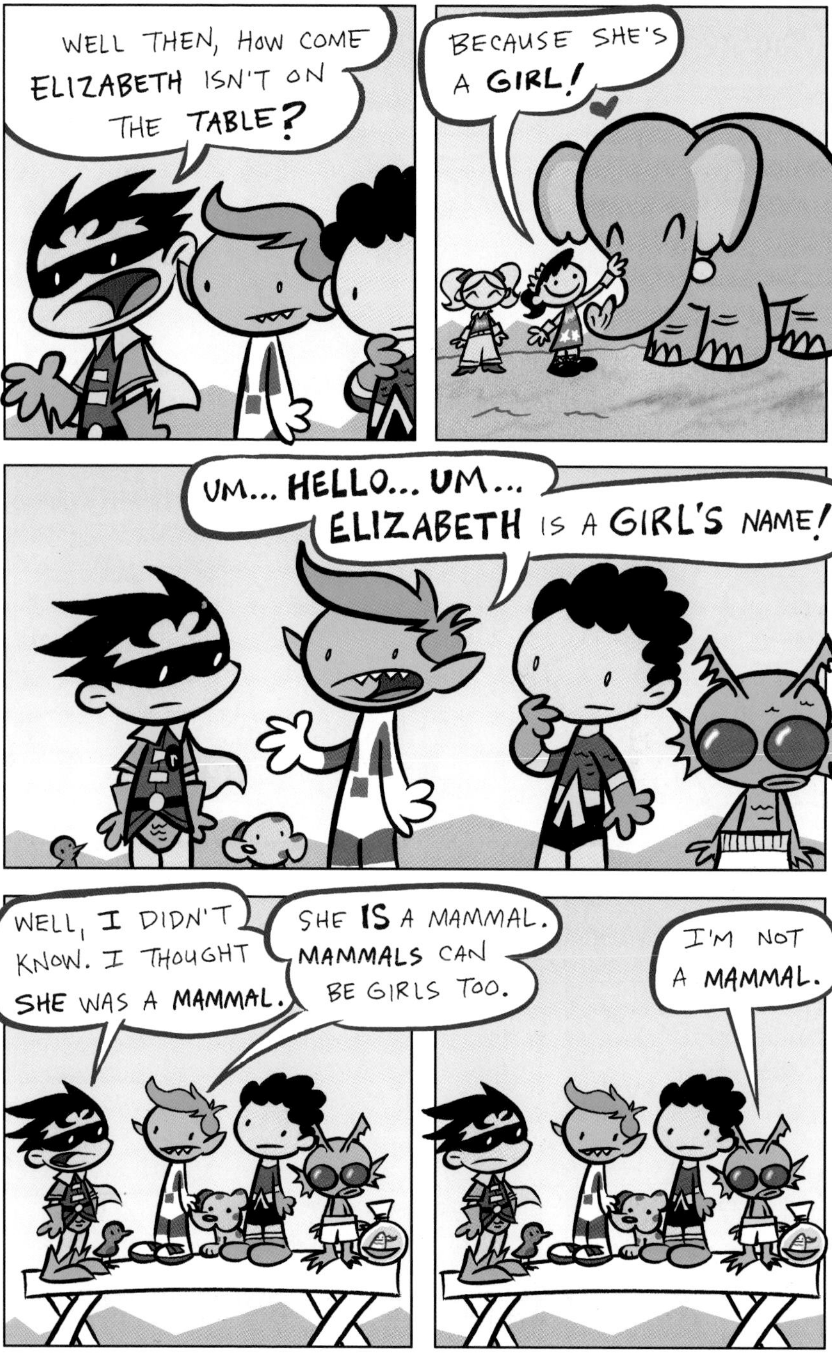
WELL THEN, HOW COME ELIZABETH ISN'T ON THE TABLE?
BECAUSE SHE'S A GIRL!
UM... HELLO... UM... ELIZABETH IS A GIRL'S NAME!
WELL, I DIDN'T KNOW. I THOUGHT SHE WAS A MAMMAL.
SHE IS A MAMMAL. MAMMALS CAN BE GIRLS TOO.
I'M NOT A MAMMAL.

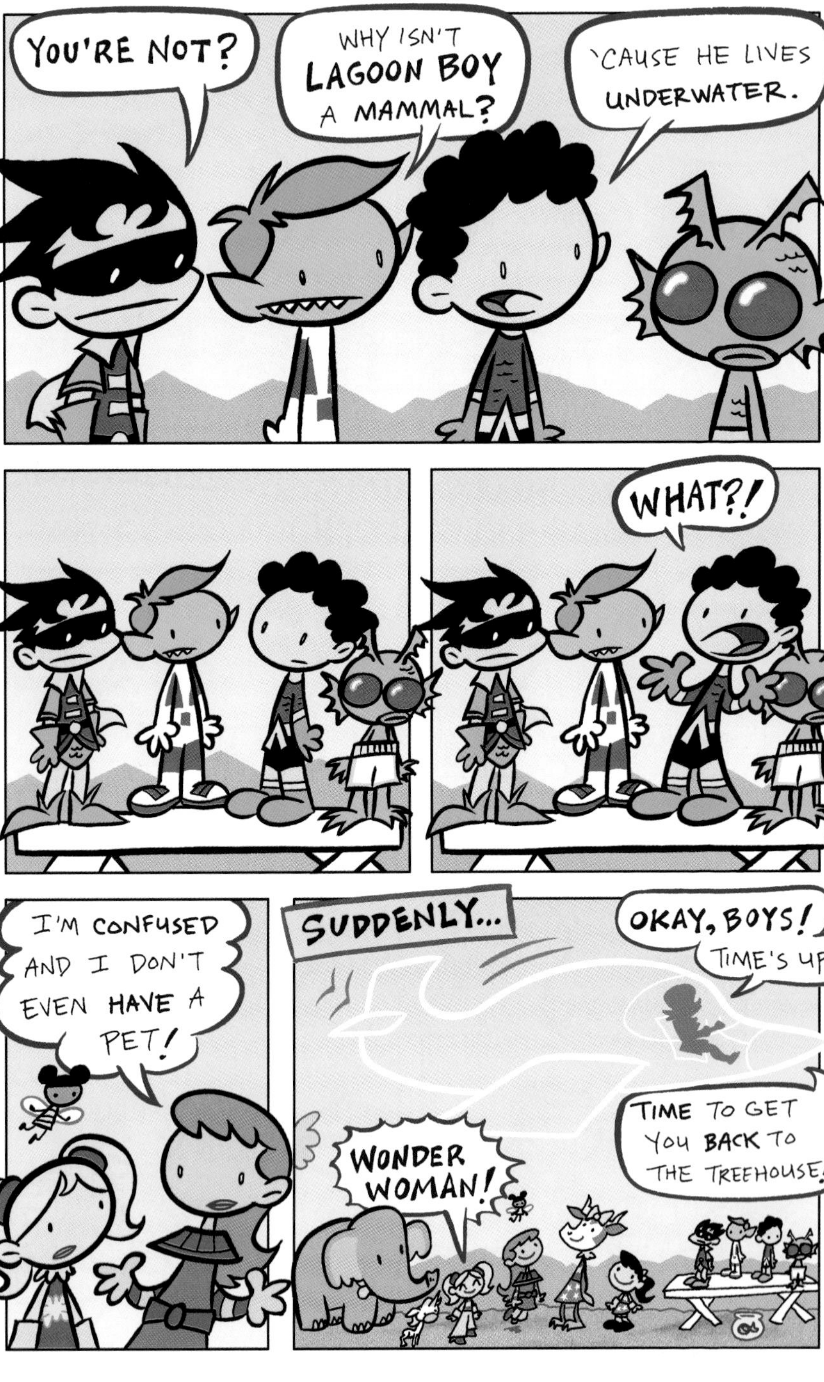
YOU'RE NOT?
WHY ISN'T LAGOON BOY A MAMMAL?
'CAUSE HE LIVES UNDERWATER.
WHAT?!
I'M CONFUSED AND I DON'T EVEN HAVE A PET!
SUDDENLY...
OKAY, BOYS! TIME'S UP!
TIME TO GET YOU BACK TO THE TREEHOUSE!
WONDER WOMAN!

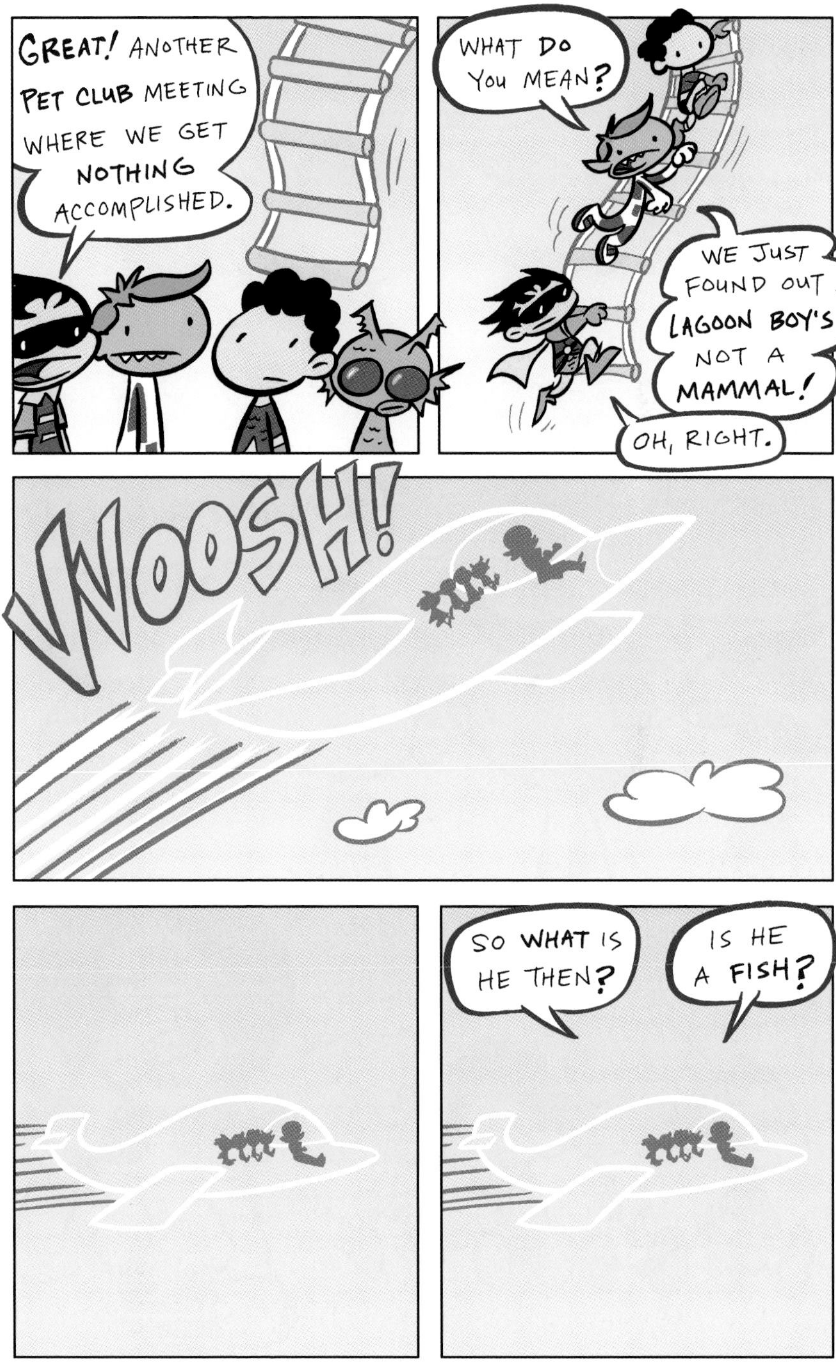
GREAT! ANOTHER PET CLUB MEETING WHERE WE GET NOTHING ACCOMPLISHED.
WHAT DO YOU MEAN?
WE JUST FOUND OUT LAGOON BOY'S NOT A MAMMAL!
OH, RIGHT.
WOOSH!
SO WHAT IS HE THEN?
IS HE A FISH?

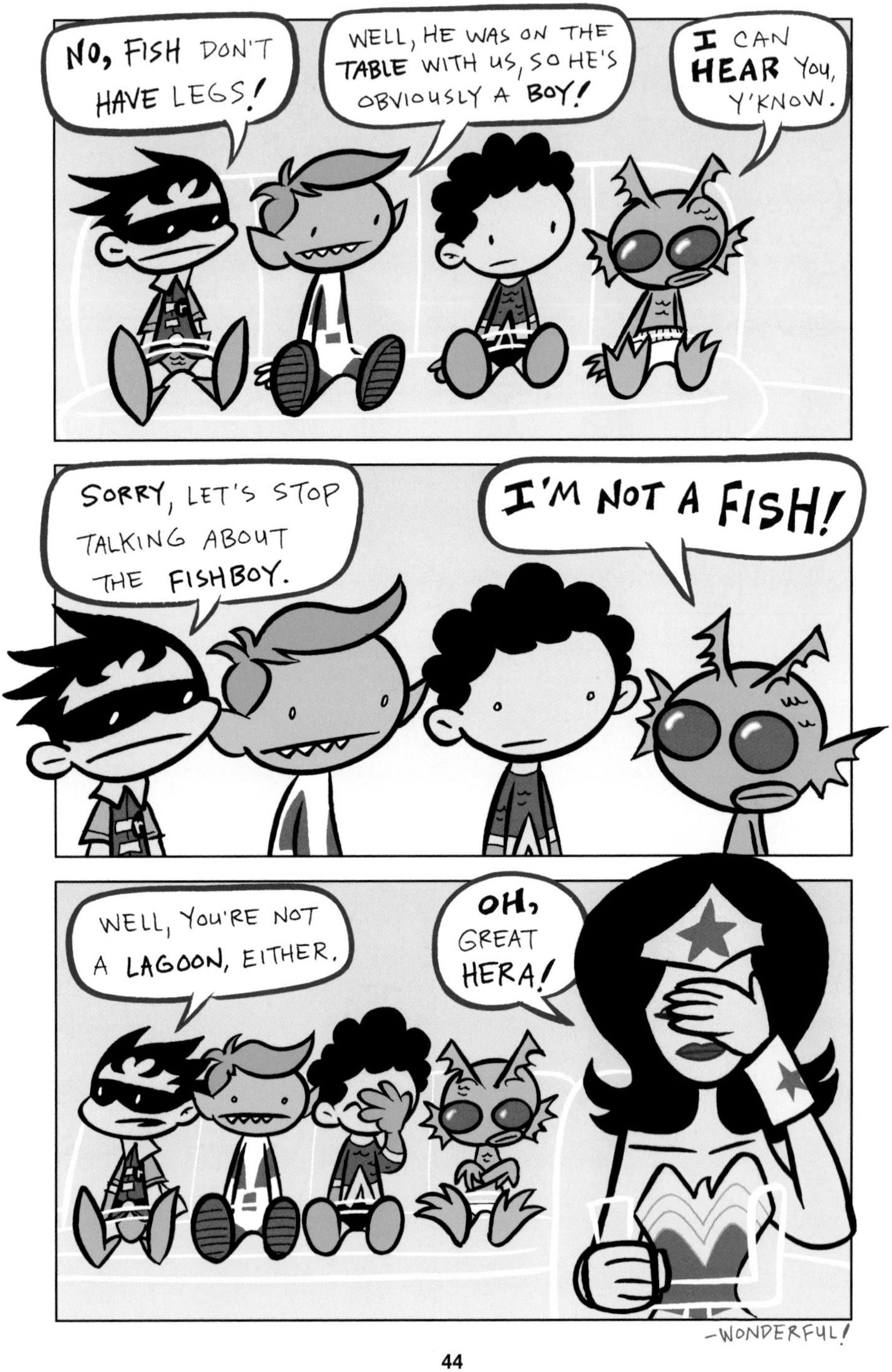
NO, FISH DON'T HAVE LEGS!
WELL, HE WAS ON THE TABLE WITH US, SO HE'S OBVIOUSLY A BOY!
I CAN HEAR YOU, Y'KNOW.
SORRY, LET'S STOP TALKING ABOUT THE FISHBOY.
I'M NOT A FISH!
WELL, YOU'RE NOT A LAGOON, EITHER.
OH, GREAT HERA!

-WONDERFUL!

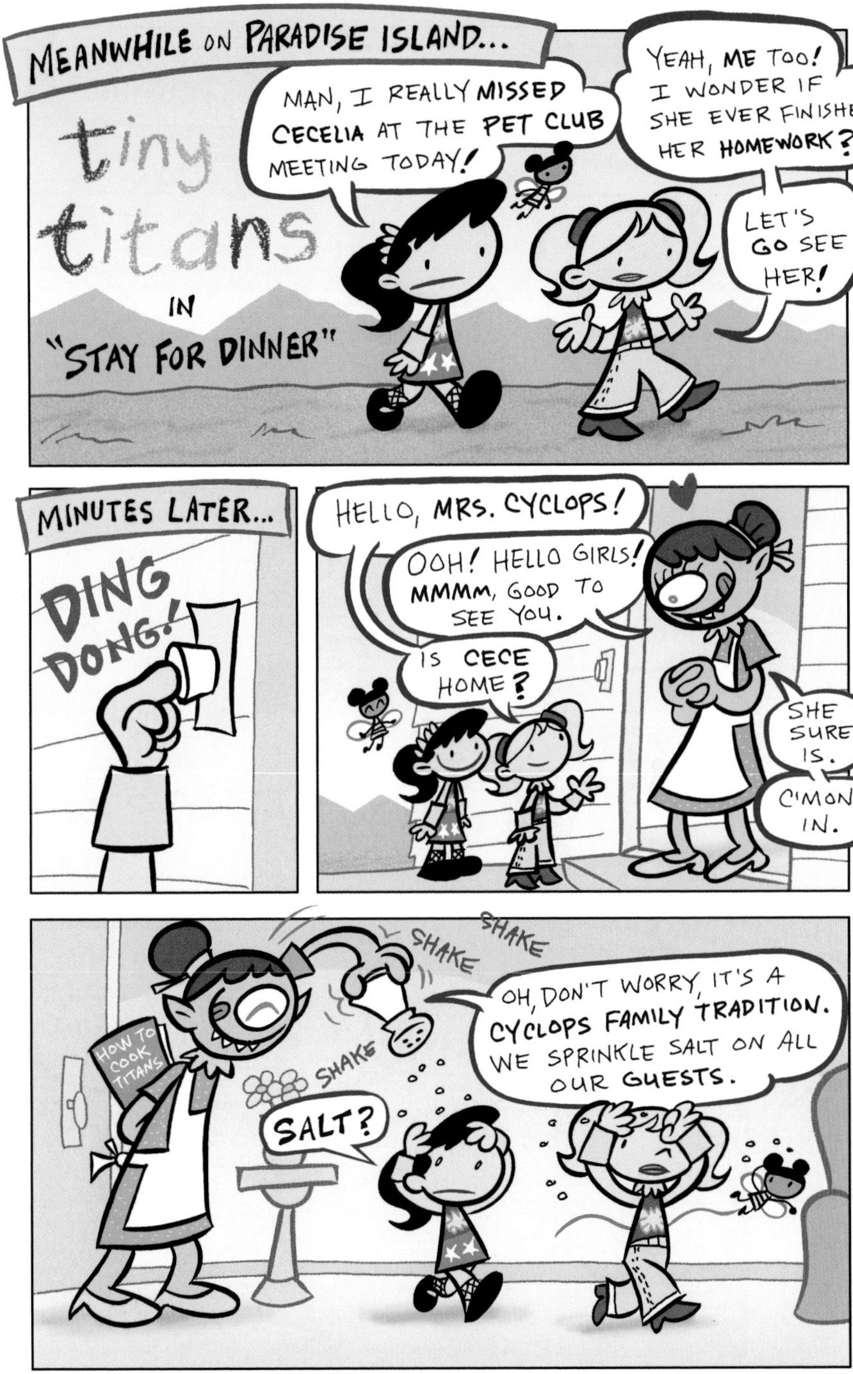
MEANWHILE ON PARADISE ISLAND...
tiny titans
IN
"STAY FOR DINNER"
MAN, I REALLY MISSED CECELIA AT THE PET CLUB MEETING TODAY!
YEAH, ME TOO! I WONDER IF SHE EVER FINISHED HER HOMEWORK?
LET'S GO SEE HER!
MINUTES LATER...
DING DONG!
HELLO, MRS. CYCLOPS!
OOH! HELLO GIRLS! MMMM, GOOD TO SEE YOU.
IS CECE HOME?
SHE SURE IS.
C'MON IN.
SHAKE
SHAKE
SHAKE
HOW TO COOK TITANS
OH, DON'T WORRY, IT'S A CYCLOPS FAMILY TRADITION. WE SPRINKLE SALT ON ALL OUR GUESTS.
SALT?

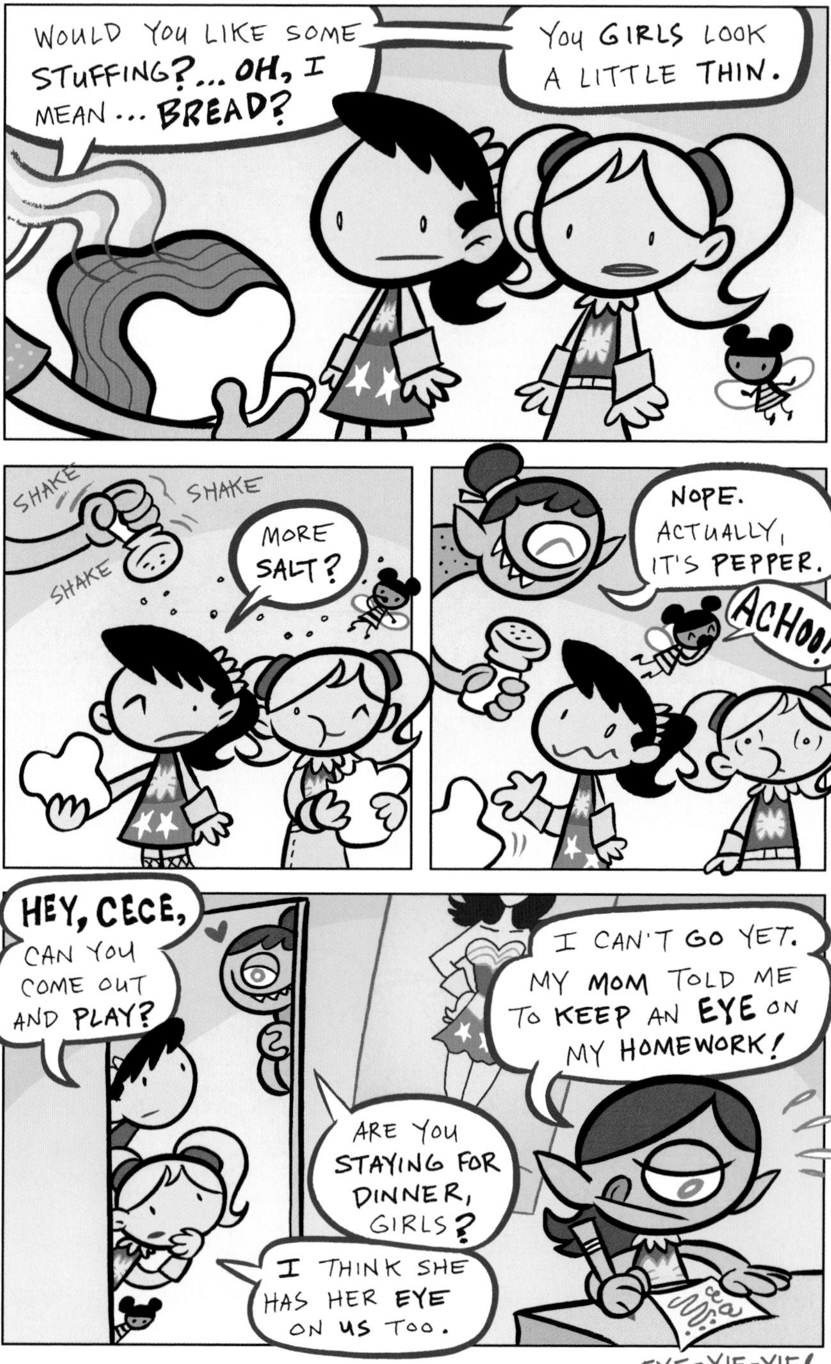
WOULD YOU LIKE SOME STUFFING?... OH, I MEAN ... BREAD?
YOU GIRLS LOOK A LITTLE THIN.
SHAKE
SHAKE
SHAKE
MORE SALT?
NOPE. ACTUALLY, IT'S PEPPER.
ACHOO!
HEY, CECE, CAN YOU COME OUT AND PLAY?
I CAN'T GO YET. MY MOM TOLD ME TO KEEP AN EYE ON MY HOMEWORK!
ARE YOU STAYING FOR DINNER, GIRLS?
I THINK SHE HAS HER EYE ON US TOO.
EYE-YIE-YIE!

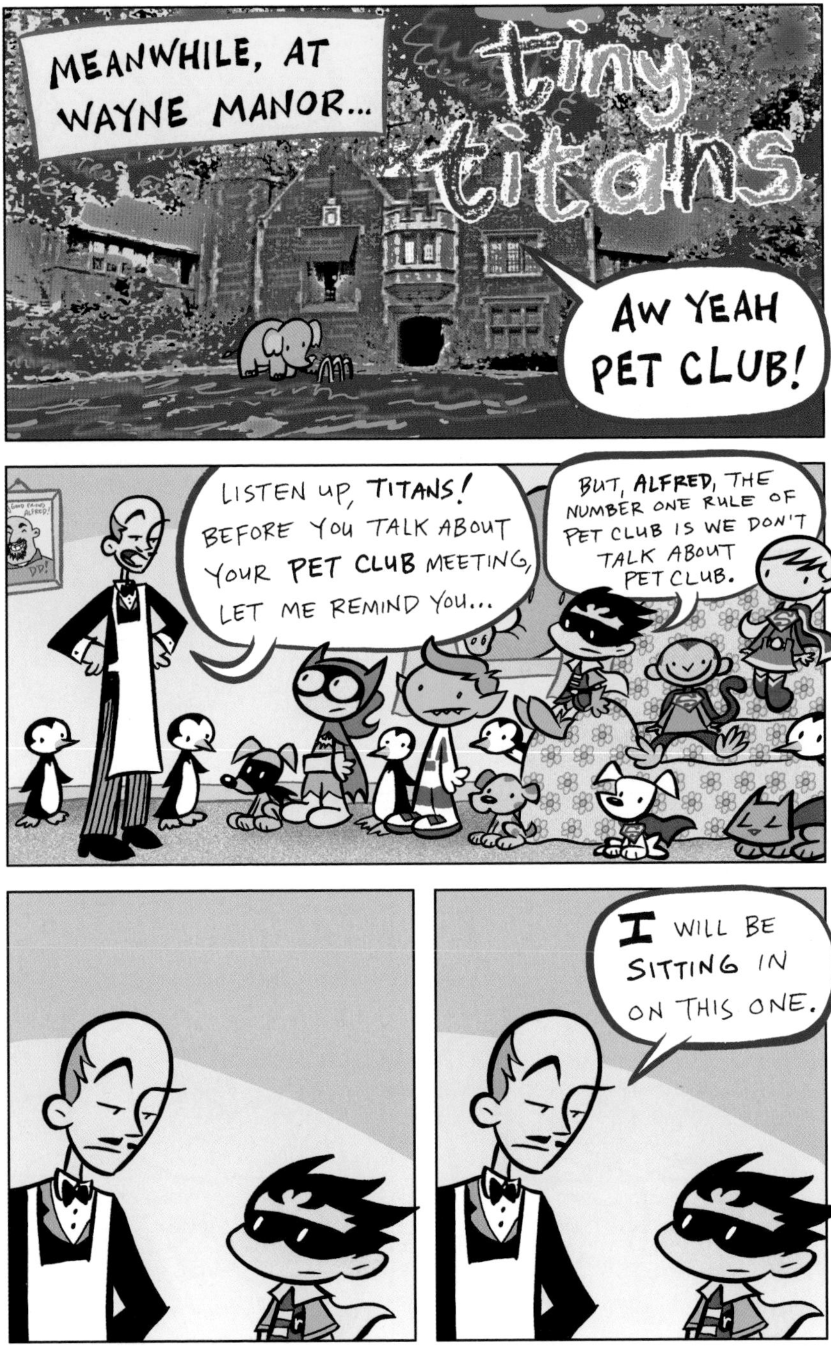
MEANWHILE, AT WAYNE MANOR...
tiny titans
AW YEAH PET CLUB!
LISTEN UP, TITANS! BEFORE YOU TALK ABOUT YOUR PET CLUB MEETING, LET ME REMIND YOU...
BUT, ALFRED, THE NUMBER ONE RULE OF PET CLUB IS WE DON'T TALK ABOUT PET CLUB.
I WILL BE SITTING IN ON THIS ONE.

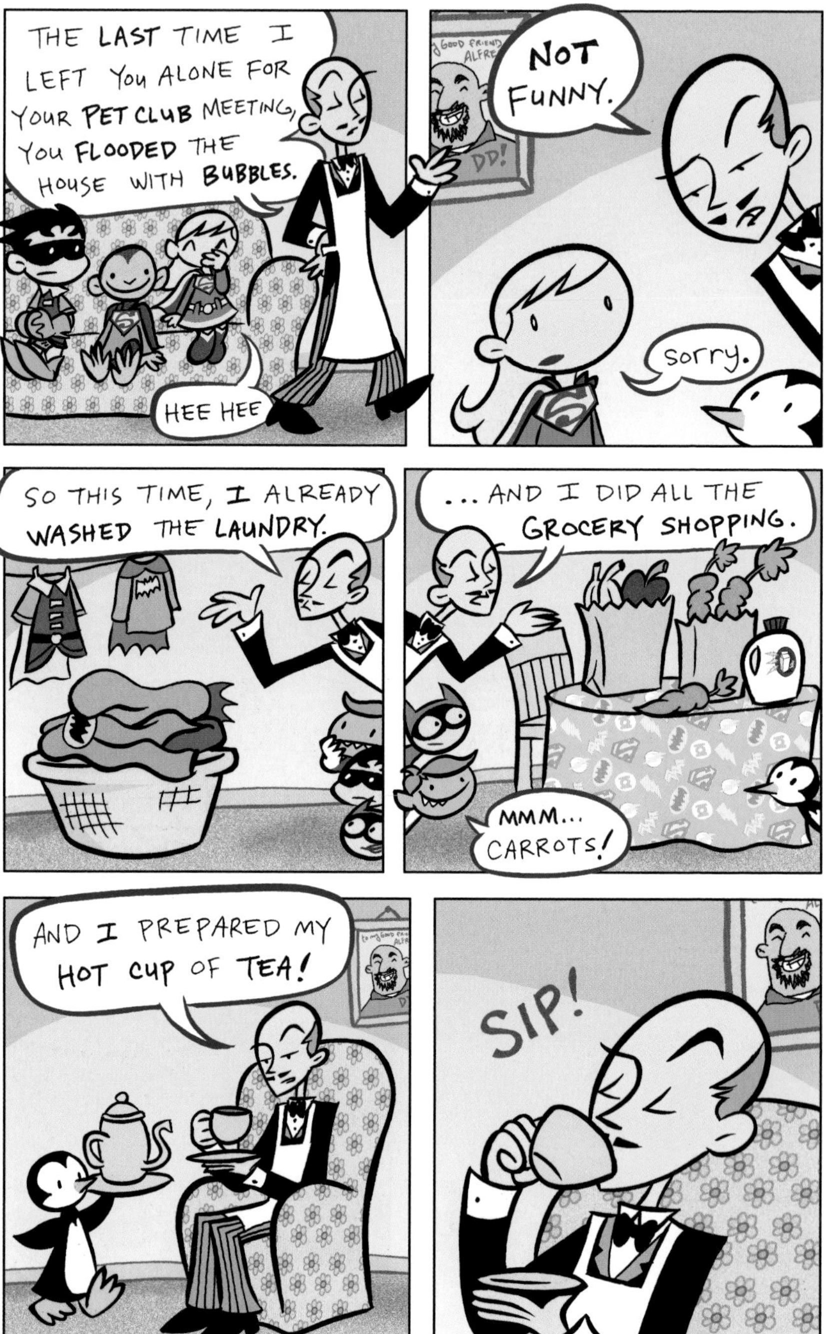
THE LAST TIME I LEFT YOU ALONE FOR YOUR PET CLUB MEETING, YOU FLOODED THE HOUSE WITH BUBBLES.
HEE HEE
NOT FUNNY.
SORRY.
SO THIS TIME, I ALREADY WASHED THE LAUNDRY.
... AND I DID ALL THE GROCERY SHOPPING.
MMM... CARROTS!
AND I PREPARED MY HOT CUP OF TEA!
SIP!

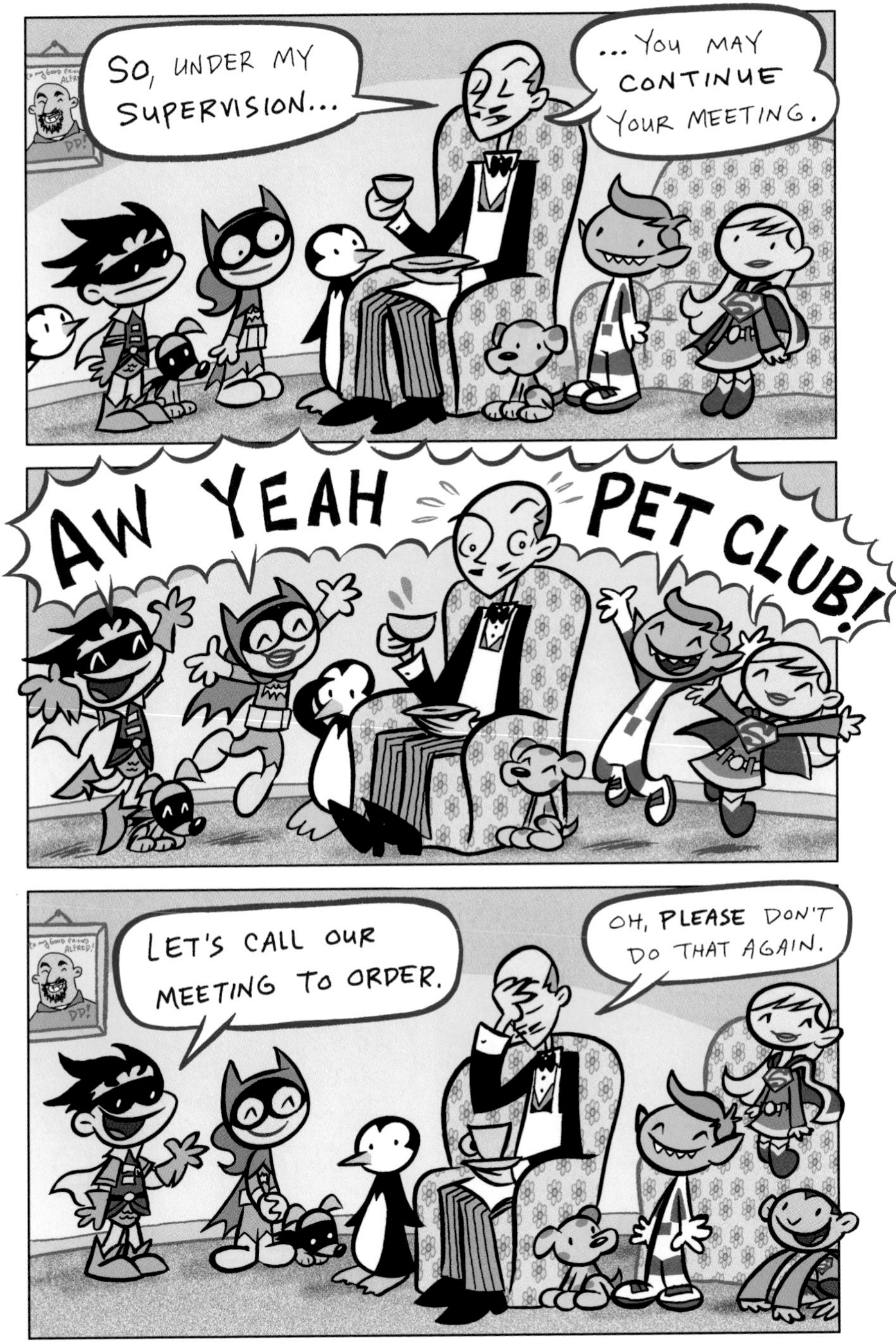
SO, UNDER MY SUPERVISION...
...YOU MAY CONTINUE YOUR MEETING.
AW YEAH PET CLUB!
LET'S CALL OUR MEETING TO ORDER.
OH, PLEASE DON'T DO THAT AGAIN.

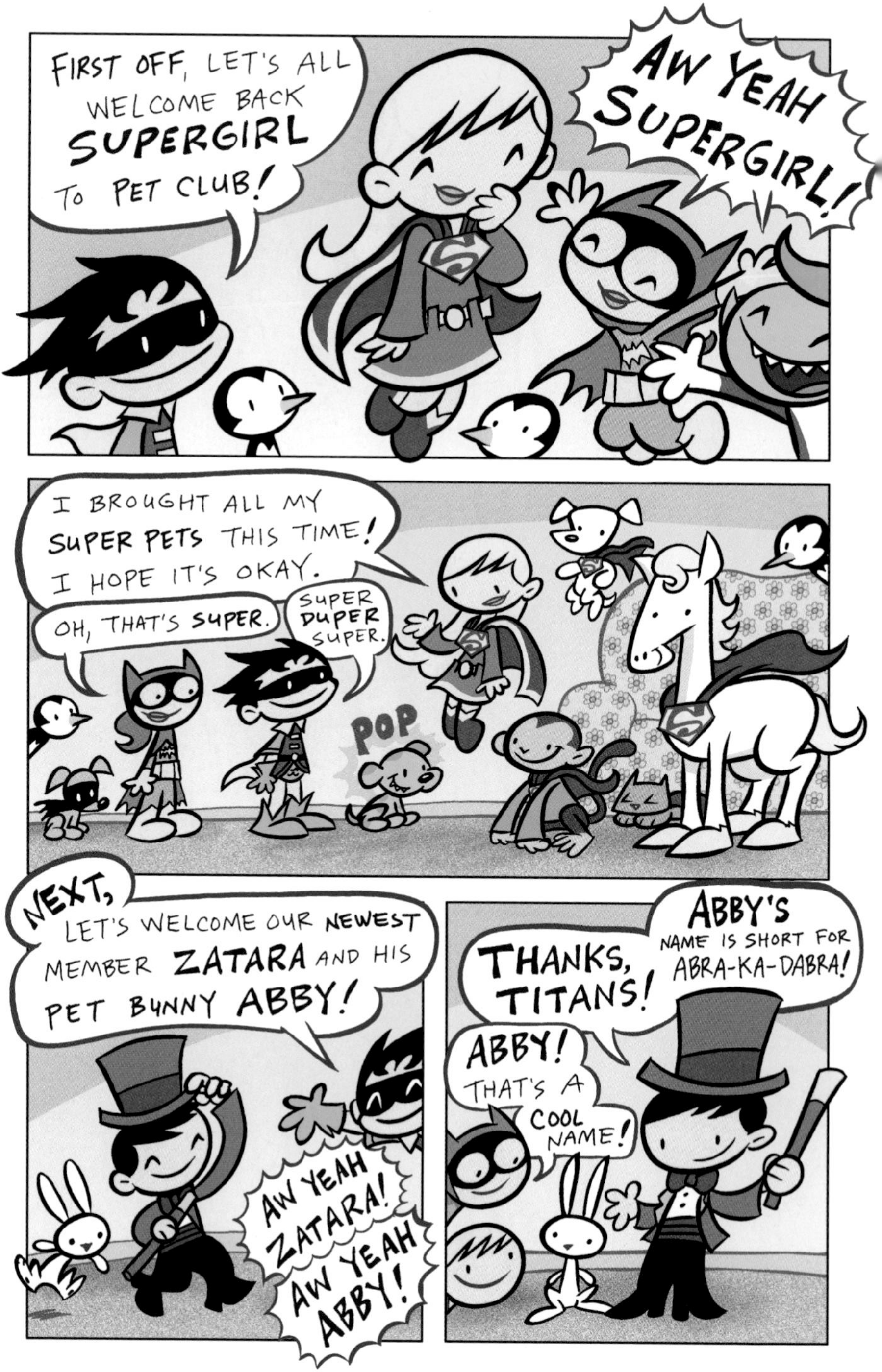
FIRST OFF, LET'S ALL WELCOME BACK SUPERGIRL TO PET CLUB!
AW YEAH SUPERGIRL!
I BROUGHT ALL MY SUPER PETS THIS TIME! I HOPE IT'S OKAY.
OH, THAT'S SUPER.
SUPER DUPER SUPER.
POP
NEXT, LET'S WELCOME OUR NEWEST MEMBER ZATARA AND HIS PET BUNNY ABBY!
AW YEAH ZATARA! AW YEAH ABBY!
THANKS, TITANS!
ABBY'S NAME IS SHORT FOR ABRA-KA-DABRA!
ABBY! THAT'S A COOL NAME!

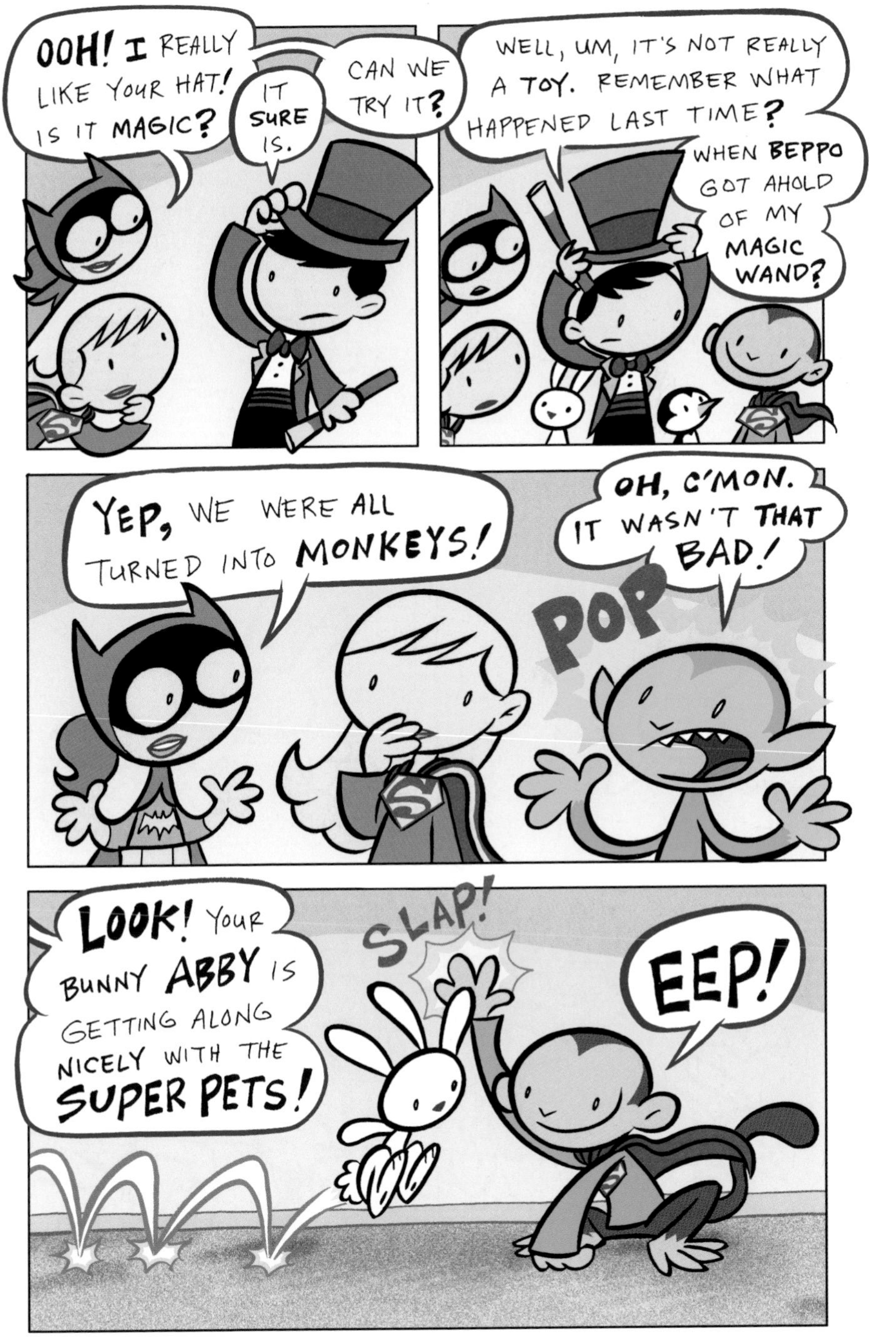
OOH! I REALLY LIKE YOUR HAT! IS IT MAGIC?
IT SURE IS.
CAN WE TRY IT?
WELL, UM, IT'S NOT REALLY A TOY. REMEMBER WHAT HAPPENED LAST TIME?
WHEN BEPPO GOT AHOLD OF MY MAGIC WAND?
YEP, WE WERE ALL TURNED INTO MONKEYS!
OH, C'MON. IT WASN'T THAT BAD!
POP
LOOK! YOUR BUNNY ABBY IS GETTING ALONG NICELY WITH THE SUPER PETS!
SLAP!
EEP!

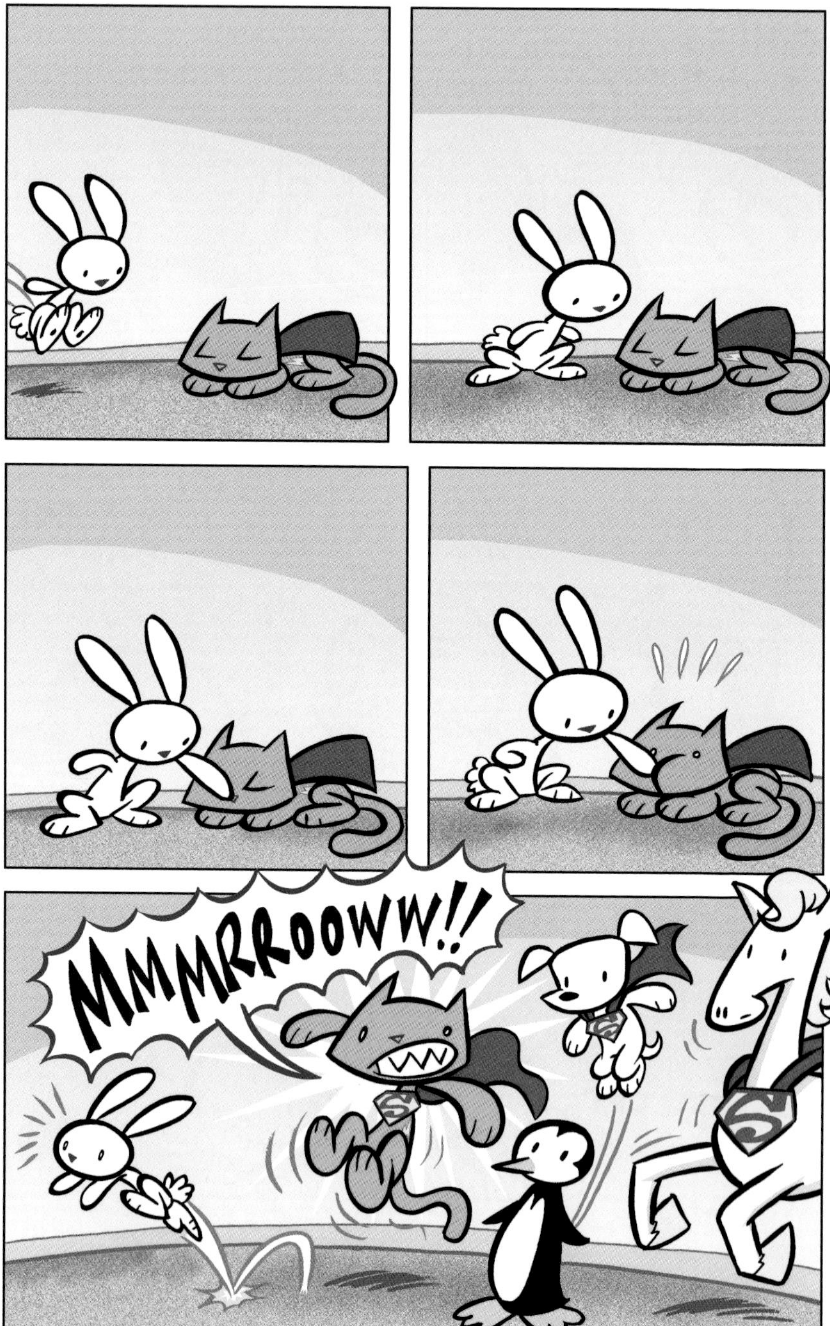
MMMRROOWW!!

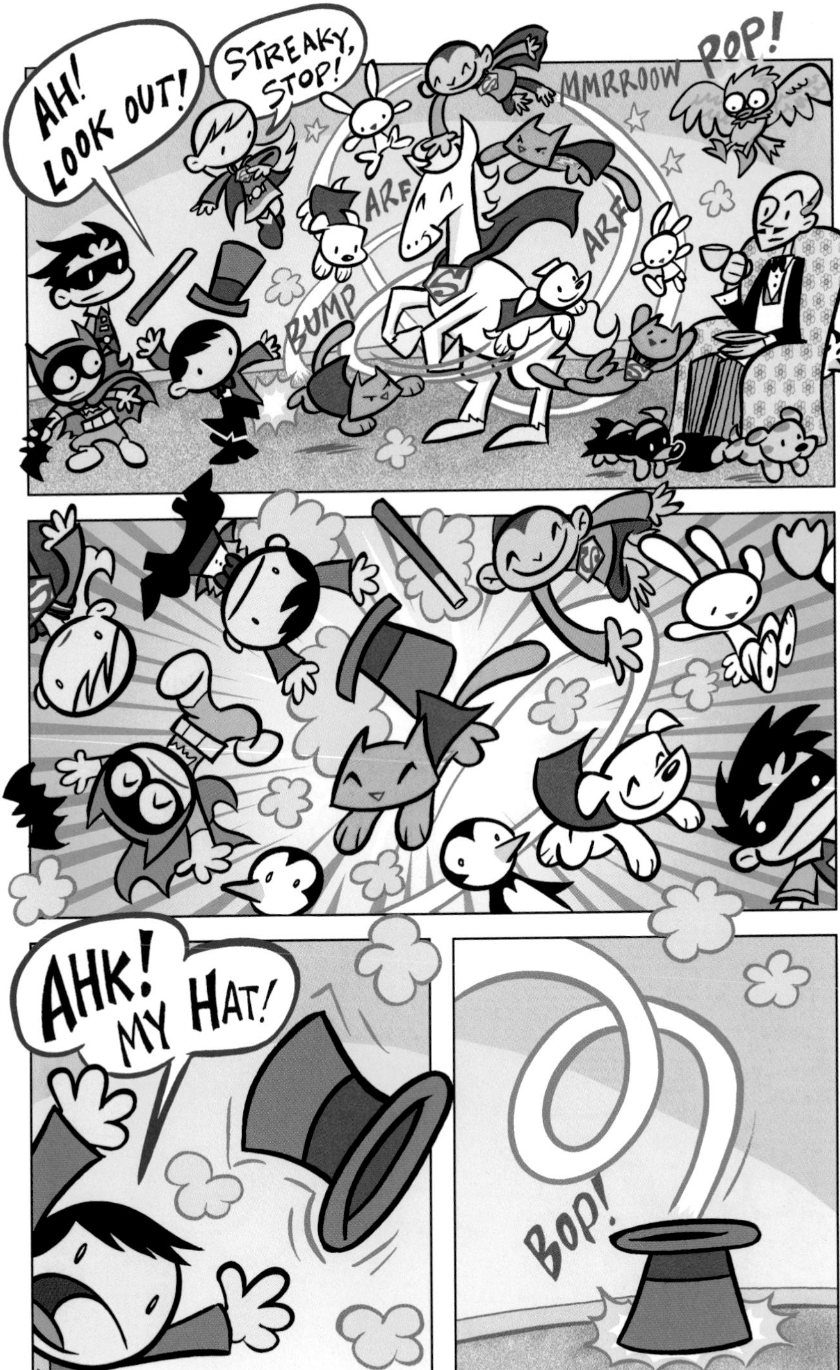
AH! LOOK OUT!
STREAKY, STOP!
MMRROOW
POP!
ARF
ARF
BUMP
AHK! MY HAT!
BOP!

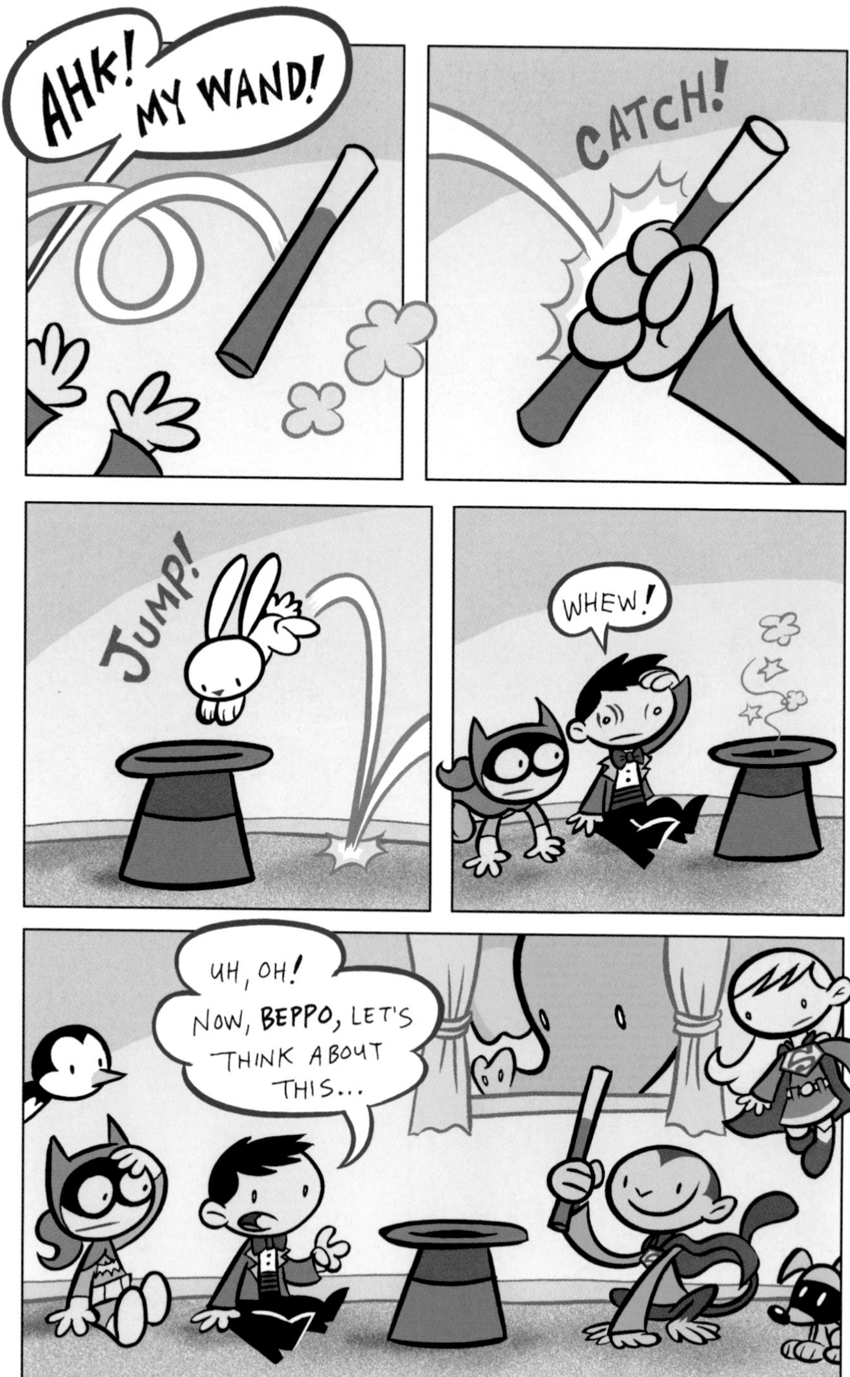
AHK! MY WAND!
CATCH!
JUMP!
WHEW!
UH, OH!
NOW, BEPPO, LET'S THINK ABOUT THIS...

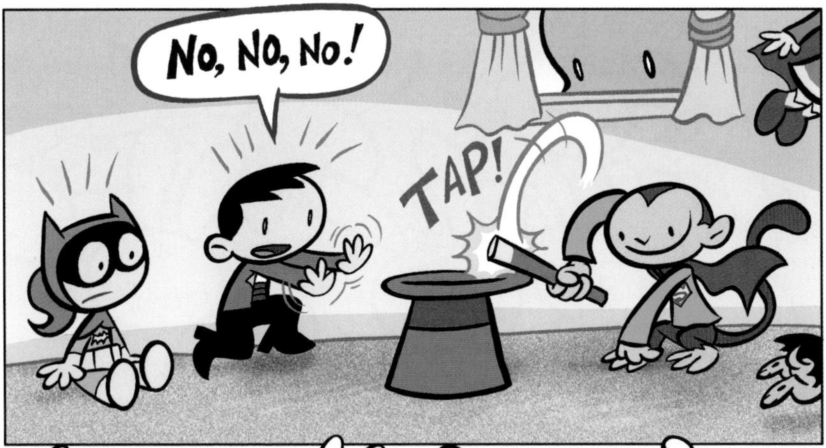
No, NO, No!
TAP!

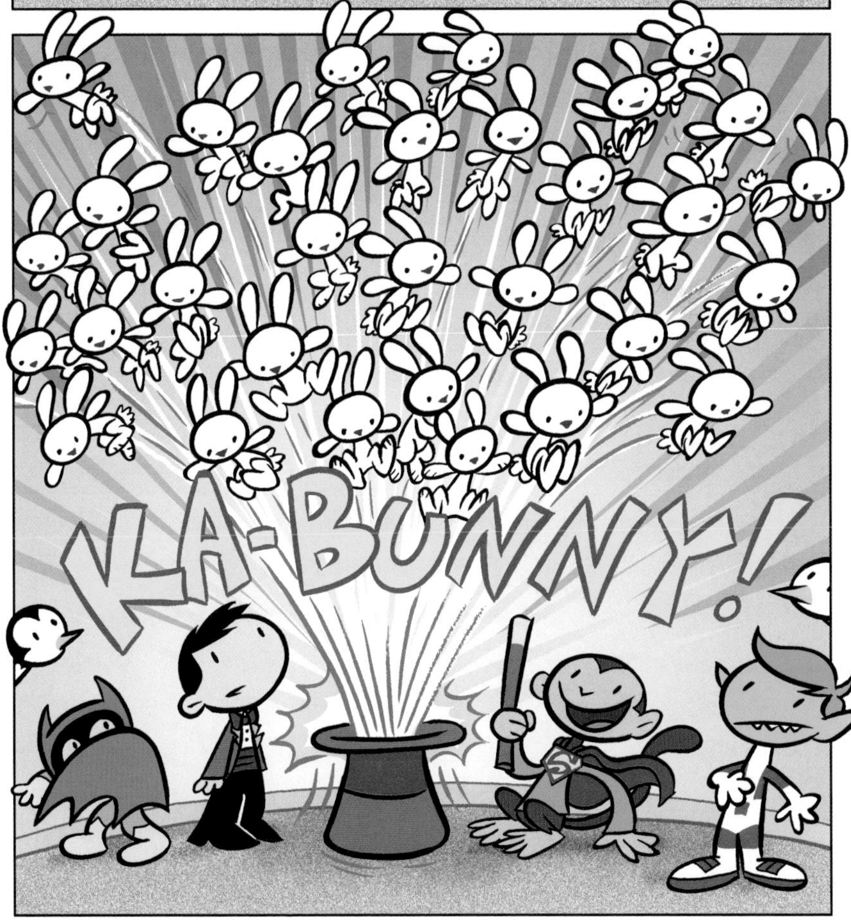
KA-BUNNY!

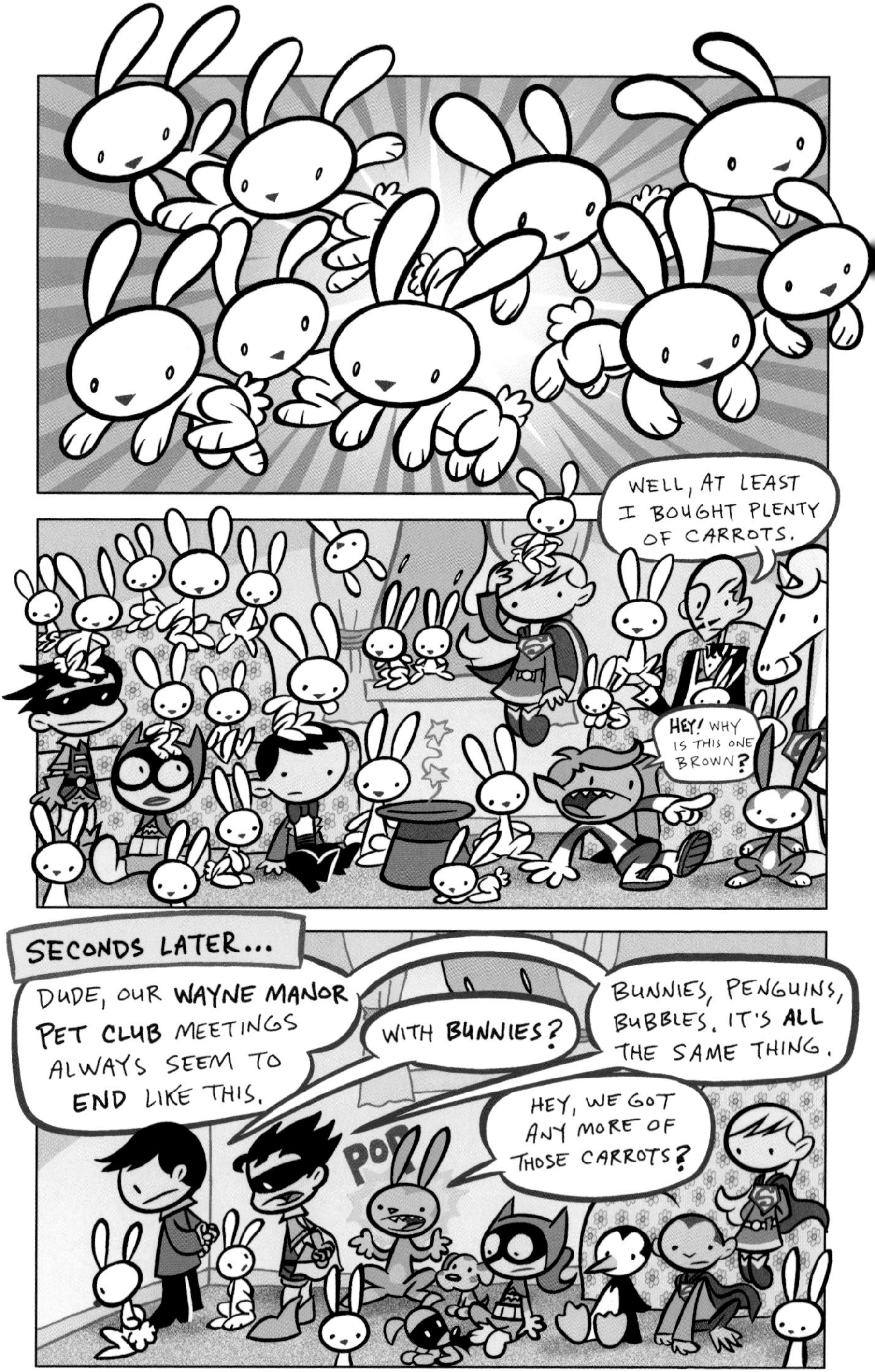

WELL, AT LEAST I BOUGHT PLENTY OF CARROTS.
HEY! WHY IS THIS ONE BROWN?
SECONDS LATER...
DUDE, OUR WAYNE MANOR PET CLUB MEETINGS ALWAYS SEEM TO END LIKE THIS.
WITH BUNNIES?
BUNNIES, PENGUINS, BUBBLES. IT'S ALL THE SAME THING.
HEY, WE GOT ANY MORE OF THOSE CARROTS?

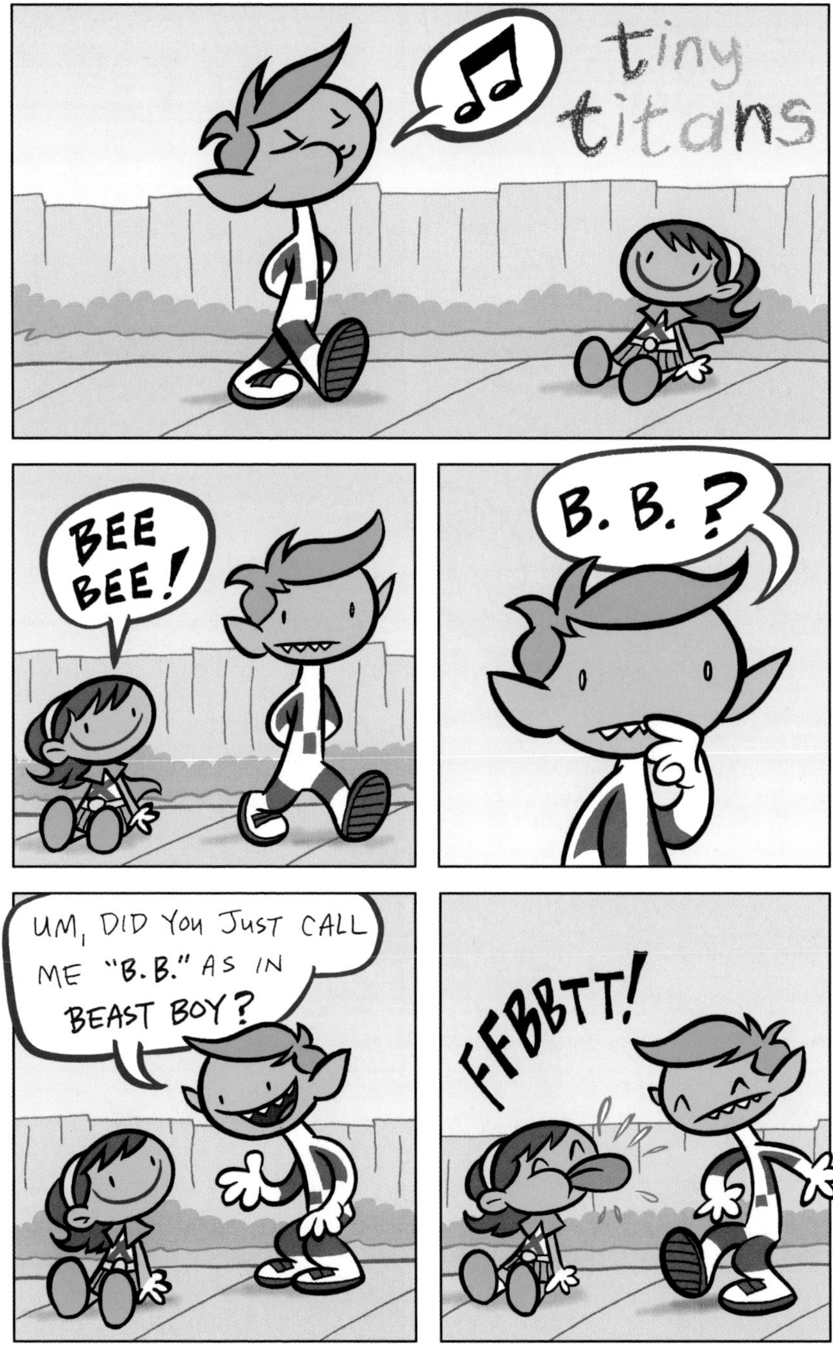
tiny titans
BEE BEE!
B. B.?
UM, DID YOU JUST CALL ME "B.B." AS IN BEAST BOY?
FFBBTT!

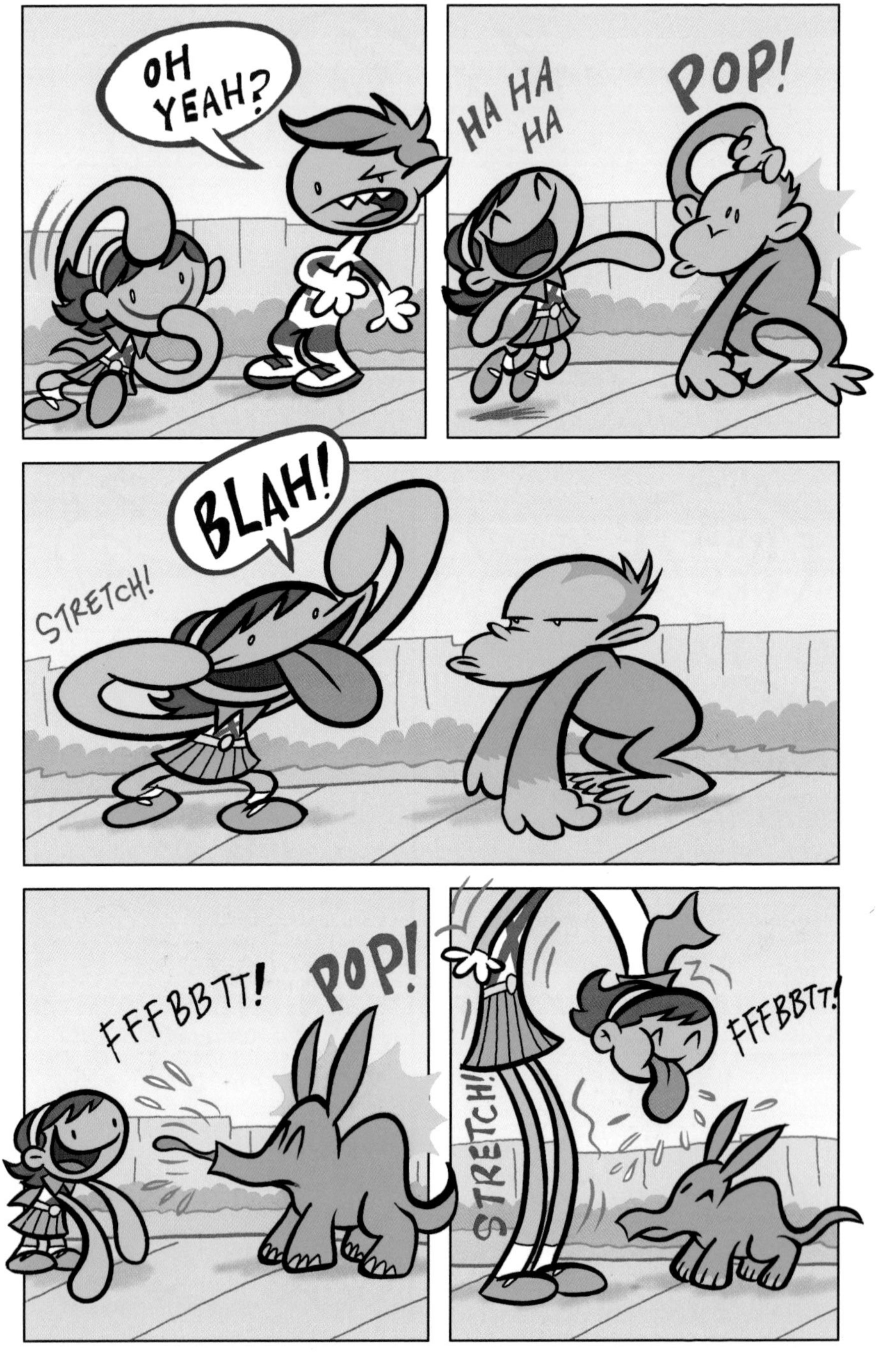
OH YEAH?
HA HA HA
POP!
BLAH!
STRETCH!
FFFBBTT!
POP!
STRETCH!
FFFBBTT!

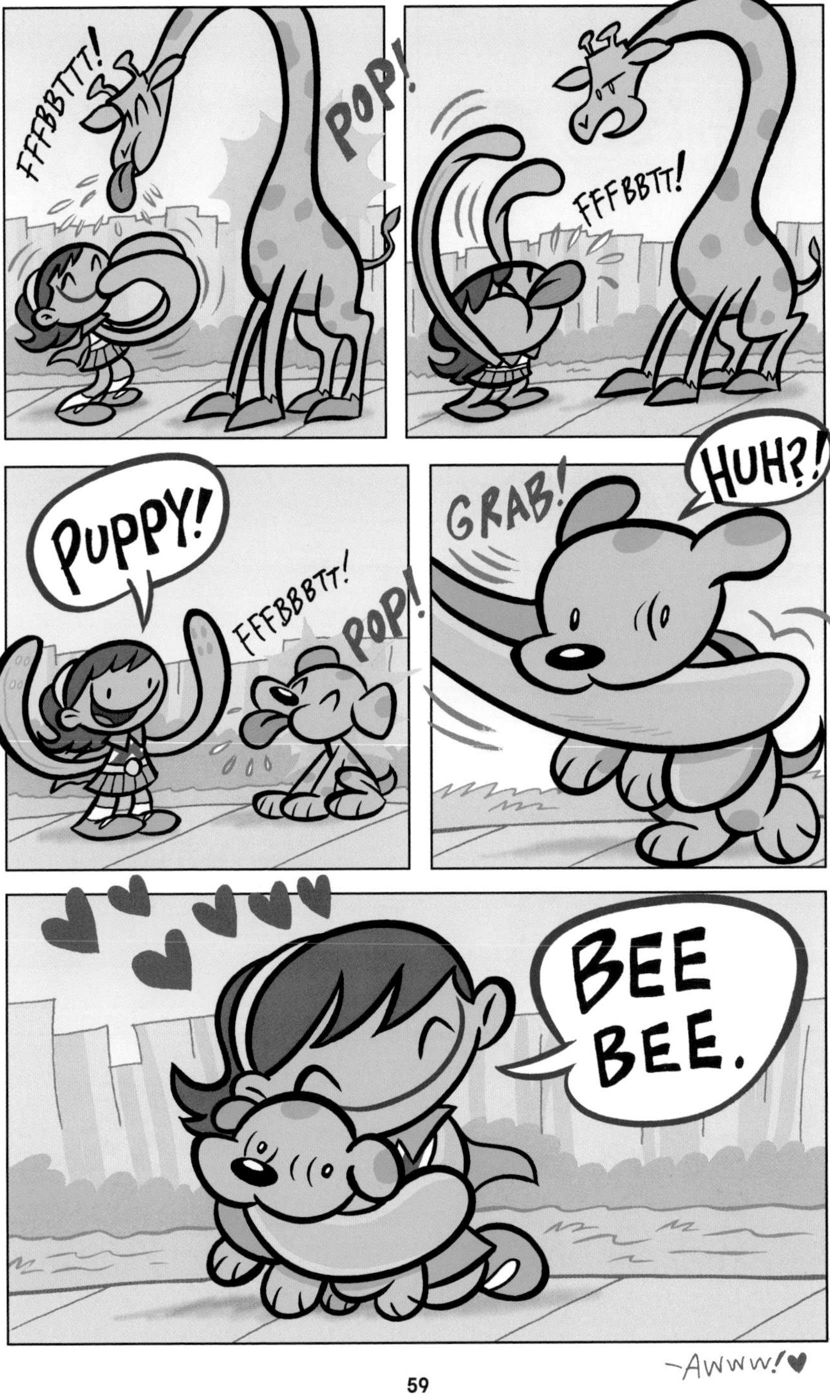
FFFBBTTT!
POP!
FFFBBTT!
PUPPY!
FFFBBBTT!
POP!
GRAB!
HUH?!
BEE BEE.
-AWWW!♥

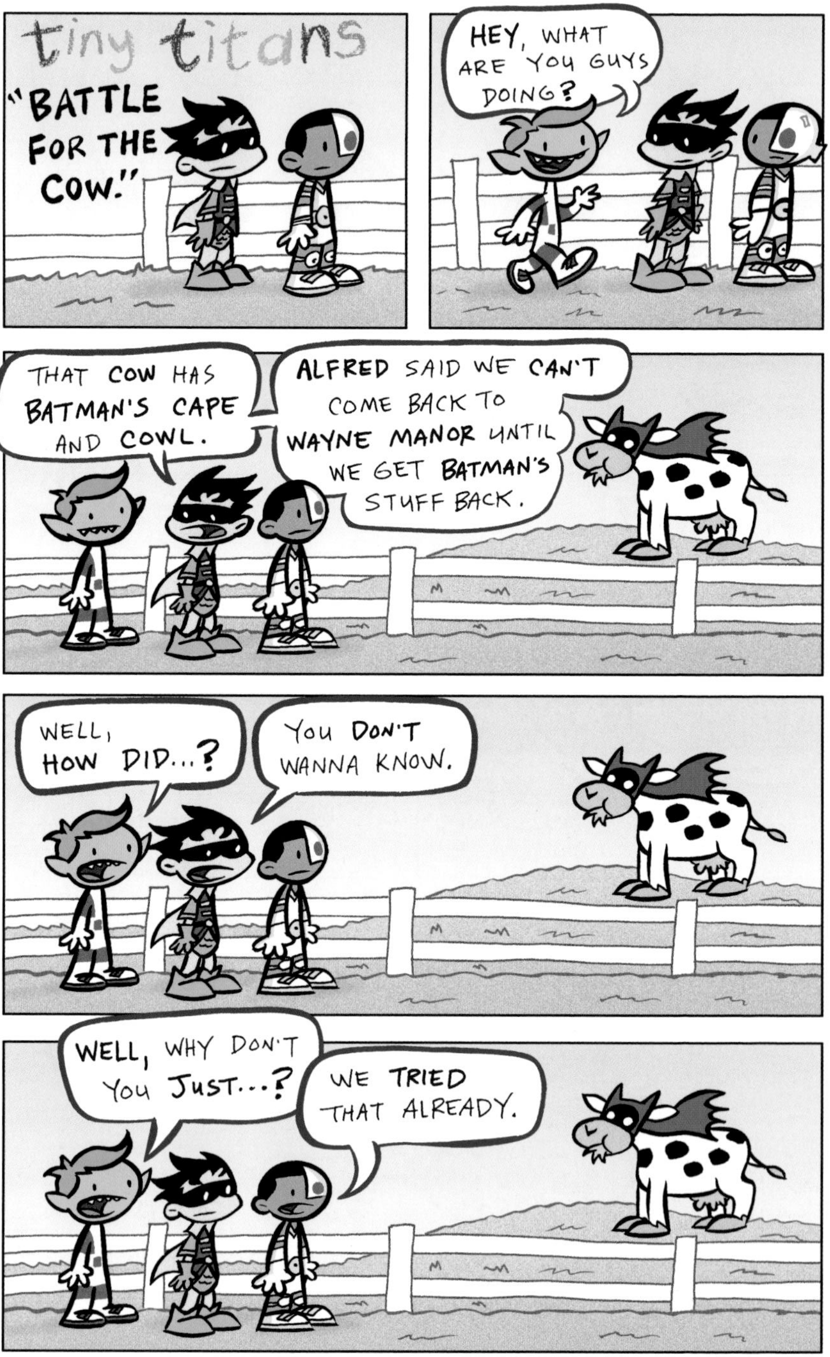
tiny titans
"BATTLE FOR THE COW."
HEY, WHAT ARE YOU GUYS DOING?
THAT COW HAS BATMAN'S CAPE AND COWL.
ALFRED SAID WE CAN'T COME BACK TO WAYNE MANOR UNTIL WE GET BATMAN'S STUFF BACK.
WELL, HOW DID...?
YOU DON'T WANNA KNOW.
WELL, WHY DON'T YOU JUST...?
WE TRIED THAT ALREADY.

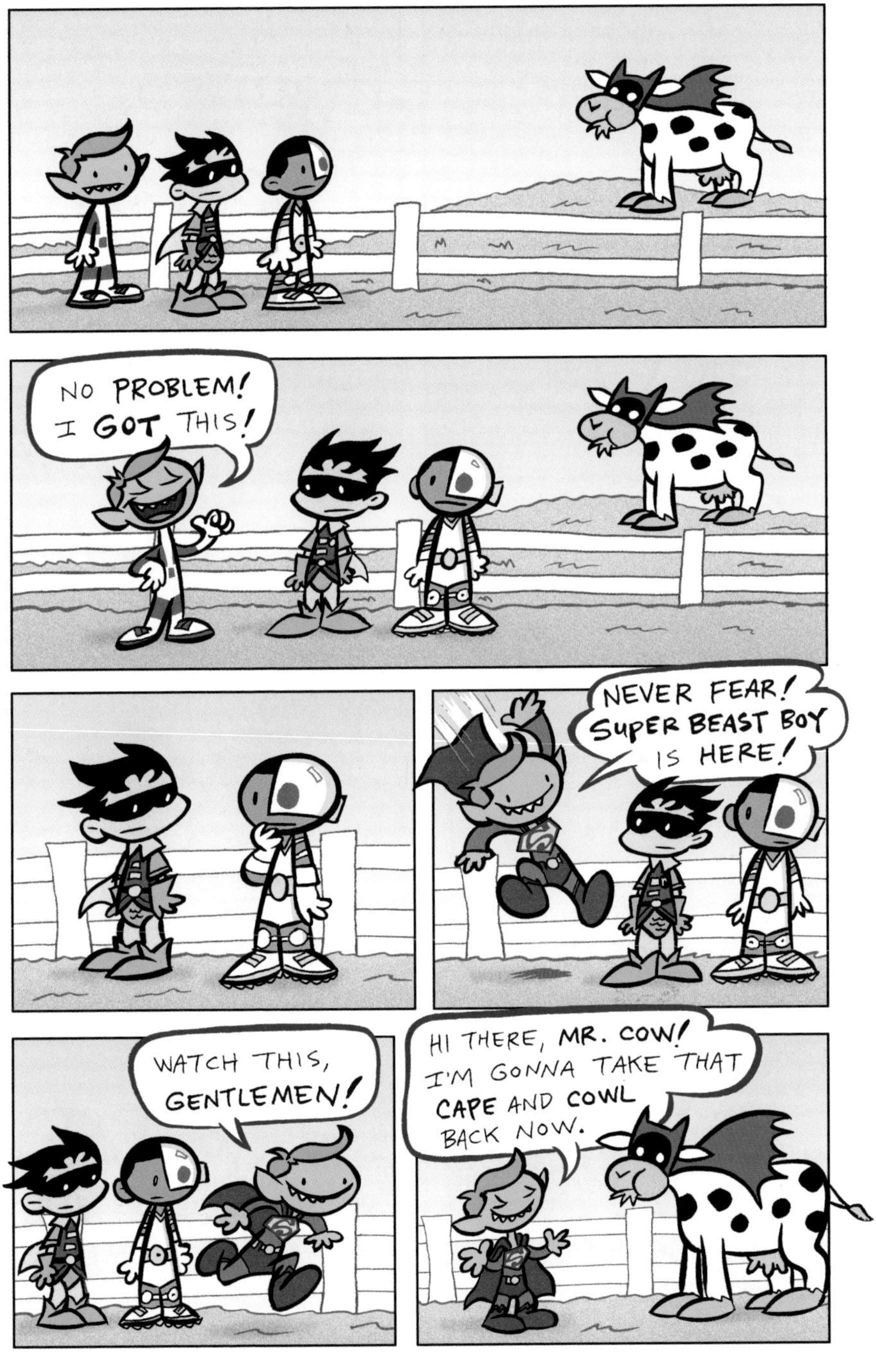
NO PROBLEM! I GOT THIS!
NEVER FEAR! SUPER BEAST BOY IS HERE!
WATCH THIS, GENTLEMEN!
HI THERE, MR. COW! I'M GONNA TAKE THAT CAPE AND COWL BACK NOW.

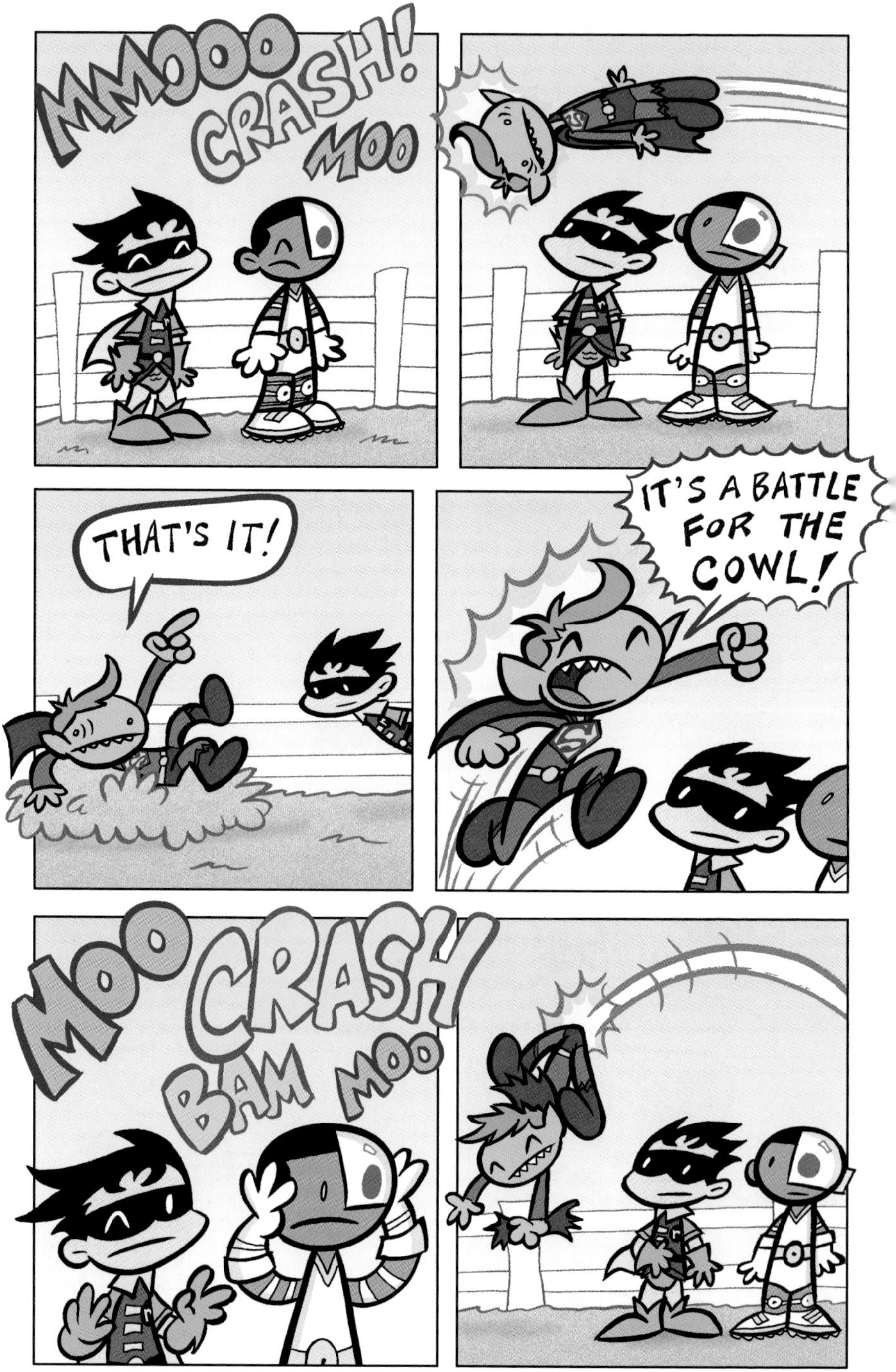
MMOOO
CRASH!
MOO
THAT'S IT!
IT'S A BATTLE FOR THE COWL!
MOO
CRASH
BAM
MOO

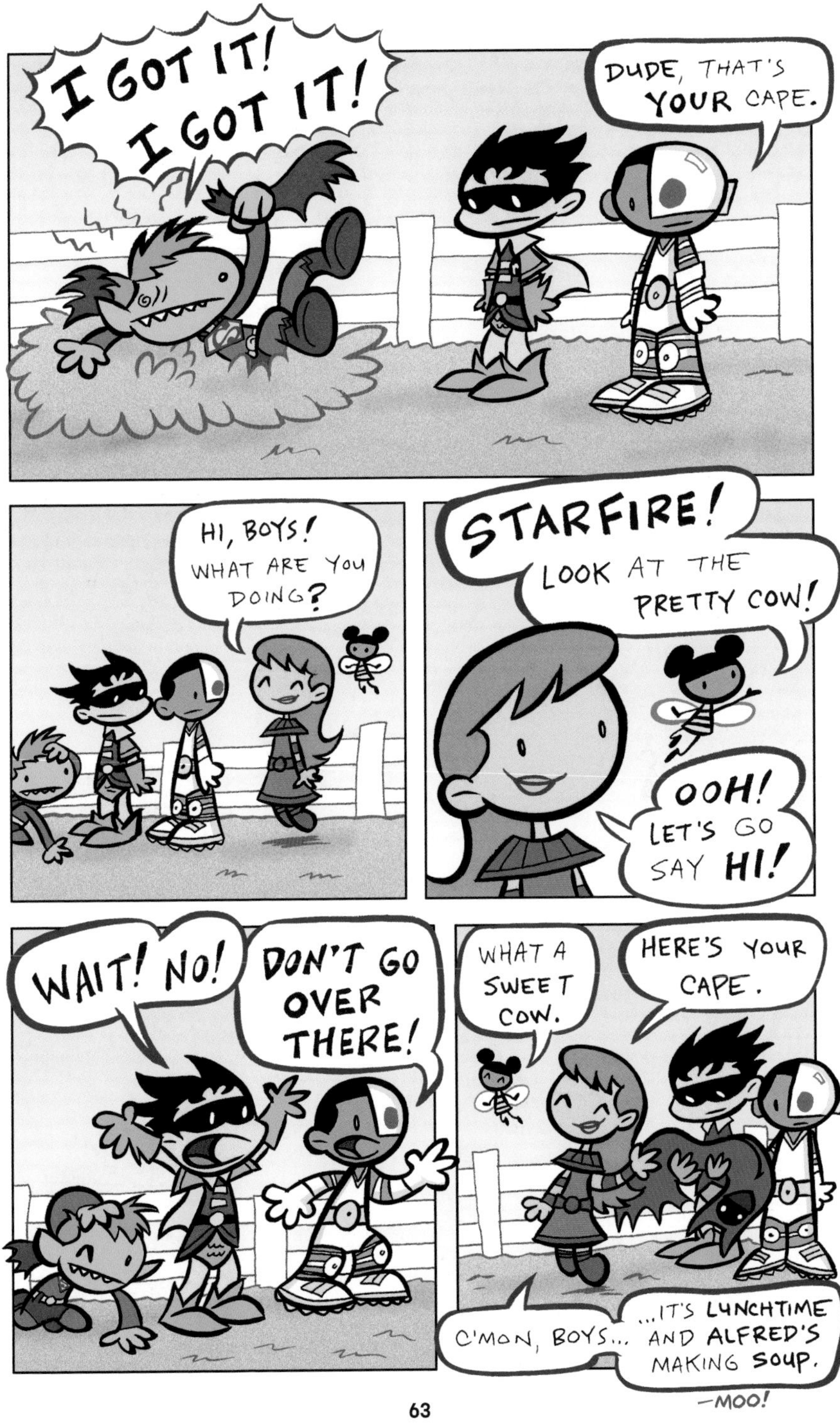
I GOT IT! I GOT IT!
DUDE, THAT'S YOUR CAPE.
HI, BOYS! WHAT ARE YOU DOING?
STARFIRE! LOOK AT THE PRETTY COW!
OOH! LET'S GO SAY HI!
WAIT! NO!
DON'T GO OVER THERE!
WHAT A SWEET COW.
HERE'S YOUR CAPE.
C'MON, BOYS...
...IT'S LUNCHTIME AND ALFRED'S MAKING SOUP.
-MOO!

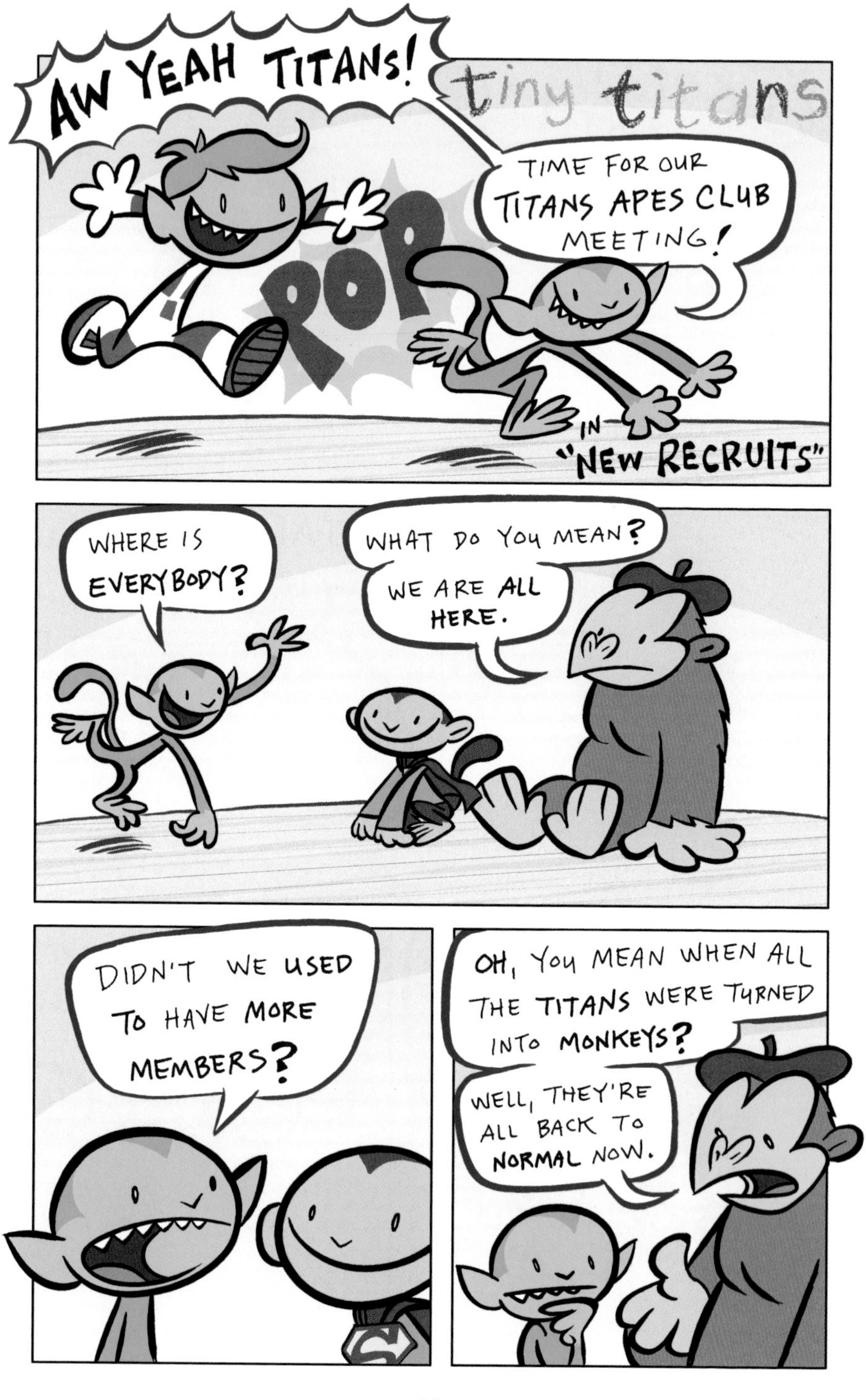
AW YEAH TITANS!
tiny titans
TIME FOR OUR TITANS APES CLUB MEETING!
POP
IN "NEW RECRUITS"
WHERE IS EVERYBODY?
WHAT DO YOU MEAN?
WE ARE ALL HERE.
DIDN'T WE USED TO HAVE MORE MEMBERS?
OH, YOU MEAN WHEN ALL THE TITANS WERE TURNED INTO MONKEYS?
WELL, THEY'RE ALL BACK TO NORMAL NOW.

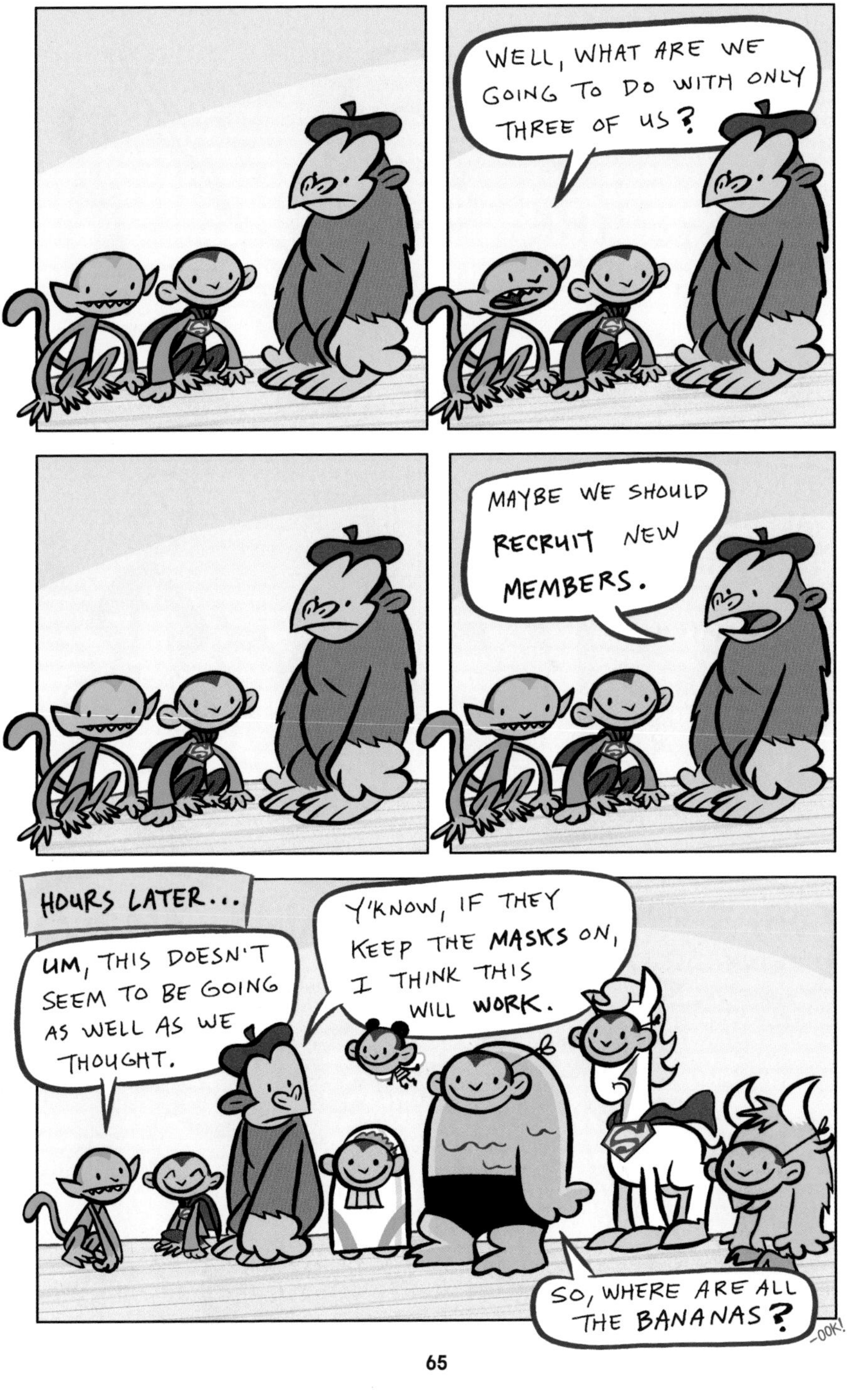
WELL, WHAT ARE WE GOING TO DO WITH ONLY THREE OF US?
MAYBE WE SHOULD RECRUIT NEW MEMBERS.
HOURS LATER...
UM, THIS DOESN'T SEEM TO BE GOING AS WELL AS WE THOUGHT.
Y'KNOW, IF THEY KEEP THE MASKS ON, I THINK THIS WILL WORK.
SO, WHERE ARE ALL THE BANANAS?
-OOK!

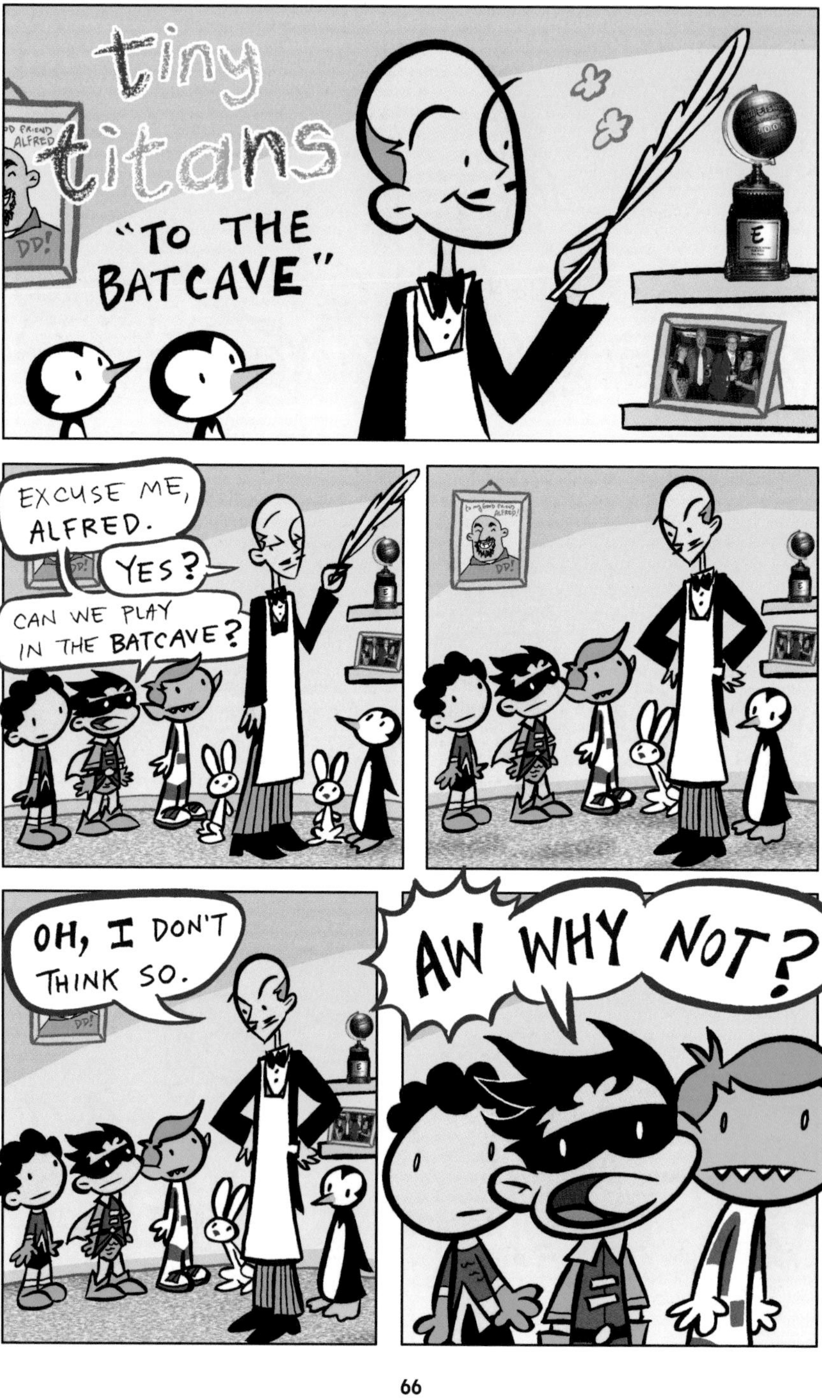
tiny titans
"TO THE BATCAVE"
EXCUSE ME, ALFRED.
YES?
CAN WE PLAY IN THE BATCAVE?
OH, I DON'T THINK SO.
AW WHY NOT?

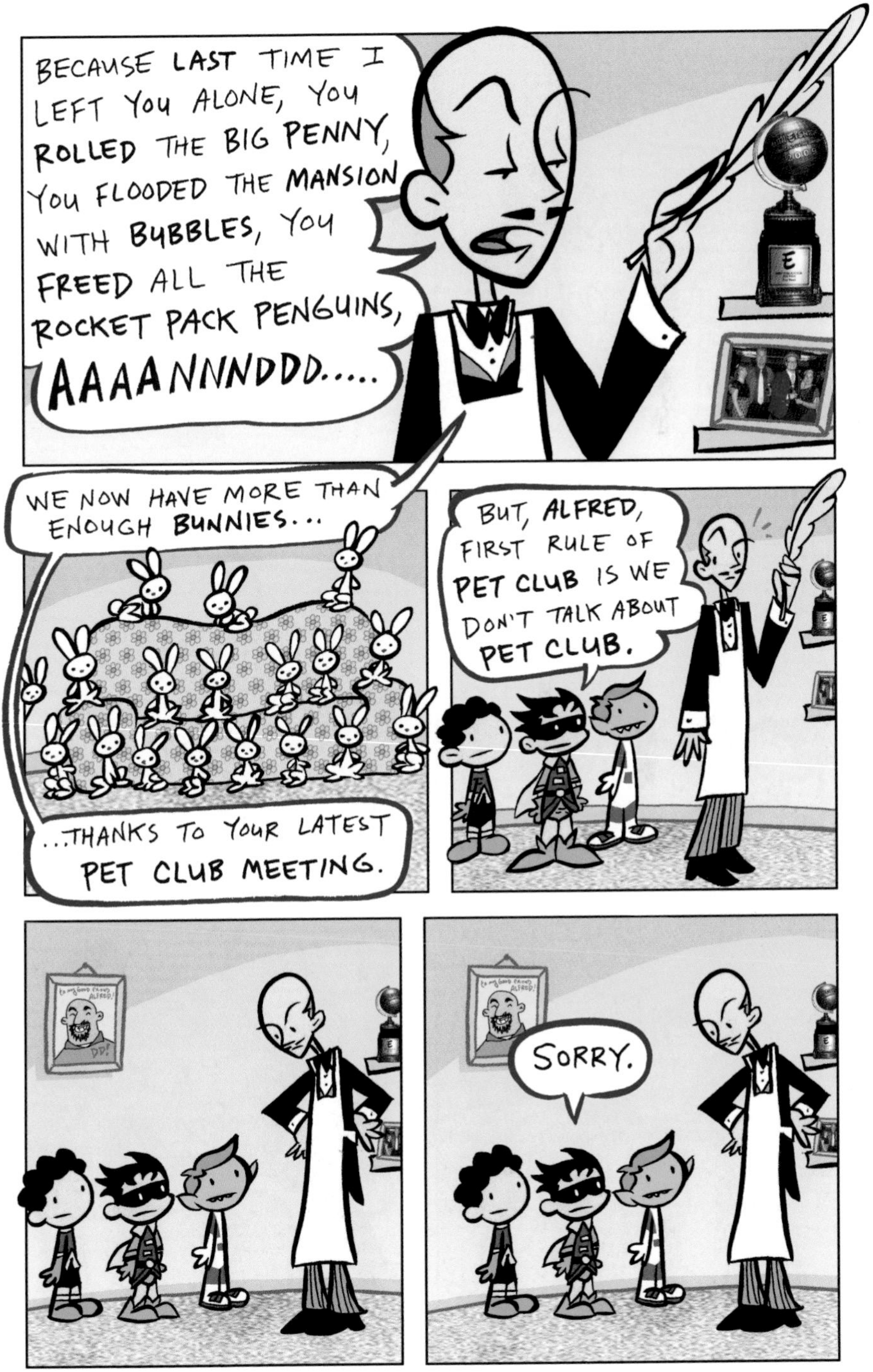
BECAUSE LAST TIME I LEFT YOU ALONE, YOU ROLLED THE BIG PENNY, YOU FLOODED THE MANSION WITH BUBBLES, YOU FREED ALL THE ROCKET PACK PENGUINS, AAAANNNDDD.....
WE NOW HAVE MORE THAN ENOUGH BUNNIES...
...THANKS TO YOUR LATEST PET CLUB MEETING.
BUT, ALFRED, FIRST RULE OF PET CLUB IS WE DON'T TALK ABOUT PET CLUB.
SORRY.

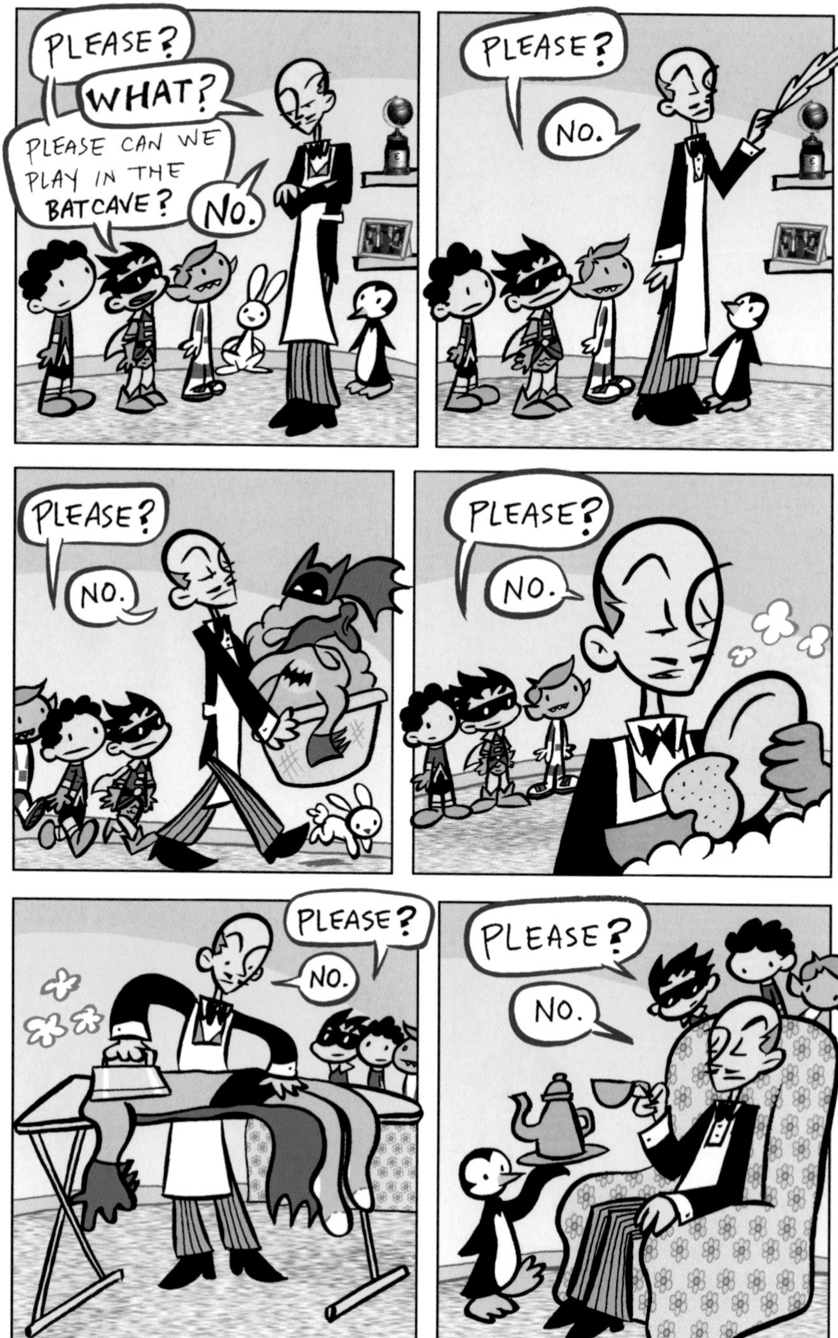
PLEASE?
WHAT?
PLEASE CAN WE PLAY IN THE BATCAVE?
NO.
PLEASE?
NO.
PLEASE?
NO.
PLEASE?
NO.
PLEASE?
NO.
PLEASE?
NO.

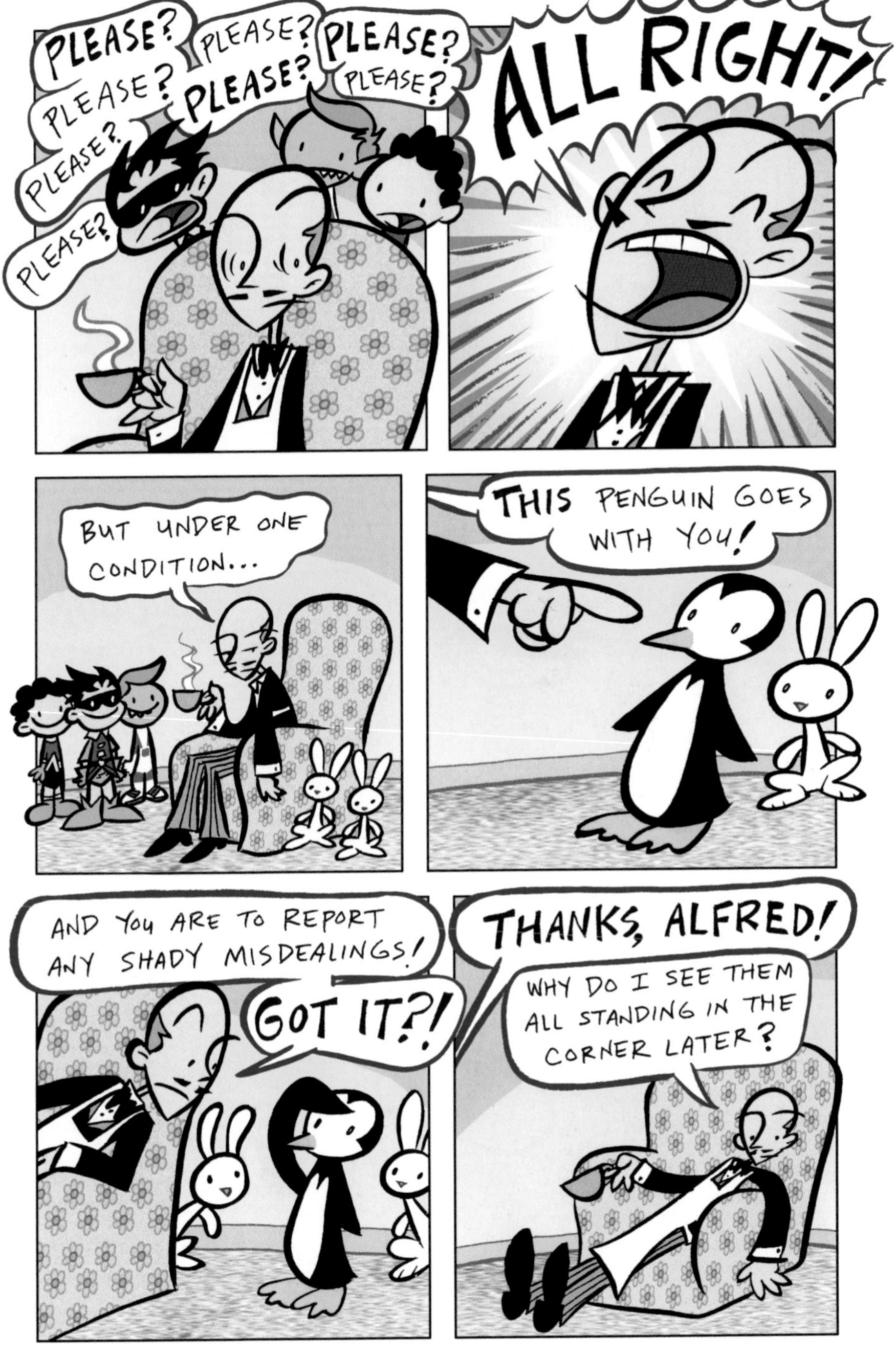
PLEASE?
PLEASE?
PLEASE?
PLEASE?
PLEASE?
PLEASE?
PLEASE?
PLEASE?
ALL RIGHT!
BUT UNDER ONE CONDITION...
THIS PENGUIN GOES WITH YOU!
AND YOU ARE TO REPORT ANY SHADY MISDEALINGS!
GOT IT?!
THANKS, ALFRED!
WHY DO I SEE THEM ALL STANDING IN THE CORNER LATER?

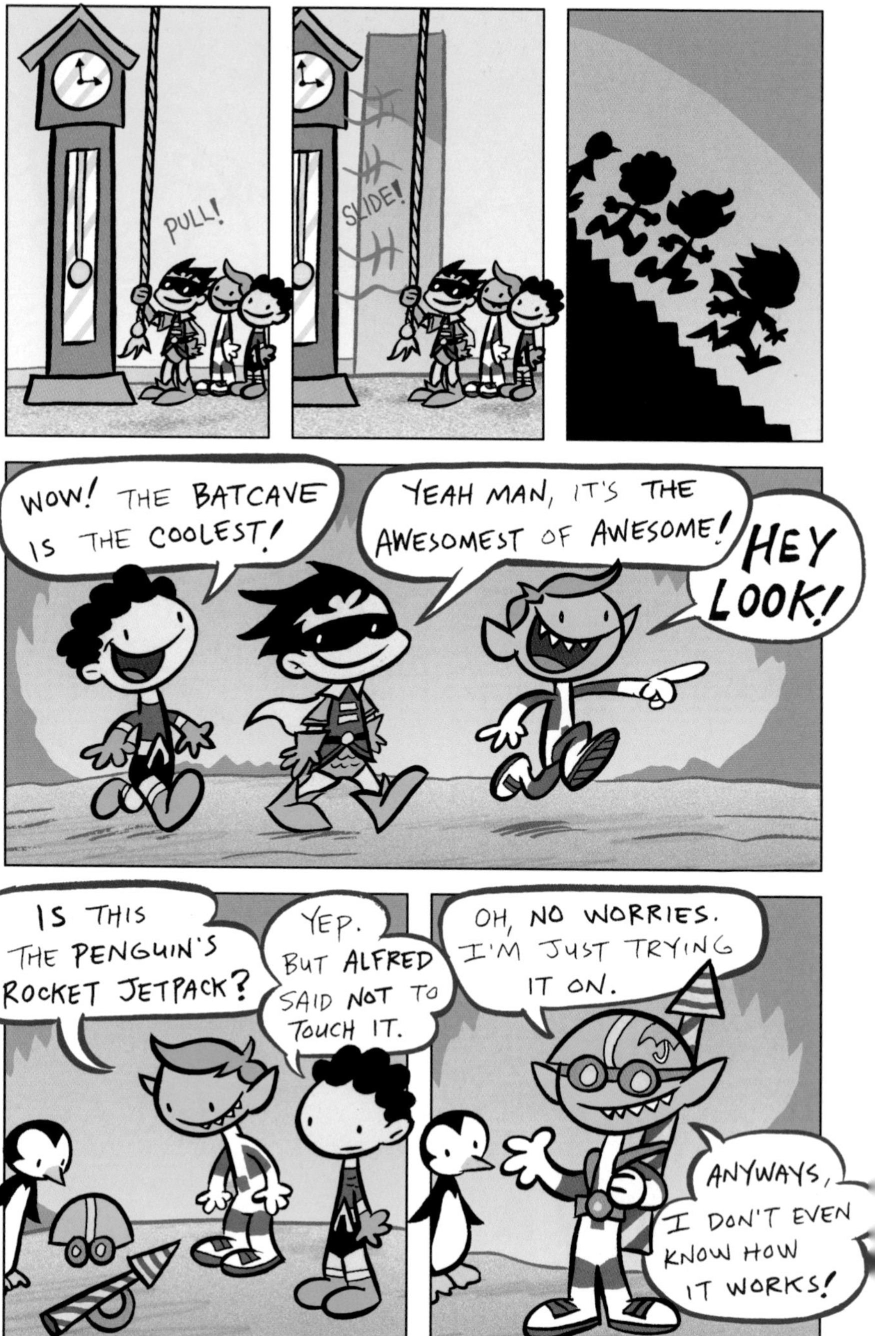
PULL!
SLIDE!
WOW! THE BATCAVE IS THE COOLEST!
YEAH MAN, IT'S THE AWESOMEST OF AWESOME!
HEY LOOK!
IS THIS THE PENGUIN'S ROCKET JETPACK?
YEP. BUT ALFRED SAID NOT TO TOUCH IT.
OH, NO WORRIES. I'M JUST TRYING IT ON.
ANYWAYS, I DON'T EVEN KNOW HOW IT WORKS!

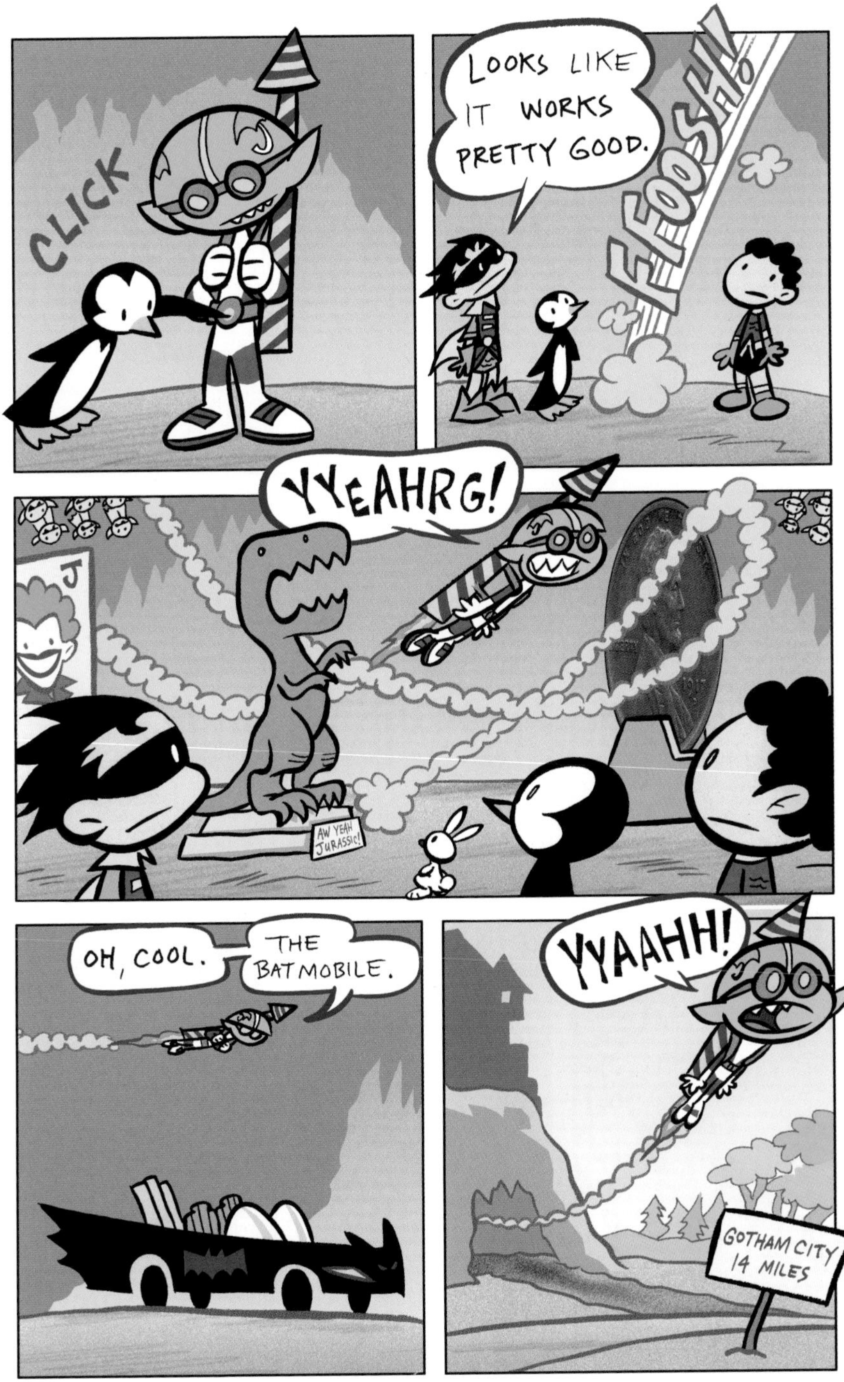
CLICK
LOOKS LIKE IT WORKS PRETTY GOOD.
FFOOSH!
YYEAHRG!
J
AW YEAH JURASSIC!
OH, COOL.
THE BATMOBILE.
YYAAHH!
GOTHAM CITY 14 MILES

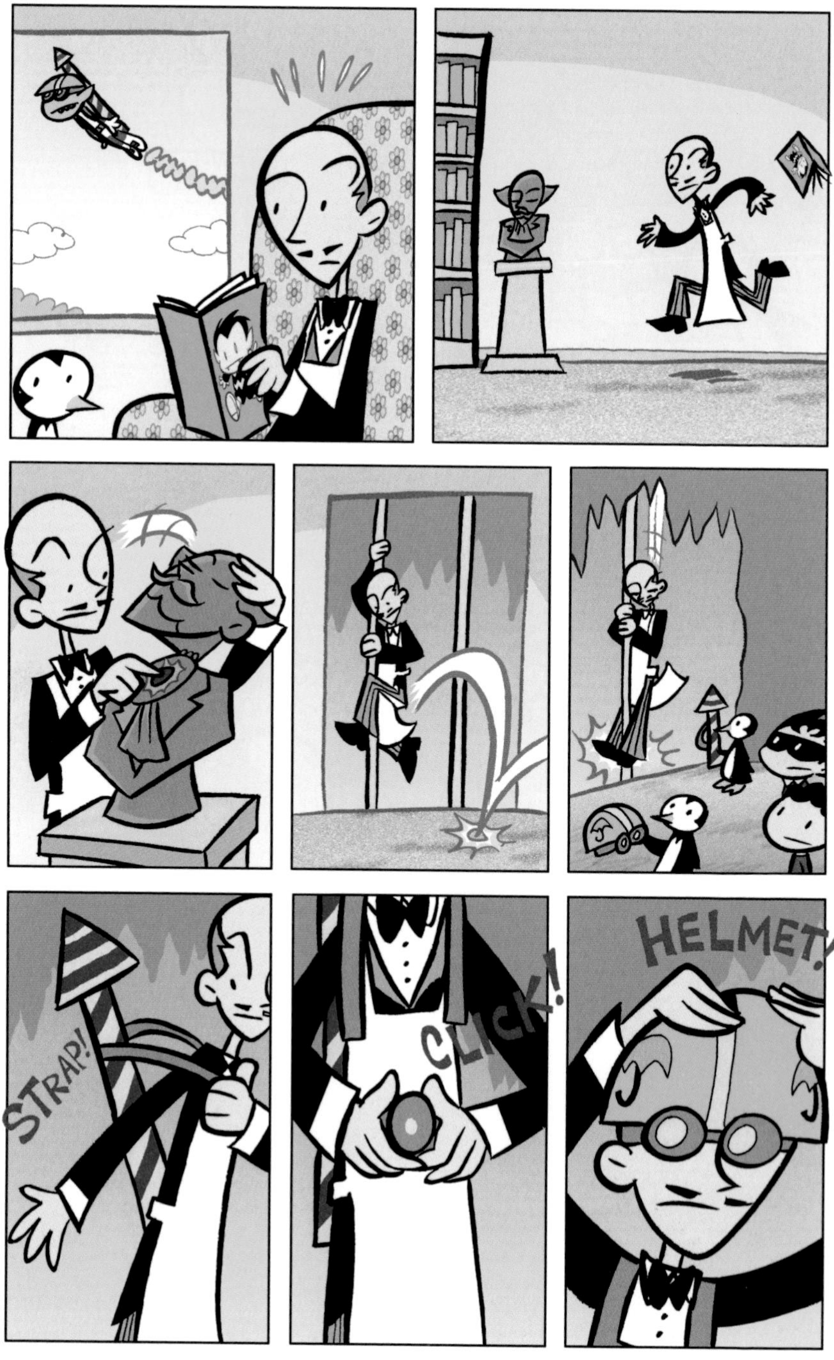
STRAP!
CLICK!
HELMET!

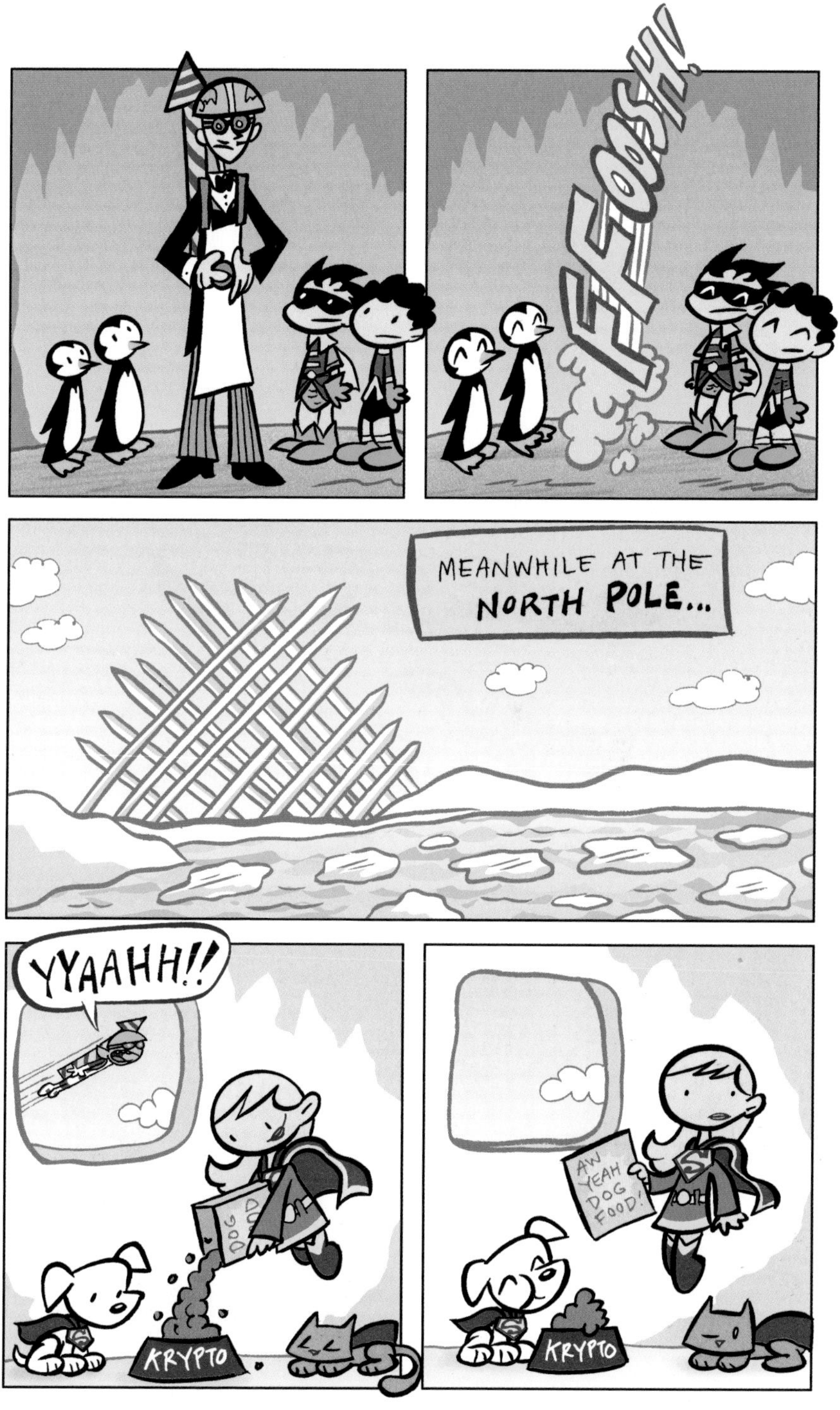
FOOSH!
MEANWHILE AT THE NORTH POLE...
YYAAHH!!
DOG FOOD
KRYPTO
AW YEAH DOG FOOD!
KRYPTO

BEAST BOY?

HI, SUPERGIRL.

ALFRED?

HELLO, MISS.

UH OH.

MINUTES LATER, BACK AT WAYNE MANOR...

HI, ROBIN!

HI, RAVEN. UM... NOW IS NOT A GOOD TIME.

THAT'S THE LAST TIME I SEND A PENGUIN TO DO A BUTLER'S JOB!

—BLAST OFF!

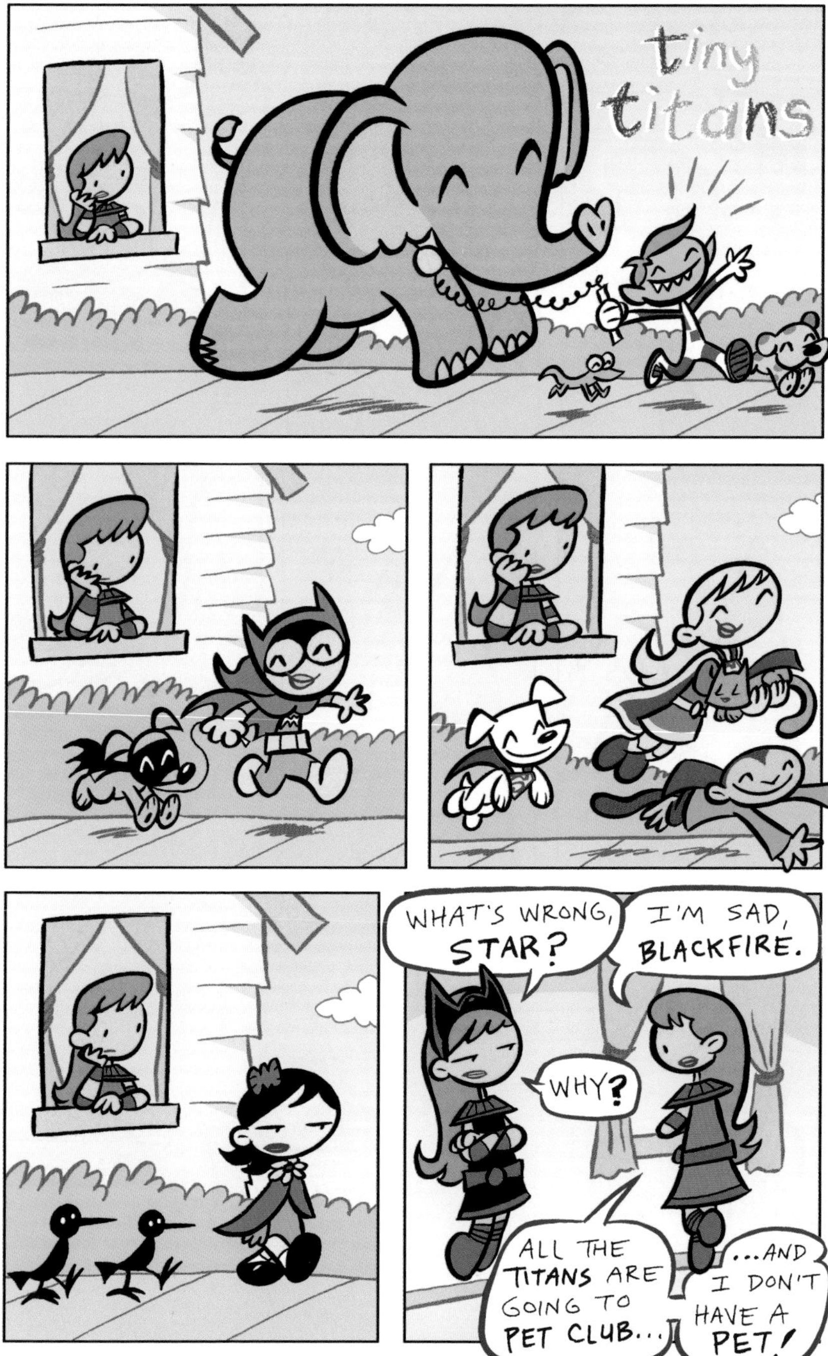
tiny titans
WHAT'S WRONG, STAR?
I'M SAD, BLACKFIRE.
WHY?
ALL THE TITANS ARE GOING TO PET CLUB...
...AND I DON'T HAVE A PET!

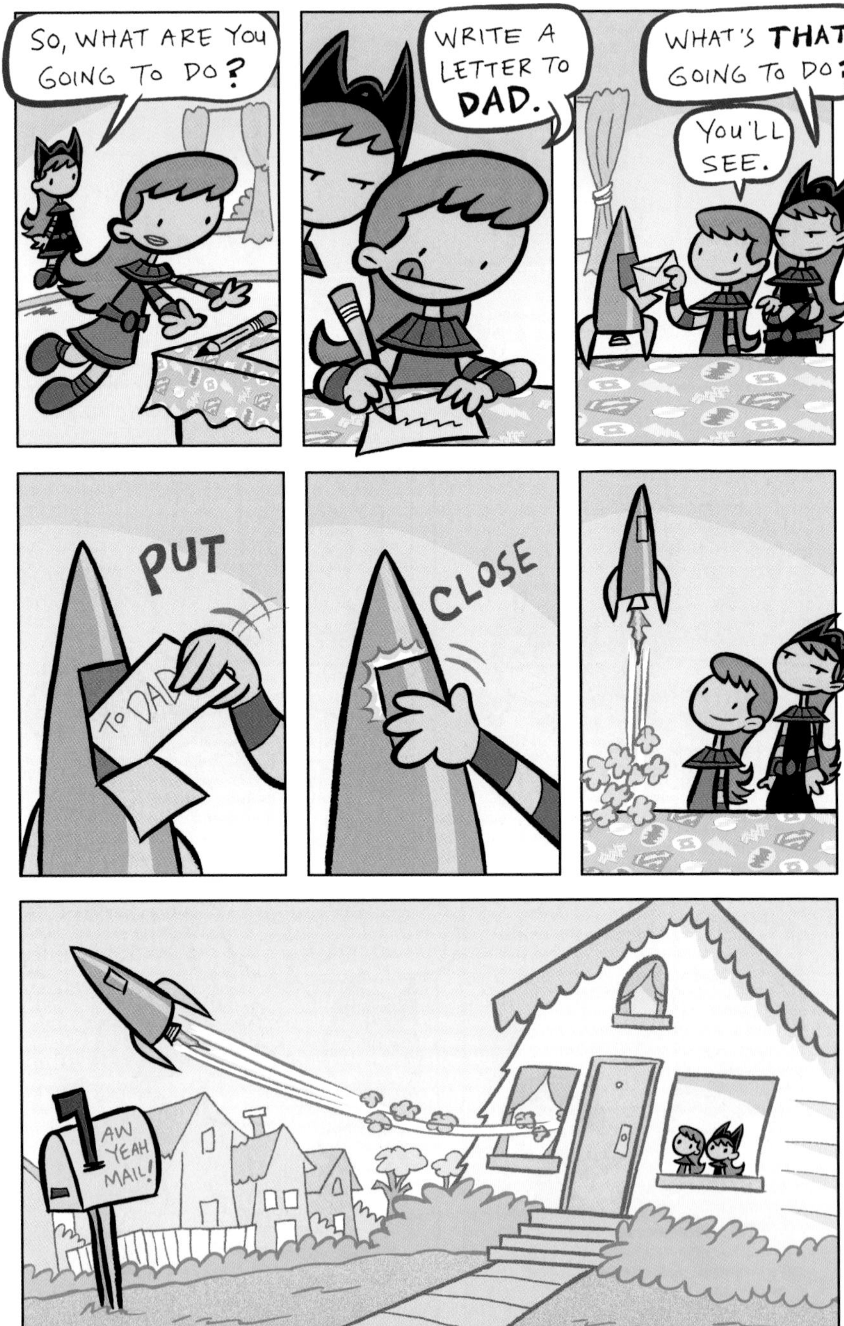
SO, WHAT ARE YOU GOING TO DO?
WRITE A LETTER TO DAD.
WHAT'S THAT GOING TO DO?
YOU'LL SEE.
PUT
TO DAD
CLOSE
AW YEAH MAIL!

WEDNESDAY
COMICS

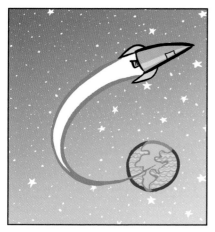

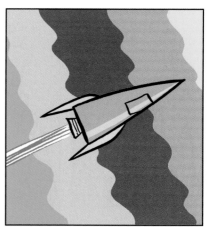

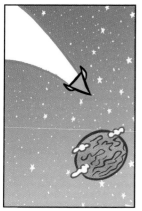

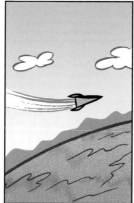

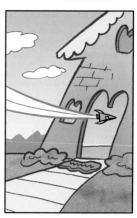

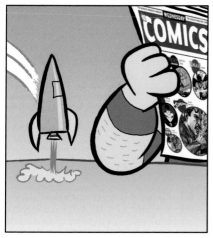

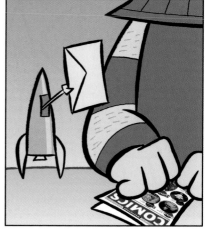

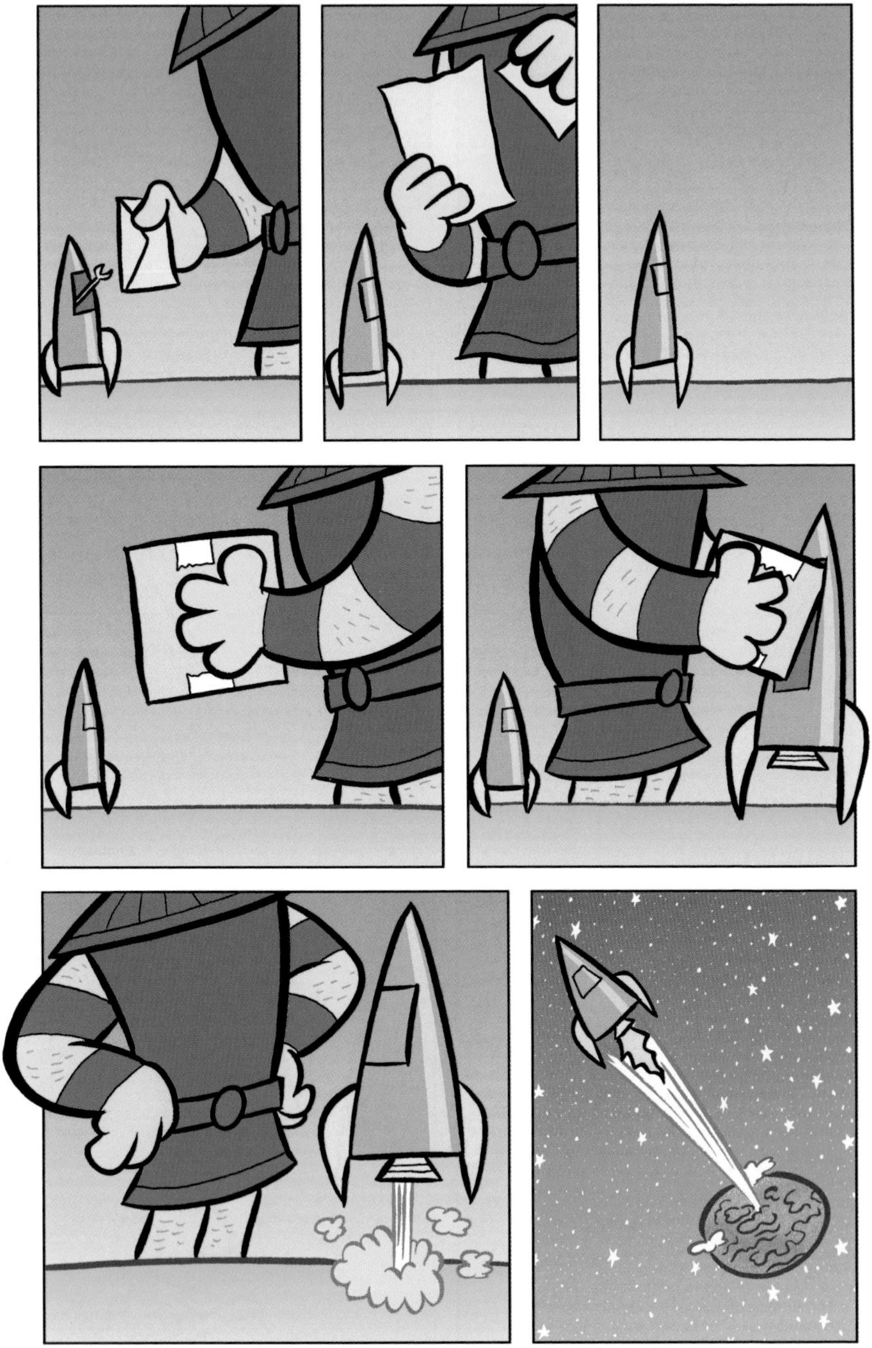

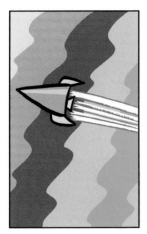

OPEN

OPEN TEAR

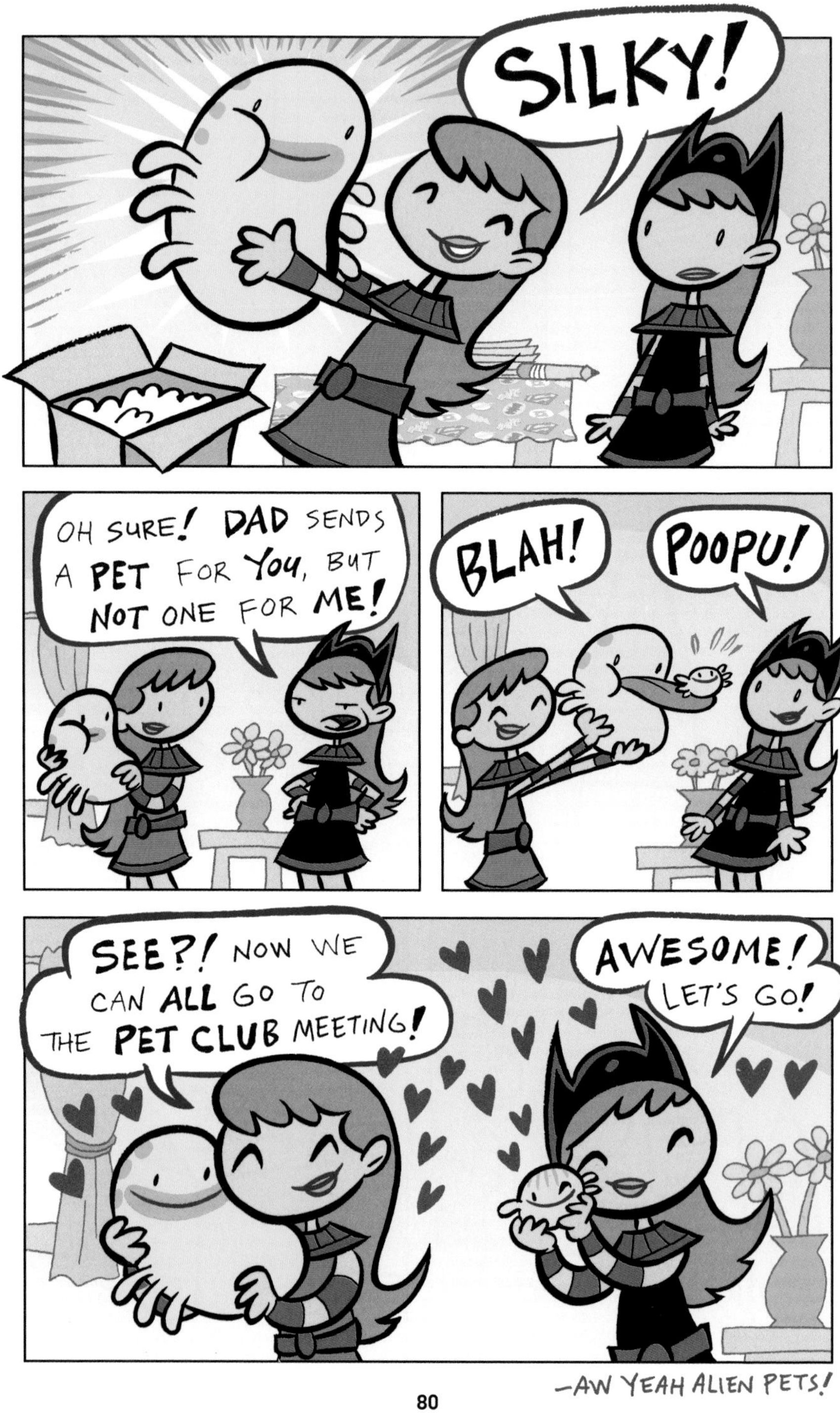
SILKY!
OH SURE! DAD SENDS A PET FOR YOU, BUT NOT ONE FOR ME!
BLAH!
POOPU!
SEE?! NOW WE CAN ALL GO TO THE PET CLUB MEETING!
AWESOME! LET'S GO!

—AW YEAH ALIEN PETS!

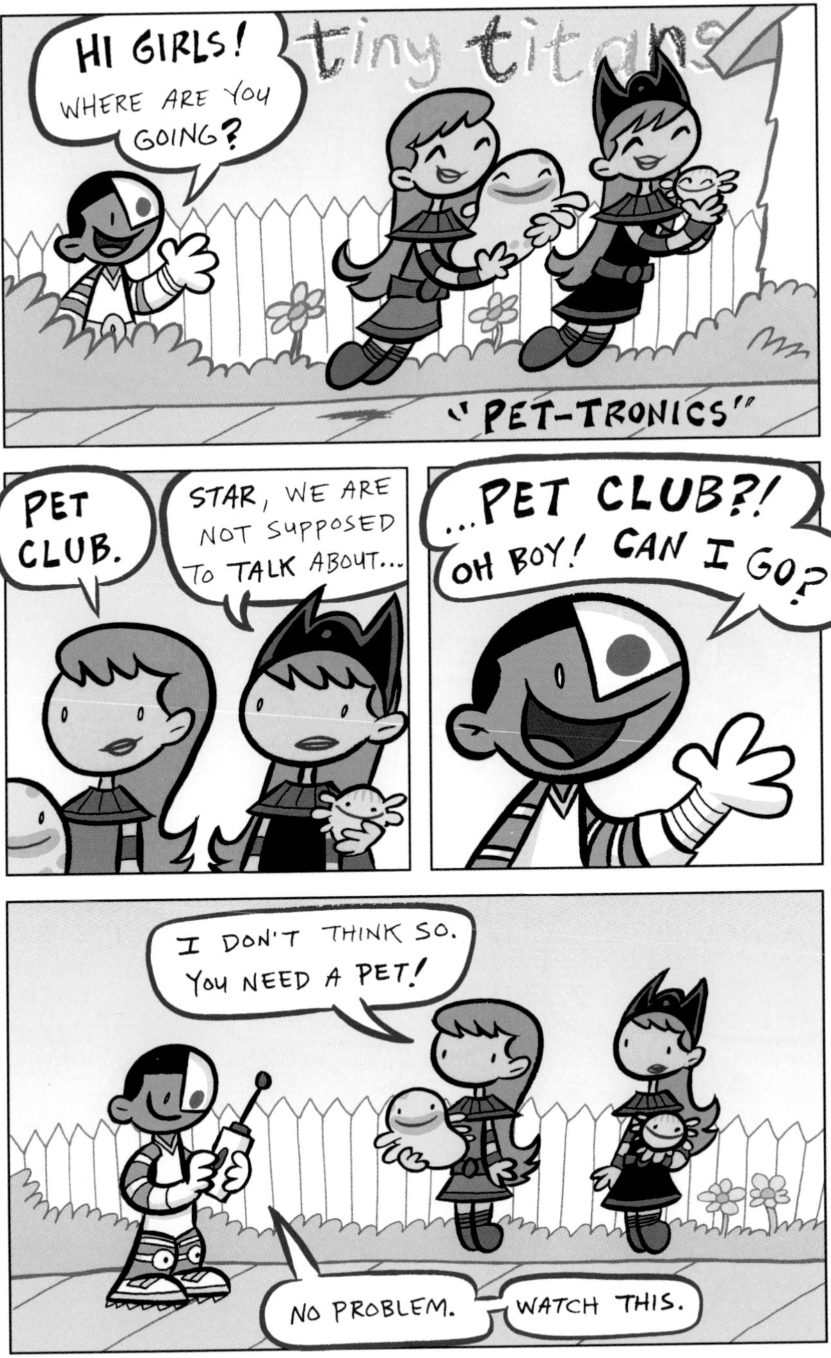
HI GIRLS! WHERE ARE YOU GOING?
tiny titans
"PET-TRONICS"
PET CLUB.
STAR, WE ARE NOT SUPPOSED TO TALK ABOUT...
...PET CLUB?! OH BOY! CAN I GO?
I DON'T THINK SO. YOU NEED A PET!
NO PROBLEM.
WATCH THIS.

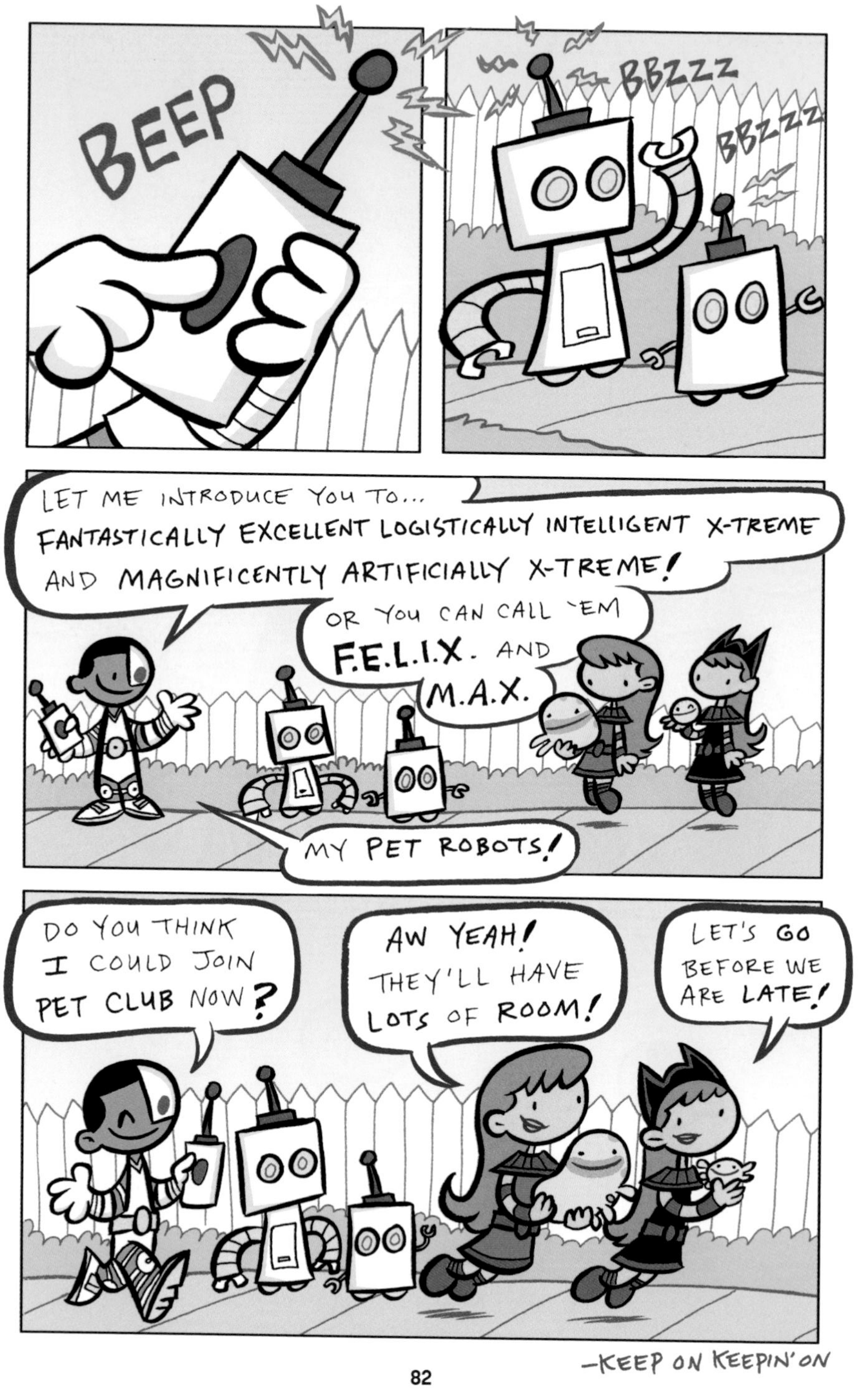
BEEP
BBZZZ
BBZZZ
LET ME INTRODUCE YOU TO... FANTASTICALLY EXCELLENT LOGISTICALLY INTELLIGENT X-TREME AND MAGNIFICENTLY ARTIFICIALLY X-TREME!
OR YOU CAN CALL 'EM F.E.L.I.X. AND M.A.X.
MY PET ROBOTS!
DO YOU THINK I COULD JOIN PET CLUB NOW?
AW YEAH! THEY'LL HAVE LOTS OF ROOM!
LET'S GO BEFORE WE ARE LATE!

—KEEP ON KEEPIN' ON

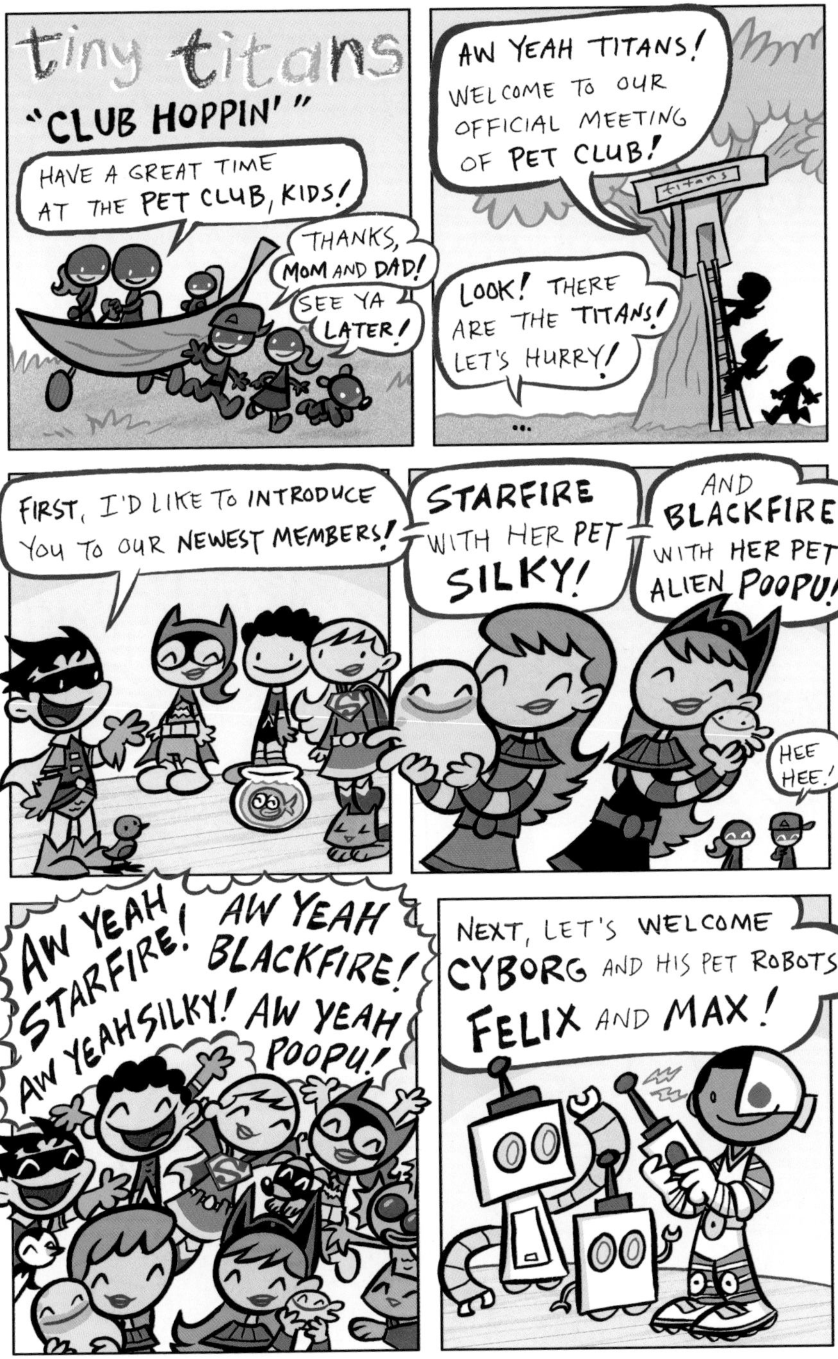
tiny titans
"CLUB HOPPIN'"
HAVE A GREAT TIME AT THE PET CLUB, KIDS!
THANKS, MOM AND DAD!
SEE YA LATER!
AW YEAH TITANS! WELCOME TO OUR OFFICIAL MEETING OF PET CLUB!
LOOK! THERE ARE THE TITANS! LET'S HURRY!
...
FIRST, I'D LIKE TO INTRODUCE YOU TO OUR NEWEST MEMBERS!
STARFIRE WITH HER PET SILKY!
AND BLACKFIRE WITH HER PET ALIEN POOPU!
HEE HEE!
AW YEAH STARFIRE! AW YEAH BLACKFIRE! AW YEAH SILKY! AW YEAH POOPU!
NEXT, LET'S WELCOME CYBORG AND HIS PET ROBOTS FELIX AND MAX!

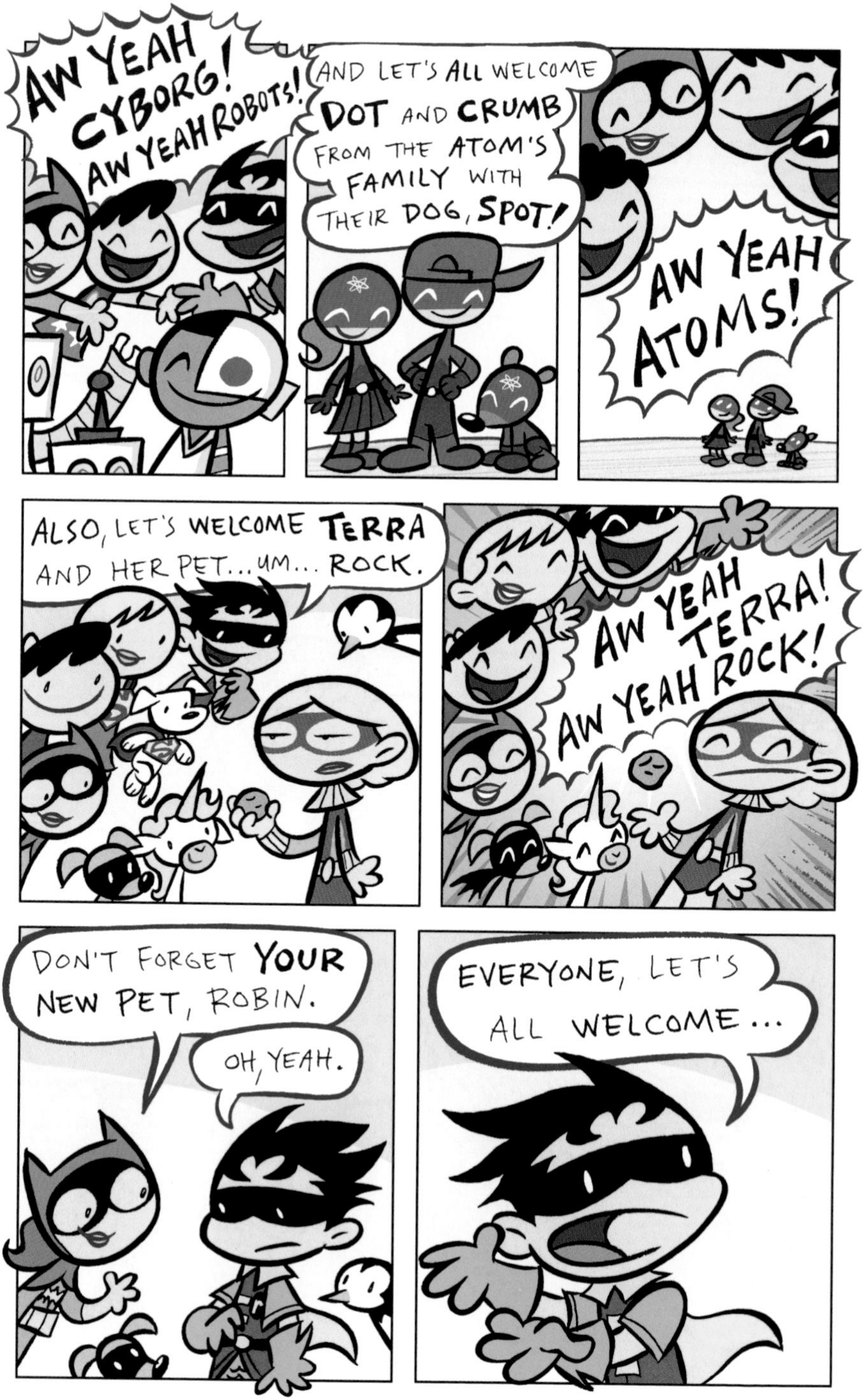
AW YEAH CYBORG! AW YEAH ROBOTS!
AND LET'S ALL WELCOME DOT AND CRUMB FROM THE ATOM'S FAMILY WITH THEIR DOG, SPOT!
AW YEAH ATOMS!
ALSO, LET'S WELCOME TERRA AND HER PET...UM... ROCK.
AW YEAH TERRA! AW YEAH ROCK!
DON'T FORGET YOUR NEW PET, ROBIN.
OH, YEAH.
EVERYONE, LET'S ALL WELCOME...

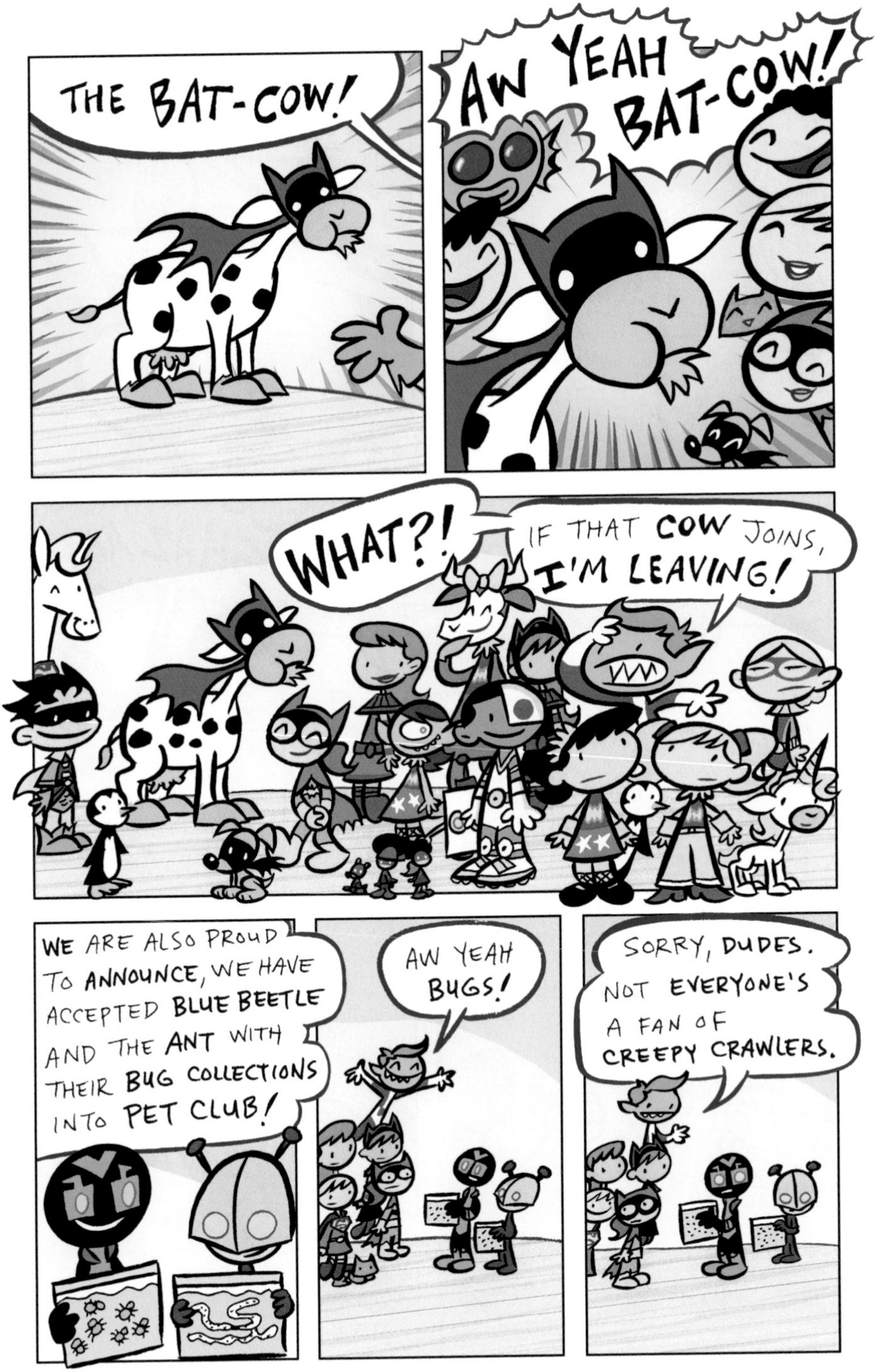
THE BAT-COW!
AW YEAH BAT-COW!
WHAT?!
IF THAT COW JOINS, I'M LEAVING!
WE ARE ALSO PROUD TO ANNOUNCE, WE HAVE ACCEPTED BLUE BEETLE AND THE ANT WITH THEIR BUG COLLECTIONS INTO PET CLUB!
AW YEAH BUGS!
SORRY, DUDES. NOT EVERYONE'S A FAN OF CREEPY CRAWLERS.

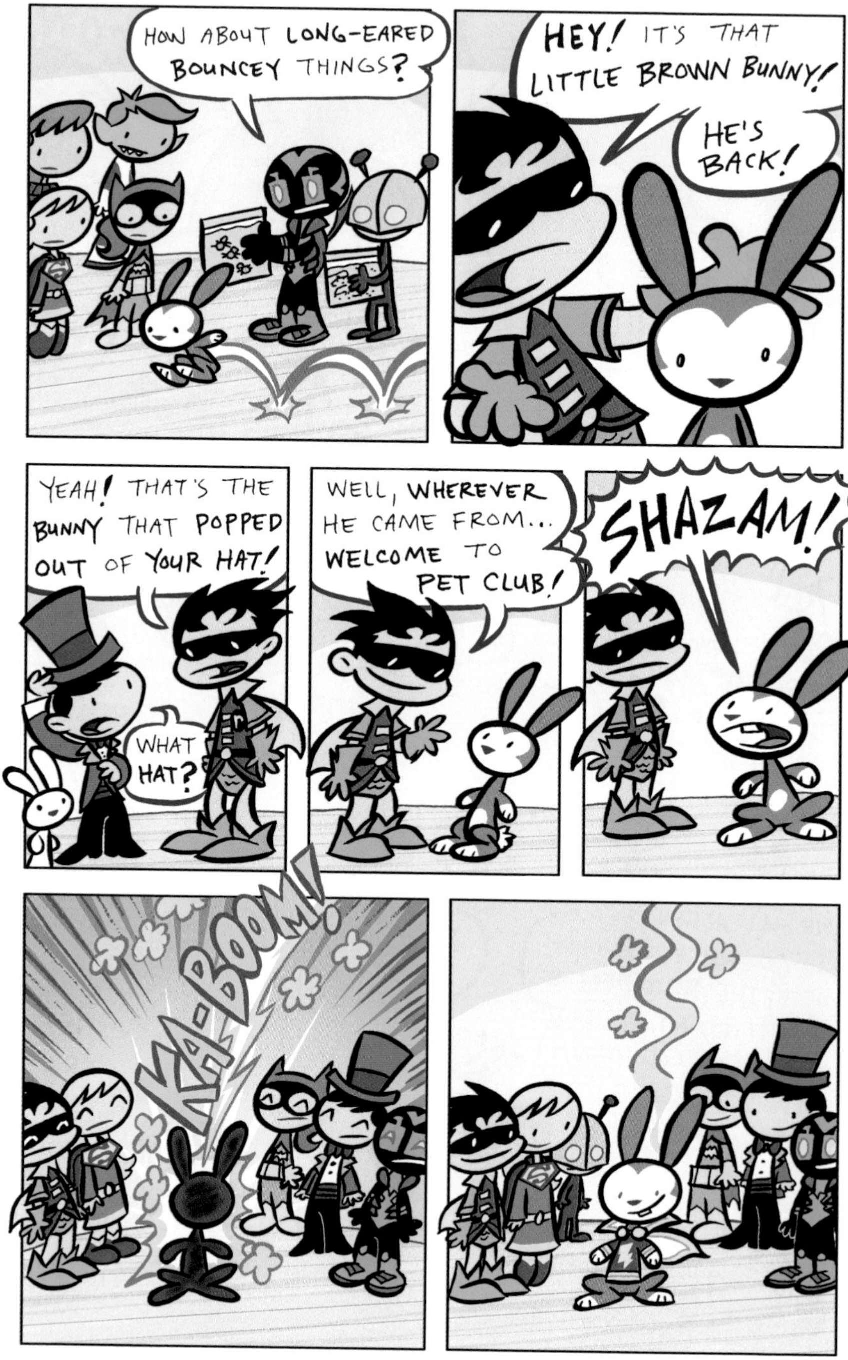
HOW ABOUT LONG-EARED BOUNCEY THINGS?
HEY! IT'S THAT LITTLE BROWN BUNNY!
HE'S BACK!
YEAH! THAT'S THE BUNNY THAT POPPED OUT OF YOUR HAT!
WHAT HAT?
WELL, WHEREVER HE CAME FROM... WELCOME TO PET CLUB!
SHAZAM!
KA-BOOM!

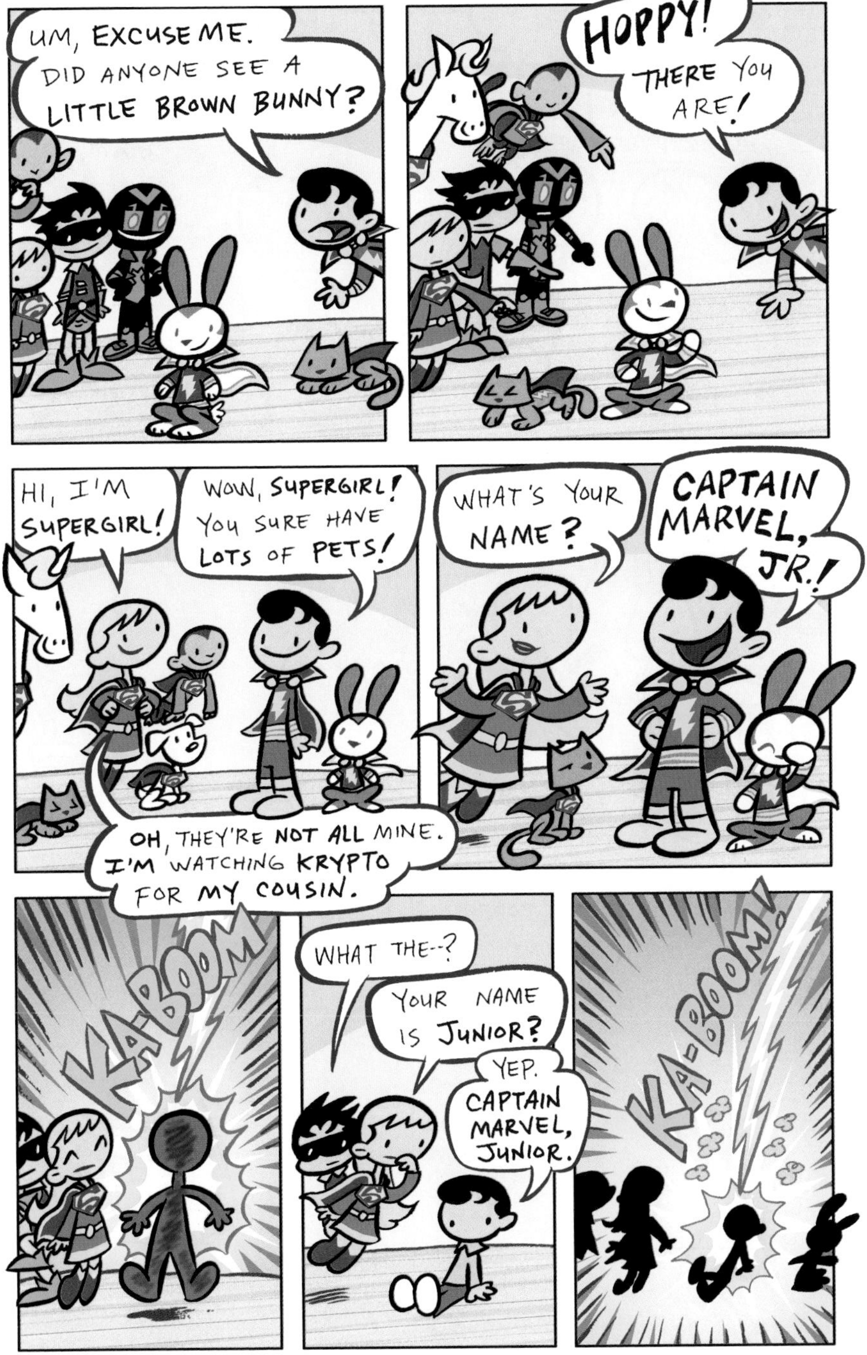
UM, EXCUSE ME. DID ANYONE SEE A LITTLE BROWN BUNNY?
HOPPY! THERE YOU ARE!
HI, I'M SUPERGIRL!
WOW, SUPERGIRL! YOU SURE HAVE LOTS OF PETS!
OH, THEY'RE NOT ALL MINE. I'M WATCHING KRYPTO FOR MY COUSIN.
WHAT'S YOUR NAME?
CAPTAIN MARVEL, JR.!
KA-BOOM
WHAT THE--?
YOUR NAME IS JUNIOR?
YEP. CAPTAIN MARVEL, JUNIOR.
KA-BOOM!

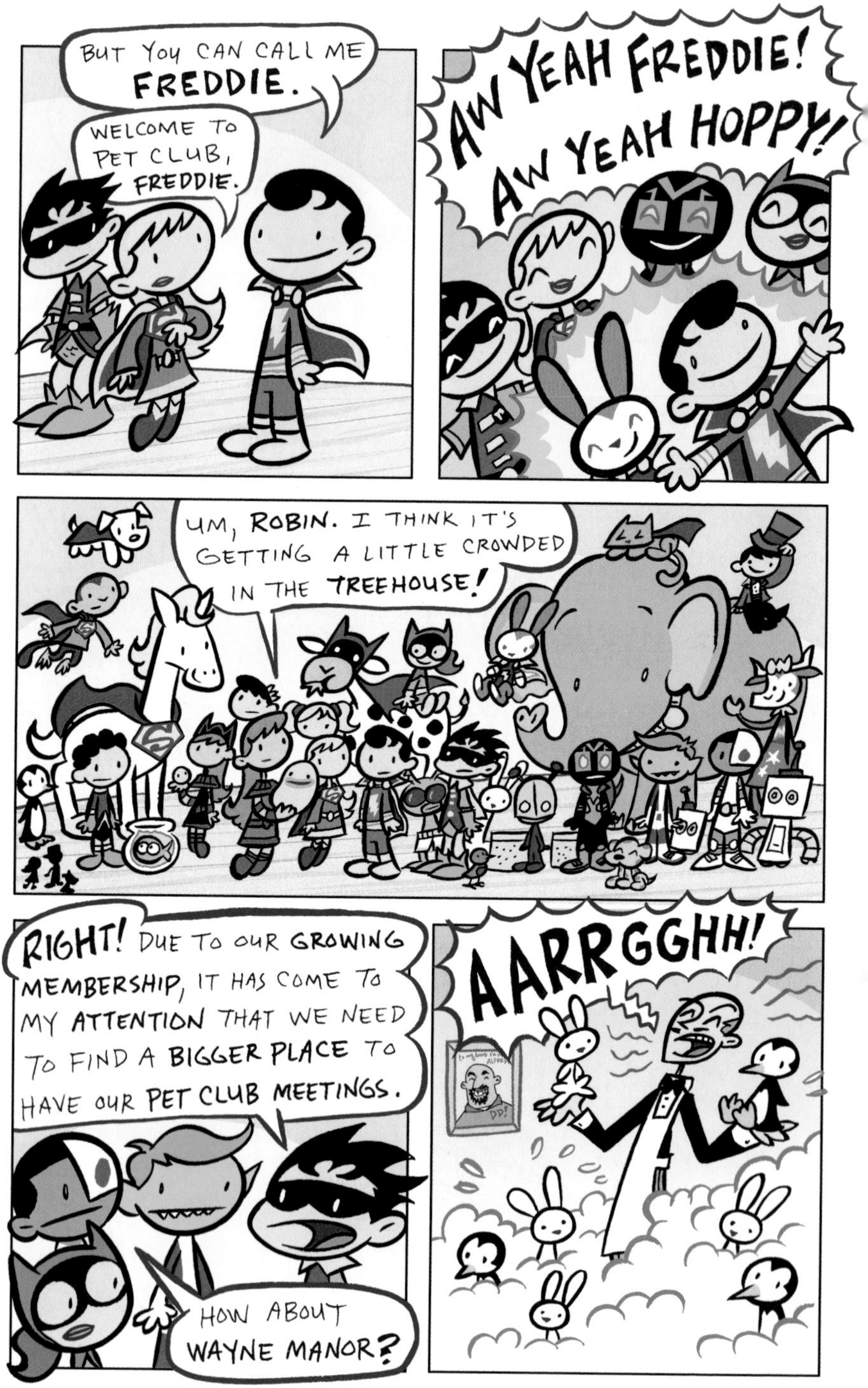
BUT YOU CAN CALL ME FREDDIE.
WELCOME TO PET CLUB, FREDDIE.
AW YEAH FREDDIE!
AW YEAH HOPPY!
UM, ROBIN. I THINK IT'S GETTING A LITTLE CROWDED IN THE TREEHOUSE!
RIGHT! DUE TO OUR GROWING MEMBERSHIP, IT HAS COME TO MY ATTENTION THAT WE NEED TO FIND A BIGGER PLACE TO HAVE OUR PET CLUB MEETINGS.
HOW ABOUT WAYNE MANOR?
AARRGGHH!

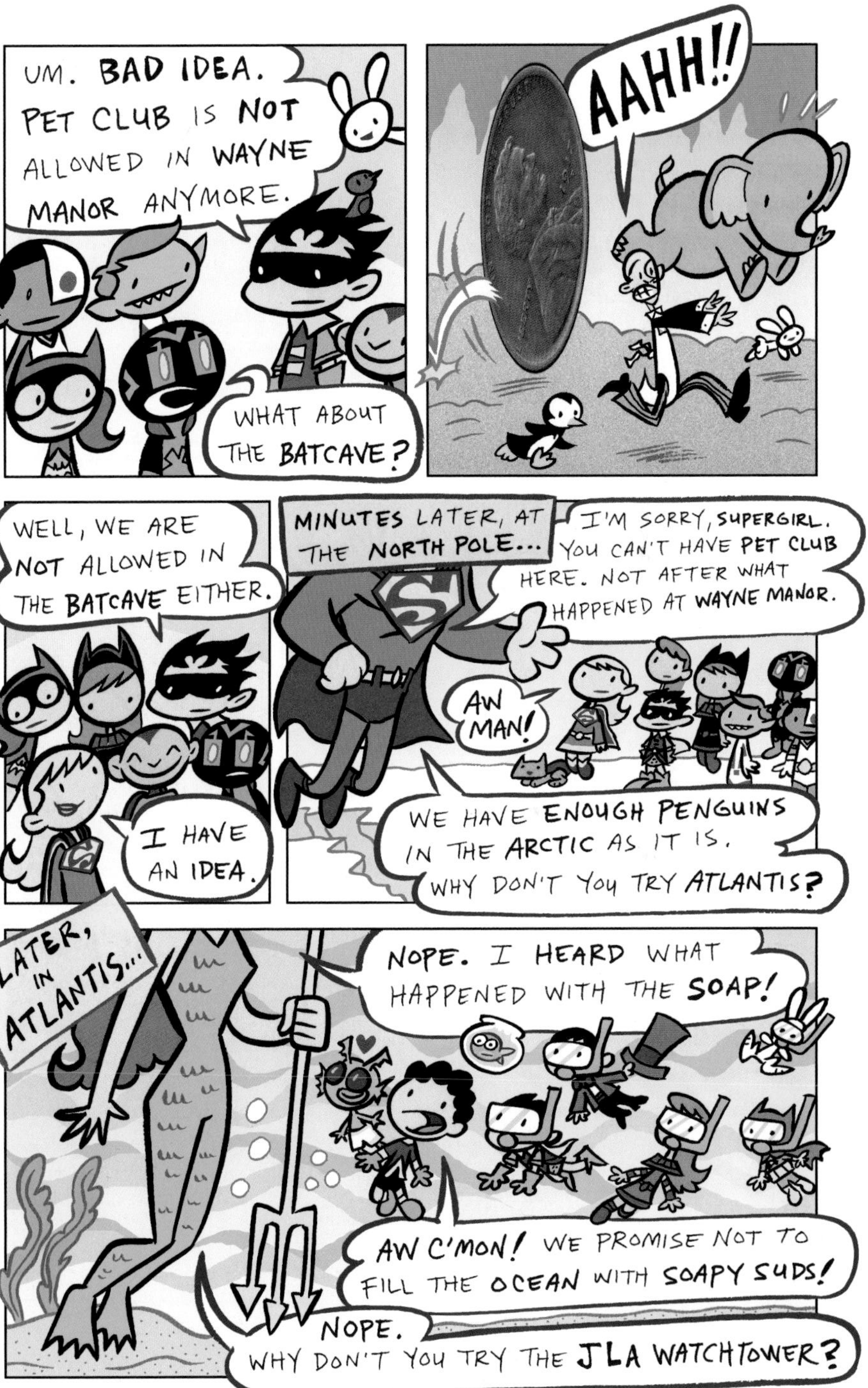
UM. BAD IDEA. PET CLUB IS NOT ALLOWED IN WAYNE MANOR ANYMORE.
WHAT ABOUT THE BATCAVE?
AAHH!!
WELL, WE ARE NOT ALLOWED IN THE BATCAVE EITHER.
I HAVE AN IDEA.
MINUTES LATER, AT THE NORTH POLE...
I'M SORRY, SUPERGIRL. YOU CAN'T HAVE PET CLUB HERE. NOT AFTER WHAT HAPPENED AT WAYNE MANOR.
AW MAN!
WE HAVE ENOUGH PENGUINS IN THE ARCTIC AS IT IS. WHY DON'T YOU TRY ATLANTIS?
LATER, IN ATLANTIS...
NOPE. I HEARD WHAT HAPPENED WITH THE SOAP!
AW C'MON! WE PROMISE NOT TO FILL THE OCEAN WITH SOAPY SUDS!
NOPE. WHY DON'T YOU TRY THE JLA WATCHTOWER?

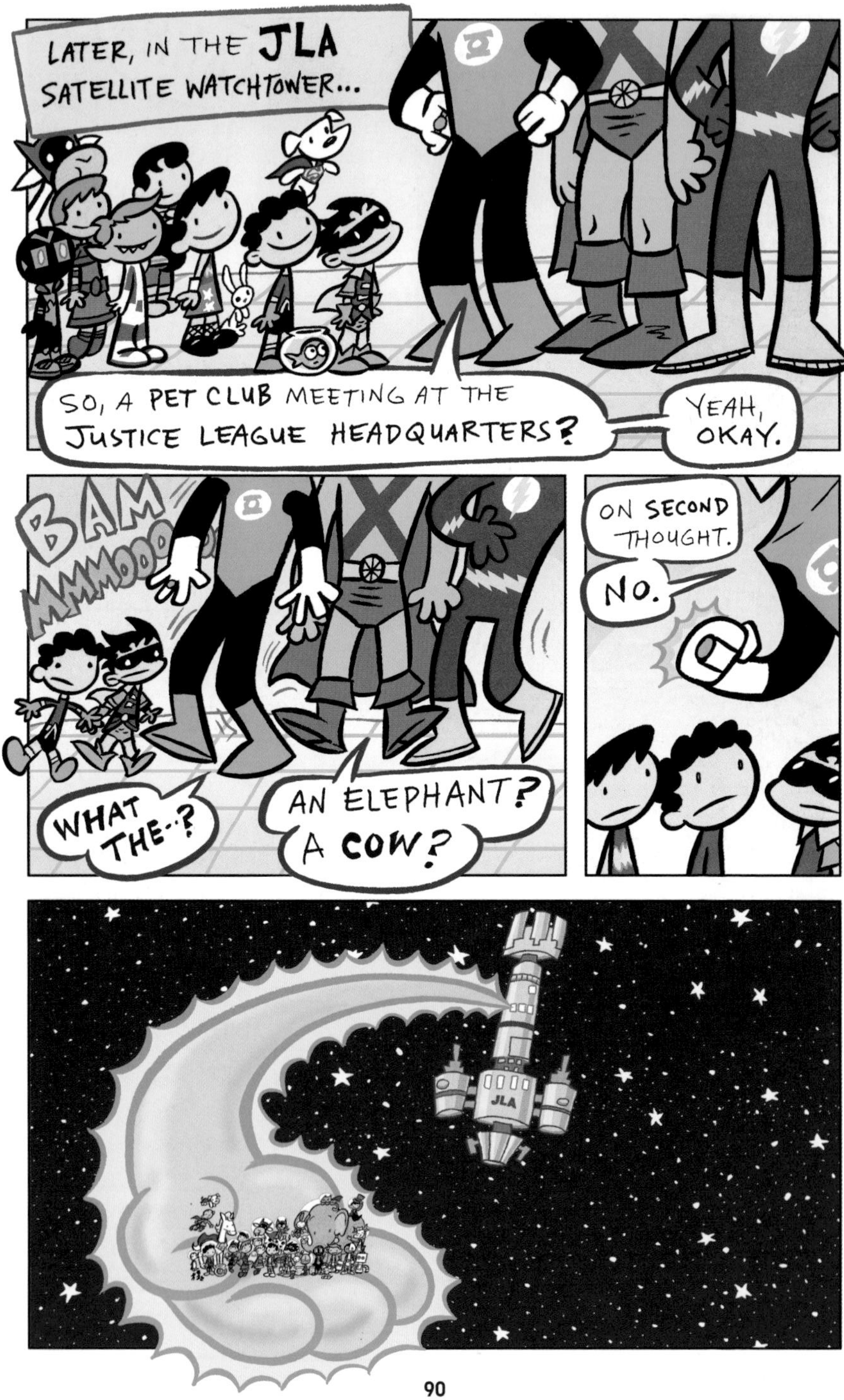
LATER, IN THE JLA SATELLITE WATCHTOWER...
SO, A PET CLUB MEETING AT THE JUSTICE LEAGUE HEADQUARTERS?
YEAH, OKAY.
BAM
MMMOOO
WHAT THE..?
AN ELEPHANT? A COW?
ON SECOND THOUGHT.
NO.
JLA

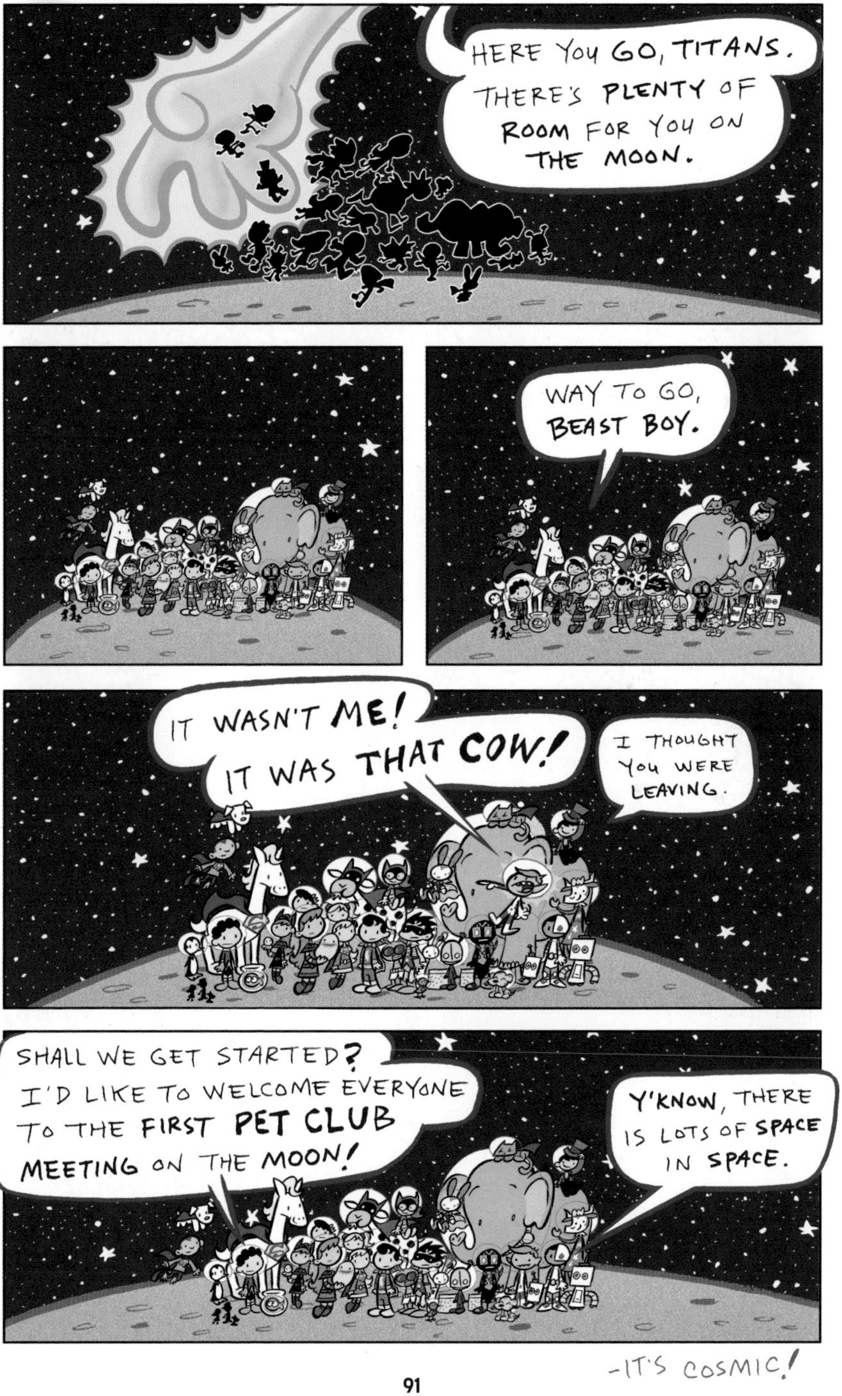
HERE YOU GO, TITANS. THERE'S PLENTY OF ROOM FOR YOU ON THE MOON.
WAY TO GO, BEAST BOY.
IT WASN'T ME! IT WAS THAT COW!
I THOUGHT YOU WERE LEAVING.
SHALL WE GET STARTED? I'D LIKE TO WELCOME EVERYONE TO THE FIRST PET CLUB MEETING ON THE MOON!
Y'KNOW, THERE IS LOTS OF SPACE IN SPACE.
-IT'S COSMIC!

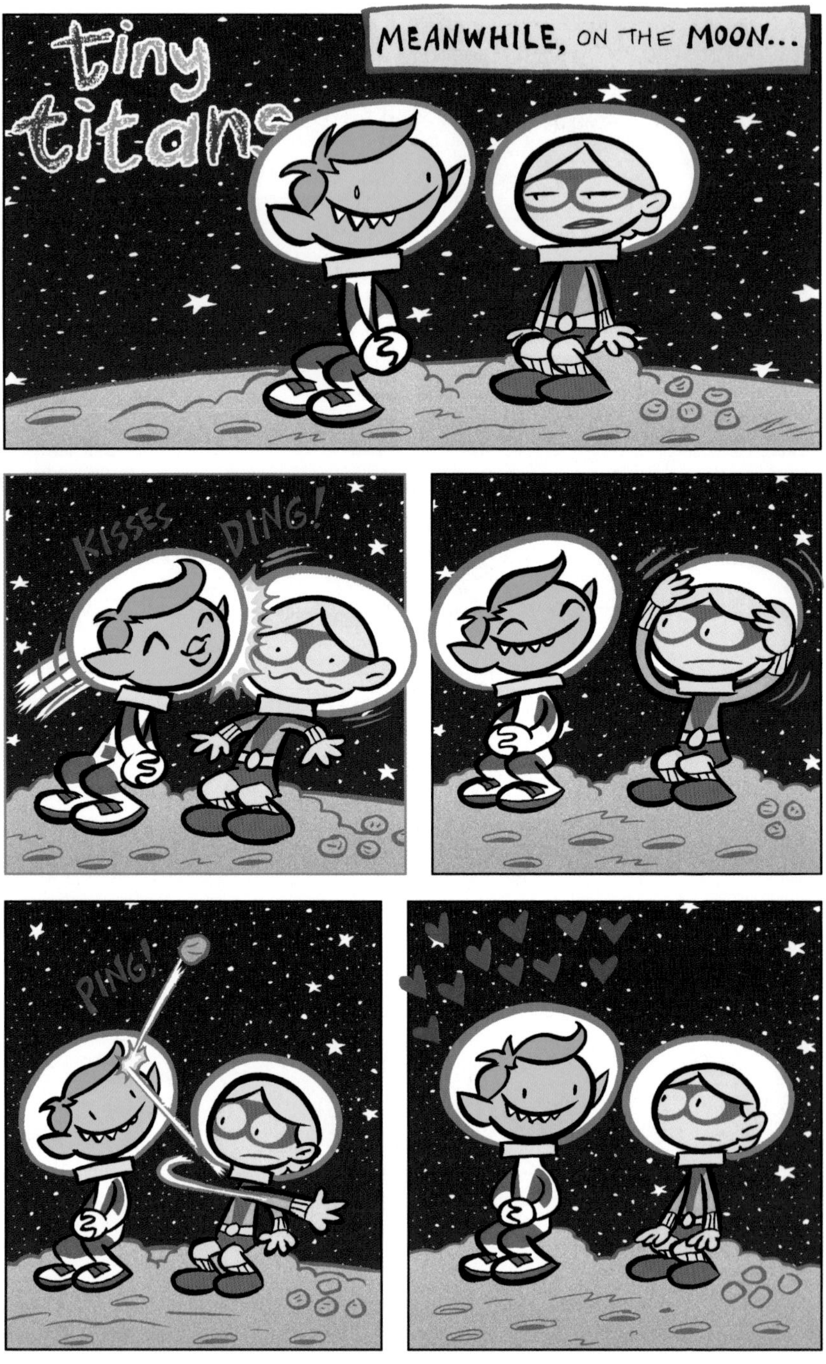
tiny titans
MEANWHILE, ON THE MOON...
KISSES
DING!
PING!

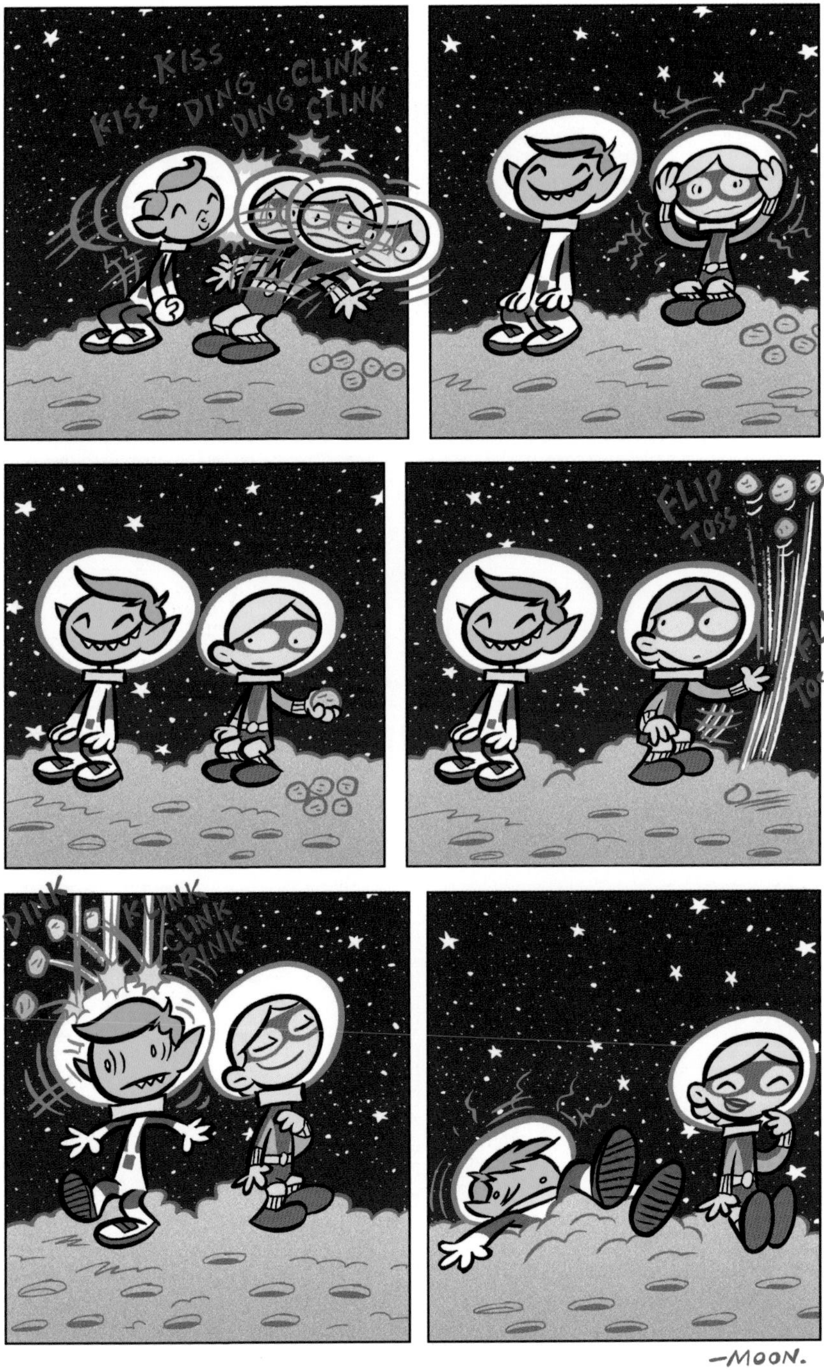
KISS
KISS
DING
DING
CLINK
CLINK
FLIP
TOSS
FLIP
TOSS
DINK
KLINK
CLINK
RINK
-MOON.

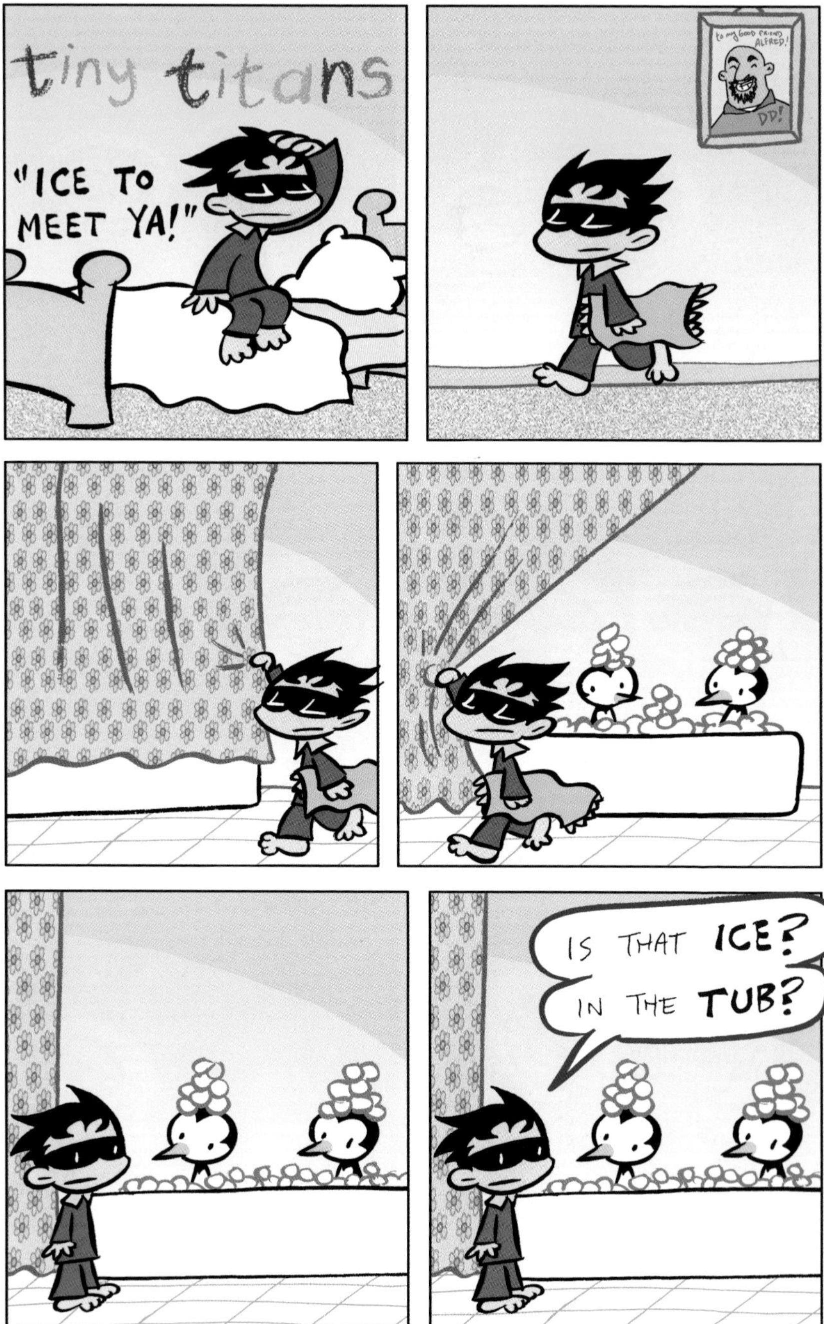
tiny titans
"ICE TO MEET YA!"
to my GOOD FRIEND ALFRED!
DD!
IS THAT ICE?
IN THE TUB?

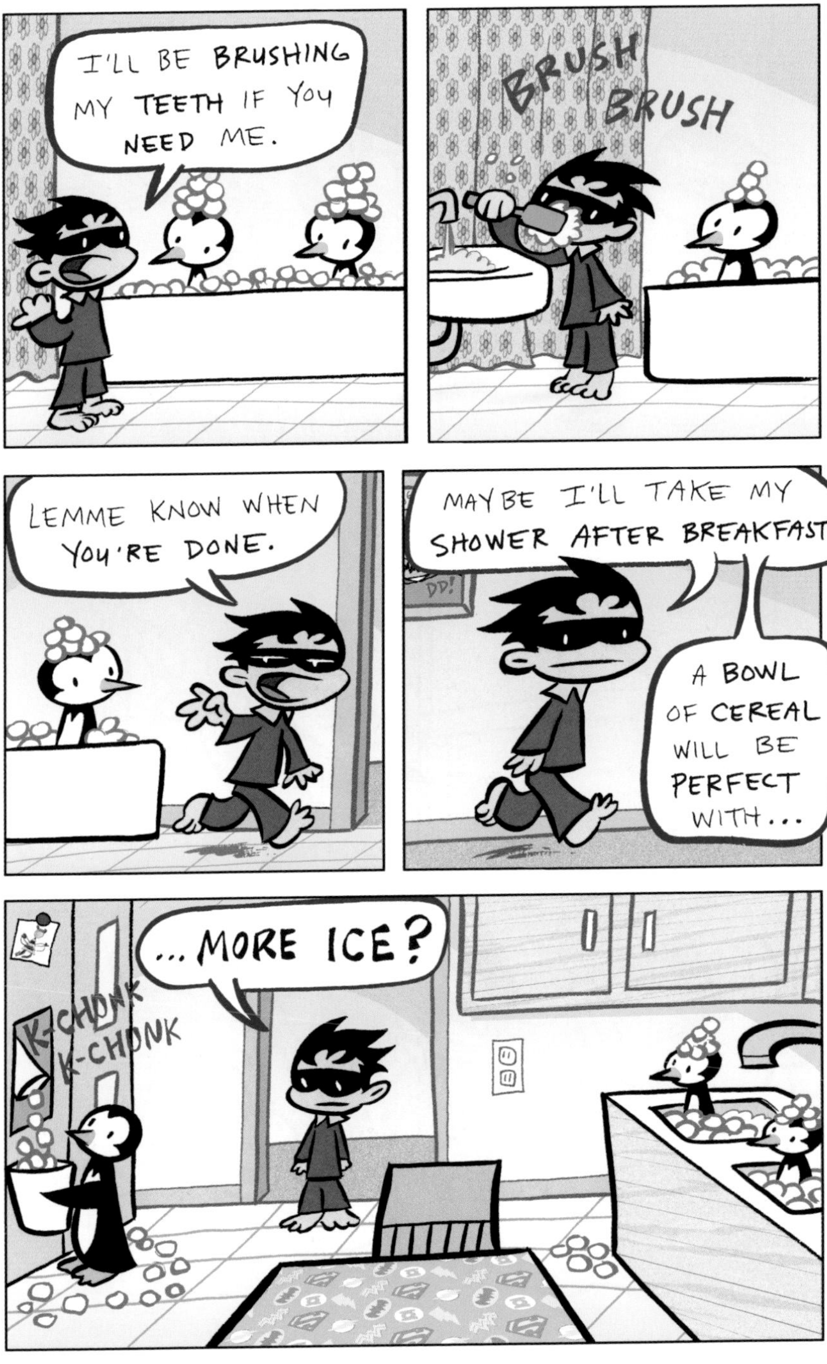
I'LL BE BRUSHING MY TEETH IF YOU NEED ME.
BRUSH
BRUSH
LEMME KNOW WHEN YOU'RE DONE.
MAYBE I'LL TAKE MY SHOWER AFTER BREAKFAST.
A BOWL OF CEREAL WILL BE PERFECT WITH...
...MORE ICE?
K-CHONK
K-CHONK

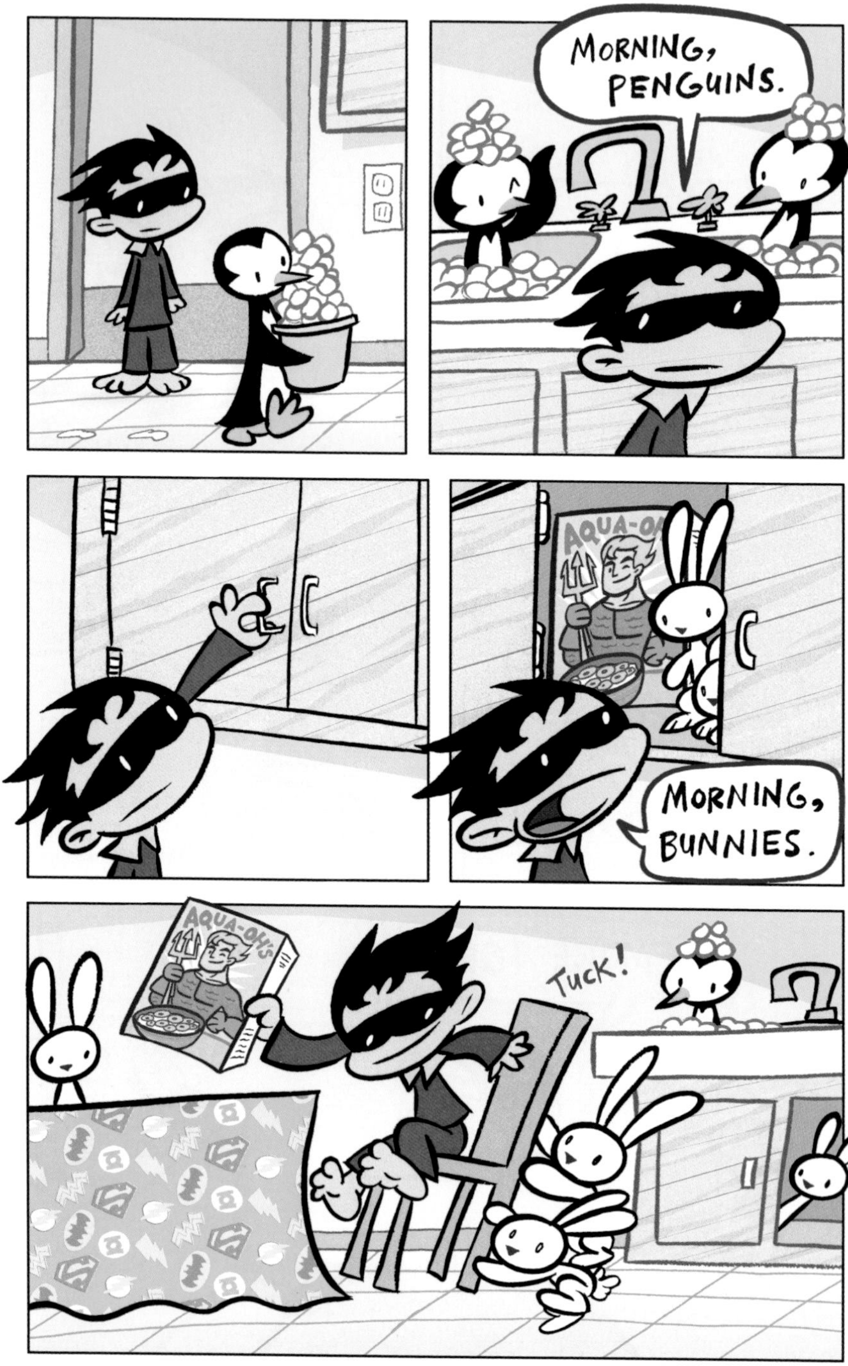
MORNING, PENGUINS.
MORNING, BUNNIES.
AQUA-OH'S
TUCK!

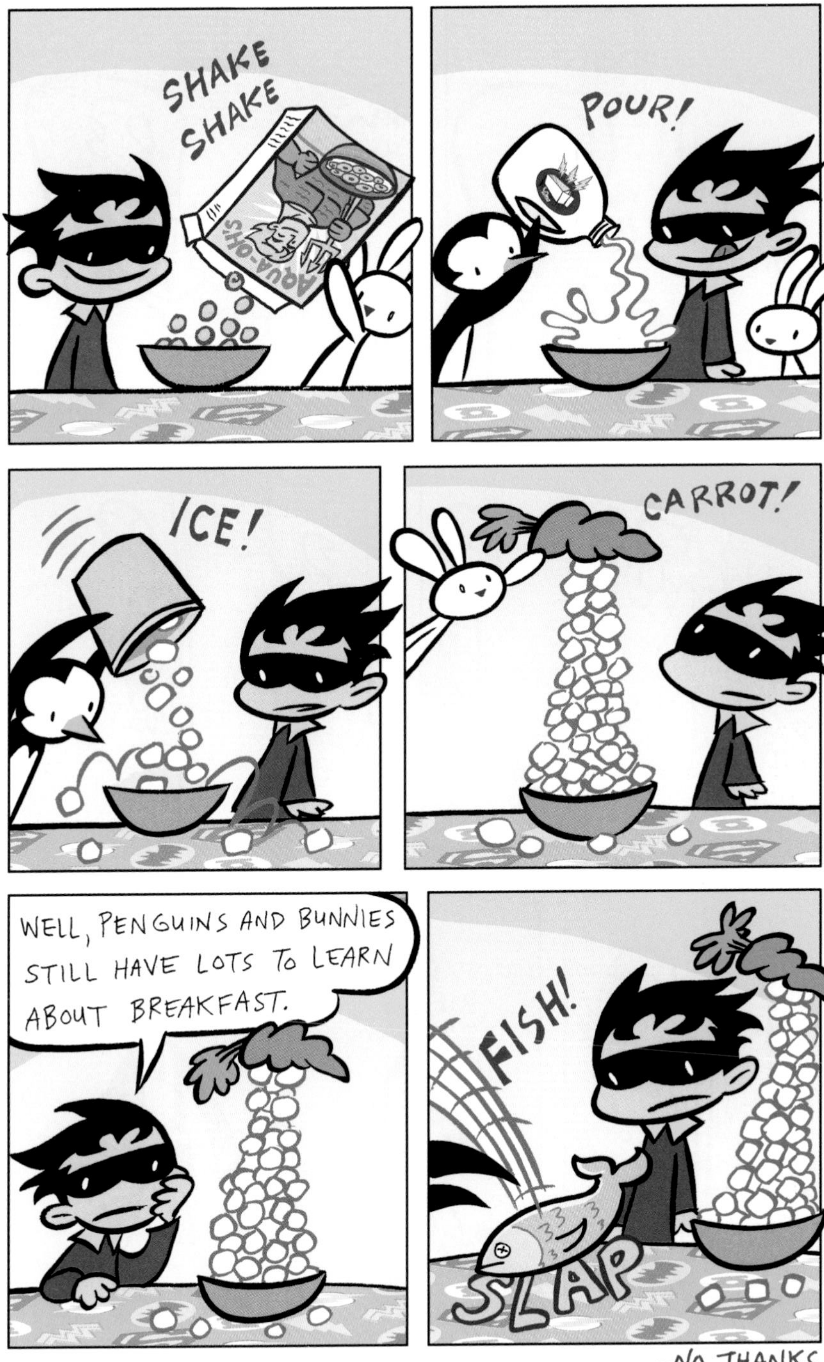
SHAKE
SHAKE
AQUA-OHS
POUR!
ICE!
CARROT!
WELL, PENGUINS AND BUNNIES STILL HAVE LOTS TO LEARN ABOUT BREAKFAST.
FISH!
SLAP
-NO THANKS

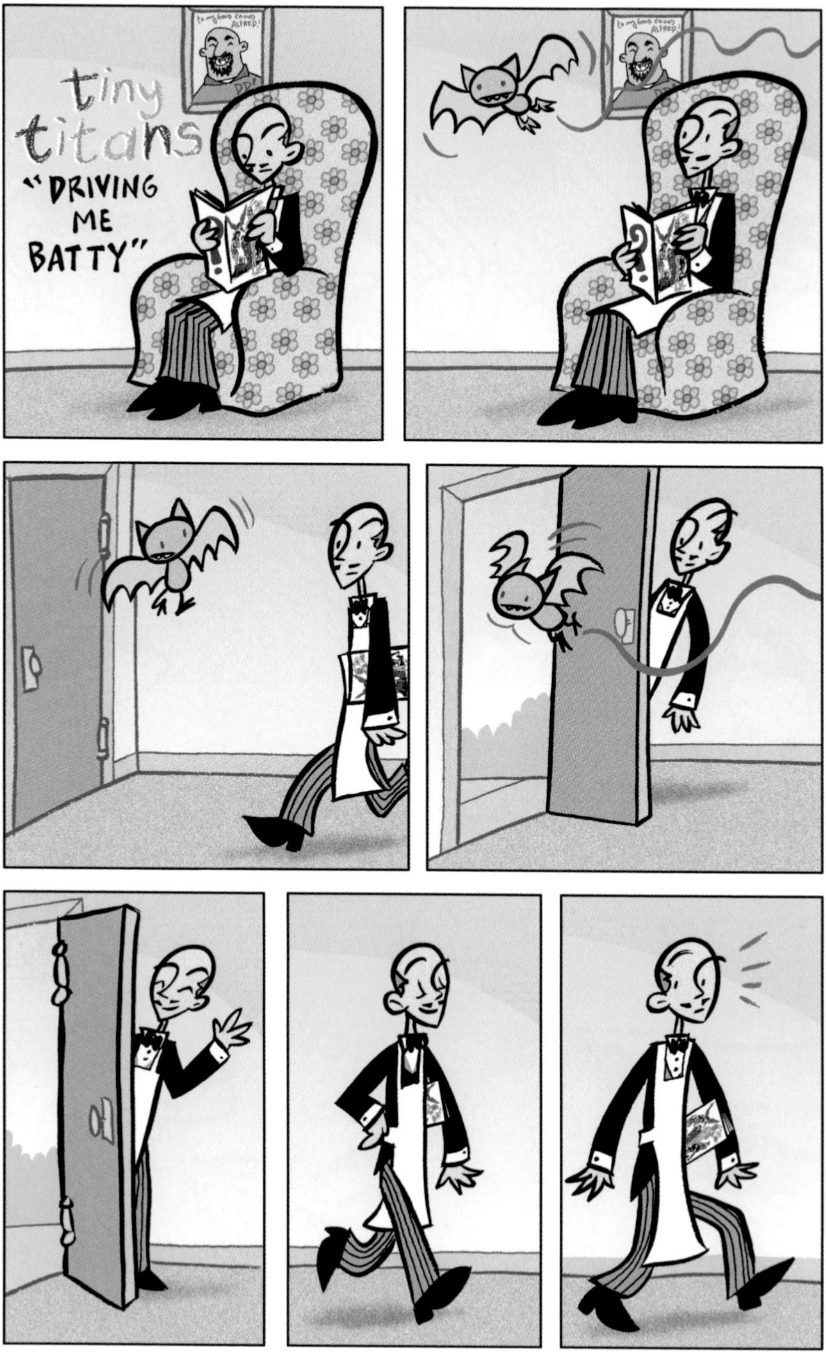
tiny titans
"DRIVING ME BATTY"
to my good friend ALFRED!

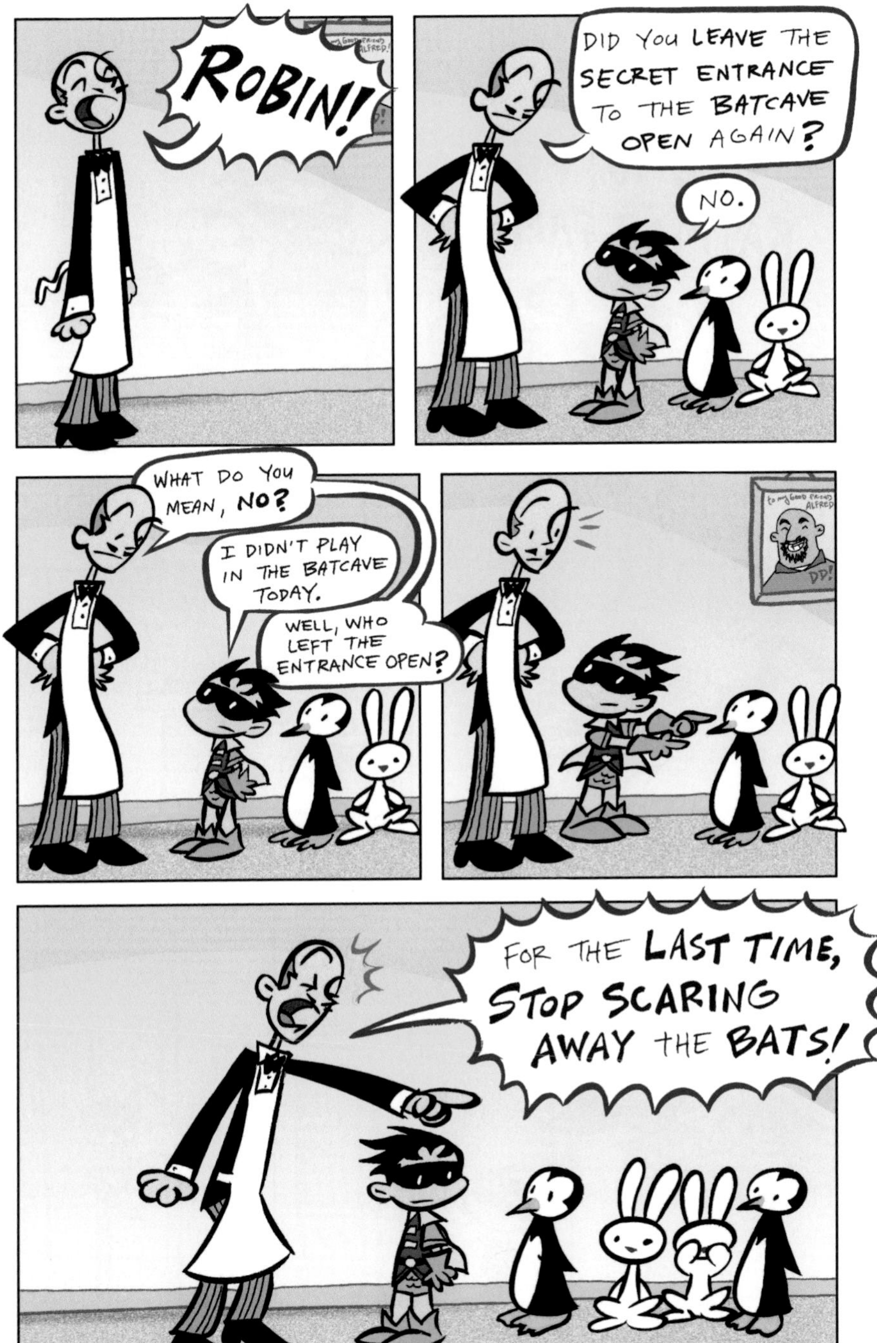

ROBIN!
DID YOU LEAVE THE SECRET ENTRANCE TO THE BATCAVE OPEN AGAIN?
NO.
WHAT DO YOU MEAN, NO?
I DIDN'T PLAY IN THE BATCAVE TODAY.
WELL, WHO LEFT THE ENTRANCE OPEN?
FOR THE LAST TIME, STOP SCARING AWAY THE BATS!

—NOCTURNAL

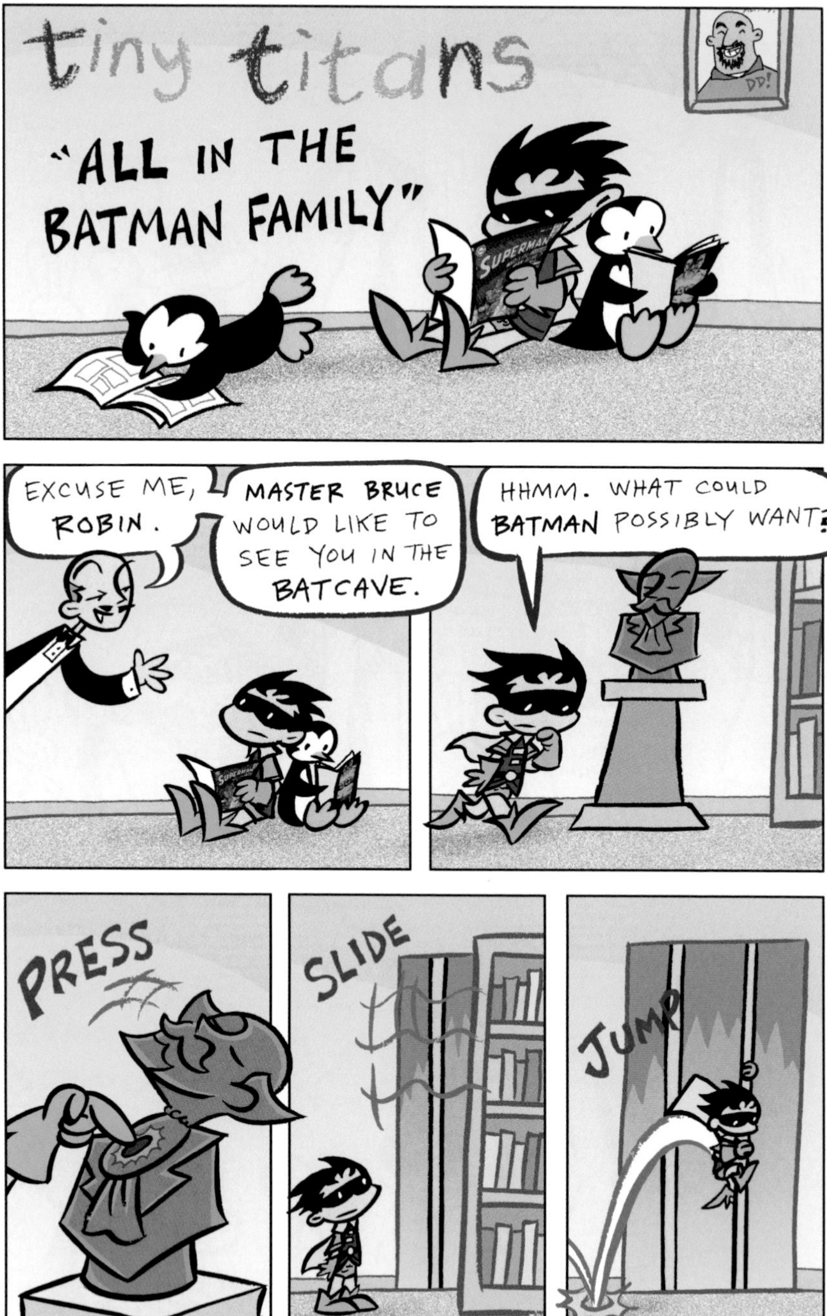
tiny titans
"ALL IN THE BATMAN FAMILY"
DD!
SUPERMAN
EXCUSE ME, ROBIN.
MASTER BRUCE WOULD LIKE TO SEE YOU IN THE BATCAVE.
SUPERMAN
HHMM. WHAT COULD BATMAN POSSIBLY WANT?
PRESS
SLIDE
JUMP

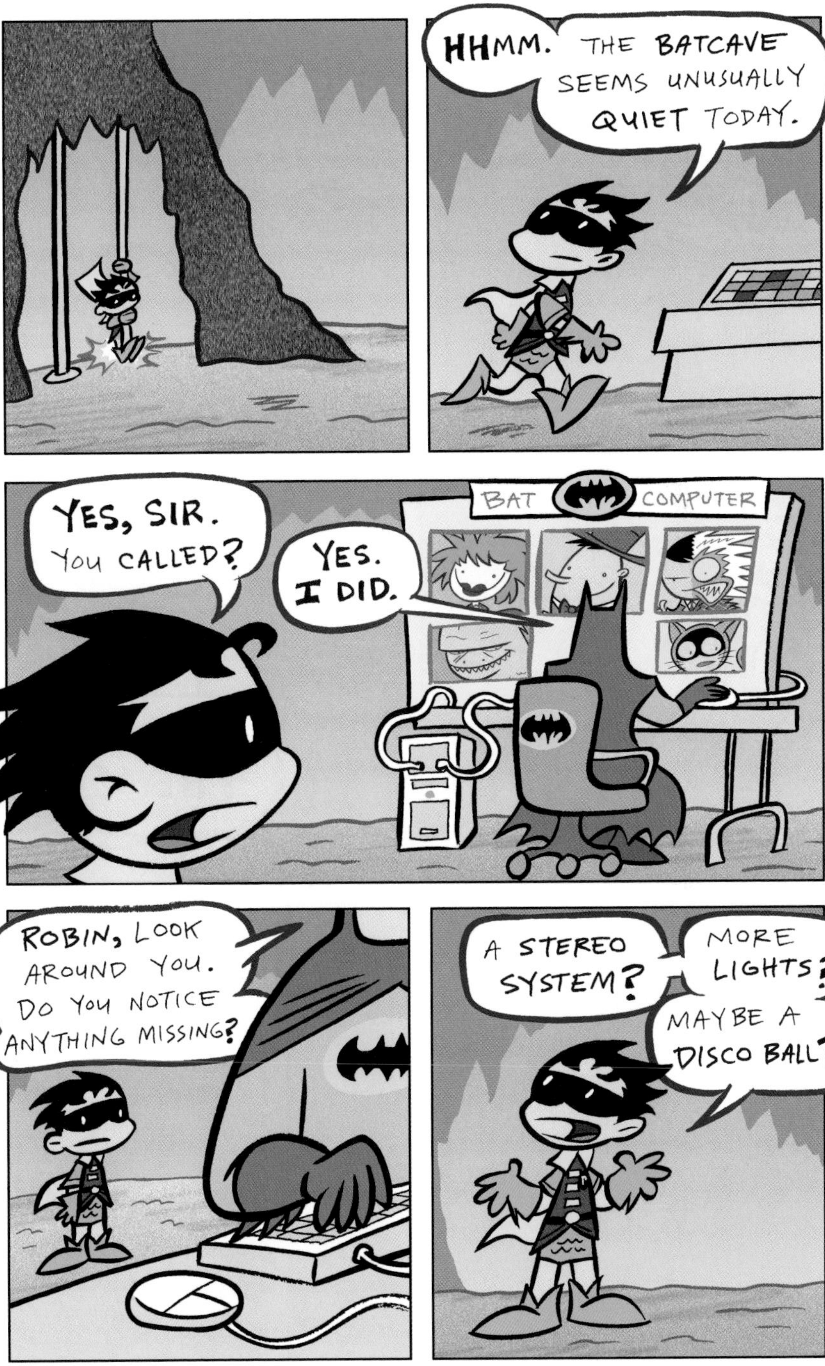
HHMM. THE BATCAVE SEEMS UNUSUALLY QUIET TODAY.
YES, SIR. YOU CALLED?
YES. I DID.
BAT COMPUTER
ROBIN, LOOK AROUND YOU. DO YOU NOTICE ANYTHING MISSING?
A STEREO SYSTEM?
MORE LIGHTS?
MAYBE A DISCO BALL?

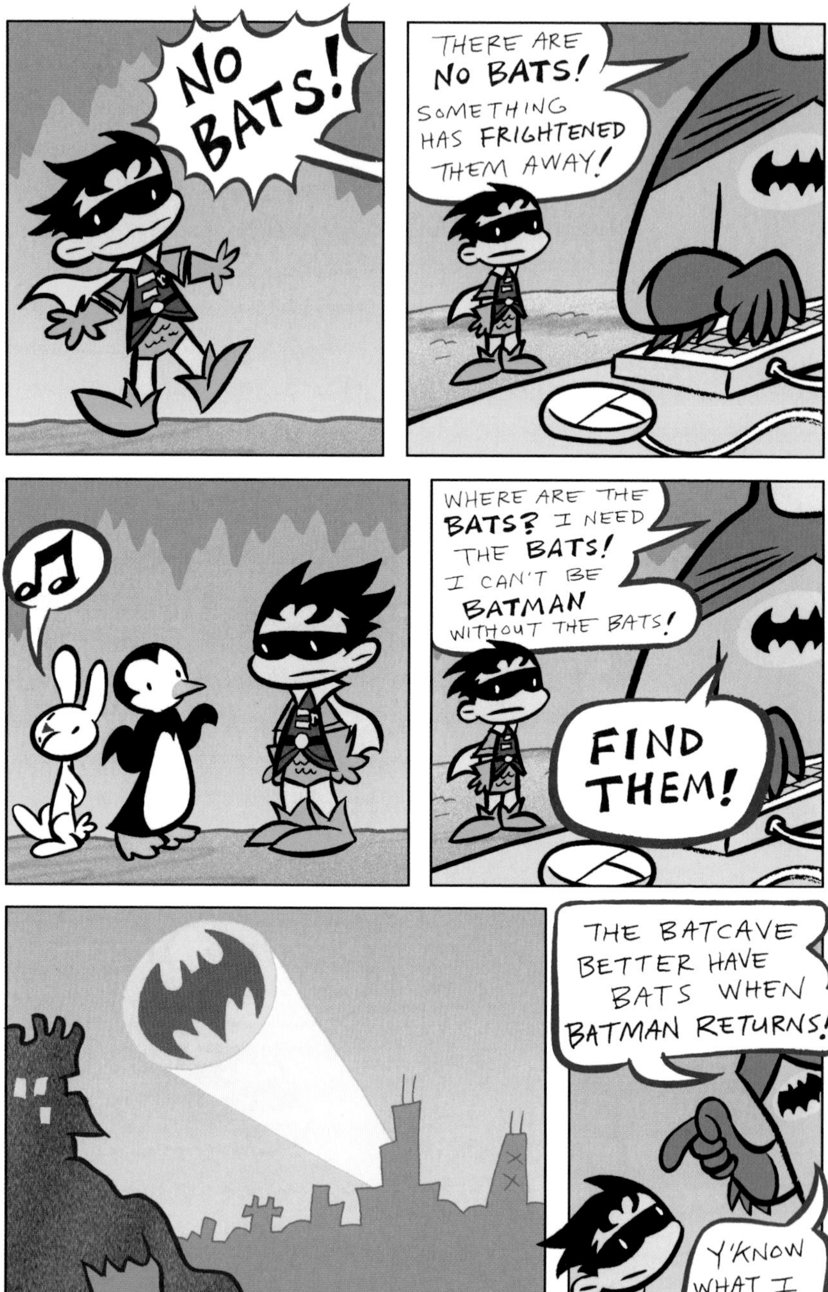
NO BATS!
THERE ARE NO BATS! SOMETHING HAS FRIGHTENED THEM AWAY!
WHERE ARE THE BATS? I NEED THE BATS! I CAN'T BE BATMAN WITHOUT THE BATS!
FIND THEM!
THE BATCAVE BETTER HAVE BATS WHEN BATMAN RETURNS!
Y'KNOW WHAT I MEAN.

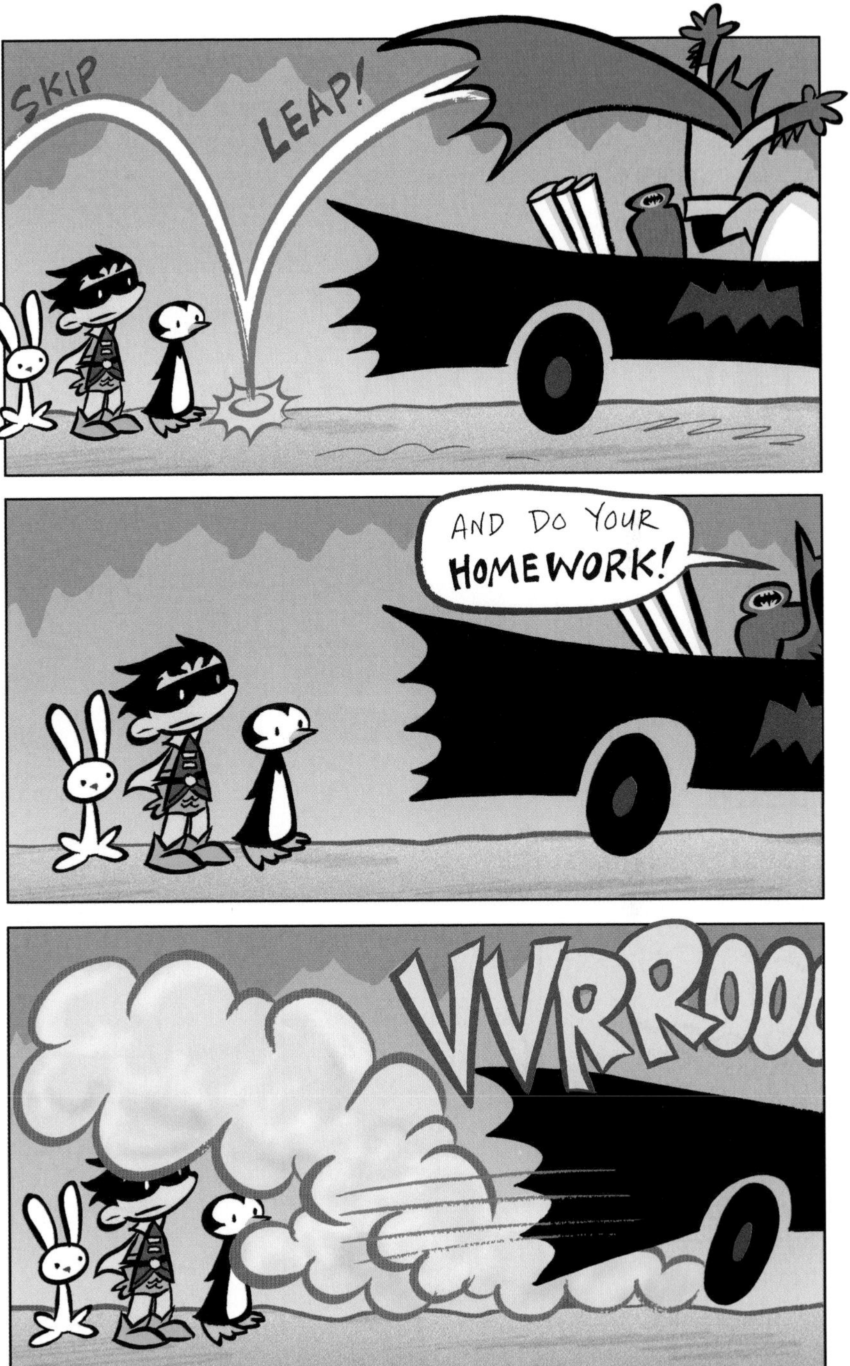
SKIP
LEAP!
AND DO YOUR HOMEWORK!
VVROO

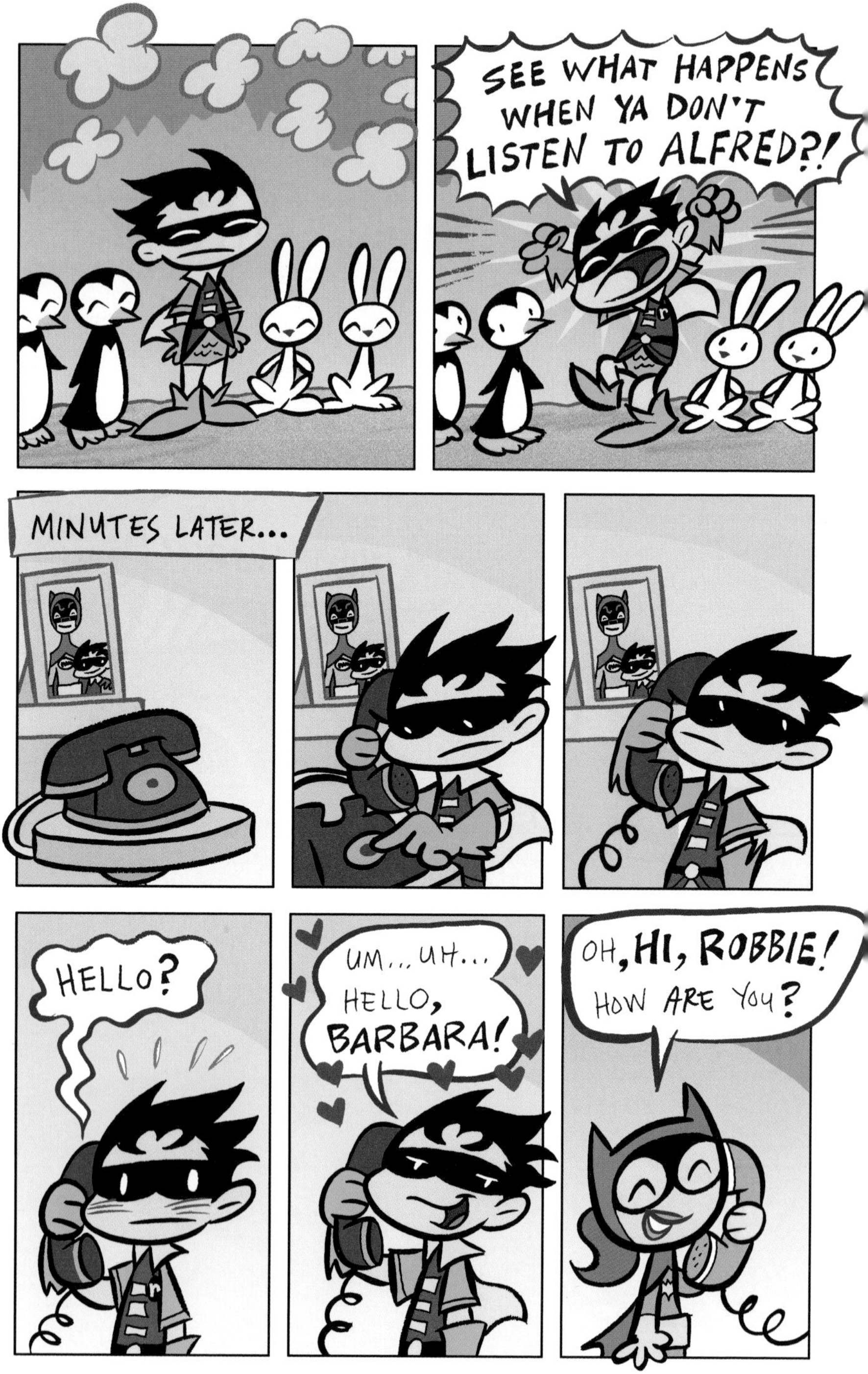
SEE WHAT HAPPENS WHEN YA DON'T LISTEN TO ALFRED?!
MINUTES LATER...
HELLO?
UM... UH... HELLO, BARBARA!
OH, HI, ROBBIE! HOW ARE YOU?

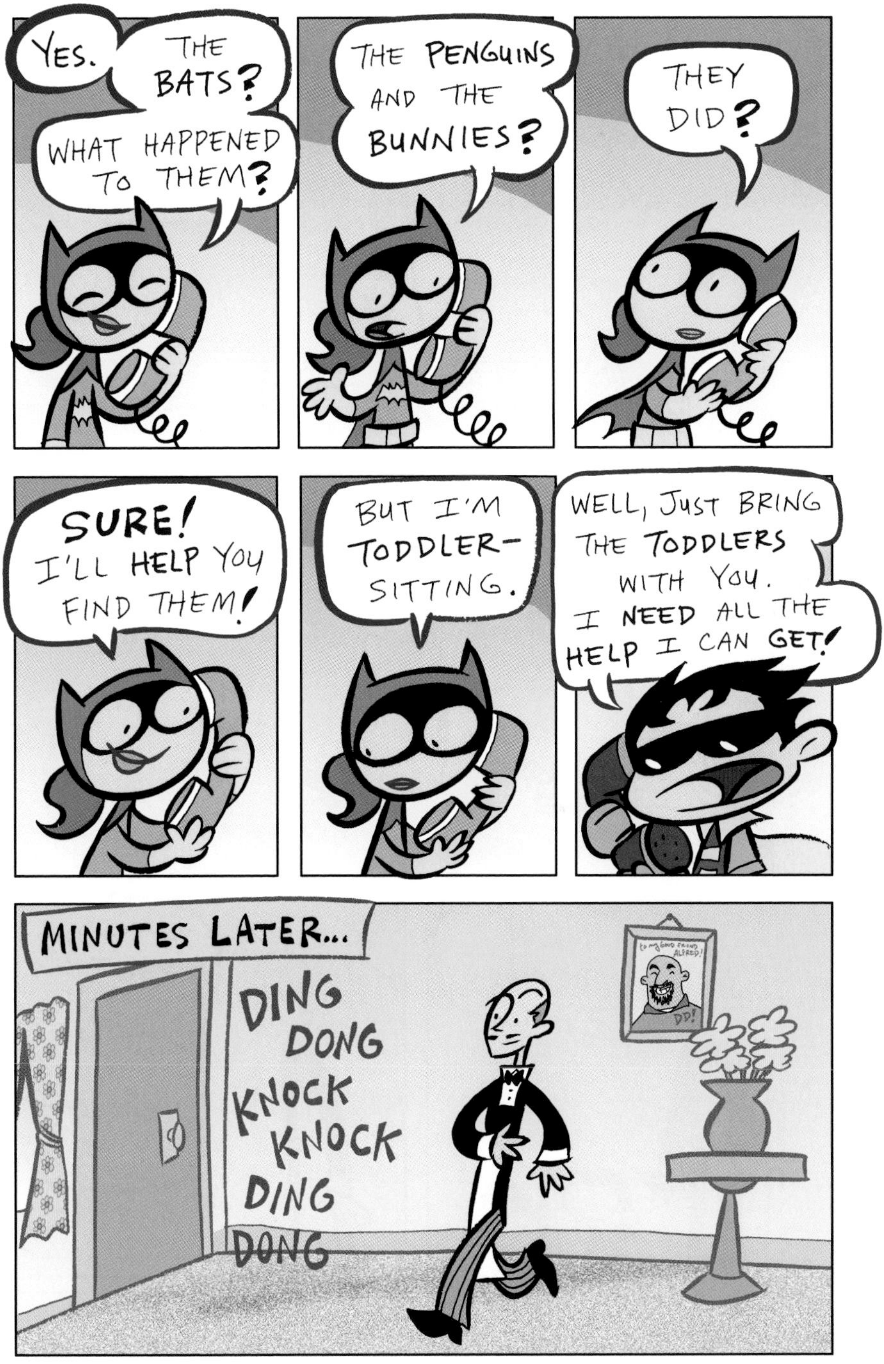
YES.
THE BATS?
WHAT HAPPENED TO THEM?
THE PENGUINS AND THE BUNNIES?
THEY DID?
SURE! I'LL HELP YOU FIND THEM!
BUT I'M TODDLER-SITTING.
WELL, JUST BRING THE TODDLERS WITH YOU. I NEED ALL THE HELP I CAN GET!
MINUTES LATER...
to my GOOD FRIEND ALFRED!
DD!
DING DONG KNOCK KNOCK DING DONG

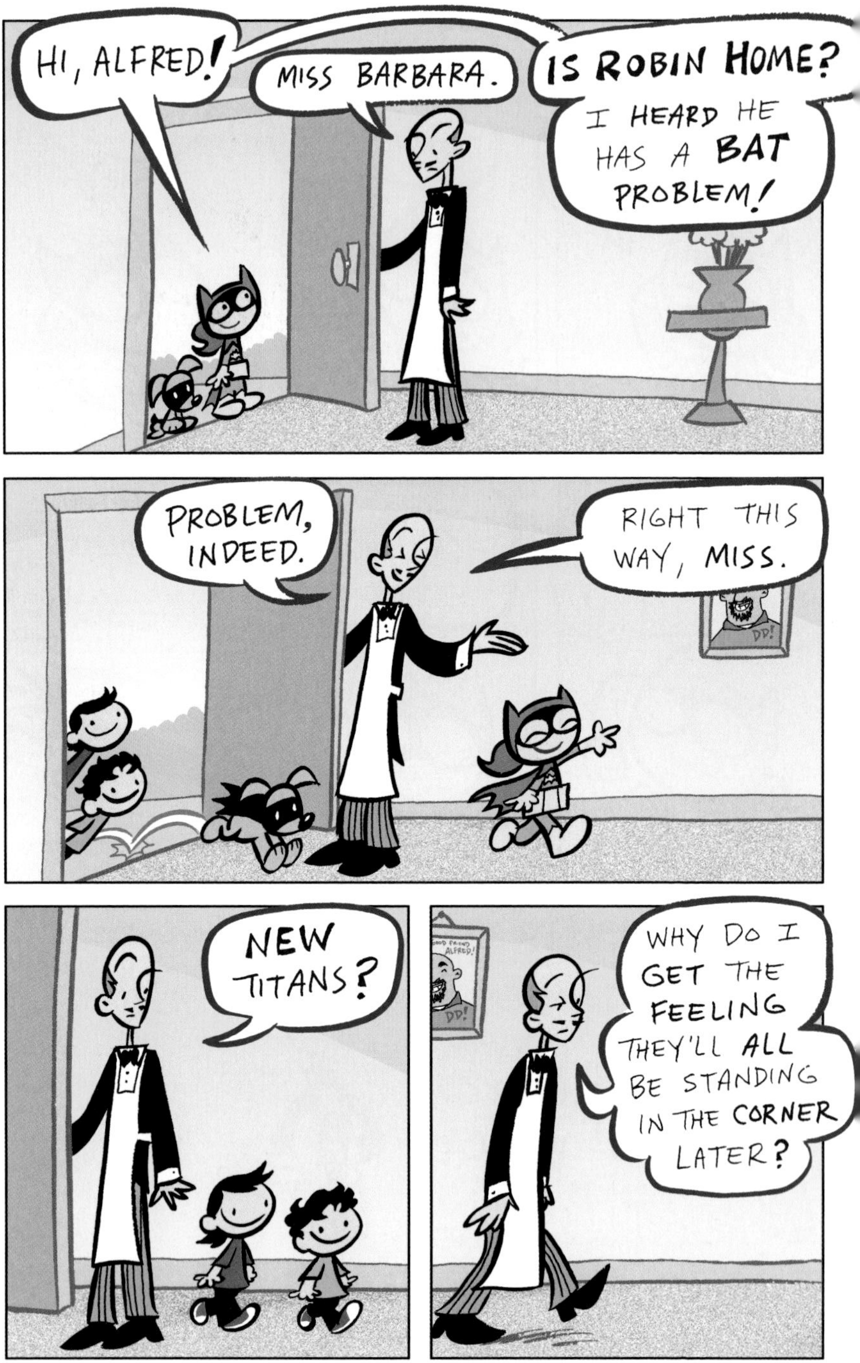
HI, ALFRED!
MISS BARBARA.
IS ROBIN HOME?
I HEARD HE HAS A BAT PROBLEM!
PROBLEM, INDEED.
RIGHT THIS WAY, MISS.
NEW TITANS?
WHY DO I GET THE FEELING THEY'LL ALL BE STANDING IN THE CORNER LATER?

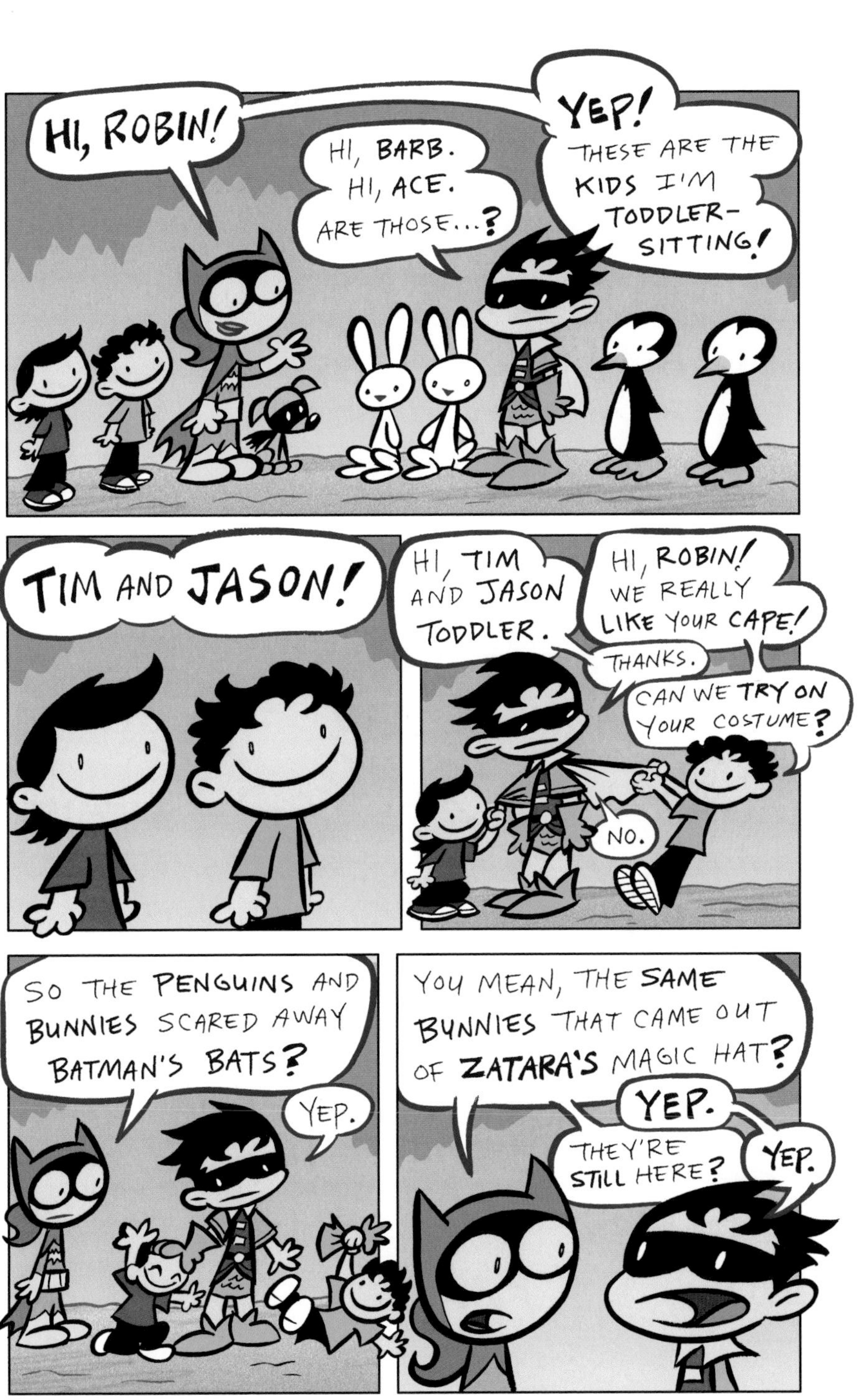
HI, ROBIN!
HI, BARB. HI, ACE. ARE THOSE...?
YEP! THESE ARE THE KIDS I'M TODDLER-SITTING!
TIM AND JASON!
HI, TIM AND JASON TODDLER.
HI, ROBIN! WE REALLY LIKE YOUR CAPE!
THANKS.
CAN WE TRY ON YOUR COSTUME?
NO.
SO THE PENGUINS AND BUNNIES SCARED AWAY BATMAN'S BATS?
YEP.
YOU MEAN, THE SAME BUNNIES THAT CAME OUT OF ZATARA'S MAGIC HAT?
YEP.
THEY'RE STILL HERE?
YEP.

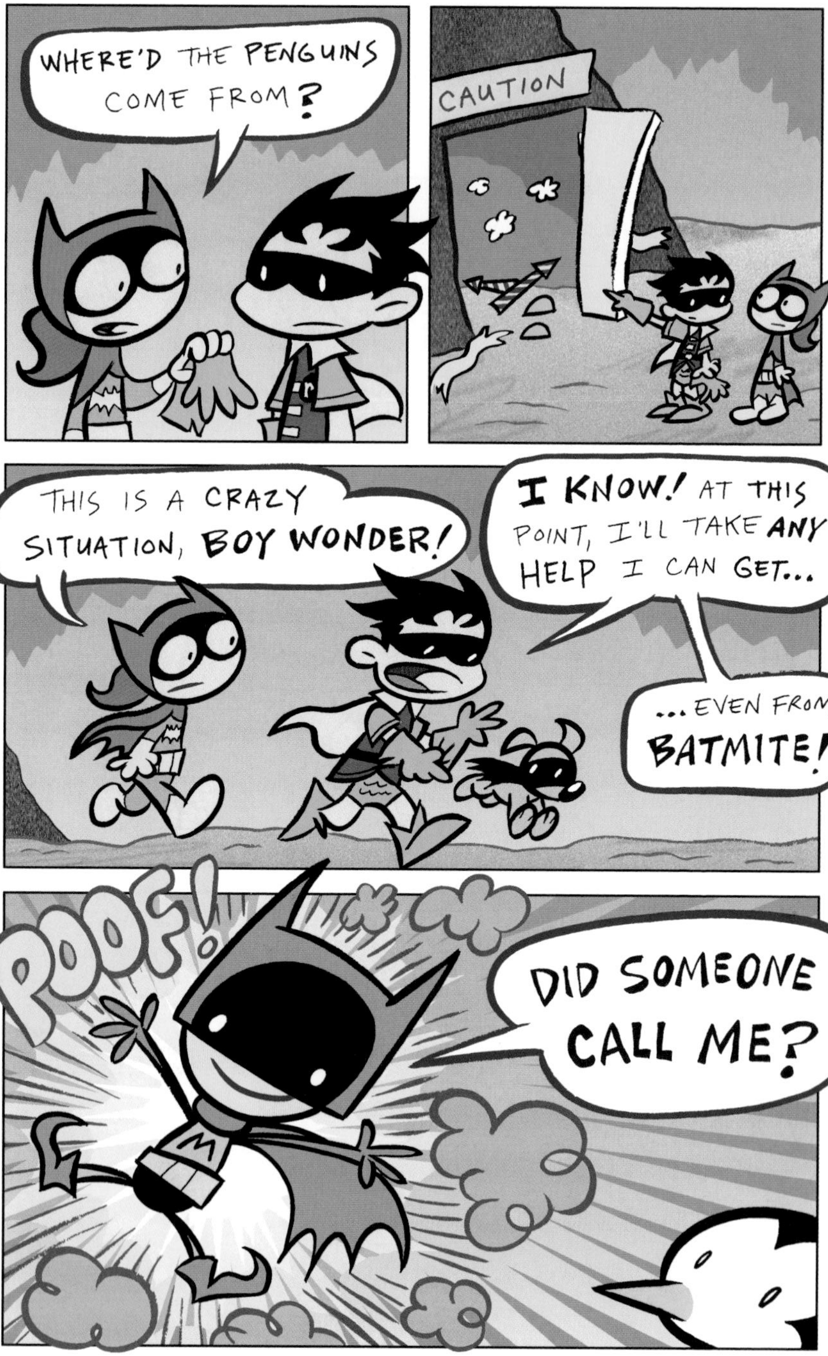
WHERE'D THE PENGUINS COME FROM?
CAUTION
THIS IS A CRAZY SITUATION, BOY WONDER!
I KNOW! AT THIS POINT, I'LL TAKE ANY HELP I CAN GET...
...EVEN FROM BATMITE!
POOF!
DID SOMEONE CALL ME?

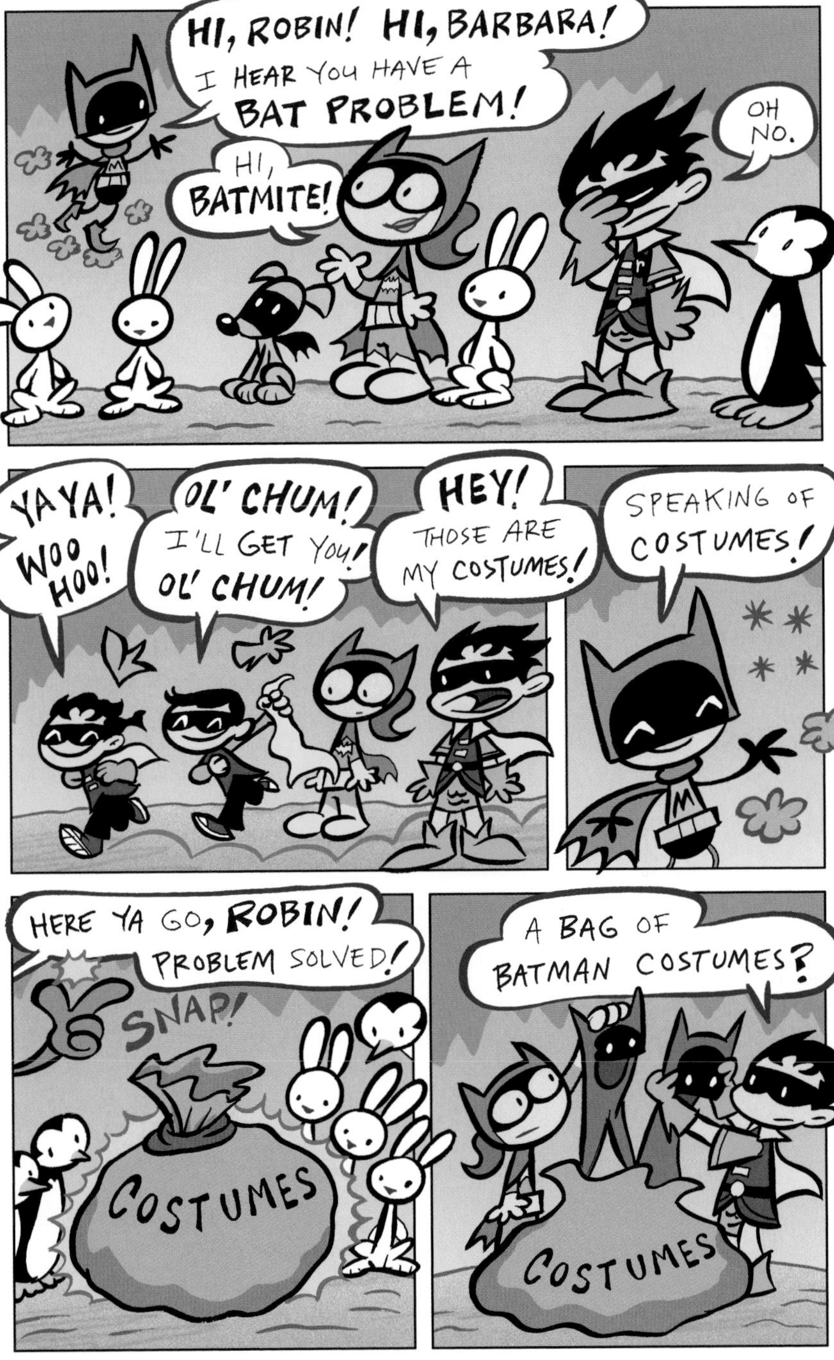
HI, ROBIN! HI, BARBARA! I HEAR YOU HAVE A BAT PROBLEM!
HI, BATMITE!
OH NO.
YAYA! WOO HOO!
OL' CHUM! I'LL GET YOU! OL' CHUM!
HEY! THOSE ARE MY COSTUMES!
SPEAKING OF COSTUMES!
HERE YA GO, ROBIN! PROBLEM SOLVED!
SNAP!
COSTUMES
A BAG OF BATMAN COSTUMES?
COSTUMES

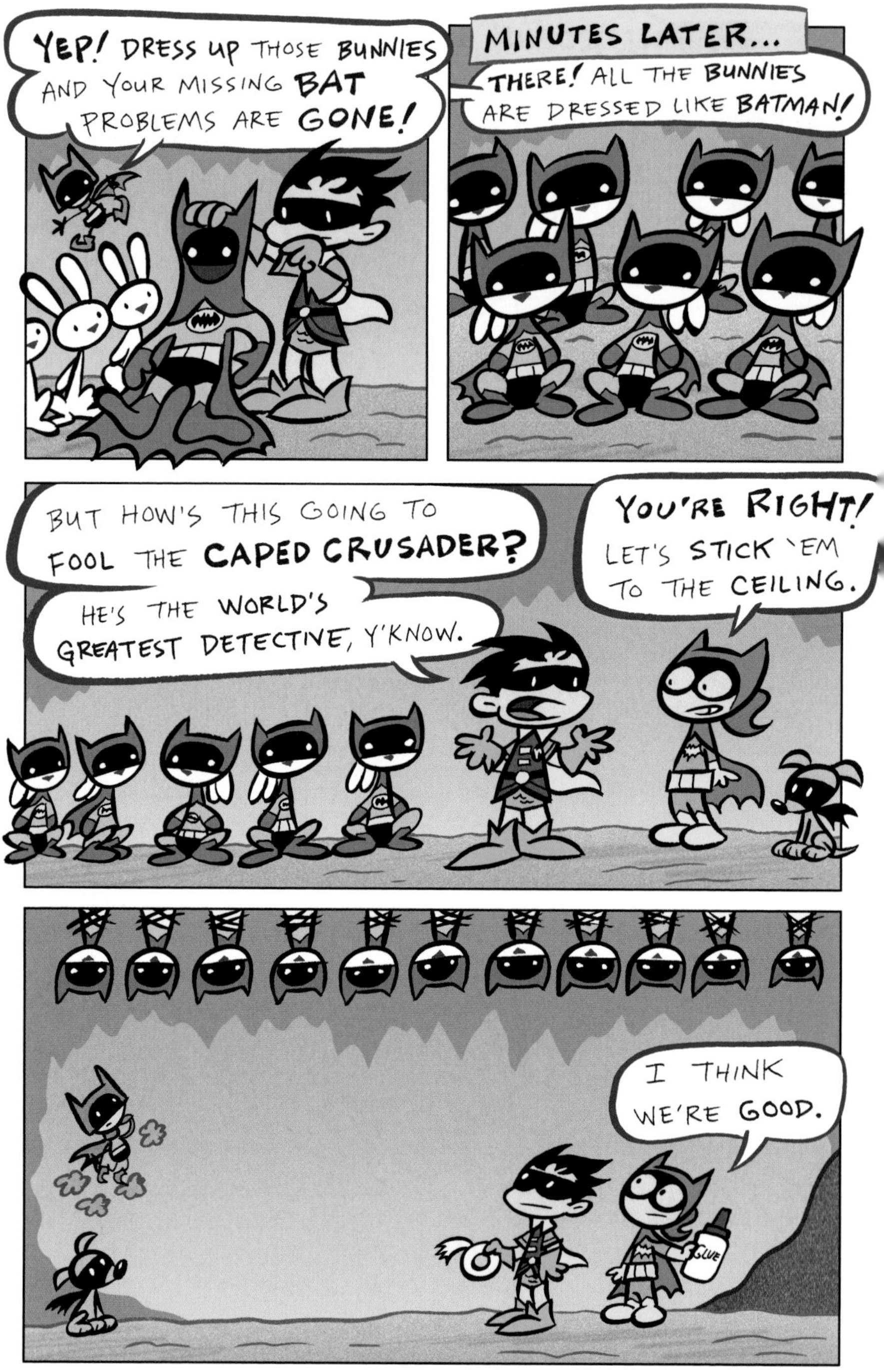
YEP! DRESS UP THOSE BUNNIES AND YOUR MISSING BAT PROBLEMS ARE GONE!
MINUTES LATER...
THERE! ALL THE BUNNIES ARE DRESSED LIKE BATMAN!
BUT HOW'S THIS GOING TO FOOL THE CAPED CRUSADER?
HE'S THE WORLD'S GREATEST DETECTIVE, Y'KNOW.
YOU'RE RIGHT! LET'S STICK 'EM TO THE CEILING.
I THINK WE'RE GOOD.
GLUE

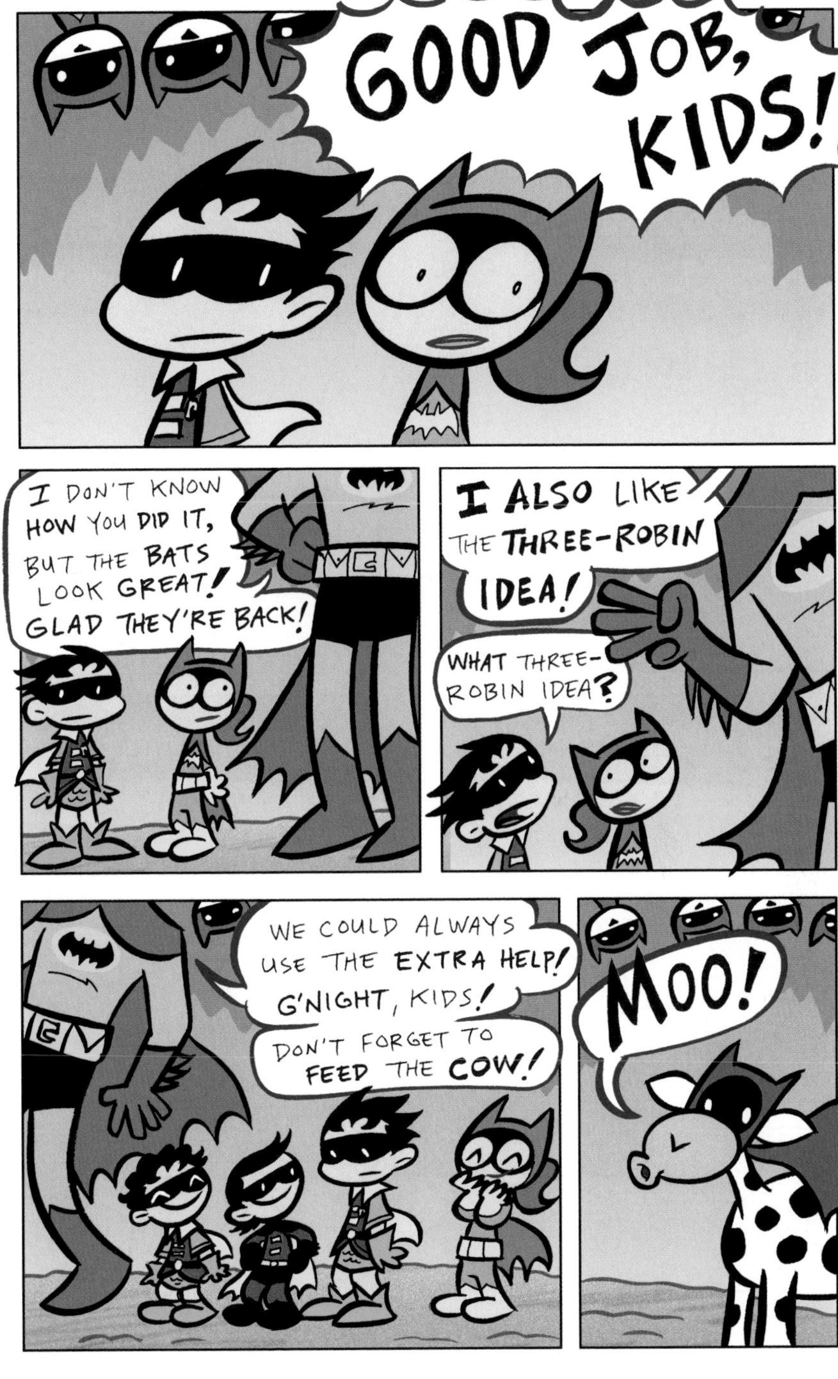
GOOD JOB, KIDS!
I DON'T KNOW HOW YOU DID IT, BUT THE BATS LOOK GREAT! GLAD THEY'RE BACK!
I ALSO LIKE THE THREE-ROBIN IDEA!
WHAT THREE-ROBIN IDEA?
WE COULD ALWAYS USE THE EXTRA HELP!
G'NIGHT, KIDS!
DON'T FORGET TO FEED THE COW!
MOO!

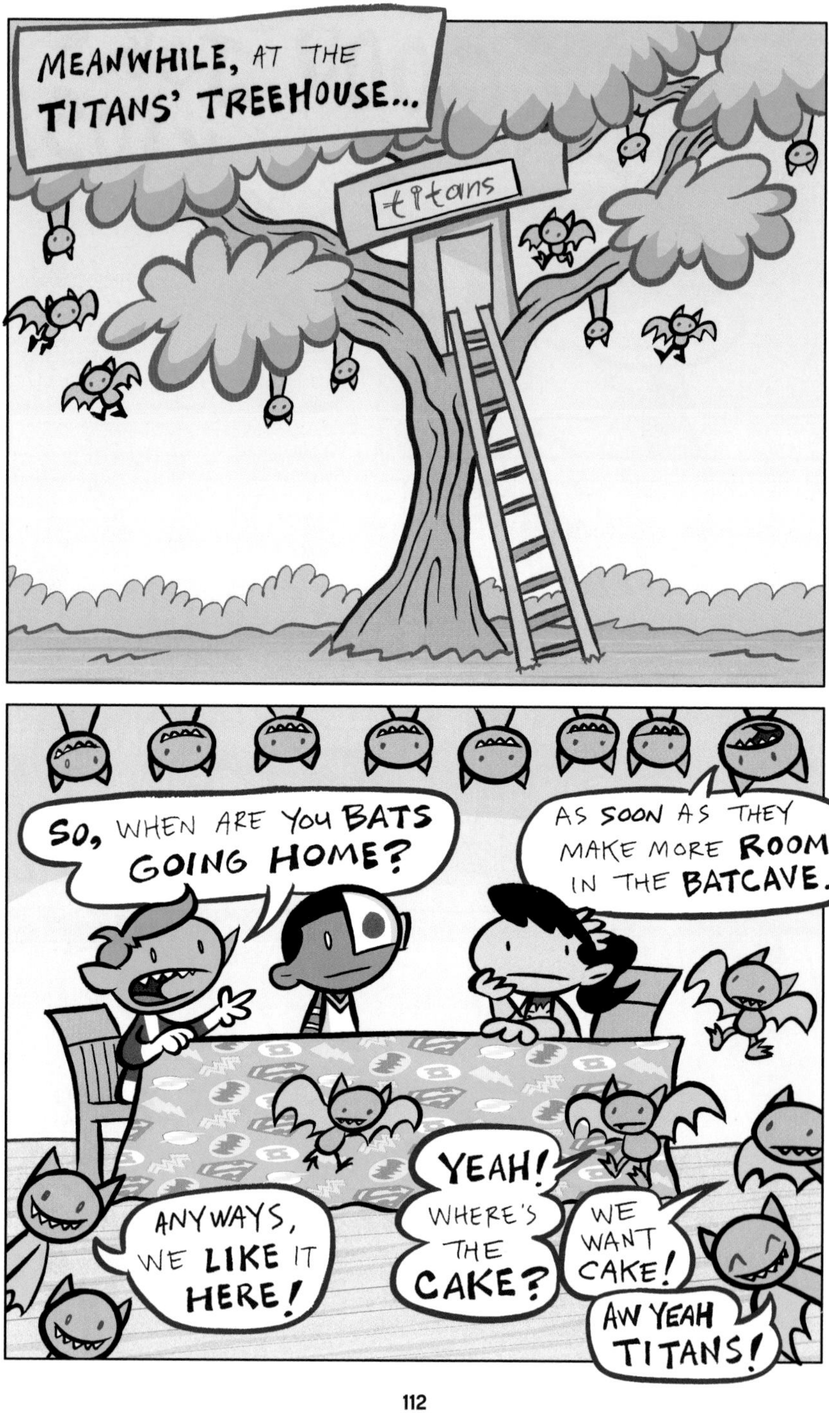
MEANWHILE, AT THE TITANS' TREEHOUSE...
titans
SO, WHEN ARE YOU BATS GOING HOME?
AS SOON AS THEY MAKE MORE ROOM IN THE BATCAVE.
ANYWAYS, WE LIKE IT HERE!
YEAH!
WHERE'S THE CAKE?
WE WANT CAKE!
AW YEAH TITANS!

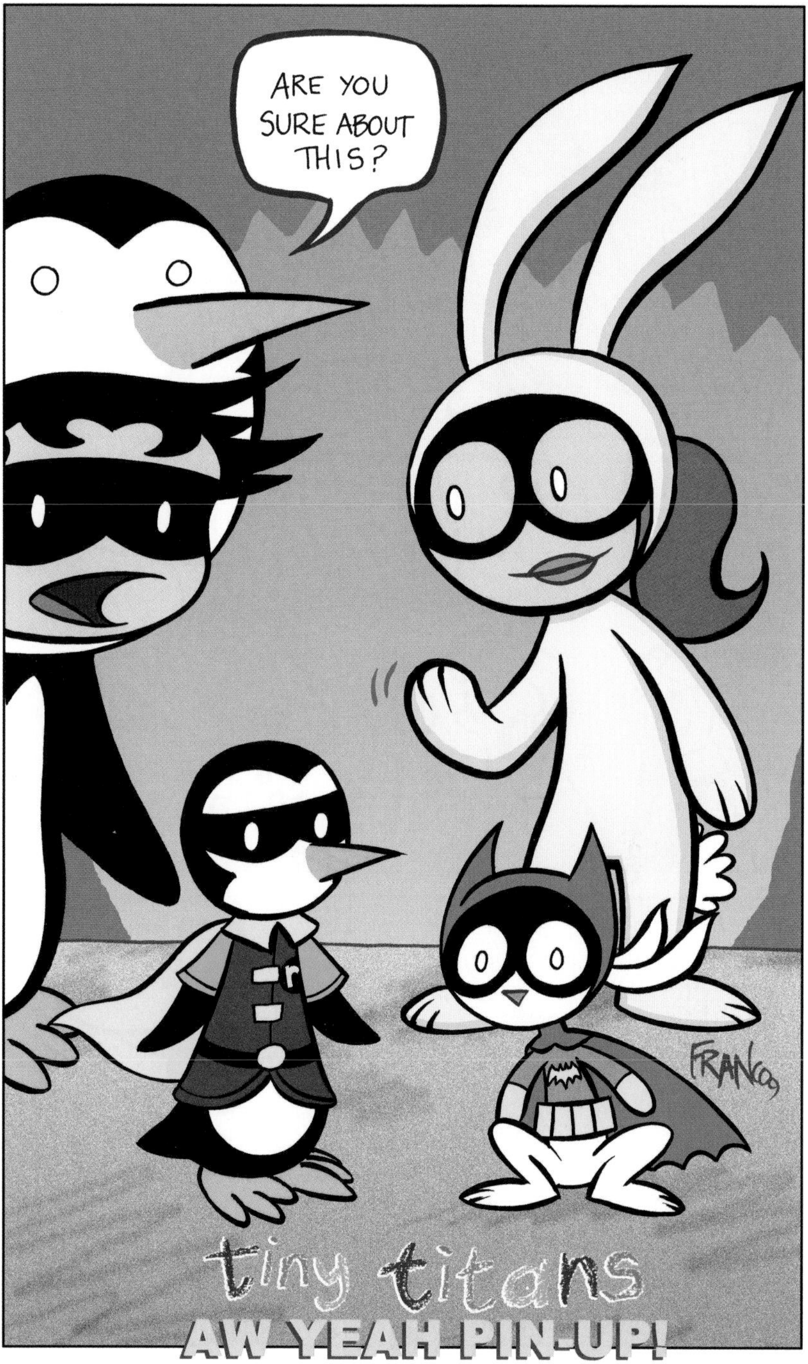
ARE YOU SURE ABOUT THIS?
FRANCO9
tiny titans
AW YEAH PIN-UP!

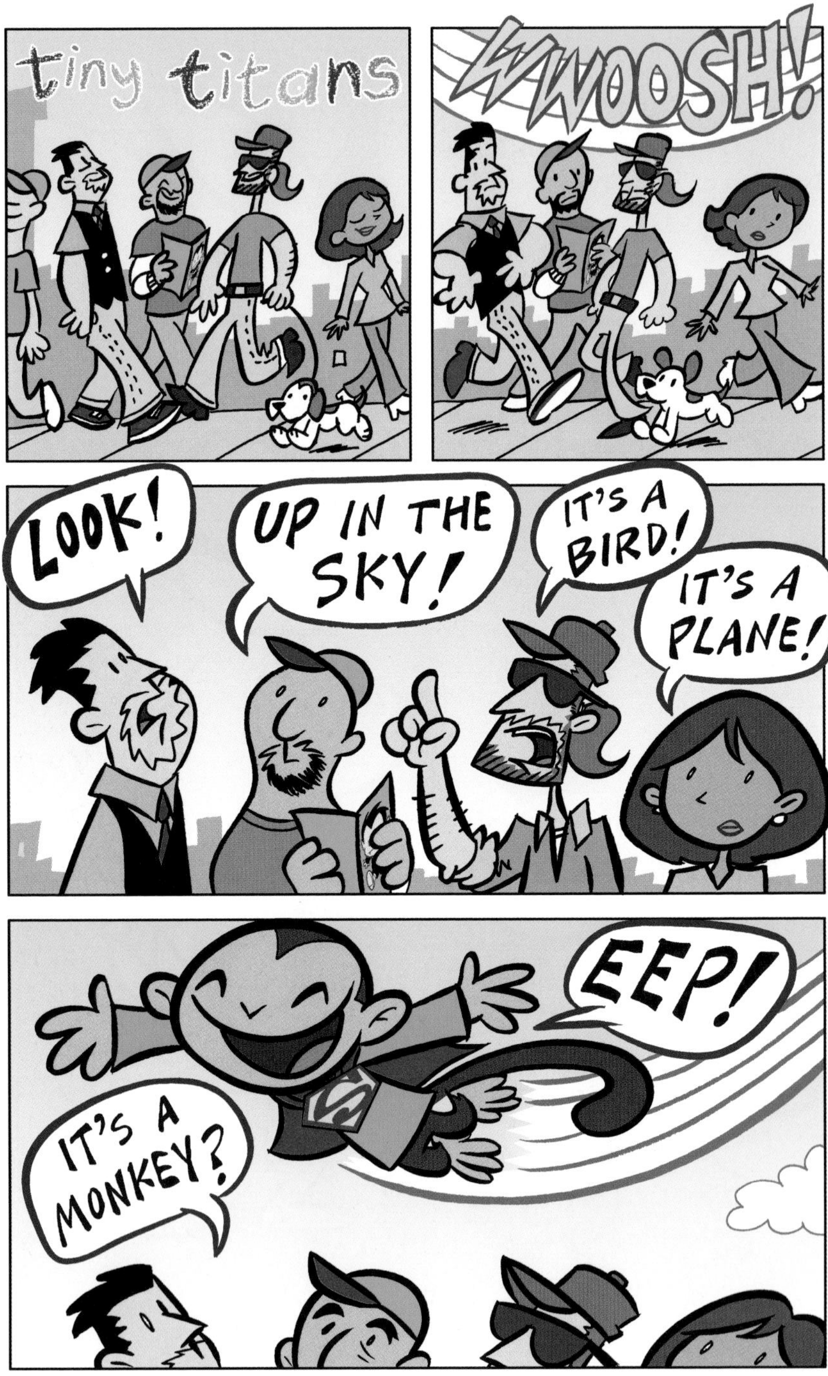
tiny titans
WWOOSH!
LOOK!
UP IN THE SKY!
IT'S A BIRD!
IT'S A PLANE!
EEP!
IT'S A MONKEY?

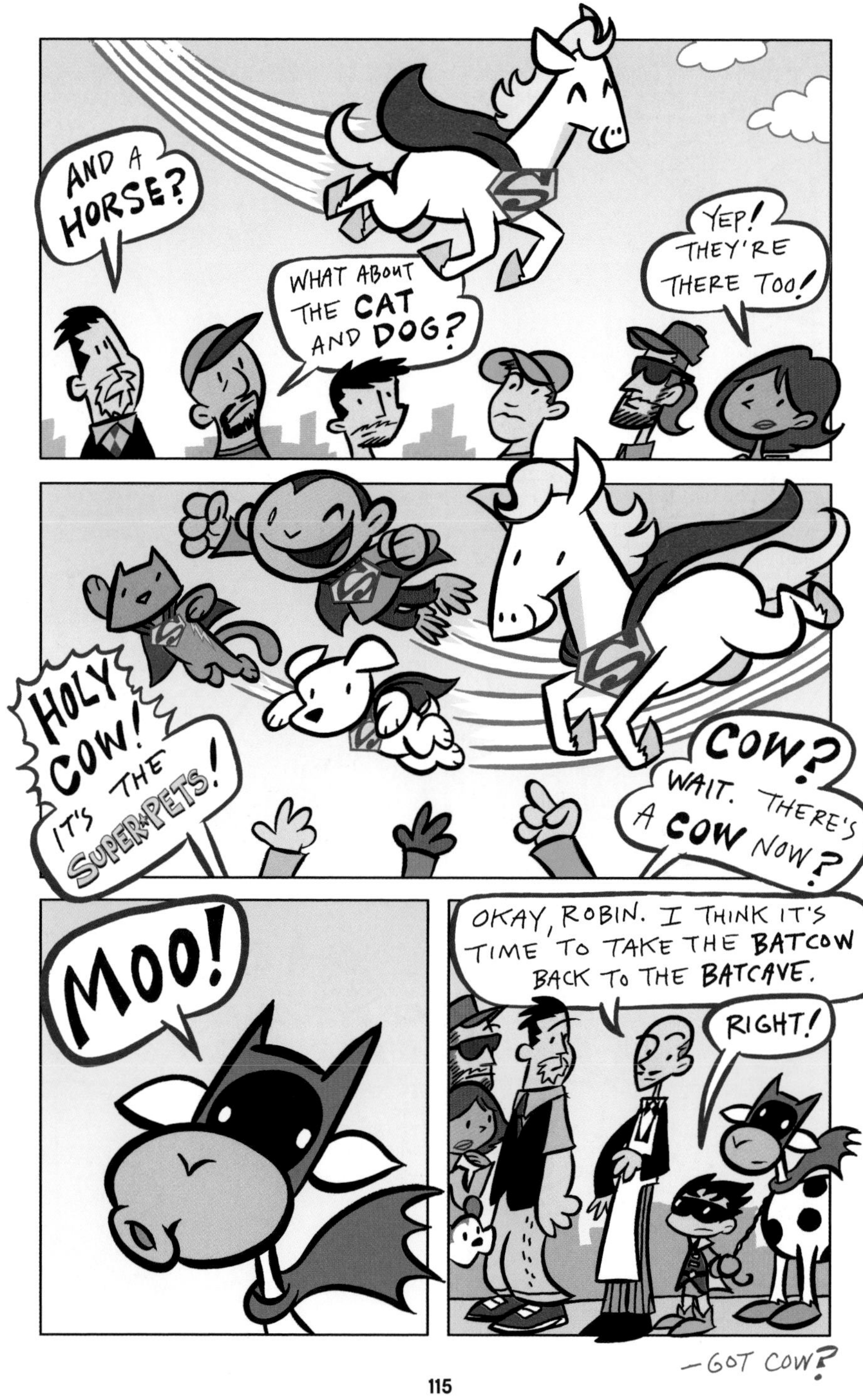
AND A HORSE?
WHAT ABOUT THE CAT AND DOG?
YEP! THEY'RE THERE TOO!
HOLY COW! IT'S THE SUPER-PETS!
COW? WAIT. THERE'S A COW NOW?
MOO!
OKAY, ROBIN. I THINK IT'S TIME TO TAKE THE BATCOW BACK TO THE BATCAVE.
RIGHT!

—GOT COW?

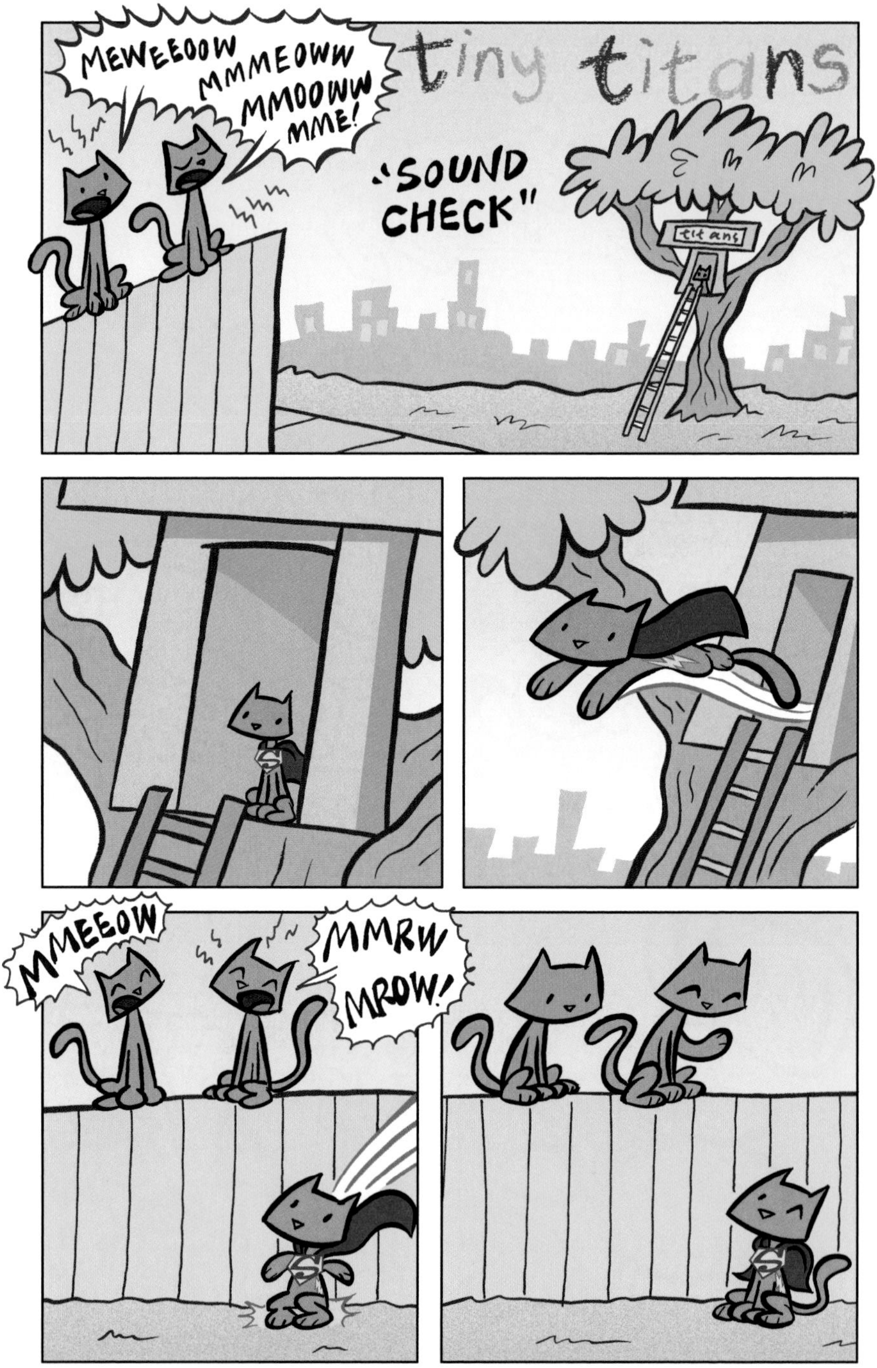

MEWEEOOW
MMMEOWW MMOOWW MME!
tiny titans
"SOUND CHECK"
titans
MMEEEOW
MMRW MROW!

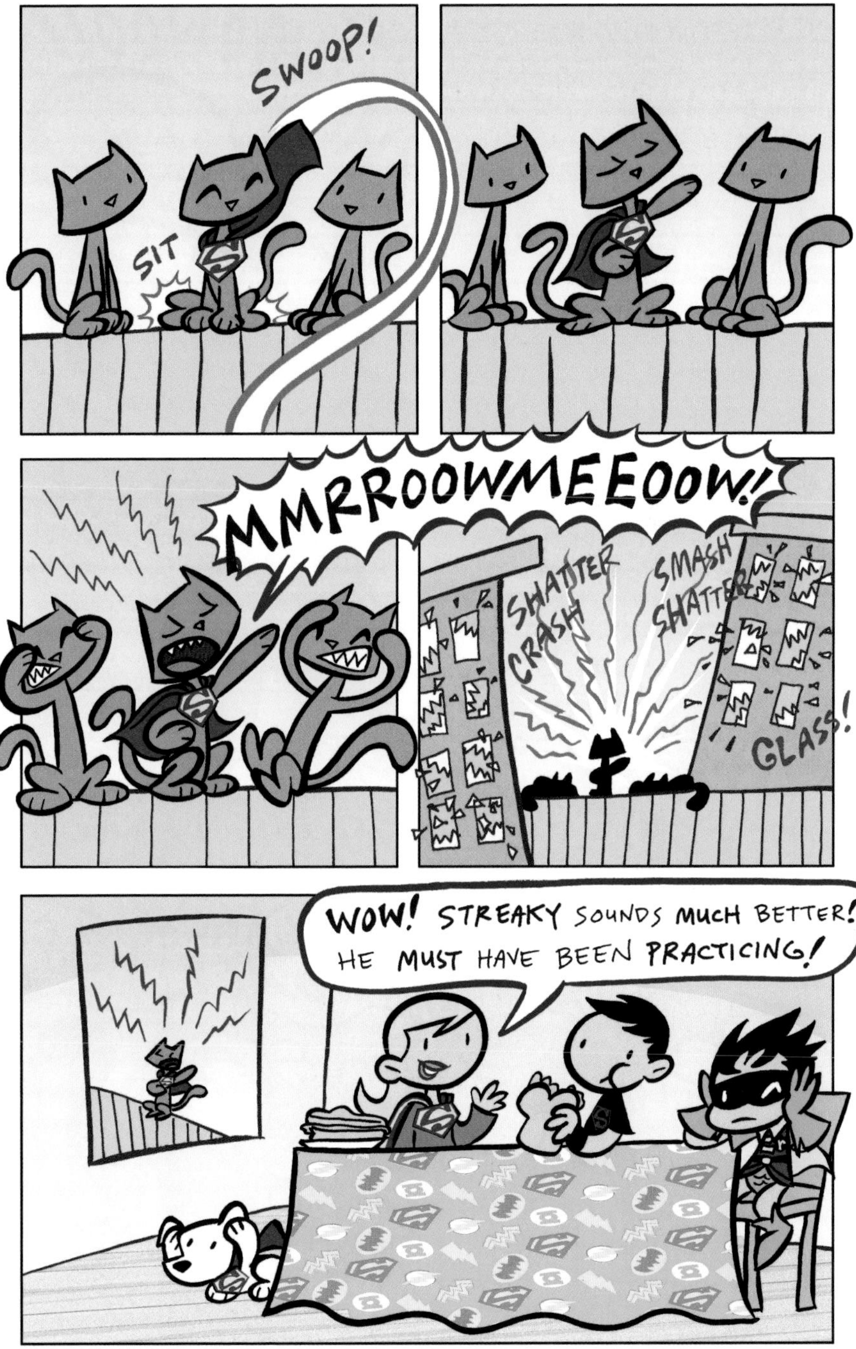
SWOOP!
SIT
MMRROOWMEEOOW!
SHATTER
CRASH
SMASH
SHATTER
GLASS!
WOW! STREAKY SOUNDS MUCH BETTER! HE MUST HAVE BEEN PRACTICING!

—TUNE A TUNA.

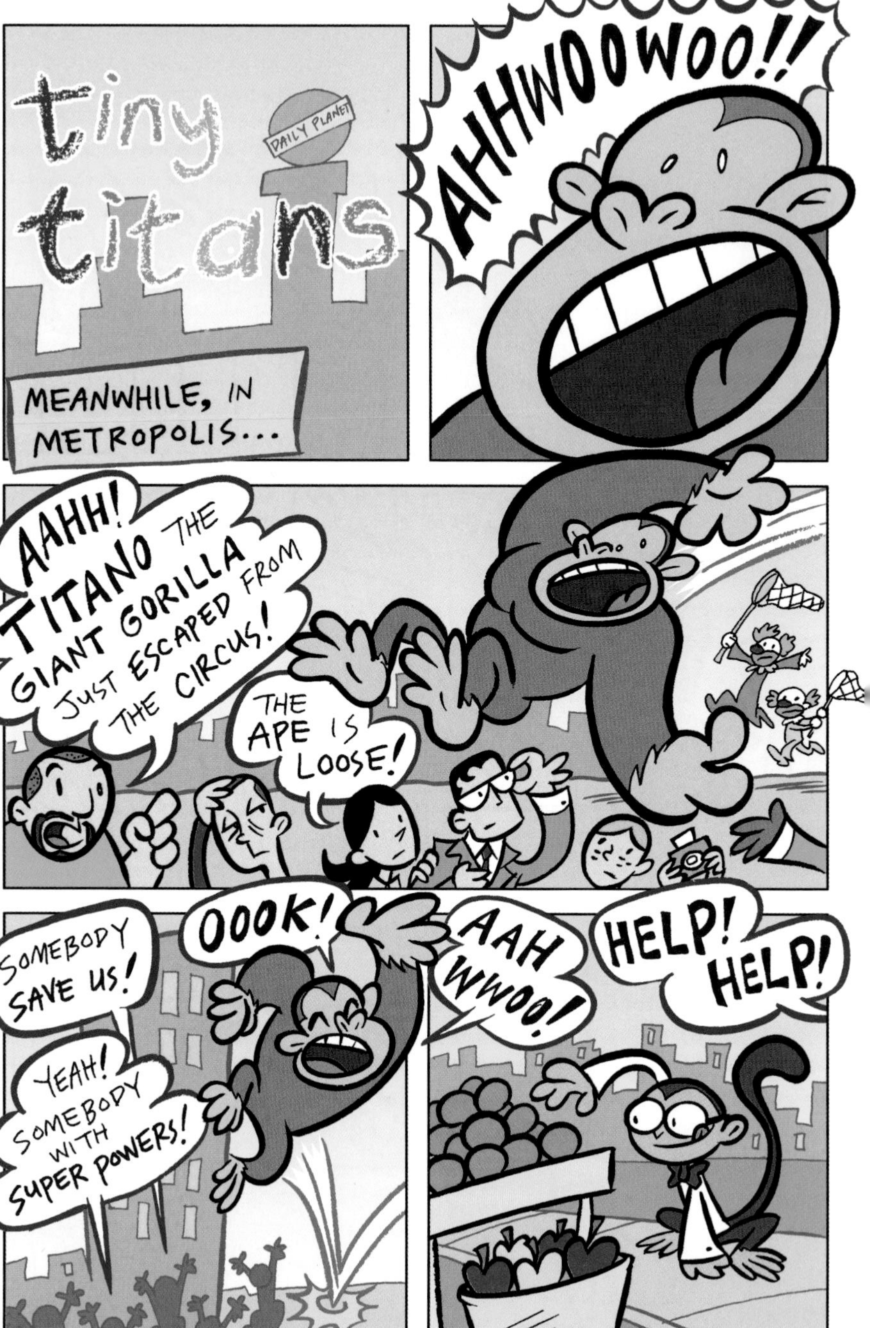
tiny titans
DAILY PLANET
MEANWHILE, IN METROPOLIS...
AHHWOOWOO!!
AAHH! TITANO THE GIANT GORILLA JUST ESCAPED FROM THE CIRCUS!
THE APE IS LOOSE!
SOMEBODY SAVE US!
OOOK!
YEAH! SOMEBODY WITH SUPER POWERS!
AAH WWOO!
HELP! HELP!

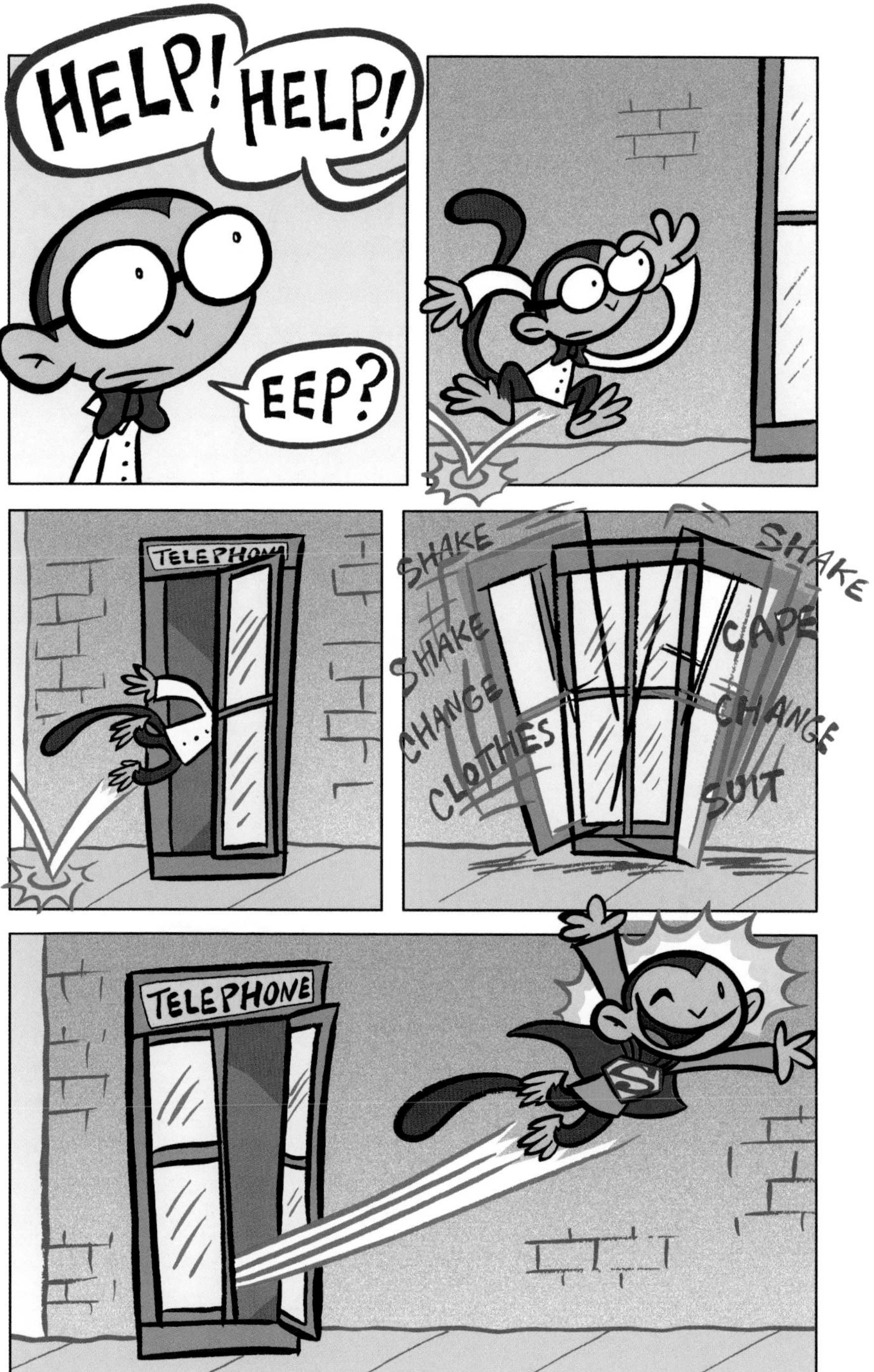
HELP! HELP!
EEP?
SHAKE
SHAKE
SHAKE
CHANGE
CLOTHES
CAPE
CHANGE
SUIT
TELEPHONE

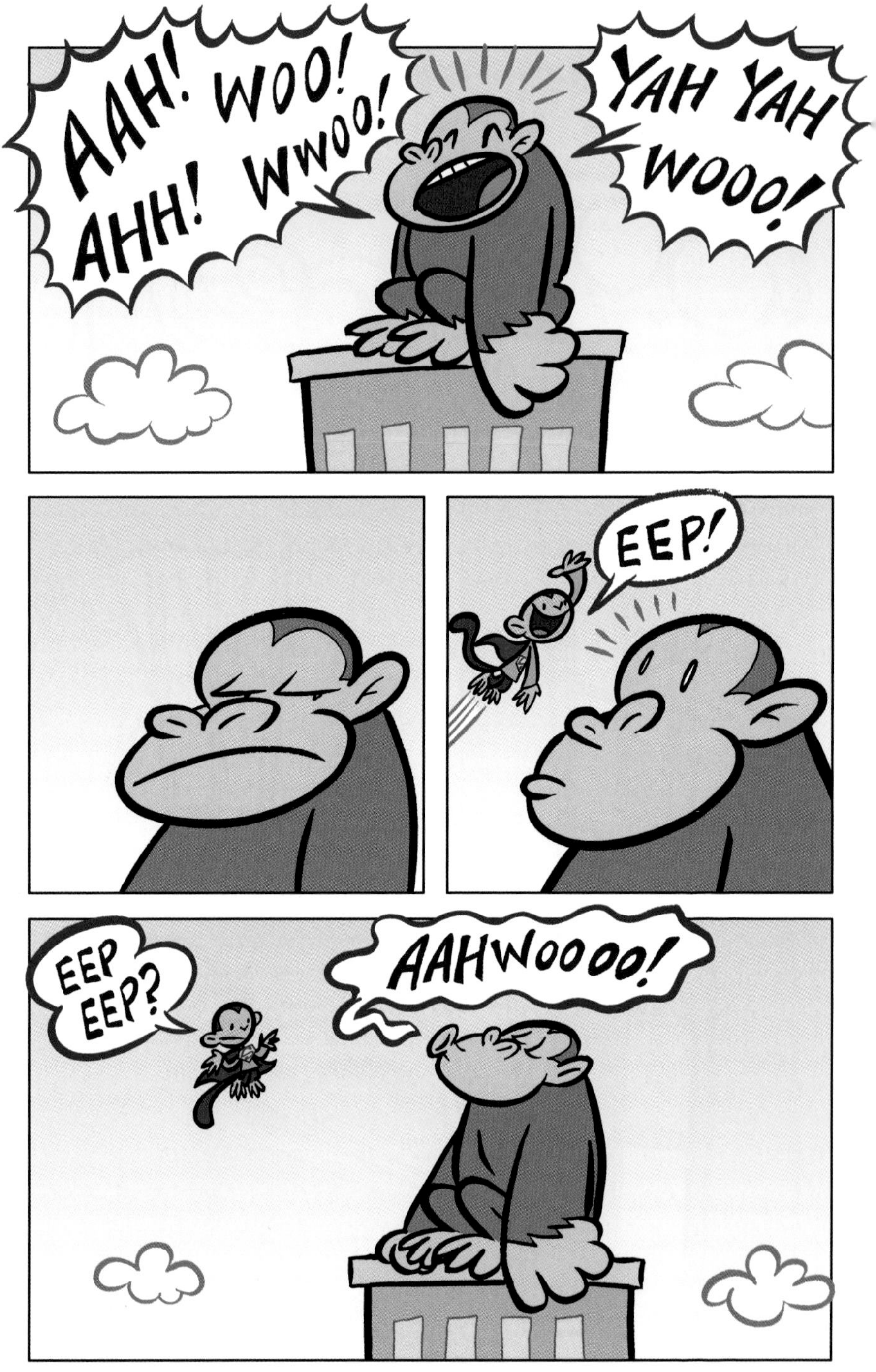

AAH! AHH! WOO! WWOO!
YAH YAH WOOO!
EEP!
EEP EEP?
AAHWOOOO!

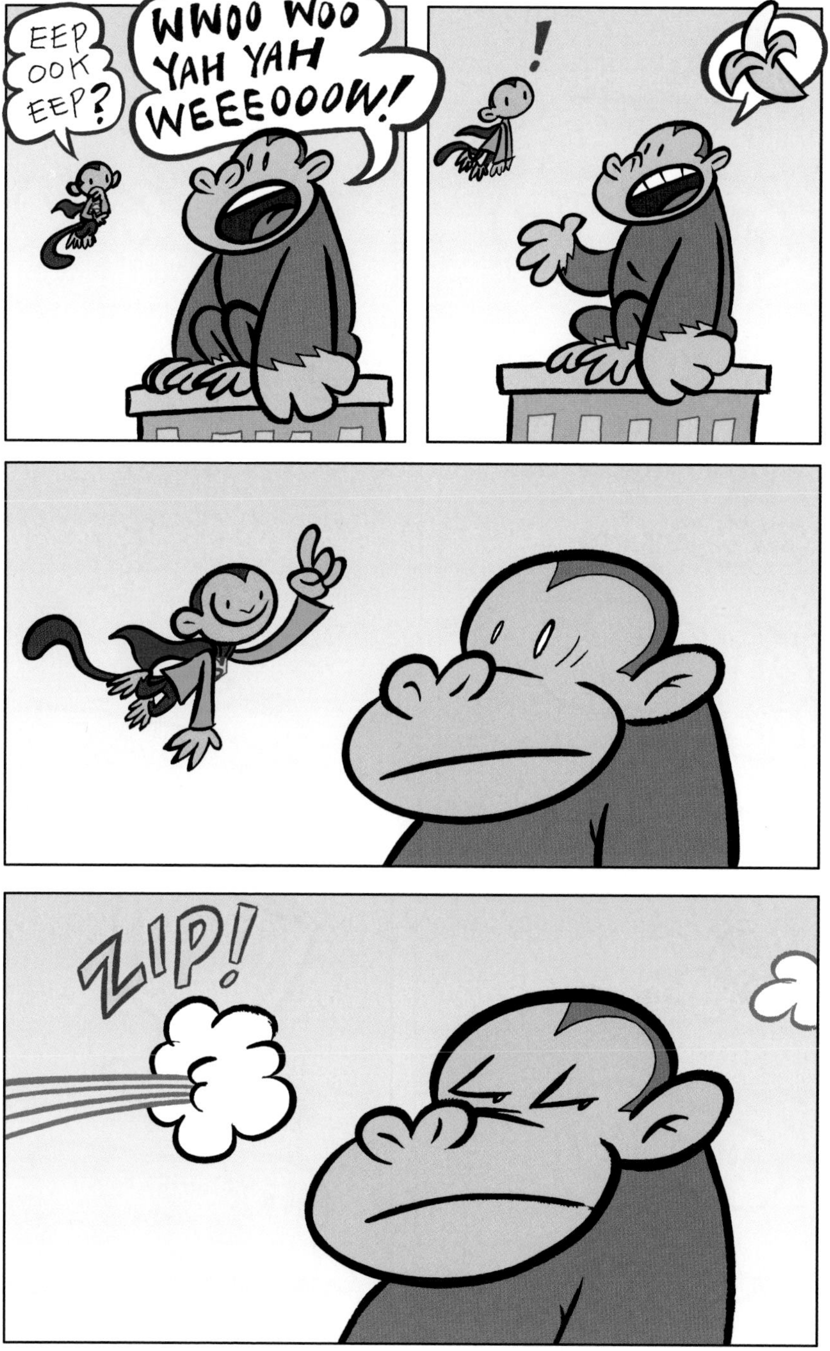
EEP OOK EEP?
WWOO WOO YAH YAH WEEEOOOW!
!
ZIP!

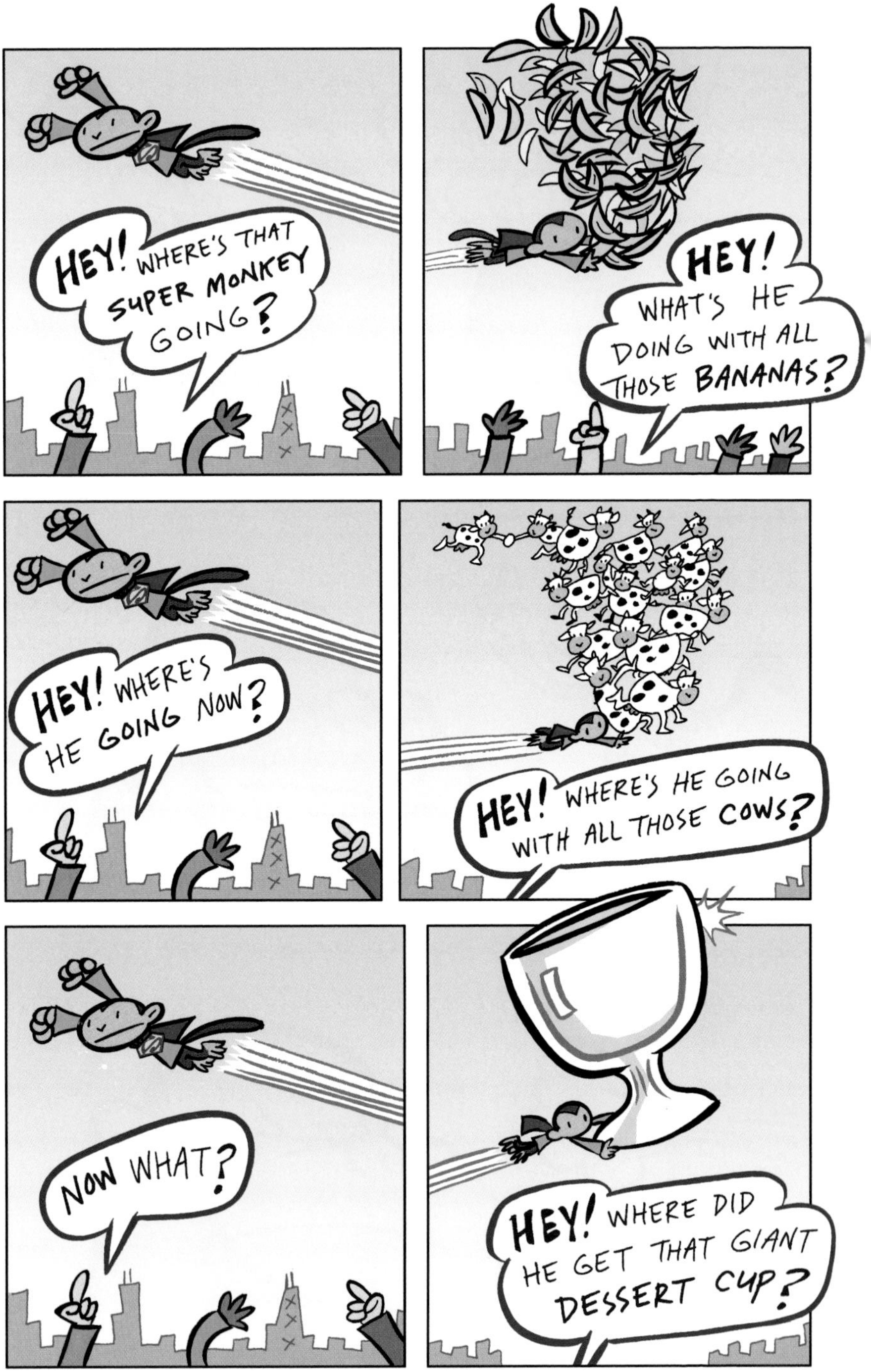
HEY! WHERE'S THAT SUPER MONKEY GOING?
HEY! WHAT'S HE DOING WITH ALL THOSE BANANAS?
HEY! WHERE'S HE GOING NOW?
HEY! WHERE'S HE GOING WITH ALL THOSE COWS?
NOW WHAT?
HEY! WHERE DID HE GET THAT GIANT DESSERT CUP?

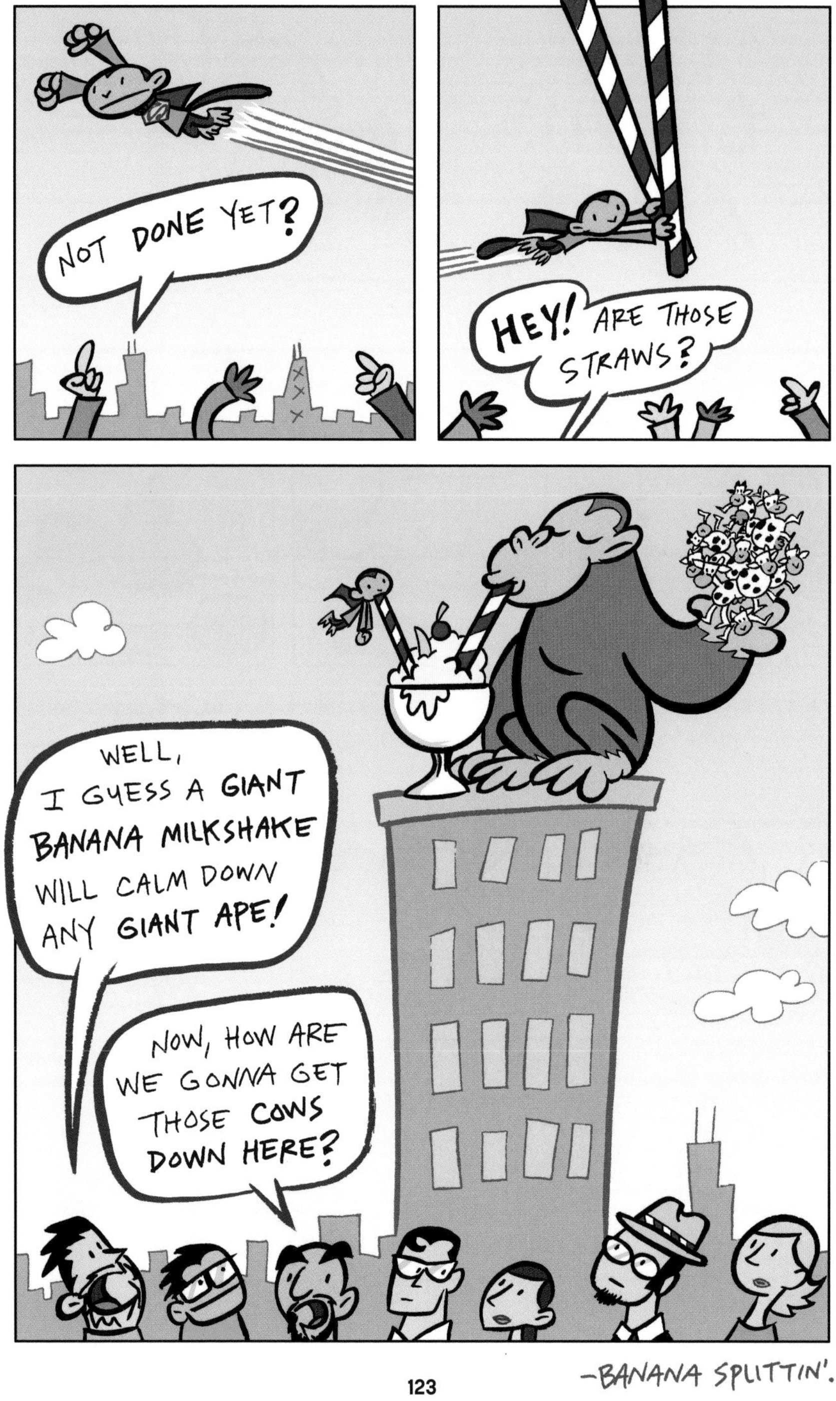
NOT DONE YET?
HEY! ARE THOSE STRAWS?
WELL, I GUESS A GIANT BANANA MILKSHAKE WILL CALM DOWN ANY GIANT APE!
NOW, HOW ARE WE GONNA GET THOSE COWS DOWN HERE?

–BANANA SPLITTIN'.

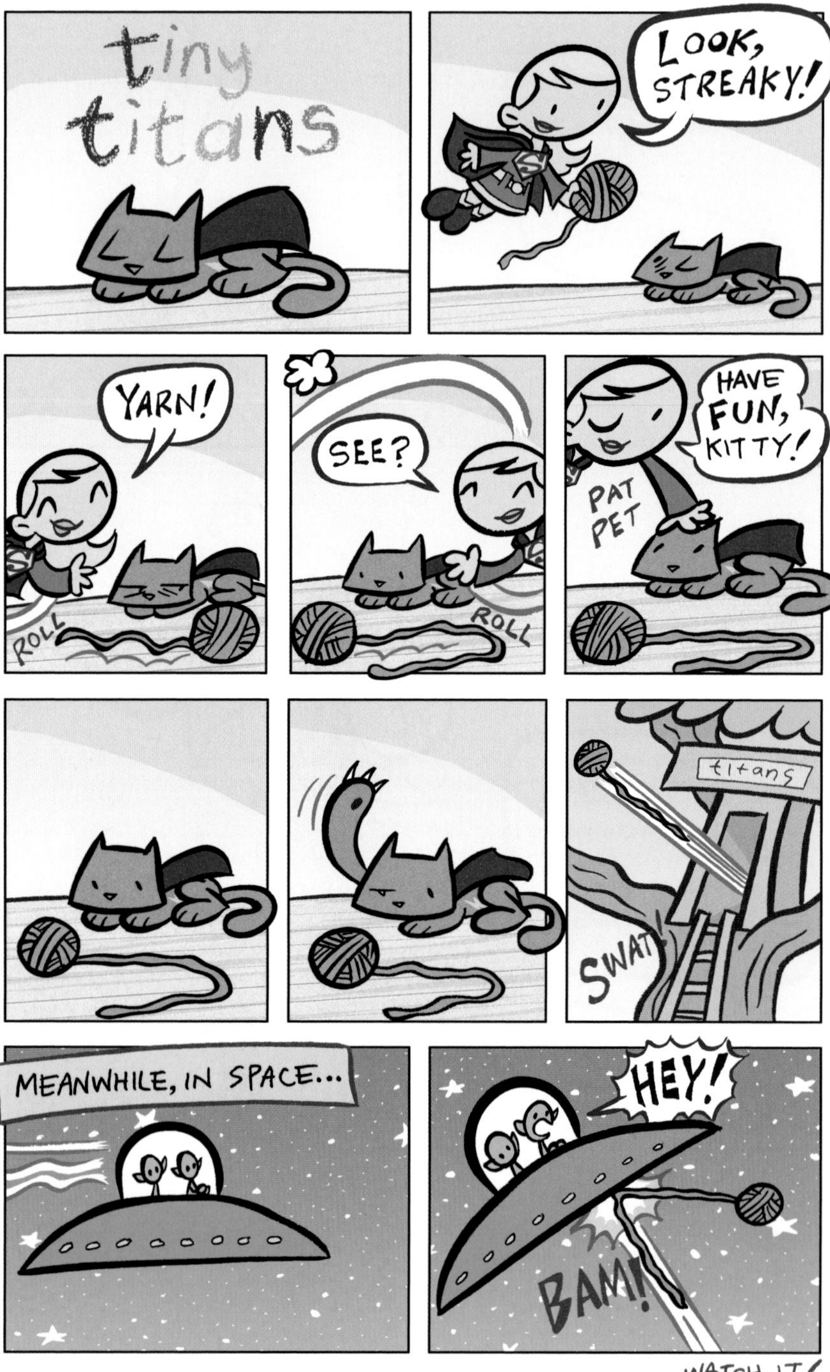
tiny titans
LOOK, STREAKY!
YARN!
ROLL
SEE?
ROLL
PAT PET
HAVE FUN, KITTY!
titans
SWAT!
MEANWHILE, IN SPACE...
HEY!
BAM!
—WATCH IT!

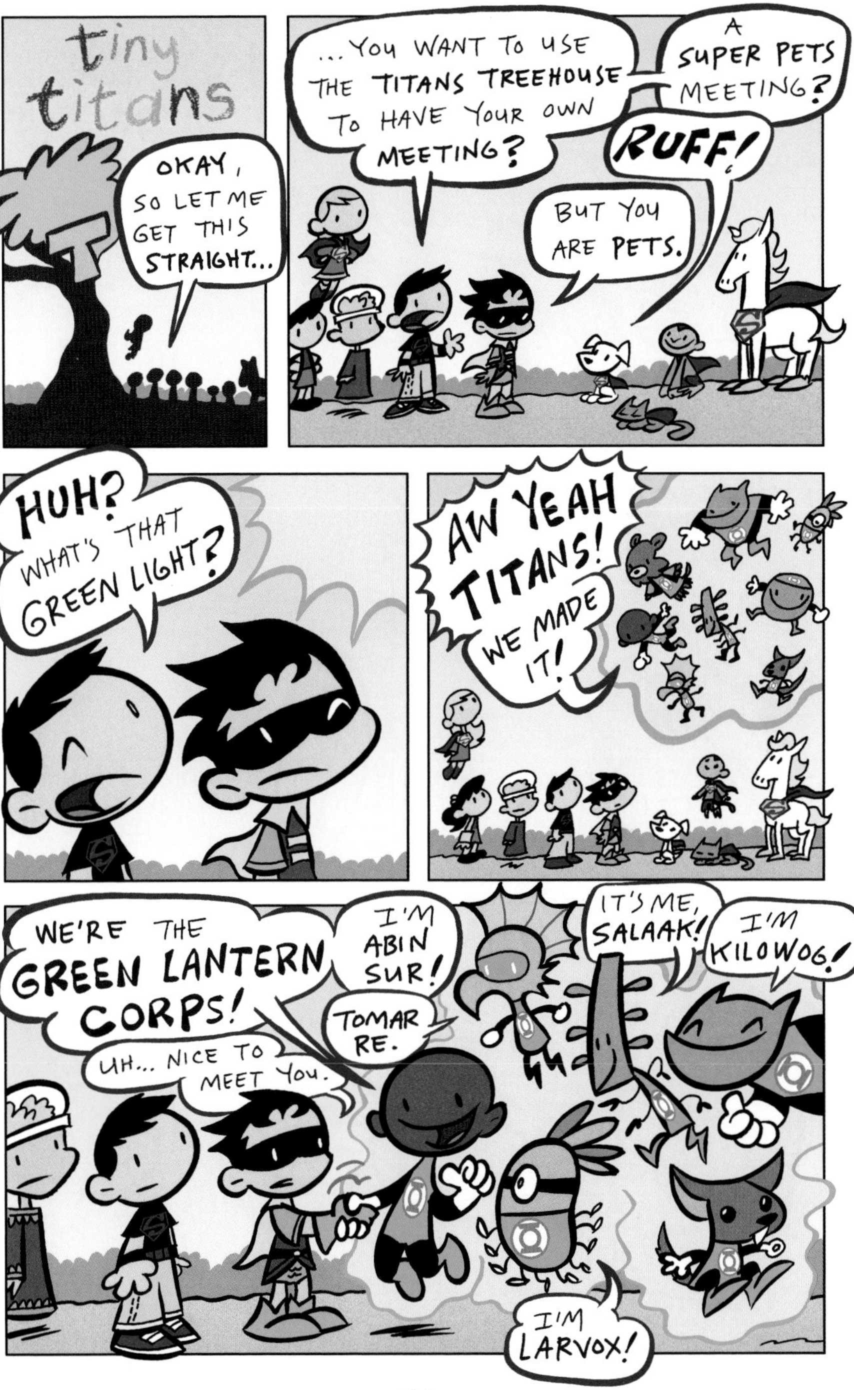
tiny titans
OKAY, SO LET ME GET THIS STRAIGHT...
...YOU WANT TO USE THE TITANS TREEHOUSE TO HAVE YOUR OWN MEETING?
A SUPER PETS MEETING?
RUFF!
BUT YOU ARE PETS.
HUH? WHAT'S THAT GREEN LIGHT?
AW YEAH TITANS!
WE MADE IT!
WE'RE THE GREEN LANTERN CORPS!
I'M ABIN SUR!
TOMAR RE.
IT'S ME, SALAAK!
I'M KILOWOG!
UH... NICE TO MEET YOU.
I'M LARVOX!

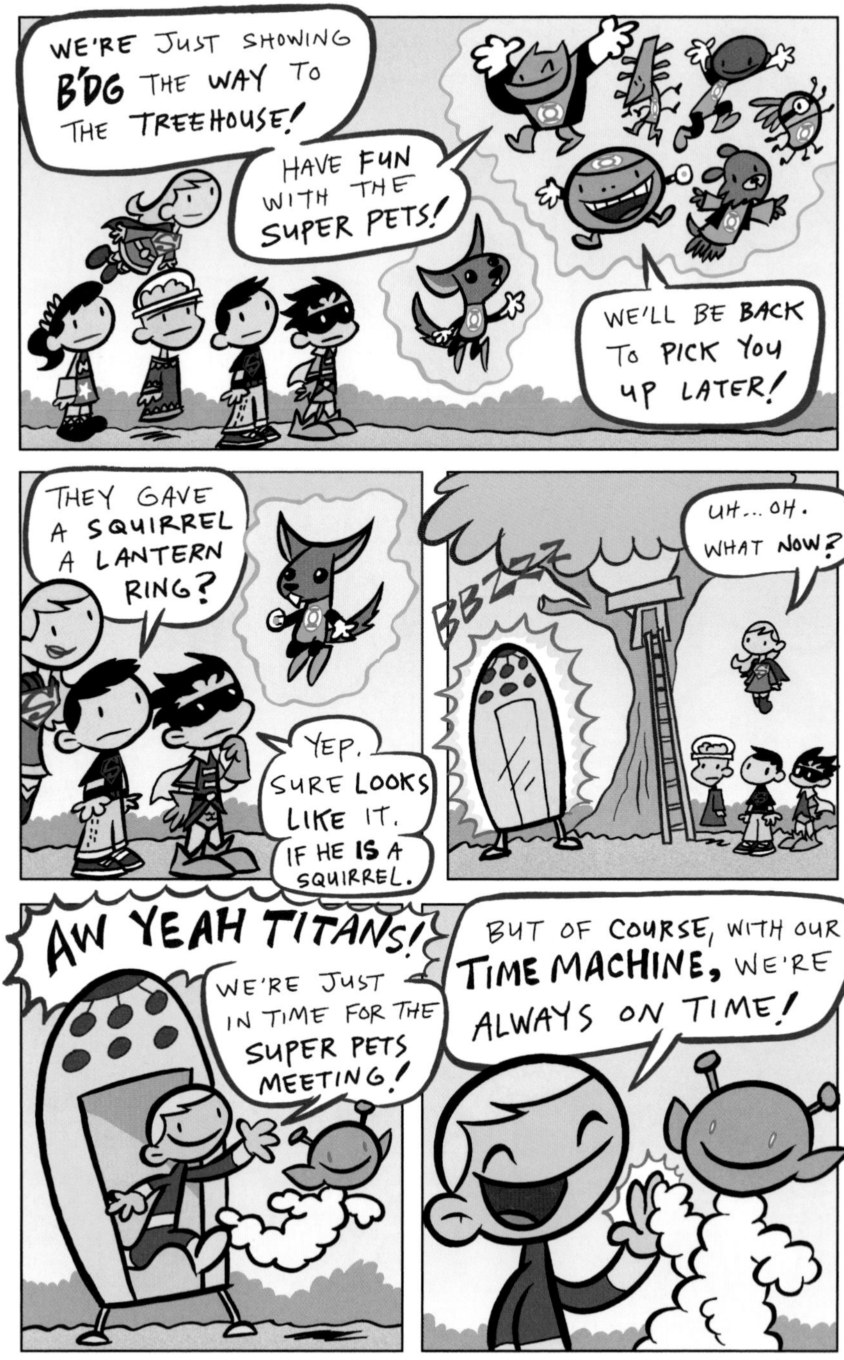
WE'RE JUST SHOWING B'DG THE WAY TO THE TREEHOUSE!
HAVE FUN WITH THE SUPER PETS!
WE'LL BE BACK TO PICK YOU UP LATER!
THEY GAVE A SQUIRREL A LANTERN RING?
YEP. SURE LOOKS LIKE IT. IF HE IS A SQUIRREL.
BBZZZ
UH... OH. WHAT NOW?
AW YEAH TITANS!
WE'RE JUST IN TIME FOR THE SUPER PETS MEETING!
BUT OF COURSE, WITH OUR TIME MACHINE, WE'RE ALWAYS ON TIME!

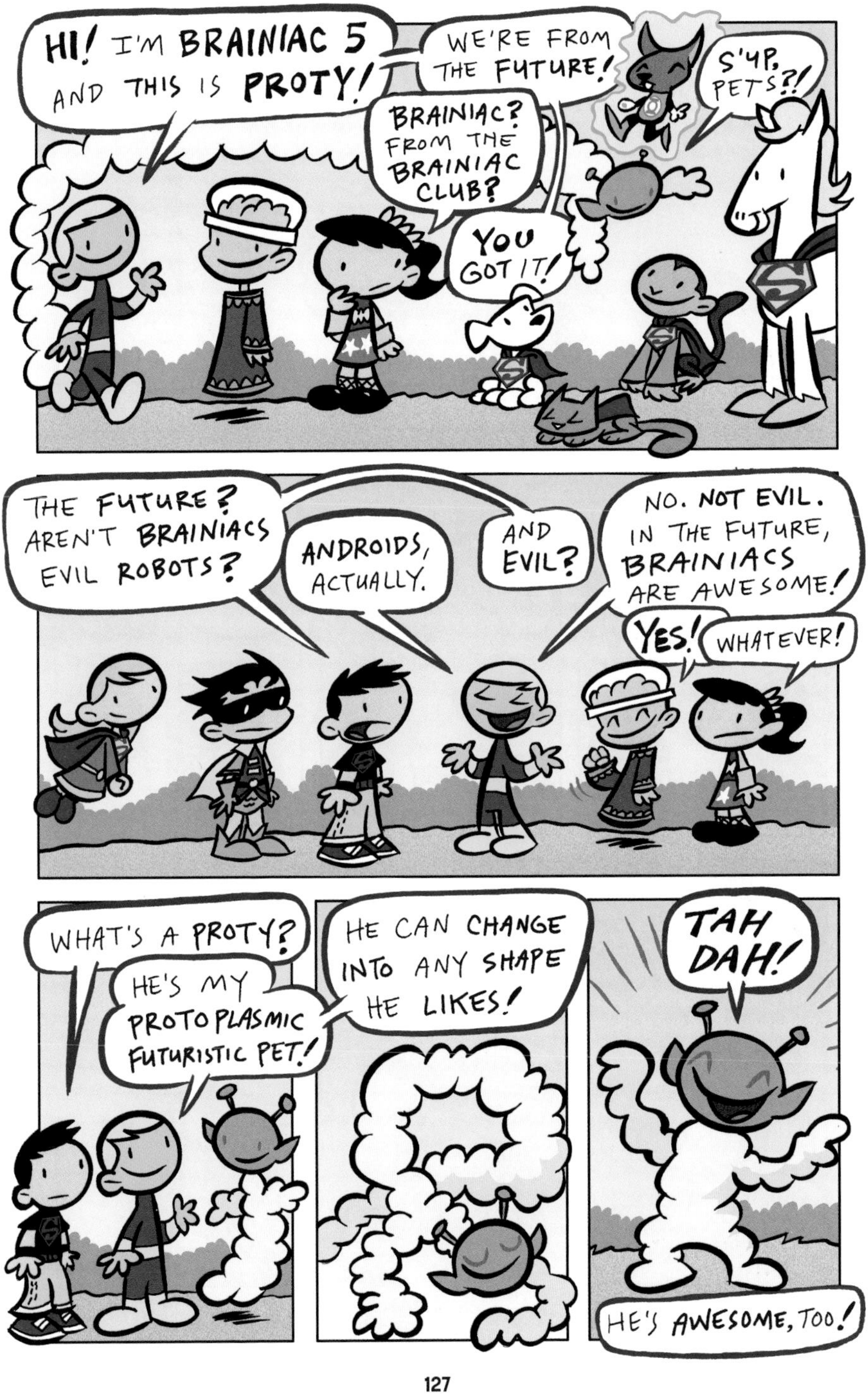
HI! I'M BRAINIAC 5 AND THIS IS PROTY!
WE'RE FROM THE FUTURE!
S'UP, PETS?!
BRAINIAC? FROM THE BRAINIAC CLUB?
YOU GOT IT!
THE FUTURE? AREN'T BRAINIACS EVIL ROBOTS?
ANDROIDS, ACTUALLY.
AND EVIL?
NO. NOT EVIL. IN THE FUTURE, BRAINIACS ARE AWESOME!
YES!
WHATEVER!
WHAT'S A PROTY?
HE'S MY PROTOPLASMIC FUTURISTIC PET!
HE CAN CHANGE INTO ANY SHAPE HE LIKES!
TAH DAH!
HE'S AWESOME, TOO!

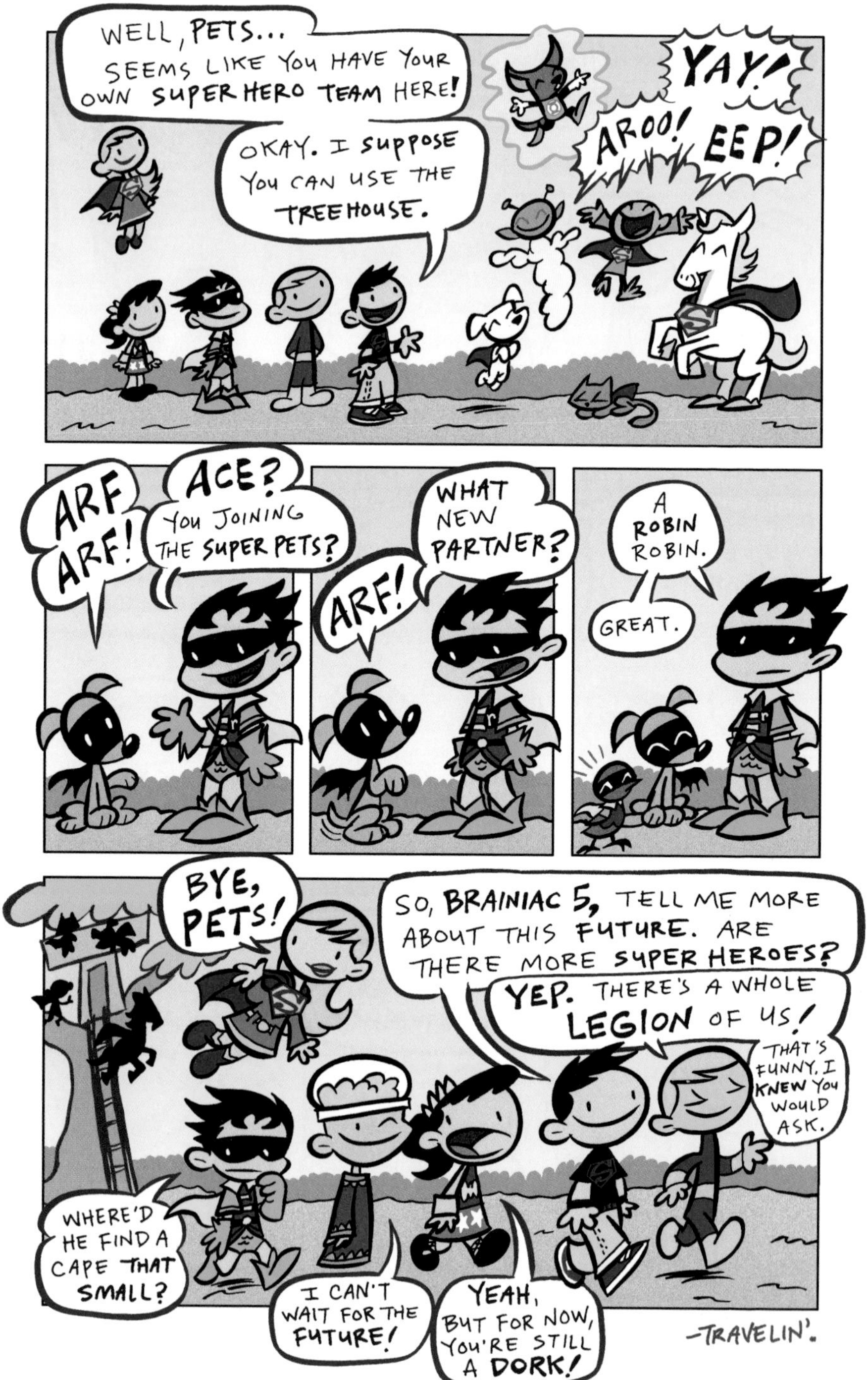
WELL, PETS... SEEMS LIKE YOU HAVE YOUR OWN SUPERHERO TEAM HERE!
OKAY. I SUPPOSE YOU CAN USE THE TREEHOUSE.
YAY!
AROO!
EEP!
ARF ARF!
ACE? YOU JOINING THE SUPER PETS?
ARF!
WHAT NEW PARTNER?
A ROBIN ROBIN.
GREAT.
BYE, PETS!
SO, BRAINIAC 5, TELL ME MORE ABOUT THIS FUTURE. ARE THERE MORE SUPER HEROES?
YEP. THERE'S A WHOLE LEGION OF US!
THAT'S FUNNY. I KNEW YOU WOULD ASK.
WHERE'D HE FIND A CAPE THAT SMALL?
I CAN'T WAIT FOR THE FUTURE!
YEAH, BUT FOR NOW, YOU'RE STILL A DORK!
-TRAVELIN'.

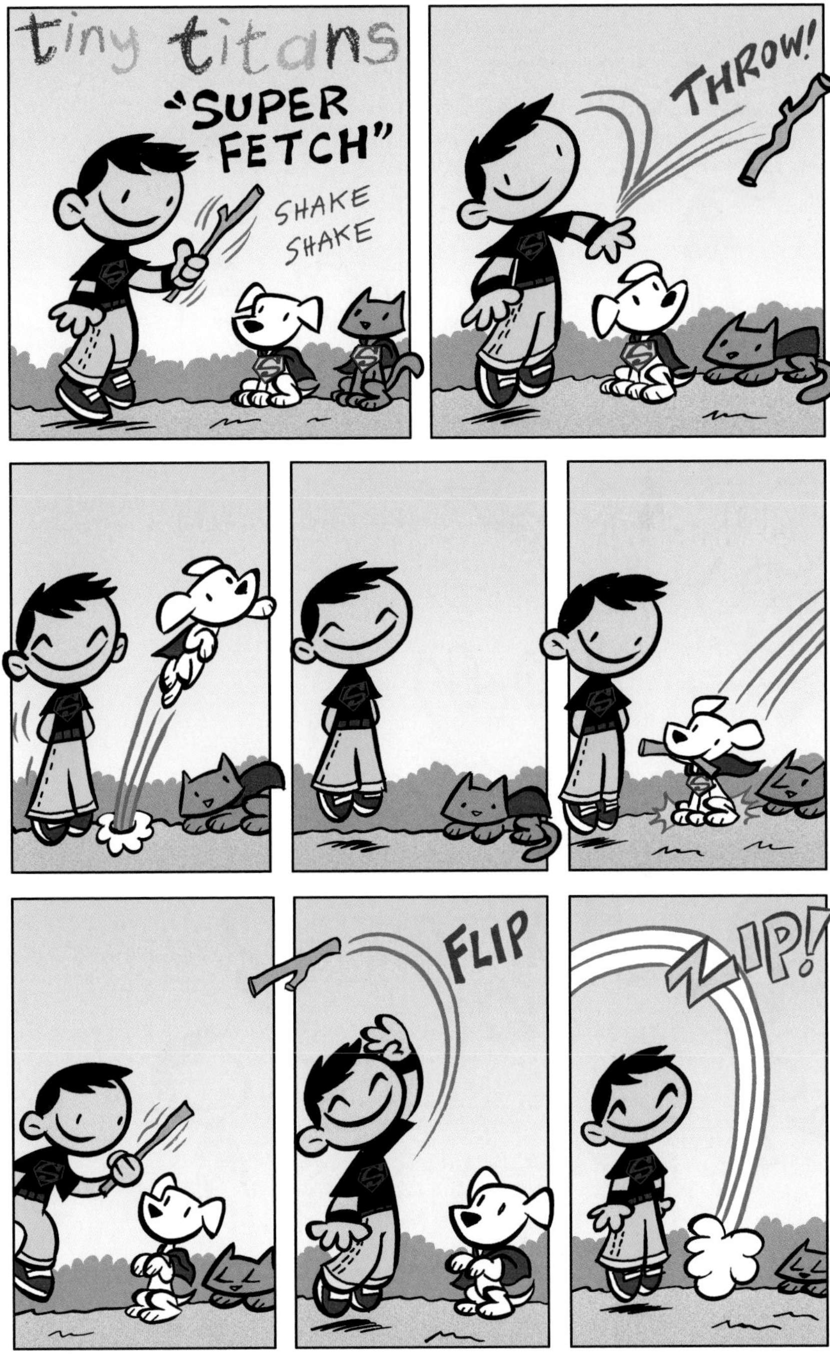
tiny titans
"SUPER FETCH"
SHAKE SHAKE
THROW!
FLIP
ZIP!

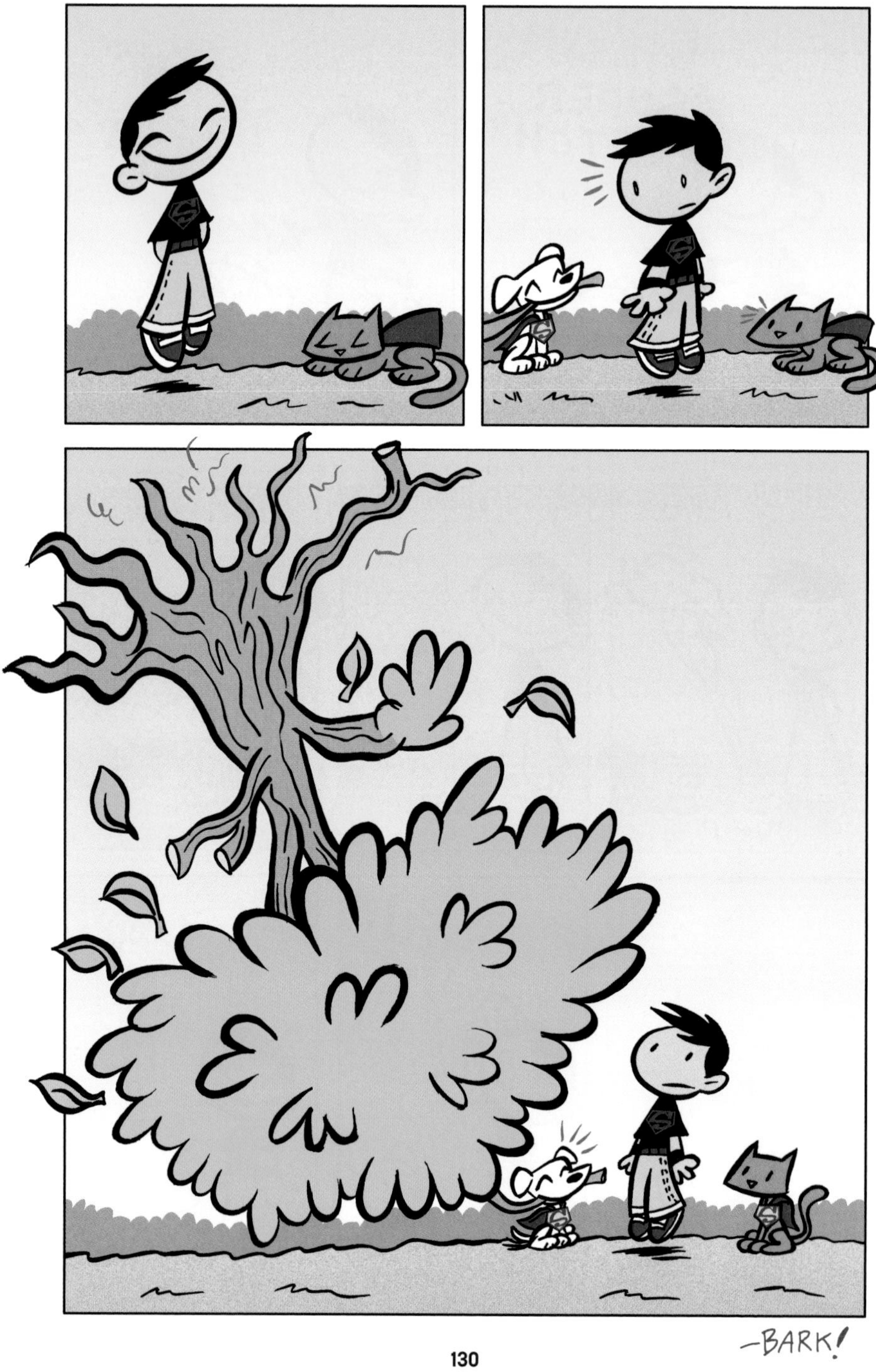
-BARK!

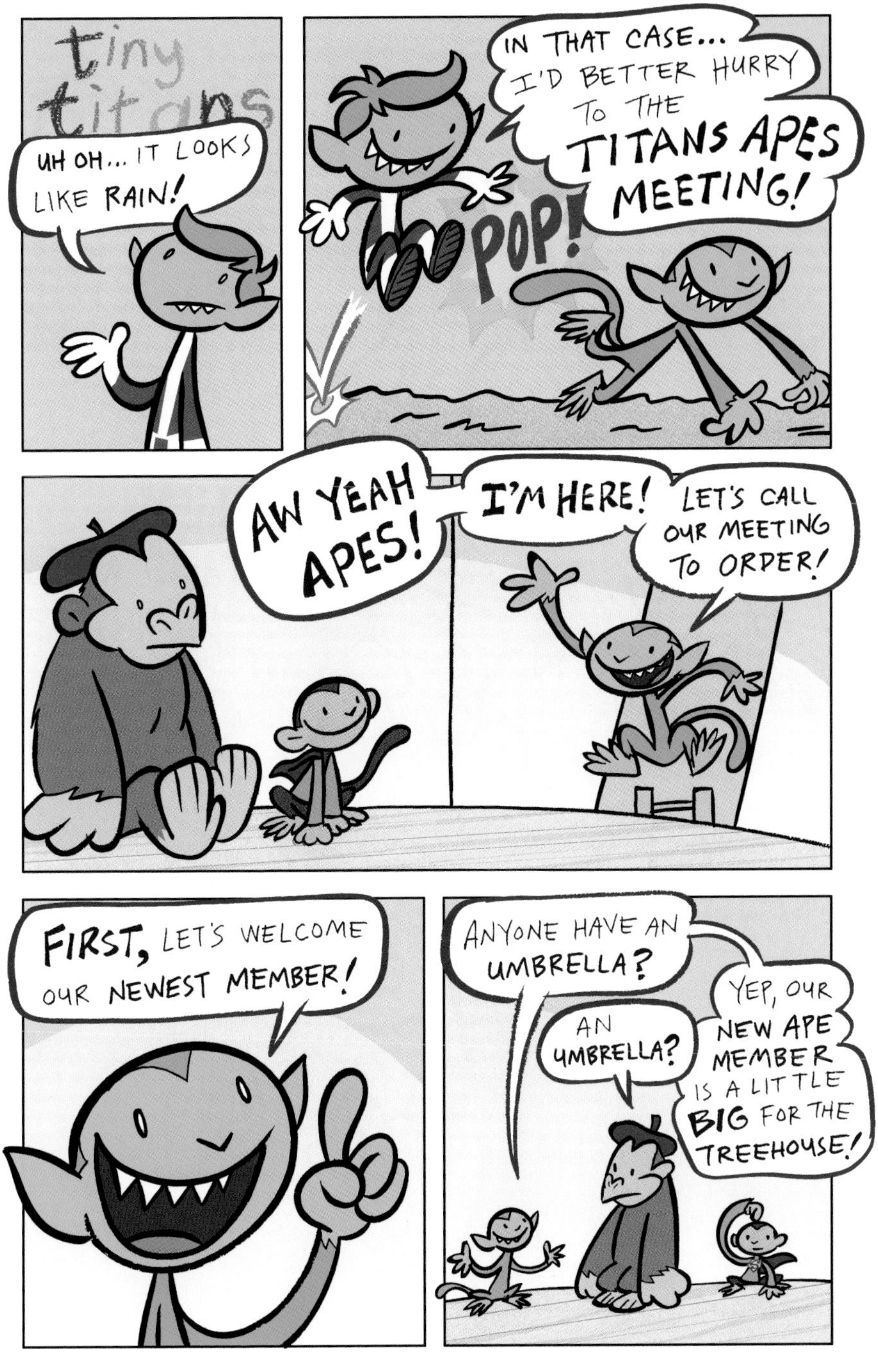
tiny titans
UH OH... IT LOOKS LIKE RAIN!
IN THAT CASE... I'D BETTER HURRY TO THE TITANS APES MEETING!
POP!
AW YEAH APES!
I'M HERE!
LET'S CALL OUR MEETING TO ORDER!
FIRST, LET'S WELCOME OUR NEWEST MEMBER!
ANYONE HAVE AN UMBRELLA?
AN UMBRELLA?
YEP, OUR NEW APE MEMBER IS A LITTLE BIG FOR THE TREEHOUSE!

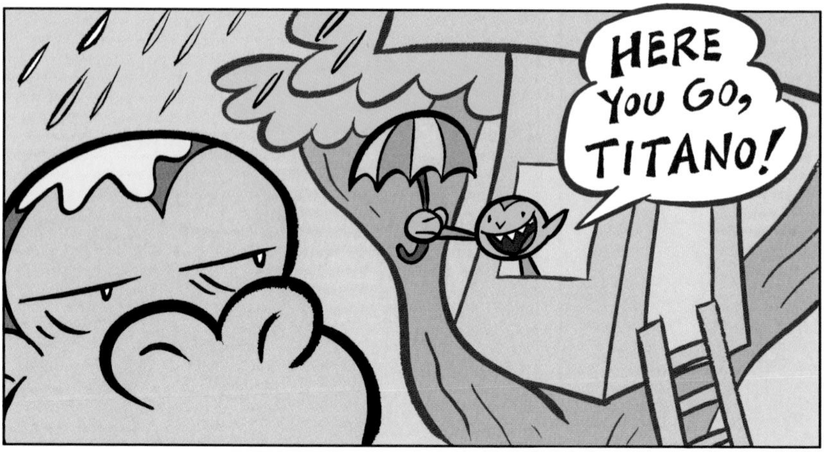
HERE YOU GO, TITANO!

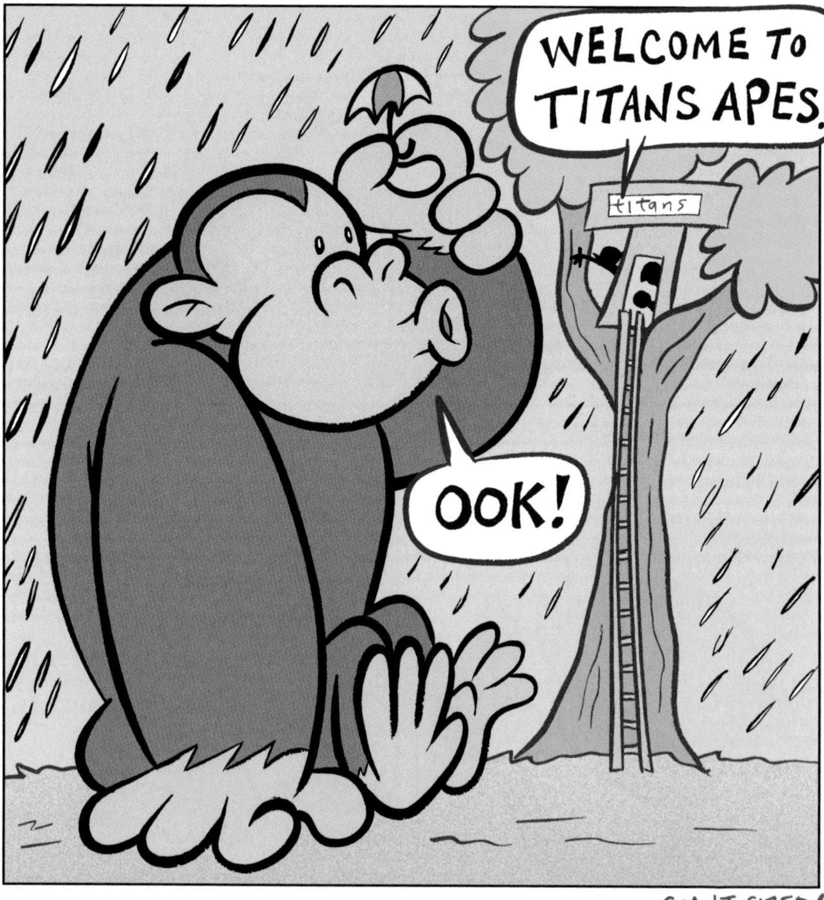
WELCOME TO TITANS APES!
titans
OOK!

—GIANT SIZED!

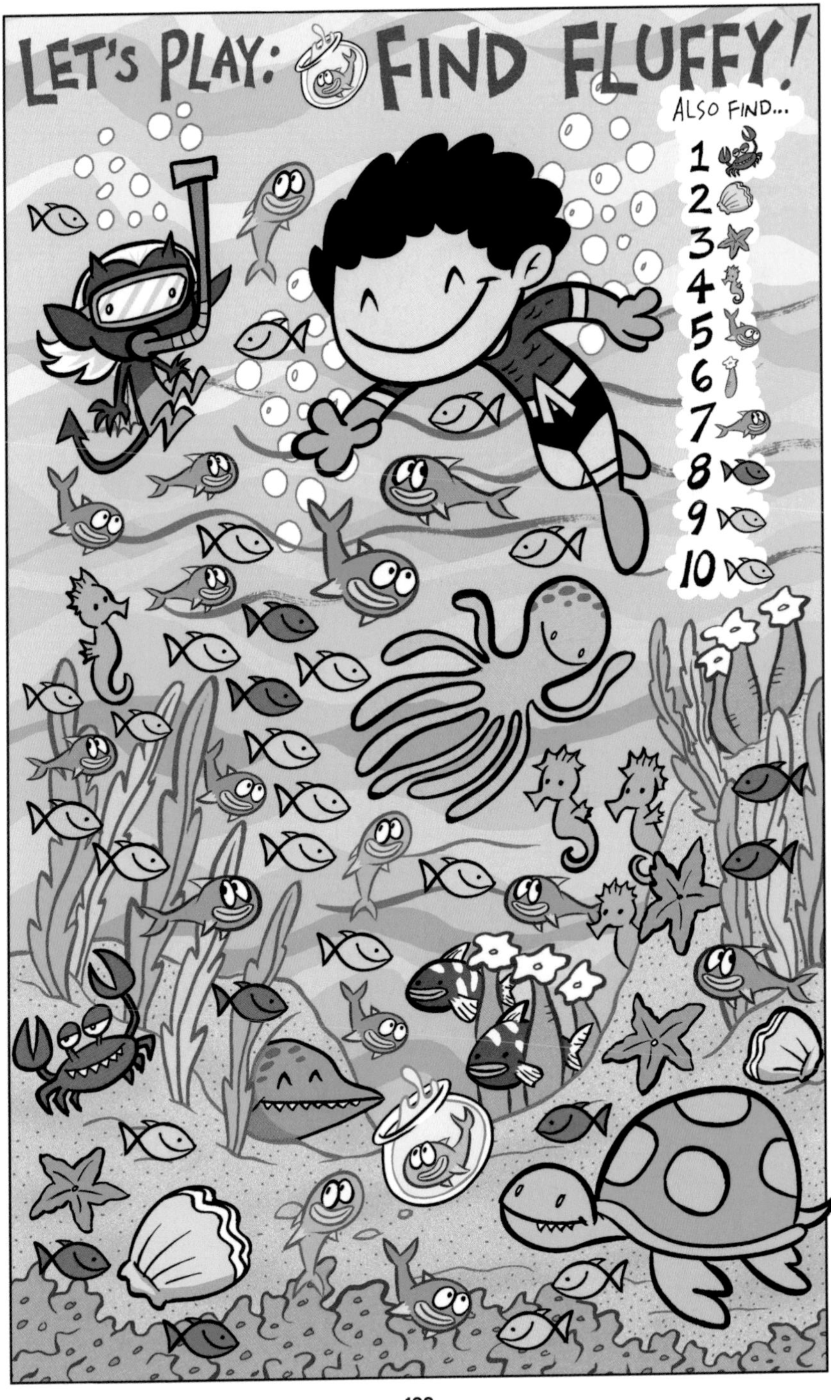
LET'S PLAY: FIND FLUFFY!
ALSO FIND...
1
2
3
4
5
6
7
8
9
10

tiny titans puzzler!

WELCOME TO THE **PET CLUB** WORD SEARCH!

E	F	E	S	O	C	S	P	K	G	L	Q	H	Q	U
L	R	C	Y	P	R	R	N	N	A	C	A	P	L	A
I	F	A	Z	P	L	J	F	E	H	O	C	R	J	C
Z	D	L	Z	E	L	O	I	A	V	N	C	F	R	O
A	Q	X	I	B	W	E	K	B	K	A	N	L	X	C
B	R	R	D	S	N	B	M	A	Q	M	R	E	Q	O
E	Q	K	C	L	E	S	S	U	M	Y	M	M	I	J
T	S	T	R	E	A	K	Y	U	K	B	E	T	M	A
H	S	A	N	P	E	T	C	L	U	B	W	K	R	O
X	K	Y	R	T	A	S	O	Q	Y	Q	Y	O	R	X
C	X	O	W	U	E	M	J	M	T	F	B	Q	R	F
K	R	J	X	V	D	P	F	R	W	I	F	M	Q	L
P	L	R	N	S	N	I	U	G	N	E	P	U	J	D
H	A	Y	X	L	I	K	Y	S	V	U	C	V	L	P
E	Q	C	U	V	G	R	J	L	X	D	D	X	F	F

Find these words in the puzzle above!

PETCLUB
ELIZABETH
BEPPO
RAVENS

PENGUINS
STREAKY
FLUFFY
ACE

ROBINS
COCO
JIMMYMUSSEL
ALPACA

AW YEAH TITANS!

134

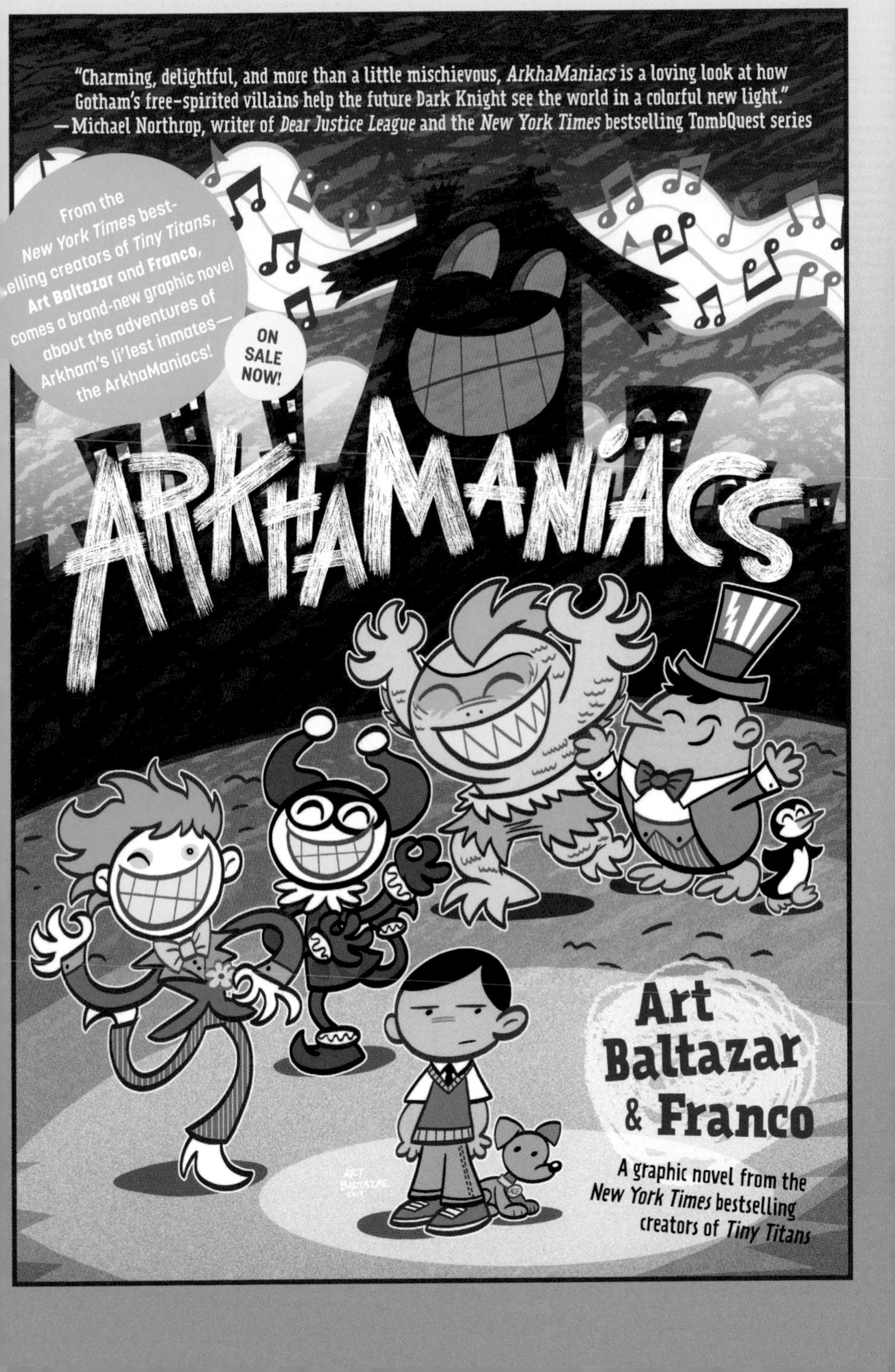
"Charming, delightful, and more than a little mischievous, *ArkhaManiacs* is a loving look at how Gotham's free-spirited villains help the future Dark Knight see the world in a colorful new light."
—Michael Northrop, writer of *Dear Justice League* and the *New York Times* bestselling TombQuest series
From the *New York Times* best-selling creators of *Tiny Titans*, **Art Baltazar** and **Franco**, comes a brand-new graphic novel about the adventures of Arkham's li'lest inmates—the ArkhaManiacs!
ON SALE NOW!
ARKHAMANIACS
Art Baltazar & Franco
A graphic novel from the *New York Times* bestselling creators of *Tiny Titans*

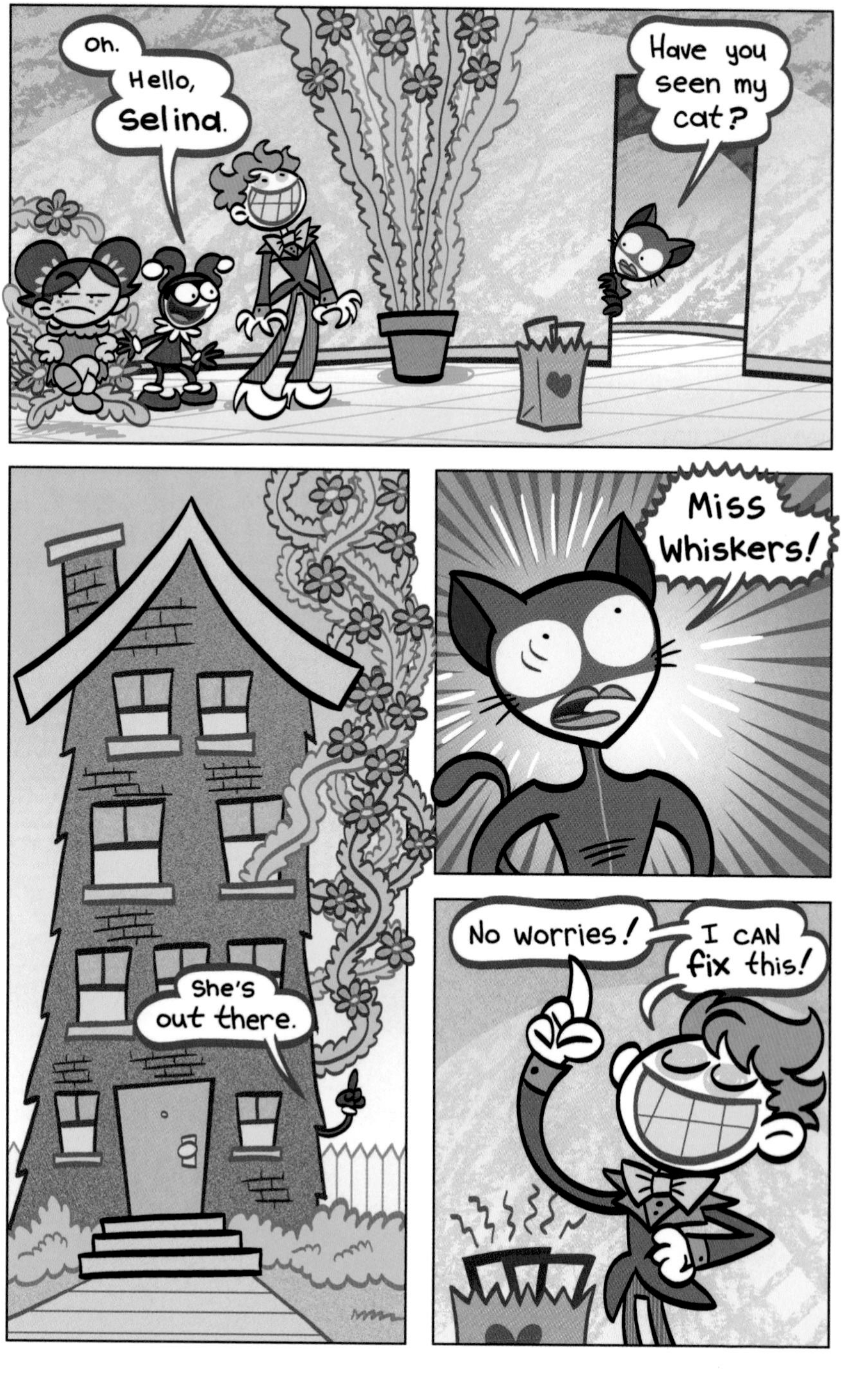

Oh.
Hello, Selina.
Have you seen my cat?
She's out there.
Miss Whiskers!
No worries!
I CAN fix this!

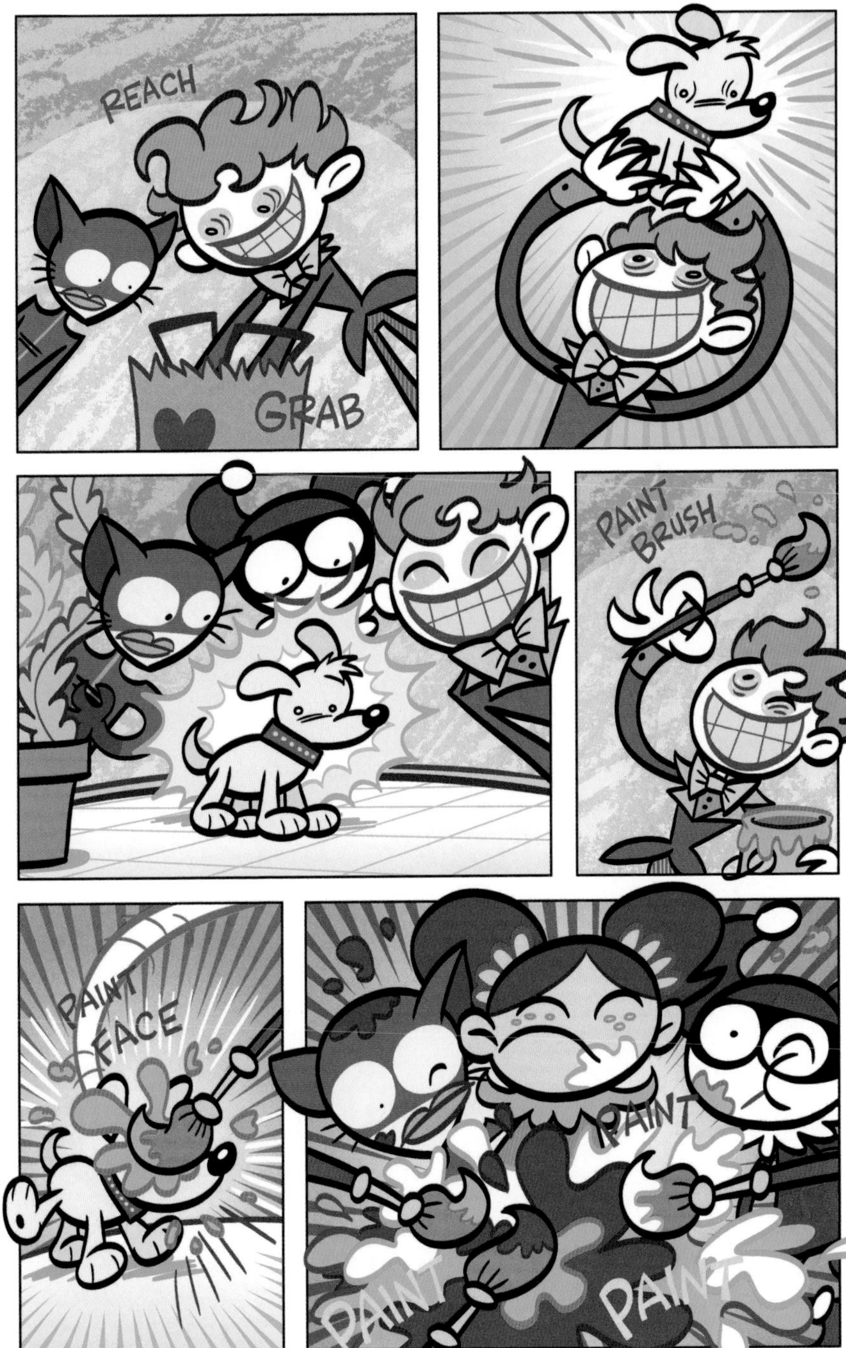
REACH
GRAB
PAINT BRUSH
PAINT FACE
PAINT
PAINT
PAINT

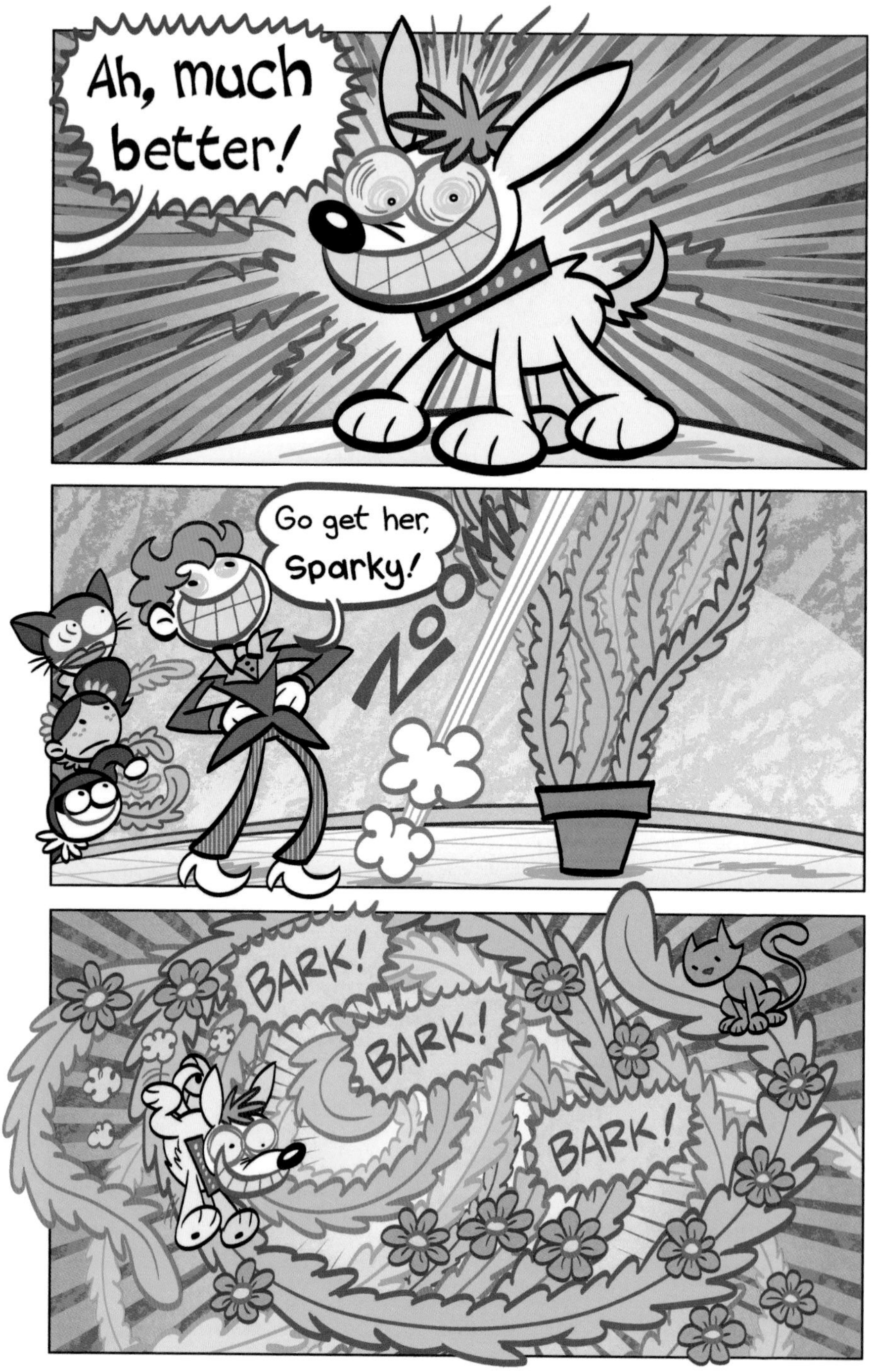
Ah, much better!
Go get her, Sparky!
ZOOM
BARK!
BARK!
BARK!

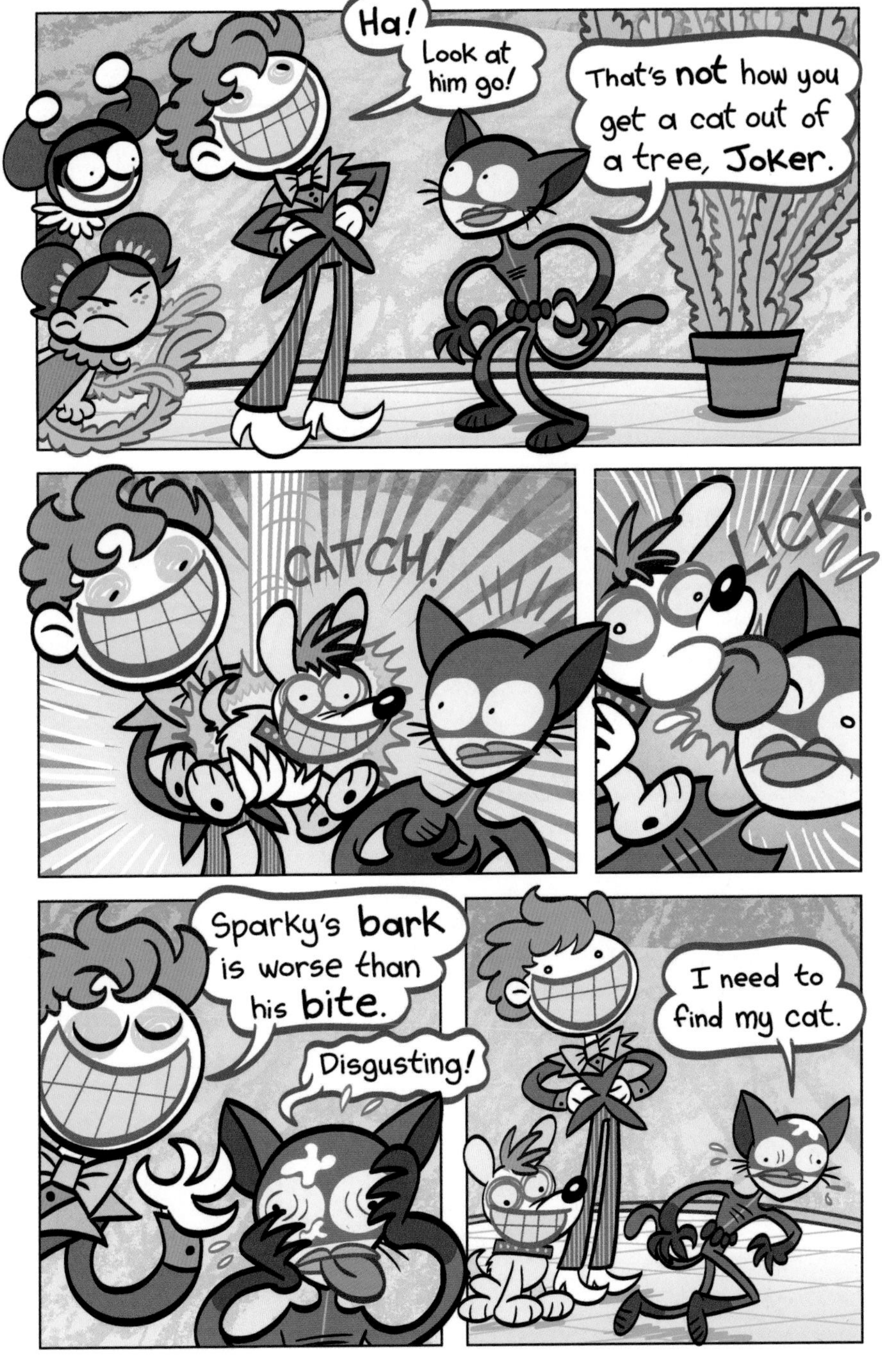
Ha!
Look at him go!
That's **not** how you get a cat out of a tree, **Joker**.
CATCH!
LICK!
Sparky's **bark** is worse than his **bite**.
Disgusting!
I need to find my cat.

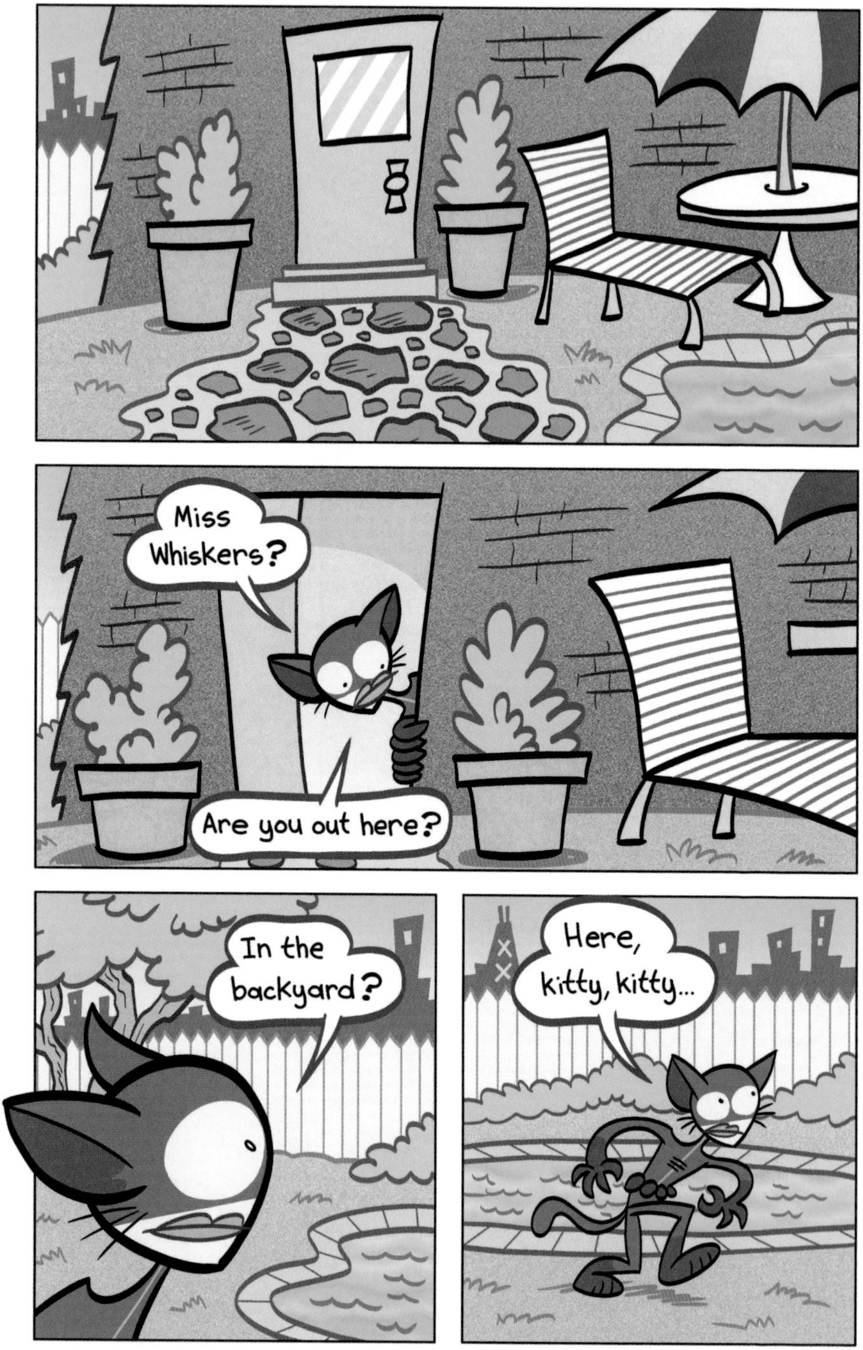
Miss Whiskers?
Are you out here?
In the backyard?
Here, kitty, kitty...

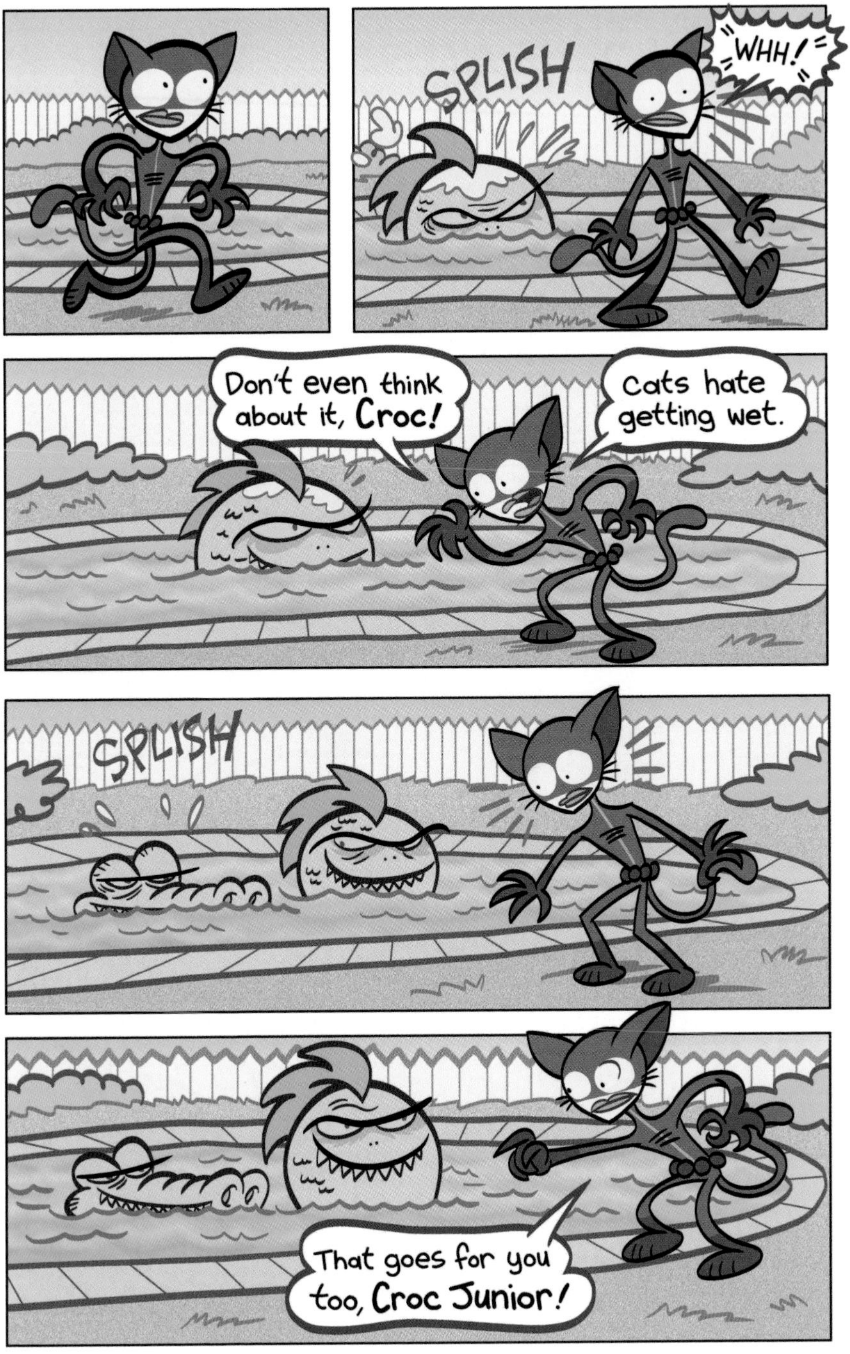
SPLISH
WHH!
Don't even think about it, Croc!
Cats hate getting wet.
SPLISH
That goes for you too, Croc Junior!

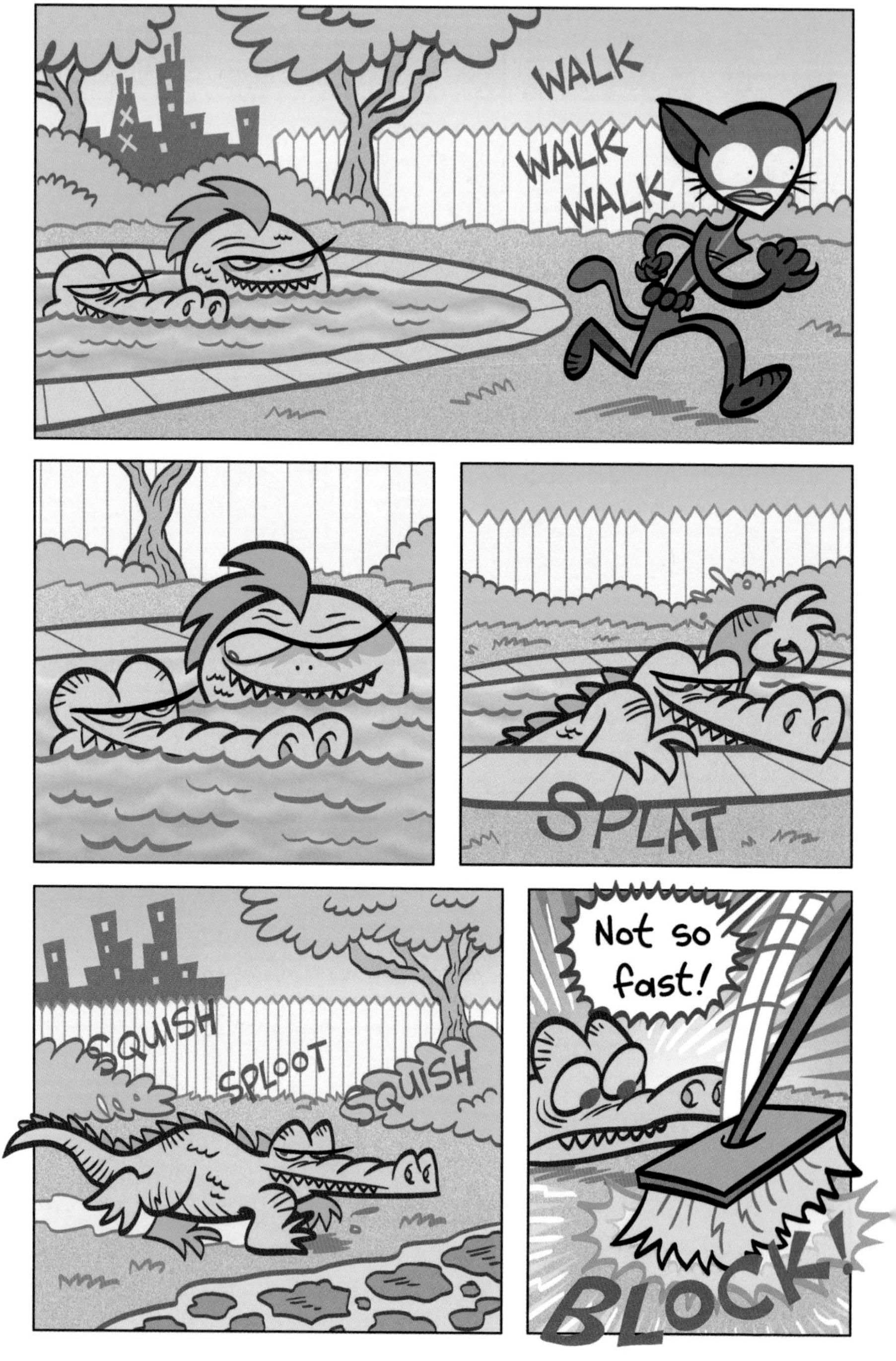
WALK
WALK
WALK
SPLAT
SQUISH
SPLOOT
SQUISH
Not so fast!
BLOCK!

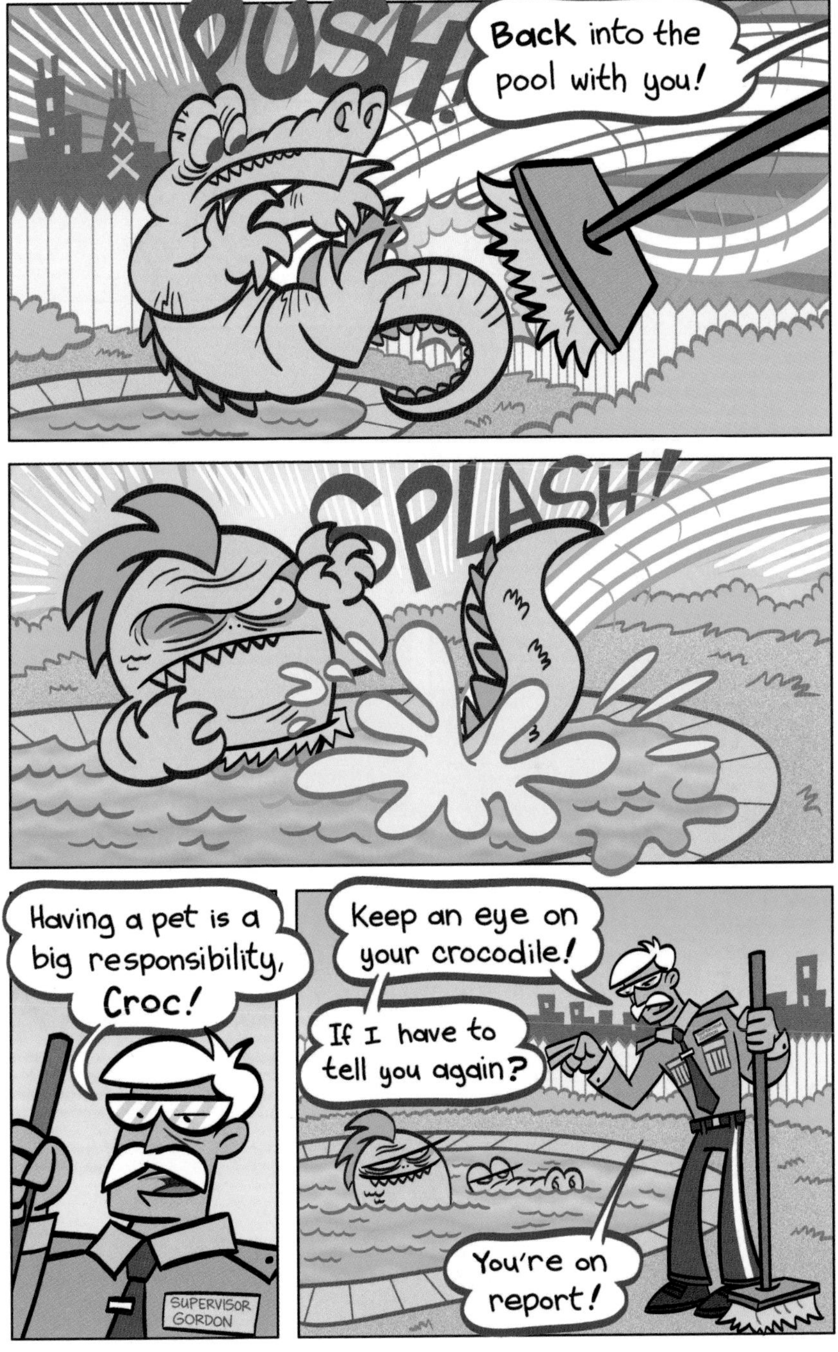
PUSH!
Back into the pool with you!
SPLASH!
Having a pet is a big responsibility, Croc!
SUPERVISOR GORDON
Keep an eye on your crocodile!
If I have to tell you again?
You're on report!

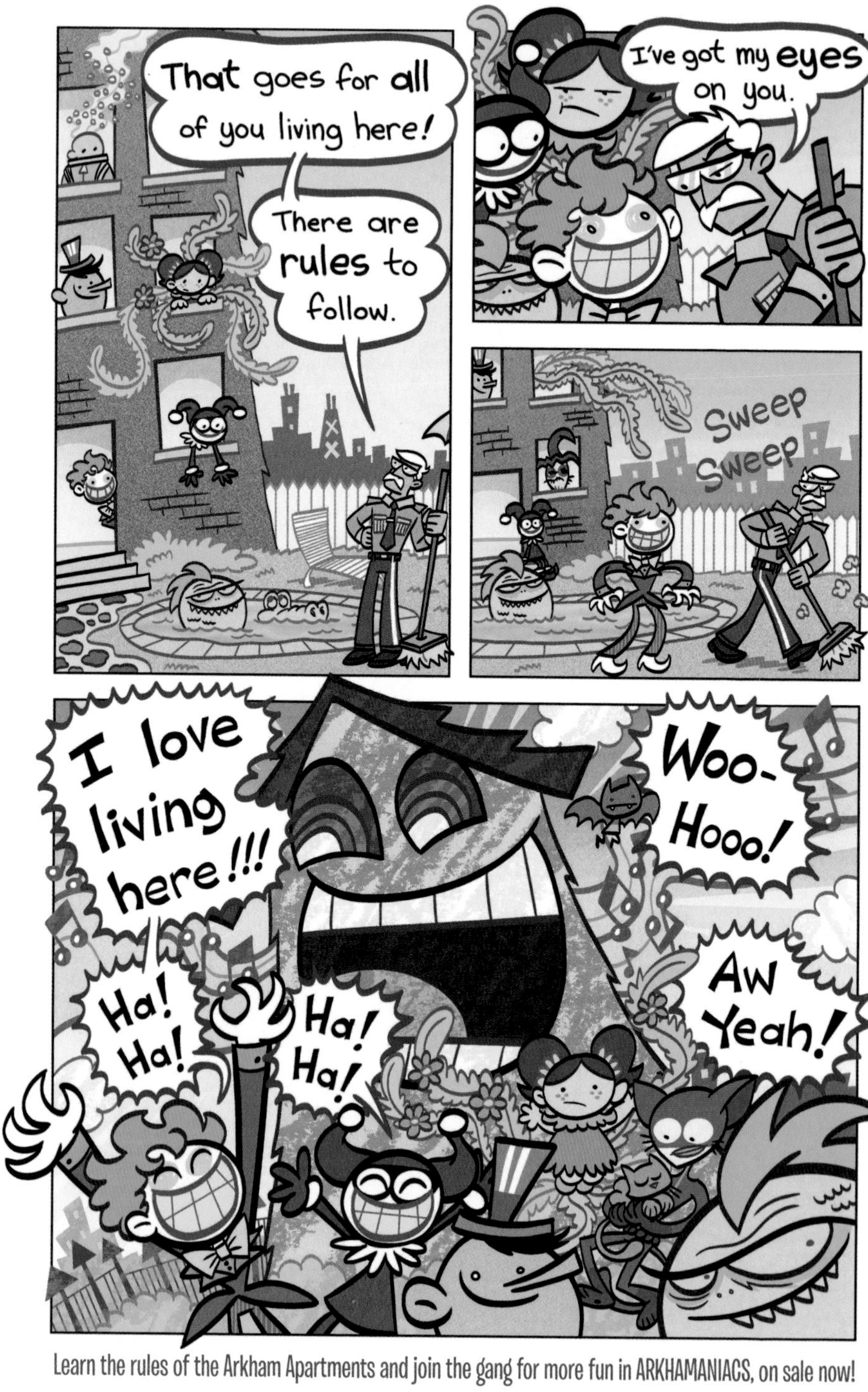
That goes for all of you living here!
There are rules to follow.
I've got my eyes on you.
Sweep Sweep
I love living here!!!
Woo-Hoooo!
Ha! Ha!
Ha! Ha!
Aw Yeah!

Learn the rules of the Arkham Apartments and join the gang for more fun in ARKHAMANIACS, on sale now!